The Cowboy Imports a Bride

By Cora Seton

To Lois and Eberle, who have cheered me on since the beginning.

Author's Note

The Cowboy Imports a Bride is Volume 3 in the **Cowboys of Chance Creek** series, set in the fictional town of Chance Creek, Montana. To find out more about Cab, Rose, Hannah, Mia, Fila, Ethan, Autumn, Jamie, Claire, Rob, Morgan and other Chance Creek inhabitants, look for the rest of the books in the series, including:

Look for the **Heroes of Chance Creek** series, too:

The SEALs of Chance Creek Series:

A SEAL's Oath

A SEAL's Vow

A SEAL's Pledge

A SEAL's Consent

Sign up for my newsletter HERE.

www.coraseton.com/sign-up-for-my-newsletter

Chapter One

"I **'M GOING TO MAKE THIS SHORT AND SWEET."** Holt Matheson stalked into the dining room and hung his cowboy hat on the back of the nearest chair. He braced his hands against the walnut dining room table and looked from one to the other of his grown children, who sat two per side in varying degrees of boredom and irritation. All of them were dusty from the day's work. Usually Holt convened these meetings right after dinner. Today it was barely two in the afternoon—and they'd been summoned inside smack in the middle of their ranching chores.

"I have four sons ranging in age from 28 to 33. Four sons," he repeated, slapping his hand on the polished surface of the table. "And not one single daughter-in-law or grandchild in sight. What the hell is wrong with all of you?"

Rob Matheson, the youngest of the four, tilted his chair back on two legs and laced his hands behind his neck, exchanging a puzzled glance with his oldest brother, Jake. Normally Holt stuck to tried and true subjects: get up before the sun and don't stop working until it's dark; don't turn your back on an unbroken horse; just because you elect a government doesn't mean it isn't out to get you; and his perennial favorite—take your darn boots off before you enter the house.

Marriage was a new topic at the Matheson table.

"You saying you want us to go knock someone up?" Ned drawled. Rob coughed to cover his laugh. Second eldest, Ned always could get away with baiting their father. If he'd said that, he'd more than likely be flat on the floor by now. As the afternoon sun slanted through the windows, a fly droned somewhere out of sight. It was August, hotter than hell, and as usual his father refused to turn on the air-conditioning.

"I'm saying I'm starting to wonder if you all are batting for the wrong team," Holt said, straightening up. His rectangular belt buckle, emblazoned with a bald eagle, glinted in the sunlight.

"Holt," Lisa chided from the opposite end of the table. "Set a good example for the children."

Rob bit back another laugh. After thirty-four years of marriage to his father, his mother was still trying to civilize him. He rubbed a hand across his forehead and added his voice to the discussion. "What's wrong, Dad—you need some more cheap labor?"

Ned snorted. "More like free labor."

Luke, only a year older than Rob, grinned, flashing white teeth against his tanned skin. All four Matheson boys were blond and blue-eyed. They got their height and broad shoulders from their father, but their mother's

Viking heritage won out as far as hair was concerned. When they were together, they attracted a lot of female attention. Rob didn't mind that one bit—as long as most of it was directed his way.

"Show some respect!" Holt boomed. "You get paid plenty." The room fell silent. It was true their father paid them—if you counted a roof over their heads, three meals a day and housekeeping service as payment. They each received a small spending allowance as well, but nothing to write home about. Holt kept them in line by keeping them cash-poor. "Now I've heard plenty about your exploits down at the Dancing Boot, and I've seen more than one pretty filly creeping out of here on a Sunday morning who didn't look like she was heading to church, so I'll assume that it's possible I'll one day have a grandchild, but I'm getting mighty impatient waiting for that day to come. By the time I was Rob's age I had four sons!"

Holt caught each of their gazes in turn and let his point sink home. "I can't force you to marry, but I can lay out a few enticements in your path. So here's how it's going to be. The first one of you who brings home a bride will get 200 acres near the river to do with exactly as you see fit."

Jake sat up straight, and Rob understood why: 200 acres was nothing to sneeze at. A man could do a lot with 200 acres. "No meddling?" he asked.

Holt's eyebrows lowered. "When do I ever meddle?"

"When do you not meddle, you old coot?" Lisa said. "You run our children's lives like they were still in diapers." Holt shot her a hard look but she didn't back down.

"No meddling," Holt confirmed after a long moment. "200 acres to the first one who gets a girl to the altar and marries her. Now get back to work."

He strode from the room. Lisa pushed her chair back from the table, stood up and followed him. Rob wondered if the rest of his brothers felt as blindsided as he did. 200 acres. All his own. What could he do with 200 acres if his father kept his nose out of it?

He wasn't sure. But he wanted like hell to find out.

"I WON'T BE ABLE to make it on Saturday after all."

Morgan Tate closed her eyes at her father's words. Clutching the cell phone to her ear, she checked to make sure her office door was shut. Barely bigger than a broom closet, it was still a mark of how far she'd risen at Cassidy Wineries. Assistant Manager of the distillery—a far cry from the grunt work she used to do when she joined the company ten years ago. In three days the company was unveiling the first vintage produced entirely under her supervision. She'd hoped her father would come to the tasting room for the celebration being hosted in its honor.

"Why not?" She tried to keep the anger out of her voice. When did he ever come to anything she invited him to? She shouldn't be surprised he'd back out now.

"It's Linda—she's pregnant." Pride rang out clearly in his voice. "Everyone's coming to celebrate!"

Linda. His other daughter. His *real* daughter. The one

he'd had under the sanction of marriage—not the one he'd fathered during an illicit affair with a student. As always, Morgan felt the sting of shame of her birth. She was used to being kept in the shadows, though—the child no one had wanted. The daughter her father wished would disappear. He might never say as much, and he still did his duty by her when it suited him, but more than once he'd hinted that he wouldn't take it amiss if she moved to Toronto, or even to the United States— anywhere far from Victoria.

She forced herself to take a deep, steadying breath, twirling a strand of her thick, long dark hair around one finger. "Congratulations, Dad. I know you'll be a terrific grandfather."

Of course Linda would beat her to motherhood, too. Linda seemed to make it her life's work to be the perfect daughter—the daughter Edward Tate could be proud of. She'd beat Morgan in grades, looks, scholarships, jobs, marriage and now this. Not that they ever talked—of course not—but her father made sure to keep her up-to-the-minute on his true children's exploits. She was sure he didn't go trumpeting her successes to them.

"Yes, well." Edward cleared his throat, obviously impatient to end the call. He'd managed to weasel out of another occasion, so now he'd head back to his ivory tower to work on his precious research. Studying other cultures was far more interesting than learning about your own daughter. He spent more time with his graduate students than he ever spent with her.

"Okay. See you soon," she said.

The phone clicked before she even finished the sentence.

Damn, damn, damn. Why did she always do this? Seek approval from the one man determined never to give it to her? It'd been worse in the weeks since she'd learned her mother died. Aria Cruz had always been out of reach, too, living with her husband and children in Chance Creek, Montana, but at least Morgan knew that when she did come to Victoria to visit—one month out of every year—she'd focus her complete attention on her. Aria had loved her. Not enough to risk ruining her marriage to Alex Cruz, of course. She'd only been twenty the year she'd spent in Victoria, studying anthropology at UVic. Swept away by a much older, distinguished professor, she'd gotten pregnant that fall, had the baby in the spring, and left her infant with Edward's parents to raise when she returned in September to Montana and married Alex.

Morgan had always known the truth of her parentage. She'd always known she came last—after the legitimate children of her mother and father's marriages. She'd learned to be a realist—to depend only on herself. But she couldn't help hoping that one day—just once—she'd come first with her father.

With any man.

If she was smart, she thought as she tucked her cell phone back in her pocket, she'd turn her back on men all together. Stay single.

Join a nunnery, even.

But her biological clock was ticking with a vengeance

these days. Now that she'd reached this milestone in her career, it suddenly became obvious how much the rest of her life was lagging behind. Maybe it was meeting her half-brother and sister in Montana for the first time last month when she went to find out why her mother missed her yearly visit.

Maybe it was her mother's death.

She stared out the window that overlooked the Cassidy vineyards. She'd half-known that something bad had happened before she arrived in Montana. Her mother had never let her down like that before. Then her worst fears were confirmed when Aria's daughter, Claire, told her their mother was dead. She hadn't been prepared for the grief that had come and gone in waves ever since. Aria was far from a perfect mother—but she was Morgan's mother, nonetheless. Now she was gone, and more than ever Morgan found herself alone in the world.

At least she'd come to know Claire and Ethan during that trip—the children Aria had never allowed her to meet during her lifetime. They'd known nothing about her, of course, or of her father, Edward. They'd been angry at first, but soon absolved her of their mother's sins and welcomed her to the family.

Her last few days in Montana had been some of the happiest she'd known—shot through with grief over Aria's death. Ethan and his wife, Autumn, and Claire and her intended, Jamie Lassiter, lived on the Cruz ranch and were working together to build a guest ranch business. She'd also met Cab Johnson, county sheriff, and Rose Bellingham and Tracey Richards, who helped Autumn out with the inside chores.

Most importantly, she'd met Rob Matheson, the handsomest cowboy in all Montana. The man who took her breath away. He'd grown up on the ranch next door to the Cruzes, and was fast friends with Ethan, Cab and Jamie.

She wanted to go back to Chance Creek. She wanted a life like Ethan and Autumn's—or Claire and Jamie's. She wanted a husband, children on the way. She wanted her own business, too—a winery she controlled from top to bottom.

Everyone else was getting exactly what they wanted.

Why couldn't she?

"ROB, SHE'S HERE—she'll be landing at the airport in a couple of minutes!" Claire Cruz called out of the window of her Honda Civic.

She'd driven the long lane up to the Matheson house so fast she'd raised a trail of dust that must be visible for miles, Rob thought, startled out of his nap in the shade of the verandah. Unlike his brothers who'd leapt up from their father's bizarre challenge raring to get to the next block of ranch chores, he'd decided to put his feet up for a while and think things through. The nap just kind of snuck up on him.

Now he sat up straight, as alert as an eagle looking for prey. "Who's here? What are you talking about?" Claire lived on the ranch next door and they'd grown up side-by-side like brother and sister. He'd never seen her this excited about anything. Her sleek, dark bob swung against her jaw as she leaned out the window and beckoned to him.

"Morgan! She just arrived. She came early to surprise everyone. Hop in, you can ride with me!"

Rob was off the porch in a flash. He hadn't seen Morgan Tate in weeks, not since she'd flown back to Canada.

"Why the hell didn't she call me?" he demanded as he climbed into Claire's teeny-tiny car, already wishing for the leg room of his Chevy truck. You'd think now that Claire was settling down with Jamie on the Cruz ranch she'd get herself a decent set of wheels.

"Like I said, it's supposed to be a surprise. I didn't know how to lure you out to the airport without telling you, though. Hurry up. She's waiting!"

Excitement and desire tightened Rob's gut. Morgan. Here in Chance Creek. More than two whole weeks early for Claire and Jamie's wedding.

"Last time I talked to her, she told me there was no way she could take any time off work. She said she could only come here for the weekend of the wedding," he said, gazing out the window as Claire made a tight u-turn and headed back out the lane. Luckily it was only fifteen minutes to the airport. Ten, the way Claire was driving.

"I think she was leading you on so she could surprise you better," Claire said. She seemed thrilled at the prospect of seeing her half-sister. Which made sense. After Claire got over her initial shock and anger at finding her mother had a daughter she'd never told anyone about, Claire had embraced her sister, only to have her leave again. He wondered if the happiness on her face was mirrored on his own.

"She's going to help me with all the last minute details about the wedding," she added.

"You don't get to hog her the whole time, though," Rob said, comfortably. Two years older than him, Claire used to boss him around as much as she did Ethan when they were kids. Once he got bigger than her, however, he'd had his revenge through multiple practical jokes over the years. He never got tired of giving her a hard time.

Still, he was happy for her and Jamie, and looked forward to their wedding, not the least because it meant that Morgan would be in town again.

Except she was already here.

Rob ran a hand through his hair and looked down at the jeans and t-shirt he wore. He'd worked all morning and he suddenly became aware how ripe he was. Hell, if he'd known Morgan was coming he'd have spiffed up a bit. Put on a fresh shirt at least.

"She won't mind your stink," Claire said.

"She won't notice my stink under your stink," Rob said, elbowing her. The car's path wobbled.

"Hey, watch it." Claire got the Civic back under control and soon they were pulling into the airport parking lot. The Chance Creek Regional Airport had been refurbished a few years back and it sported a modern glass and granite façade.

Inside, though, it still was the same pokey little terminal it had always been. She tugged him down the single long corridor to the point beyond which airport security blocked their way.

"That's her flight," Claire called out, pointing to a line of people spilling into the building from an airplane boarding ramp. "We made it just in time."

Rob realized he hadn't told anyone back at the ranch he was leaving. His father had asked him to sort out the equipment stored in the south stable this afternoon. Luckily it wasn't an important job. If Holt was in some kind of all-fired hurry, he would have to find someone else to do it. With three brothers, there was always someone to fill in for him.

He craned his neck as each passenger came through the entrance. Each time he was disappointed. Morgan must be sitting near the rear of the plane.

The number of passengers slowed to a trickle and then stopped.

"Where is she?" Rob demanded, turning on Claire. He caught her wide smile and his stomach sank.

Damn it.

"Got you! You should have seen your face when I said she was here," Claire crowed. "Ooooh, Rob's in love!"

"Stow it," Rob said, jamming his fists in his pockets and trying to restrain himself from picking Claire up, shoving her into a suitcase and sending her to Timbuktu.

"Come on—you play jokes on other people all the time. What's wrong? You can dish it out, but you can't take it?" Claire danced around him, enjoying her triumph all too much.

"If you don't shut your trap, I'm going to dish something out," Rob said, turning on his heel back the way they'd come. Claire's laughter followed him. She was right, though; he had put many people in the same spot he was now. He was sure some day this would seem funny to him, too.

But not now. He was aching for Morgan, and she was a thousand miles away.

He stopped in his tracks when Ethan, Autumn, Claire, Jamie, Cab—hell, even Ned, Jake and Luke—appeared before him, all laughing fit to burst.

What the hell?

"Got it all on camera!" Ethan hollered, holding up the cell phone Rob knew Claire had bought him a couple of months back. Someone must have finally showed Ethan how to use it.

"Very funny." Okay, he could see why Ethan would want to film his humiliation—he'd made a movie of Ethan's drunken rant about the qualities necessary for a ranch wife last spring, and posted it on the Internet as a wife-wanted ad. The movie had gone viral, and Autumn had been one of the women to answer the ad. She'd been all set to write a scathing article for the magazine she worked for about cowboys and their arrogance when she arrived in Montana. Instead, she and Ethan fell in love.

He'd expected gratitude. Not retaliation.

"Should we send it to Morgan? Show her how much you looooove her?" Jamie asked, knocking back his cowboy hat, the better see Rob. His dark hair was falling into his eyes as usual. A bit shorter than Rob and Ethan, Jamie's model-good looks still caught the eye of every woman who walked by.

Rob supposed he deserved that, too. After all, he had screwed up Jamie's proposal to Claire with a well-timed practical joke, as well.

"No—don't get her hopes up," Claire chimed in. "Morgan deserves a real man. One who isn't afraid of commitment."

"You mean a guy who can date a woman more than two weeks running?" Rose said, laughing like she knew all about it. Well, she did, didn't she?

Everyone did.

"Has he ever dated anyone for two weeks running?" Cab said. The sheriff had way too much time on his hands if he could show up at the airport for this. Usually the large man held his peace, but this time he seemed all too happy to throw his lot in with the rest of these jokers.

Everyone else laughed.

Ethan looked the sheriff up and down. "Hey, I've got an idea, Cab. Why don't *you* date Morgan? Get her to move to Montana for good. If Rob here keeps going after her, she'll end up running away to Alaska or something."

Rob stiffened. *Cab? Dating Morgan?* "Hey!"

They all ignored him. "Cab's perfect," Claire said, turning an appraising eye on the big man. "You'd be part of the family, then. You know, after the two of you got married."

Married? Cab and Morgan? Rob fought to keep his hands from clenching into fists.

Cab appeared to consider this. "She's awfully pretty," he agreed. "Got a good head on her shoulders, too."

"Lay off!" Rob couldn't keep his voice from rising.

"Why—you getting serious about her?" Cab goaded him.

"Serious? Rob?" Claire said. "That'll be the day."

Feeling like an unbroken horse caught in a corral, Rob glared at all of them. "I can be serious."

Everybody laughed like he'd uttered a terrific joke. Damn it, wasn't anyone going to back him up?

He saw Autumn lingering behind Ethan. Despite her months on the Cruz ranch, she still stood out from the rest. Her long, brown hair and elfin face always made her look a little other-worldly. He knew from experience she didn't like practical jokes—didn't like it when people got laughed at—and now he understood why. It sucked being on the receiving end, didn't it? Why had he ever become such a prankster?

Well, he knew exactly why, didn't he? To keep three older brothers off of his back. To keep everyone else from teasing him. He'd been different, once—too sensitive, too much of a dreamer—but that was a long time ago—a hell of a long time ago. No one messed with him now.

Not usually.

"I'm out of here," he said, and stalked off down the hall toward the exit. He realized he didn't even have his own truck to ride home in. Well, he'd be damned if he took a ride from one of his so-called friends. He hoped there'd be a cab out front when he reached the door.

There was, thank God, and he climbed in and told the driver to take him to the Dancing Boot before anyone else reached the pavement.

To hell with all of them. He could be serious. He could date a woman for more than two weeks.

He just hadn't tried it yet.

MORGAN CLICKED THROUGH HER TEXT MESSAGES to find the one she'd received from the caterer that morning. Jillian Hodgeson was probably sick of her by now, but she was determined that the event scheduled for her vintage's debut would go off without a hitch. Check and recheck every detail—that was her motto when she ran these affairs. So far it had paid off. Taking on this extra role at the winery was one of the things which brought her to the owner's attention. Elliot Cassidy was a crusty old man whom she didn't particularly like, but respected because of his position. His son, Duncan, was another matter. He was an ass.

She paused when she spotted the text Claire had sent her earlier in the day. Asking her again what she knew about the way their mother had spent her money. Morgan pressed her lips together. She knew what Claire was after. Aria had blown through large amounts of the Cruz ranch's profits, and when she and Alex died in a car accident the preceding August, Ethan and Claire had been left with a business seriously in debt. Only by taking on Jamie as a partner and turning the spread into a guest ranch had Ethan been able to refinance it and buy out Claire's share. Claire was rich now, but she couldn't let the mystery go: how had Aria spent all that money? Claire seemed sure her mother had blown it on Morgan.

Morgan had already told her a hundred times that while Aria had taken her to restaurants and bought her clothes now and then when she came to visit, she had not underwritten her day-to-day upkeep—as a child or an adult.

It must be galling to her siblings that Aria had siphoned so much money from the ranch, but it hurt her that Claire still blamed her for the loss of the cash—even if her texts were worded carefully, with plenty of assurances that she was *just curious*.

The part where Claire asked for the dates of Aria's visits really bothered her. She was afraid the dates she gave her wouldn't add up. She had realized something in the weeks since she met her half-brother and sister. When Ethan and Claire talked about their mother's yearly absences, they always talked about *months*.

Aria never stayed in Victoria more than a month, however.

Morgan could imagine how Ethan and Claire had felt when they learned their mother's shopping sprees in Europe were really visits to a daughter in Canada they didn't know she had. They must have felt betrayed— stabbed in the heart. It was a miracle they accepted her at all, let alone made friends with her, but their friendship meant more to her than she could ever express.

What if there were more secrets to find out about

Aria Cruz? What if those secrets tore her new, precious family apart? Claire seemed bent on doing that herself.

What had Aria done with the rest of her time away from home? Had she actually gone to Europe and done some shopping?

Maybe.

Maybe not.

It was the *maybe not* that left her cold. Morgan hugged her arms across her chest. Could she possibly have another half-brother or sister out there? Could one Montana girl leave a trail of children across a continent or two?

In her darkest moments, that's exactly what Morgan pictured. But no—that would require lengths of time away from home that Aria simply hadn't spent. Claire said her year away during college was the only time Aria had been gone from Montana for so many months.

So no other children. *Probably.*

Morgan dropped a hand to her own flat stomach. No children for her, either. Claire had mentioned she and Jamie were thinking of trying for a child as soon as they got married. With Autumn already pregnant, Claire said she wanted to be sure their kids were of similar ages.

"That makes it so much more fun, don't you think?" she'd commented the last time they talked on the phone.

Yes. She did think that would make it more fun. Too bad she was stuck a thousand miles away, with no husband in sight, let alone a child.

Maybe she should say yes the next time Duncan hinted around about marriage.

Shivering with disgust at the thought of marrying her boss's son, she pulled her thoughts back to Chance Creek, the Cruz ranch, and Rob Matheson. Now there was someone she'd like to have a baby with. Tall, broad-shouldered, muscled in all the right places, with hands that set her skin on fire...

She stifled a laugh. As if that would ever happen. Everyone she met in Chance Creek took her aside at one time or another to tell her Rob was bad news. A lady's man with no desire to ever settle down. She'd told them all she could handle him, and she had. They'd made out a lot, but done nothing else. Every time he tried to take things further, she stopped him cold.

No way she'd lose her heart to someone so entirely off limits.

Except she kind of already had.

She glanced back down at Claire's text again, and resolutely clicked past it. Caterer. Party. Vintage.

She had far too much work to do to think about anyone back in Chance Creek.

"BUY ME A DRINK, COWBOY?"

Rob slid his gaze over to the curvy brunette who'd taken the stool next to his at the long, wooden bar in the Dancing Boot. He squinted a little. Georgette Harris, from the next town over. Where'd she work? The feed store, that was it.

"I'm outta cash," he lied. Truth was, he had a little money left in his pocket, but only enough to keep himself drunk tonight.

"I'll buy my own drink, then. Hope you don't mind the company." She smiled at him and leaned closer, all the better to flash him some cleavage.

Pretty impressive cleavage.

"Free country," he mumbled. He'd already consumed a hefty amount of alcohol, but the sting of the afternoon's confrontation at the airport was still sharp. *Some friends.* Not one of them had defended him. No respect at all.

She laid a hand on his arm. "I've got the night off."

He frowned, trying to work that one out. The feed store wasn't open past six. "Night off from what?"

"From my boyfriend, silly. From Jessie—you know Jessie Henry."

Sure. Maybe. But he couldn't bring the man's face to mind.

She leaned even closer, her breast brushing his arm as she whispered into his ear, "Thought I'd have a little fun while he's out of town. You know what I mean?" She dropped a hand to his thigh.

Yeah. He knew exactly what she meant. Rob straightened a little and eyed her speculatively. "Why pick me?" he asked, surprising himself. Why even bother asking? Why not take the gift he'd been handed and show the lady a heck of a good time like he usually would?

"You won't be no problem tomorrow," Georgette said cheerfully. "Nor tonight. Some guys get squeamish about fooling around with another man's girl. Not you. And I know I won't get any phone calls next week wondering where I am. You'll be too busy chasing after some other guy's woman."

Wow. That was harsh. Suddenly he felt all too sober.

"Guys like you are handy," she said, as if sharing a confidence. "A girl can yank your chain, have her way with you, and kick you back into the closet when she's done. You're like a pair of high heels. Great now and then when you want a party, but useless for the day-to-day."

Rob blinked.

She must have caught his expression, because she rushed to add, "But pretty. You're real pretty, ain't you, Rob?"

"Fuck off." He stood up, slapped some cash on the bar and stalked toward the door, weaving a little before he got his bearings. Guess he was a little drunk after all.

Cab cut him off before he made it halfway across the room. He hadn't even seen the man enter the Boot.

"Tell me you're not driving," Cab said.

Rob pushed past him, into the still-warm Montana evening. Cab followed him outdoors. Aside from the music spilling out of the Boot with them, Chance Creek was already quiet. Most folks were tucked in for the night. Past nine o'clock this town shut down.

"Can't let you do that, buddy. Give me the keys."

For god's sake. His truck wasn't even in the lot— he'd taken a taxi here.

Unwilling to argue it out, Rob handed them over, and struck out on foot.

"Where you going?" Cab called after him.

"Nowhere."

Nowhere at all.

Chapter Two

MORGAN HOPPED ON ONE FOOT as she threaded a leg into the tailored pants she planned to wear to work this morning. She tried to keep her cell phone between her shoulder and her cheek, but the thing was too darn small to balance there.

"So first Mom spends twenty-four years telling me never to have children, and now she tells me I better get pregnant again right after this one's born," Autumn said in her ear. They talked most days—Autumn filling her in on all of the ranch gossip and venting her frustrations about guests and family. It was barely getting light out, but Morgan knew ranch life started early. Ethan would already be out doing his chores, and Autumn would be prepping breakfast for her guests. Often she and Autumn squeezed in a call before the day got busy.

"Why is she rushing you?" Morgan asked. "You've got tons of time." As usual when she talked to Autumn she felt a jealousy she tried to squash. Autumn had all the things she wanted—a business of her own, a husband she adored.

And a baby on the way.

Morgan couldn't believe she was still single at this age. Maybe getting married earlier and having a family would have screwed with her career. Fine—she didn't need to rewrite the past. It was the future that scared her. What did all her successes mean if there was no one to share them with?

"You're forgetting who Mom's patients are; women who can't conceive on their own. When you spend all day telling forty-something-year-old women that they're not fertile anymore and are going to have to spend thousands of dollars on invasive procedures, you tend to get a skewed view of things."

"Don't you mean fifty-something-year-old women?" Morgan asked, trying to shrug into her blouse.

"No, I mean forty-something. Even thirty-something. Don't tell me you're one of those women who thinks they have all the time in the world to start a family. There's no guarantee it'll work, no matter what your age. Even women in their twenties can have trouble conceiving. If you want kids, you need to get a move on."

Suddenly Autumn had her full attention. Morgan stood stock still, the blouse still gaping open. "What?"

"Oh, I…shoot." Morgan could picture her in the Cruz ranch Big House kitchen, whipping up breakfast. She'd be standing by the counter that separated it from the huge living room with its floor-to-ceiling windows and their incredible view of the Montana landscape. "I'm sorry, that came out all wrong. You know what my mom's like; I think I was channeling her for a minute there. Forget everything I just said. You do have plenty of time."

But Autumn's tone told her she didn't entirely believe that. "You really think I might not be able to have kids?"

"No! I don't mean that at all. Boy, I really stuck my foot in my mouth, didn't I?" Autumn paused. "Here's what Mom would say. Even if you got married next month and got pregnant right away, you wouldn't give birth until you were 33. Let's say two years later you try again. You're 36 or 37 when your second child is born. Now you're looking at forty around the corner. Two kids is plenty for most people, but no one tells women that if they want a big family, they need to start early. And let's face it—you're not getting married next month, are you?"

"N…no." Feeling like she'd been sucker punched, Morgan hastened to do up her buttons with fingers that suddenly didn't work right. Sure she was looking forward to getting married, but she had felt like she still had plenty of time to start her family. Lots of time to have two, three, even four children. She'd always wanted a houseful, and now she was too old?

"But…what if I don't get married for a couple of years?" she said.

"Then you might need the help of someone like my mom." Autumn's voice changed. "But no one's saying you even have to have kids. You have a great career, right? Oh, darn—I gotta go. Ethan just came in."

She clicked off, leaving Morgan speechless. Yes, she had a fantastic career. Sort of.

Okay, actually it sucked. Elliot Cassidy was a tyrant and Duncan was all hands and innuendos. She'd been desperate to leave for months, but was afraid if she did so, she'd have to leave Victoria, as well. The wine industry on the island was small and tight-knit. If the Cassidys heard she was looking for work elsewhere, she had no doubt they'd do their best to undermine her job search.

Besides, she wanted more than a job. She wanted to own her own winery someday, and she wanted to create vintages that would bear her name, not the Cassidys'.

She wanted a family, too. A big one.

She was sick to death of being alone.

ROB PULLED HIS HAT OFF as he paced wearily down the center aisle of the Chance Creek Lutheran Church. He slid into a pew about halfway down and leaned back against the wooden seat, thankful to take a load off.

He didn't know how long he'd walked during the night, striding along the highway as if he meant to leave Chance Creek behind him for good. When he sobered up and realized it was himself he was trying to leave behind, not the town or the people in it, he turned around and walked back again.

His feet were sore, he stank of alcohol and sweat, and he was sure if Georgette saw him now she'd run the other way screaming, but he wasn't ready to head home yet. Not until he'd thought a few more things through.

This seemed as good a place as any to do that, with its wooden floors and clean, spare lines.

He scraped the back of his hand against the stubble on his chin. He was a mess, all right. Through and through. His life today bore no resemblance to the one he'd expected to lead. Sure, he was a rancher, after a fashion. Although he acted more like his father's hired hand. But somehow he thought his life would add up to more. He'd thought he'd be respected, like his father was. That he'd be in charge...of something. That he'd have more to show for the work he did.

Instead, he was a joke.

No one took him seriously. They certainly didn't look up to him. He couldn't blame them, either. He spent his time goofing off, drinking, sleeping around, and playing jokes on everyone who came near.

"Been a while, Rob."

Startled, Rob glanced up to see Reverend Joe Halpern standing at the end of the pew.

"Sure has." He ducked his head, embarrassed to be caught here.

"Don't mind me," Joe said, as if reading his thoughts. He was a husky man in his late 60's. Out of his Sunday garb he looked like any other rancher in these parts. His jeans strained below a somewhat protruding belly. A green button-down shirt was tucked in neatly at his waist. "I'll go about my business unless you'd like some company."

Suddenly Rob found it difficult to speak. He could use a little company right now. Anything to stop the dark thoughts that chattered in his mind.

Joe nodded as if he understood. "I remember when you used to come to church like clockwork—all you Matheson boys did back then. I had the feeling you didn't mind it as much as the others, though, even though your parents had to herd the lot of you between them like so many cattle. You were only a pipsqueak and I had a full head of hair back in those days."

Rob nodded. He remembered those days, too. The reverend was right; he hadn't minded church that much when he was young. For one hour a week his brothers couldn't hassle him and no one said a word if he kept his mouth shut and daydreamed. As Halpern's voice droned on above him, he'd think about the stones he'd found in the creek that morning, how they'd got there and why there were different colors, or about the grouse he'd snuck up on, or why sometimes clouds were fat and puffy and sometimes thin as pulled cotton.

He was happiest when he was alone, and quiet—watching something. Learning about it.

But no one ever left him alone. Not for long, anyhow.

"Mind if I take a seat?" Joe prompted.

"Make yourself at home," Rob said and it occurred to him it was a particularly stupid thing to say to a man of God in his own church. Still, he slid over and made room.

"Just say the word and I'll leave you to your thoughts," Joe said. "But in my experience, when a man shows up in church at this time of the morning, dressed in the same clothes he went out in last night, he might be looking to make some changes in his life."

"Yeah," Rob said. "You got that right."

"Tell me about it." Joe settled back, his gaze fixed on the pulpit at the front of the sanctuary. Like being in confession, Rob thought, as he sat back, too. His own gaze forward. If they had some walls around them they might be Catholics. Maybe the Catholics had the right idea.

"Not much to tell," he started. "Just…this isn't who I want to be."

"Who do you want to be?"

"I don't know. A good man. Useful." That brought Georgette to mind again. Her clinging grasp and the way she'd dismissed his worth with a single word. Useless. *Useless but pretty.*

Son of a bitch. He glanced toward the ceiling. *Sorry.*

Joe nodded. "Do you have a calling?"

A calling? "Like being a preacher?" That was the last thing he'd ever be. He tried to picture himself in that pulpit, preaching a moral lesson to the congregation. The idea was laughable.

But it sparked another memory. An idea he'd had as a small boy, right in this church one Sunday morning. He'd been feeling particularly aggrieved at the way Ned and Luke liked to rush up whenever they spotted him and scare away the bird he'd been stalking, or stomp to bits the nest he'd found, or splash in the water of Chance Creek until every fish for a mile went into hiding.

With the ignorance of youth, he'd thought that if only he could stand in Halpern's pulpit, he could take on the minister's authority and turn of phrase. He could tell everyone in the congregation about all the wondrous things he saw on the Matheson ranch—the tiny bugs and the towering trees; the ceaseless life that teemed and thronged in the grasses; the ever-shifting shades of light that filtered through pine branches in the hills; the sound of the water that ran in the creek—and by telling them about it, he could teach them to know God. No one ever interrupted the reverend when he was preaching. Maybe if Rob was able to preach in his own way, people would listen to him. And if the congregation listened to him, then his family would have to listen to him, as well. And then maybe his father would stop rushing around and barking orders all the time, and his brothers would stop bickering and pushing him around and...

Beating on him.

Joe held his silence beside him and Rob was thankful for that.

No amount of talking about the natural wonders surrounding their home had stopped Ned from kicking his ass. Boys were boys, and four boys were too many for one ranch. He'd soon learned to cultivate his fists, his careless attitude and a wicked way of playing jokes that made his enemies the laughing stocks of all their friends. Ned backed off...in time.

"I'm not sure," he said finally, the memories making him raw. Coming here was a mistake. There weren't any answers for him in church.

"I think the trick is to think about who you were before the world got to you," Joe said.

Rob looked at him in surprise. A bit too close to his own train of thought.

Joe grimaced. "I see more of what goes on from that pulpit than people think," he said. "It looks like I'm the one on display—front and center for everyone to stare at when I preach. What people don't realize is from up there I can look just as hard at each and every one of them."

Huh. That put Sunday mornings in a whole new light.

"I see who's here and who's not." He elbowed Rob good-naturedly. "I see who sits next to whom. Who chooses a pew down front and who hides in the back. Who's playing hangman with his brother instead of listening to my sermon. Who's got a black eye and who's wiping away tears. The Mathesons are good people, solid citizens. Your father's done his best with his ranch and with the four of you. But every family's got its strengths and weaknesses, Rob. Your dad is loyal, strong, dependable. He's got no head for learning, though, and that's a shame. I always thought you'd head out to the University."

Rob shrugged. "What's the point? Ranching doesn't require a degree." A new soreness pained his heart. He could have won any of those scholarships they handed out in his high school. Could've been the valedictorian, probably. But Mathesons didn't get straight A's. He'd learned that soon enough.

"So you want to be a rancher?"

"What else is there?"

This time Joe did turn his head. "Everything. There's a whole world out there."

A whole world. If that was true, why did he feel so hemmed in? His entire life took place on one ranch, in the confines of his family, trussed up in their opinions of right and wrong. Suddenly he longed to be out on the highway again, striding away. "I've got no idea what I'd be if I wasn't a rancher."

Joe stood up. "You, of all the people in this congregation, can be whatever you want to be. My own father used to say that children are the only ones who show their true colors." He shrugged. "Try being the man you wanted to be when you were five. You might find it suits you best. I'll leave you to your thoughts. The Man Upstairs might have a few things he'd like to add to my lecture."

The preacher made his way forward, past the pulpit and into the small room behind it. Probably getting things set for Sunday, Rob thought as he shifted on the hard seat.

The man he wanted to be at five?

Who was that?

"ARE YOU BRINGING A GUEST on Saturday?" Duncan's grating voice cut through Morgan's thoughts. She was in the distillery room, checking the huge vats of aging wine, her first job every morning when she came to work.

"Yes." No. She hadn't found a date yet.

"I'm taking Anne Goodman." He pretended to read

the gauges on the nearest vat, but she caught him slide a look her way. Anne was considered a fine catch. Rich and beautiful.

"That's nice." She moved away, but not before she saw a triumphant smile cross Duncan's face. He must have guessed she didn't have a date. Since she'd rebuffed his advances several times, he'd taken every opportunity to show her what a mistake she'd made.

He'd also taken every opportunity to block her at work, interfering with every task, bossing her around, and generally being a pain in her ass. She knew what he was trying to say—if she wanted to get any further ahead at Cassidy's, she'd better sleep with him.

No way. She wasn't going to sleep with anyone again until she was married. She'd be damned if she repeated her mother's mistakes. She'd had a close call once a few years back that opened her eyes to how easy it would be to find herself pregnant and unmarried—like her mother had been with her. She would never subject a child to the life she'd led while she was growing up, not even if it meant staying celibate for years. Sure, this was the twenty-first century, and most of the stigma about being born to an unwed mother was gone, but when that mother went on and had a new family and left you behind—you didn't need stigma to feel as worthy as a piece of yesterday's trash.

"I would rather have gone with you," he said, sidling up to her and touching her arm. "You know I'd like to spend a lot more time with you."

"I don't think that's a good idea," she said. She

couldn't believe they were going to do this again. When would Duncan understand she wasn't going to fall for him, no matter what?

"We'd make a great pair, you and I," he went on, sliding his arm around her waist, oblivious to her disgust. "We could get married, run this winery together some day."

Ugh.

There'd been a time when she would have considered going out with him, before she knew his true nature. When she'd started, all she'd seen was a young man who shared her passion for viticulture. On the outside, Duncan looked like a catch, with his flashy smile and slick good looks. On the inside he was all vinegar and no wine. Duncan Cassidy would expect to control his wife's every move the way he controlled the personnel who worked for the winery. He'd expect her to bow to his every whim.

"Come on, Morgan. What's holding you back? We could have a lot of fun." His hand slipped down to her ass and he gave a hard squeeze.

Morgan yelped and pushed him away. He folded his hands across his chest, blocking her path, and eyed her with all the confidence of a rich man who thinks he's holding all the cards.

Well, he was, wasn't he? What could she do, report him to Human Resources? This was a family business and Duncan was family. That meant he could do pretty much anything he damn well pleased.

"I don't think so." She wheeled around, wanting

nothing more than to be away from him.

"Dinner tonight," he called at her retreating back.

"Nope!"

"I'm not asking you—I'm telling you. Dad wants to take you out and celebrate. At the Rotunda." He named a brand new restaurant that was getting great reviews. Morgan's shoulders slumped. She couldn't turn down Elliot Cassidy, even if Duncan was a lecherous twit.

"What time?" she said finally.

"Eight o'clock. We'll pick you up."

"No—I'll take my own…" but when she turned around, Duncan was gone.

Damn it, a night with Elliot and Duncan after working with them all day? This was a nightmare.

Nope. Not a nightmare.

Just her life.

WHEN ROB TRUDGED the long dirt track up to the ranch house he felt like he'd been gone for a year rather than a night. Every muscle in his body ached and he couldn't wait for a long shower.

"Where've you been?" His mother knelt in her garden beside the house he'd grown up in, a wide, two-story, clapboard affair with a verandah encircling it. "On second thought, don't tell me. I doubt I want to know."

What would she say if he told her he'd been in church? Probably that it was about time. He watched her pop a cauliflower seedling out of a flat and place it in the hole she'd dug in the rich soil of a garden bed.

Without conscious thought, he paced over to join

her and knelt down, too. She handed him a trowel and he prepared the next hole while she eased another plant out of its container. "Needed to do some thinking," he said.

"Some drinking, too, by the smell of it." Lisa wrinkled her nose, but patted him on the arm to let him know she was teasing.

"Thinking it's maybe time for a change," he said.

"You have something in mind?"

He dug another hole as she set the seedling into the first one and filled dirt in around its sides.

"Not really. But I can't keep on the way I've been."

A wistful smile played on her lips as she worked beside him. "We haven't done this in years. Do you remember when you used to help me in the garden?"

Sure he did. Back in grade school, his mother used to require him to help weed her vegetable garden at least once a week. The most hated chore on the ranch—at least among the menfolk—it was always passed off onto the youngest child who could competently complete the task.

In other words, Rob.

He hadn't hated the chore, though. He'd liked the feel of dirt between his fingers, and the way the vegetable plants looked bigger and happier as soon as he cleared the weeds away. His mother would chatter to him about the different plants, including the flowers that bordered her square garden. She didn't require him to answer back much, so he'd let his attention wander, half-listening to her, half-daydreaming in the warm sun, his mind slipping away to the hows and whys of seeds, dirt, water, and bees.

Ned walked past on the way to the main house, probably raiding the fridge between chores. He did a double-take when he spotted Rob beside his mother.

Here it comes, thought Rob.

"Just like old times," Ned called out. "The flower-sissy's back!" He laughed as he continued on and clattered up the steps to the house. Beside him, his mother tsked.

But in his mind Rob was seven again, on a spring-morning recess at the small public school in Chance Creek. A crisp wind blew down from the hills. The ground was damp beneath his feet from the receding snow. His classmate, Daniel Warden, waved at a green point breaking through the dirt.

"Look—it's a tulip."

"No, it's not, it's a crocus," Rob had corrected him without thinking.

Daniel, a hot-tempered boy who couldn't bear to be wrong, had shoved him, hard. "Who cares what it's called, you flower-sissy!"

Of course the name stuck.

His own brothers thought it was hilarious and taunted him about it for days, rubbing crocuses into his face when their parents were out of sight, pushing him into his mother's newly dug flowerbeds when they ran to the house for mealtimes. The next time his mother called him to work in the garden, Rob had hid in the hayloft and refused to come out. He'd taken a paddling for it when he came in for supper, and then hid the following day, as well. When Lisa finally tracked him down and got the truth out of him, she'd sighed, and sent him on his way.

She'd never asked him to weed the garden again.

And Rob devised a suitable revenge on Daniel. His first practical joke. He slipped out of bed early one morning, picked a handful of tulips and hid them in his backpack until he reached school. There he slipped inside before the first bell rang, snuck into his classroom and left them on his teacher's desk—along with a note:

To Mrs. Ramsey, from Daniel Warden.

When the bell rang and he filed back into the classroom with the rest of the students, Mrs. Ramsey was holding the tulips, a smile on her face. "Look at what Daniel brought me," she said, lifting them high.

"You teacher-loving, flower-sissy," Rob drawled, as loudly as he could.

That particular whipping was worth it. And that practical joke was the start of a life-long run of tormenting first his enemies, and then his friends. He learned fast that a good shock or scare kept everyone at arm's length.

"I've forgiven folks for plenty of things in my life," Lisa said, breaking into his thoughts. She sat back on her heels and gazed at him from under her cream-colored cowboy hat. "But the way your father and brothers destroyed your love for the garden, for everything natural," she waved a hand to encompass the whole ranch, "is something I've found it hard to forgive. I've found it hard to forgive myself for letting it happen."

He looked down at his hands in the dirt. Remembered the peace of working in the garden. Remembered his early days exploring the ranch and all its wonders.

The man he wanted to be when he was five.

"They might have stopped me back then, but they can't stop me now," he said. He wasn't the smallest kid on a playground full of bullies anymore. And while he couldn't name his calling, he knew it wasn't being low man on the totem pole on a ranch that already had four other men to run it.

He leaned over and kissed his mother on the cheek. "Don't give up on me yet."

She tousled his hair. "Never."

AT EIGHT O'CLOCK, Elliot Cassidy's black Lincoln Town Car pulled up in front of her apartment and Morgan let herself into the back seat. She'd been on these dinner dates with the Cassidys before and she knew what to expect. Elliot would be in the driver's seat. Duncan riding shotgun. She'd take her lowly place in back and play second fiddle to them for the rest of the night.

At the restaurant, Elliot would send back the first wine, demanding something better, while Duncan would dictate to her what she should order. The remainder of the meal would be spent listening to them pick apart the service, the food, other wineries, and their own employees. By the time she returned home she'd have a migraine and a strong desire to slit her throat.

As she slid onto the seat and fastened her seatbelt,

the car pulled away from the curb.

"Only the two of us tonight," Duncan said, and she looked up with a start, her heart beginning to pound when she took in the empty passenger seat.

"Where's your father?"

"He thought we young folks might like an evening to ourselves." Duncan smiled into the rear view mirror, a self-satisfied smirk she longed to slap right off his face.

"Forget it. Take me home."

"I don't think so." Duncan pushed down on the gas pedal and the car leaped forward. Glancing out the window, Morgan saw they weren't headed downtown.

"Where are we going?"

"You'll see." He sped up again. He was driving way too fast for this neighborhood. Had he been drinking?

Probably.

"Duncan, I'm serious. Take me home."

"Relax, Tate. You're always so uptight. Maybe if you were getting some you wouldn't be such a bitch."

Getting some? She hoped he didn't think he'd be getting some tonight.

She stealthily unlocked the door and gripped the handle. She couldn't jump out of a moving vehicle but sooner or later he'd have to slow down. No way was she going to let him whisk her out of the city to some private place where she would be at his mercy. She knew all too well that men would use their strength against her, given half a chance.

Against her will, a memory of the night she and Claire had gone after Daniel Ledstrom flashed into her mind. Daniel—Claire's ex—had taken thousands of dollars of interior design supplies from her home and stashed them in the garage of his mother's vacant house. Claire thought she knew where he'd put them, and when they'd gone to check it out, they'd been cornered by Daniel and two of his thug friends. Morgan closed her eyes against the memories of the man who'd tossed her over his shoulder, hauled her into the house and dumped her on a bed. When he'd climbed on top of her, she'd thought she'd never get away. He'd torn her blouse open—touched her…

When she finally felt the car decelerate, she took her chance. Before Duncan had even pulled to a stop at the light, she clawed her seatbelt off, flung the door open, and leaped out. Her head down, she raced onto the sidewalk and down the street. It was quiet here—an industrial area. She had to hide before Duncan circled around the block.

Fishing her phone out of her purse, Morgan dialed information and asked to be put through to a cab company. She didn't stop moving and she didn't dial 911. Getting the police involved wouldn't solve anything since Duncan hadn't actually done anything yet. Plus it would get her fired, and without a recommendation from the only employer she'd had for a decade, she'd be toast. She'd have to figure out what to do about that tomorrow; right now, she needed to get home. Darting down an alley, she turned a corner and checked the street-signs.

"Hello," she said when her call was put through. Fighting for breath, she kept running. "I need a cab.

Fast."

A screech of tires warned her Duncan was trolling the streets. She ducked down another alley and hid behind a dumpster. Duncan might drive up and down the area for a while, but he'd never get out and search on foot. He was too lazy.

Besides, he'd know right where to find her tomorrow. Time to update that résumé.

Half an hour later, a taxi dropped her off in front of her building and she climbed out, nearly weak with relief. Duncan hadn't found her before the cab arrived. She was out forty dollars, and she dreaded what the morning would bring, but she was home.

Safe.

But as she walked into the covered garage under her three story complex, toward the entrance to her unit, she stifled a gasp when she saw a man loitering by her door. She stopped, ready to run, until she recognized him.

Rob.

Shocked, she lifted a hand to her hair. She was sweaty and disheveled from her dash through the streets of Victoria. Her pants were wrinkled and her blouse awry. What a time for the cowboy to show up on her doorstep.

Slowly, she approached him. "Rob? What are you doing here?"

He unfolded himself from where he'd been leaning against the wall. "I was in the neighborhood. Thought I'd stop by."

She raised an eyebrow. She was still trembling from

her close call. Only twenty minutes ago she'd needed all her defenses against Duncan. Now the man she'd longed for was closing in on her, fast. She needed a moment to transition.

She didn't get one.

"I couldn't stay away from you any longer," he said, bending down to give her a kiss that made her toes curl with desire, once she pushed Duncan from her mind. She forced herself to stay in the moment, to be conscious of only Rob. His smell, the taste of his mouth on hers, the strength in the arms that held her. She closed her eyes and leaned against him, letting everything else go. Rob Matheson was easy on the eyes, with a body made for touching. After a few moments, it was all she could do not to melt against him right here and now.

Easy, tiger. Remember your rules. Better not get him—or yourself—too hot and bothered.

She pulled away. "Come on in."

"Thanks." He finally released her and picked up a black suitcase. "Hope you don't mind me showing up like this out of the blue. I had a sudden gap in my schedule."

"Really?" She didn't think ranchers got gaps in their schedules. "Is everything all right back at home?" She unlocked the door and showed him inside her small apartment. Lugging his gear, Rob followed her into the entryway and down a short hall to the living room. Her kitchenette hugged one wall, separated from the rest of the room by a counter. Her one bedroom and bathroom opened off to the side.

"I like your place. It's…nice," Rob said, putting down his suitcase. He seemed out of place in the confines of her little apartment. The cowboy was larger than life, and her living room was oh so small.

"You mean it's tiny," Morgan said, trying to wrap her head around his presence here. Somehow Rob demanded wide skies and open land. He didn't belong in a city like Victoria. "It's cheap, too. Only a thousand dollars a month."

"A thousand dollars for this?" His eyebrows shot up.

"It's expensive here."

"The money's funny, too. What's the deal with all the colors, eh?"

She had to laugh at the mixture of the Canadianism with his western drawl. Her shock at Duncan's behavior and her wild flight through the streets began to melt away. Rob was here. She was definitely safe from Duncan now. "Easier to tell apart than your U.S. money."

He sobered up. "Look, I know it's not good manners to drop in unannounced like this, but I needed to see you and…well, I needed to get away from home for a bit."

"Well, it's great to see you, too. Just a little…unexpected." Especially after the hellacious evening she'd had.

"There's something I need to ask you. Something important." He took her hand and led her over to her china-blue couch. There he hesitated, his gaze raking her from head to toe. Whatever he saw made his expression soften and he tilted her chin up and met her mouth with his own again. His kiss started out gentle, but then it intensified. He drew her in closer, one hand at the nape of her neck, the other at the small of her back.

Morgan let his kiss wash over her until she felt weak in the knees. She'd missed Rob so much—missed his touch so much. They hadn't taken things very far when she'd visited Montana, but she'd wanted to, and she knew he wanted to. It was going to be hard to hold him off this time.

When she began to think holding him off was the last thing she wanted to do, he broke off the kiss, looking as undone by it as she was. After searching her face with his gaze, he slowly knelt in front of her and pulled something out of his pocket. Her stomach flipped when she saw it was a velvet-covered jewelry case. He opened it and held up the ring inside.

"Morgan Tate, will you marry me?"

Chapter Three

"**B**EFORE YOU ANSWER, hear me out," Rob rushed to say. Morgan's eyes had widened and her face lit up, but even so he knew that reality would soon come crashing down into her consciousness. Morgan was sensible. Practical.

She'd say they didn't know each other well enough yet.

She'd be right.

"I don't know how to say everything fast enough for you to hear it all before you make up your mind," he went on. "So, just…sit there, okay?" He pointed to the couch behind her and after a moment she dutifully sat down. She still looked stunned, however. Stunned, and her happy expression was fading fast. He'd better get going with that explanation. "You don't know much about me. What you do know probably isn't flattering." He winced at the thought of what his friends had probably told her about him during her visit to Montana last month. "But…" He sighed in frustration. This was hopeless. How could he explain everything that had happened in the last two days?

"What?" Morgan said when the pause drew out. Her voice was breathless.

"This is stupid. You won't understand." What had he been thinking? That he could fly to Victoria, explain all the thoughts swirling around in his own mind, and she'd somehow get on the same page as him?

She took his hand. "I think I will. I can. Give me a chance."

"Everyone thinks I'm a joke, Morgan. I'm not." He broke off again.

"I know you're not a joke. And I'm probably one of the best listeners you'll ever come across. I've got nowhere to go tonight, and I want to hear what you have to say. Start at the beginning and tell me all of it."

She wasn't pressing him to put the ring on her finger, and she hadn't taken it and thrown it out the window, either. Unlike his brothers or father, Morgan was willing to listen to him, like she had last month when they'd gotten to know each other. He couldn't remember any other woman giving him the kind of attention she did. Usually they wanted the same thing he was after—some beer, some dancing and some sex, not necessarily in that order. Small town girls who were dying to shake off the boredom of small town life, if only for a night.

Morgan was different, so he did as she asked. In the half-light of the hall lamp—the only switch she'd turned on when they entered the apartment—he sat on her floor and told her about his life. About the freewheeling time when he'd been too young for school or work and the whole world seemed alight with beauty and mystery, about his run-ins with his brothers—especially Ned— Holt's strictness, his mother's garden, the playground fights.

He told her how he'd cultivated a reputation as a prankster and tough guy, put aside his interest in the natural world, and buckled down to life on the ranch. How he'd soothed his dissatisfaction with liquor and women, and how none of it was enough anymore.

He even told her about Georgette, going to church, and meeting his mother in the garden.

"Something's got to change," he said. "And I've got an opportunity to jump start my future. I'm afraid to tell you about it, though. The only way I can get it is by using you, and you don't deserve that."

"Tell me."

She sat as still as she had throughout his monologue, but Rob hesitated. He couldn't believe he was saying this out loud. Surely Morgan would hate him afterwards. "My Dad's offered 200 acres to the first of us who brings home a wife. I could do a lot with that land. We could do a lot with it, you and me."

She sat back and Rob knew she was thinking all the thoughts he'd wanted her to avoid. That he was using her to get the land. That he didn't really care about her.

That maybe this was one of his practical jokes.

"It isn't a joke," he said softly. "I want a chance to change. To be the man I know I can be. I wish I could say that I love you, that I want to spend every waking moment of my life with you, and ask you to marry me for real. I think I will be able to say that to you someday soon. I think…really soon." He swallowed hard at the very thought. "But we've known each other for so short a time, I can't say it yet. I'm sorry." He got to his knees again, ready to stand up and head right back out the door. He never should have said anything to Morgan. Now he'd probably blown his chance with the only woman he thought he could fall in love with someday.

"I understand," Morgan said calmly, freezing him in place. "I appreciate how honest you've been. Sit down again for a minute. Can I tell you what I want?"

He sat down, wrapped his arms around his knees and waited, his heart pounding at what she might say. This was by far the strangest conversation he'd ever had. The most liberating, too. "Definitely."

"I want three things and I'll do just about anything to get them." She looked him straight in the eye, though he had a feeling it was hard for her to do so. "First, I want a winery—which means I need a vineyard." She held up one finger. "Second, I have some money saved up, but even if I had some land, I'd still need about twenty-thousand dollars more to buy rootstock and get it started." Another finger. "And third…"

"Third…?" Rob held his breath.

"I want a baby."

Heat blossomed inside him the moment his brain processed the concept of making a baby with Morgan. Images of her in his bed, writhing beneath him, gazing at him as he joined with her, clouded his head until he couldn't think straight. Morgan wasn't saying no to his proposal. In fact, maybe she was saying… "A baby with me?"

After a moment she nodded, but when he reached for her, she intercepted him, taking his hands in hers. "Wait. I think…I think there's more to say."

"Okay." He took a breath, hoping to make his heart stop pounding. The idea of having a child with Morgan revved him up more than he could understand. Suddenly he was seeing her in a whole new light.

He'd thought of his proposal as kind of a business transaction. A short-term deal that could get them both what they wanted. He'd figured in time they might very well divorce, but there was enough land for the two of them, and by then he'd have what he wanted— independence. A business of his own.

But what if Morgan became his wife for real? Forever?

He itched to unbutton the blouse she wore—hell, to tear it off of her—and get started making that baby right now. He didn't think they'd even make it to the bedroom. If he had his way, she'd conceive right here on the living room floor.

"Rob. Rob?" Morgan was talking to him and he hadn't heard a word she'd said.

"What?" He tried to focus on her lips. No, better focus on her eyes, instead. He couldn't kiss her eyes.

Unless they were closed and she was half-naked, lying beneath him…

Damn it. He shook the thoughts from his head and tried to pay attention.

"If I'm hearing you right, you thought we could marry, get the land and split it between us. Then get divorced after a while. That's not what I want." She held his gaze. "I want to be loved. I want the kind of love that lasts a lifetime. I want laughter and affection and honor and understanding. In fact, I want more than to be loved—I want to be cherished. And I know it's too soon," she rushed on when he opened his mouth to speak. "Like you said, you don't know me that well, and I don't know you, but it seems to me that love is possible between us, and if love is, maybe something more is, as well."

Rob nodded vigorously. Something was definitely possible between them.

"And if it's possible, maybe we can go ahead and choose it."

Choose it?

"I'm not sure I follow you," he said when it seemed like she was waiting for an answer.

"What if we choose to love each other?" she tried again, leaning forward so he got the barest glimpse down the neckline of her blouse. "What if you…decided to cherish me?" Her words drifted down to a whisper, but Rob heard every one. "I mean, could you really marry me if you didn't intend to follow through? Could you stand up in front of a minister and everyone and…lie?"

Rob sat back as the cold wash of reality broke over him. Lie in front of Joe Halpern? His family? His friends?

God?

No. He couldn't. He might joke and cheat and fool

around. He might knock some idiot flat when the occasion required it. But he would not lie to God.

That's where he drew the line.

How on earth had he made it through picking out a ring, booking a flight and traveling all the way to Morgan's home without ever facing that stumbling block? He must have been crazy to think this ever could have worked.

It was hopeless.

Except…

"Say that again—the part about choosing?"

She slid off the couch and sat on the floor beside him. In the dim light he felt like a kid again, up way past his bedtime. It was dark and quiet in the apartment, aside from the whoosh of cars passing by outside now and then.

"What if we choose to love each other? What if we decided we would? What if we said that's it—we're going to be partners for the rest of our lives, and went ahead and made a marriage out of it?" She watched him, waiting for his reaction.

In a strange way it made sense. He'd never met another woman who interested him as much as Morgan. They had chemistry in spades, and she was as ambitious as he was—more, even. Could you decide to love someone?

"Think about all those people in arranged marriages," she said, touching his knee. His skin burned and he fought the urge to capture that small hand and bring it to his lips. "We'll arrange our own marriage. We'll force ourselves to be husband and wife."

The way he felt right now, no one would have to force him to do anything. "An arranged marriage," he repeated, watching the way her lips formed her words. In another minute he'd need to kiss her.

And then he'd need to do a hell of a lot more than that.

"Do you think it could work?" she asked, trying to meet his gaze again.

He leaned in for a kiss and an electric shock jolted through his body when their mouths joined. Choose to love this woman? Choose to spend his life with her?

Why not?

When he broke off the kiss, he leaned back, but kept his hand on her arm. "I need a few things, too."

"What?"

He'd swear she was as turned on as he was, and he wanted nothing more to ditch all the talking and go straight to bed. Still, these were serious matters and they deserved to be discussed.

"I want to be respected," he said, wanting to look anywhere other than at her face, but forcing himself not to turn away. He wondered if Morgan had felt like this when she stated her needs—like she was naked in public. "I'm not talking about me telling you what to do, and I'm not saying I won't ask for your input on major decision. But in matters of my business, I need to call my own shots. I need you to trust me that I'll do my best."

Morgan laughed, a happy sound. "Of course. I trust that already."

Rob's heart expanded, and some of the pain he'd felt the last couple of days slid away. "I want to try my hand at a thing or two before I decide what to do with my share of the land. I want support and an open mind."

"Got it."

"Most of all," he hesitated, not sure how to put this desire into words. "I want…"

Morgan waited. She looked eager to hear what he might say. Eager to agree to it. He took a breath and blurted it out.

"I want to be wanted."

A smile curved Morgan's lips.

"I want you," she said. "I don't imagine that will change."

"If you'll want me, I'll cherish you. I'll be the best husband I can be. The best father I can be. I swear I'll build us a life that shows you—shows you and our kids—how much you mean to me." He lifted her hand to his mouth and kissed her fingers.

"I promise I'll respect you. Lust after you." She searched his face with his gaze. "I'll stand by you no matter what may come."

Rob found himself blinking. Something huge and hard shifted in his heart. To have an ally in life—an ally who wanted him… "Even if I'm not a rancher?"

"No matter what you choose to be."

He felt as if the ground was sliding beneath his feet. As if all the walls that ever held him in gave way at once, leaving him surrounded by a world of possibilities. Freed from a lifetime of his family's strictures, Morgan's words left his future open wide. "That's the best gift you could ever give me," he said gruffly. "I'll build you that winery. I'll get you that money."

"And I'll help you do whatever you decide to do."

"Let's have lots of babies together," he said, leaning forward to brush a kiss across her cheek.

She nodded, her eyes shining. "Hold on, just a minute." She got to her feet and moved first to the kitchen, then into her bedroom. Rob waited for her, secure in his soul for the first time in his memory that everything he was doing was exactly right.

Who would have guessed when he got on that plane that his life would change like this? Could it be only twenty-four hours ago that he was back in Montana, stuck, miserable...?

When she came back she held candles that she lit and put on the narrow coffee table.

"You kneel there," she said, pointing to one side. "Put the ring there." He did what she told him, placing it on the glass surface, curious to see what she'd do next.

She took a position on the other side, and set another ring in front of her. It looked old and tarnished, definitely meant for a man.

"My mother gave me a box of jewelry last year, some things she'd inherited but didn't use. This was one of them. I always liked it." She picked it up and took his hand. In the candle-light, she looked lovely—intent and radiant. "Rob Matheson, I promise right now to bind my life to yours, forever and always, to love you, honor you, respect you, and build a life by your side. I make this pledge now…" She trailed off uncertainly.

Rob picked up the thread. "In the presence of God?" he said softly. He felt like God was here in this room. Nothing he'd ever done had felt this right.

"In the presence of God," Morgan echoed. "Forever and ever, amen." She threaded the ring onto his finger.

Rob picked up the engagement ring Rose Bellingham had helped him choose this afternoon, with many assurances he was following the right path. This darkened, quiet living room was a far cry from the bustling chrome and glass interior of the little shop in the middle of Chance Creek.

"Morgan Tate, I promise right now to bind my life to yours, forever and always, to love you, honor you, cherish you and build a life by your side. I make this pledge in the presence of God. Forever and ever, amen."

He slid the ring onto her finger.

As he stared across the table, the candles guttering between them, Rob was positive he'd spun his life on its axis and it would never be the same again. He pulled her to stand, tugged her around the table, and bent to seal the bargain with a kiss.

Yes, he would choose to love this woman. He would choose to love her right now.

MORGAN RAN HER FINGERS through her hair and checked her reflection in the mirror, gathering the courage to leave the washroom and return to the bedroom where Rob waited for her. She still felt like she was walking on air. Her own body didn't seem to belong to her. Instead it hummed and tingled and her heart beat fit to burst right out of her chest.

She had no idea what impulse made her fetch the ring and conduct her own quasi-wedding ceremony in the drab little living room of her apartment.

Of course it hadn't felt drab with the candles lit and Rob staring across the coffee table from her. It had felt magical. It still did.

And now she was going to make love to the man she'd spend the rest of her life with.

An idea that both thrilled and terrified her.

It had been a long time since she'd been with a man. A really, really long time.

And she wasn't entirely sure she should be with a man now. Hadn't she told herself she'd wait until her wedding night before she had sex again? She hesitated, staring at her reflection. Wasn't being engaged good enough? She'd promised to marry him, and he'd promised it, too.

She wanted to know what making love to Rob would be like. She'd waited long enough. Smiling, she opened the bathroom door, made her way to the bedroom and found Rob under the covers, leaning back against the headboard of her queen-sized bed.

"Thought you'd never get here." He grinned and her heart did a little flip.

"Sorry." She sat down on the end of the bed, and played with the coverlet. She was wearing a plain blue satin short nightie with spaghetti straps. She wished she'd had something sexier, but since she hadn't been with a man in such a long time, she…didn't.

"Come on over here. Let me get a better look at you." He took her hand and gently tugged it. She slid onto the bed and made her way closer to him. When he drew her into his arms, she sighed and accepted his kiss eagerly.

Soon he was ready for more, however. And when he slid her down onto her back and moved a hand up to her breast, her heart began to pound again. Was she ready for this—right now?

What if Rob changed his mind about getting married?

What if this was one of his jokes, after all?

She blocked his hand with her own, covering up the movement by lifting it to her mouth and kissing his palm. He moved it away and kissed her again, but just as she relaxed and focused on the taste of him, he slid his hand down to her neckline once more, tugging the thin cloth to the side to expose her breast to view. He pulled back, smiled in appreciation, and bent to take it into his mouth.

Morgan stiffened, and when he grazed her nipple with his tongue, she surged up and pushed him away. She hopped off the bed, gripping the nightie to her.

"What…hey—what's wrong?" Rob sat up, too, ready to come after her.

Morgan held out a hand to stop him. "I'm sorry. I'm not ready for this. I…can't."

Rob leaned back. "Are you kidding me?"

"No. I just…I thought…" She shook her head in

confusion. Sliding out of bed, she grabbed a robe from a hook on the back of her door, but he scrambled out of the bed and stopped her before she could reach for the handle and escape into the living room.

"Hold on. What's happening? You can't walk out on me without an explanation."

"We're not married yet." She hesitated, trying desperately to keep her gaze above his waist. She should have told him earlier about her vow. He was right—this wasn't fair, but she hadn't expected to still feel this way. "I don't believe in sex before marriage," she blurted, afraid if she didn't, she'd lose her nerve.

He stopped in his tracks. "Are you saying you're a virgin?"

Now she had his attention, she thought wryly. "No. I'm not a virgin. I didn't always have this attitude toward sex, but some years back I had a...scare. And the man involved was the last man I'd pick to raise a child with. I realized I had to stop fooling around, so to speak."

Rob didn't smile at her little joke. In fact, he looked downright angry. "How long's it been since you've done it?"

She felt her cheeks heat. "About five years."

"Five years?" Now he was shocked. And her neighbors knew the length of her dry spell, too, since he'd practically shouted the words.

"It's been a while," she acknowledged curtly. She felt like she'd been caught doing something perverse, instead of the opposite. Why should she have to feel bad about abstaining? She held the moral high ground. Didn't she?

Rob cocked his head, relaxing a little. "Is this about your mother?"

Damn. Nailed it right on the nose. "Yes. It's about Aria. I grew up hearing how much my birth screwed up everyone's lives. I won't do that to a child."

"But you just told me you wanted to get pregnant. You said you wanted a baby," Rob said, moving closer. "How exactly am I supposed to get that done if we don't have sex?"

"You can *get that done* on our wedding night." She couldn't believe him. Was he really trying to use her desire for a child to seduce her?

"Meanwhile, you want us to keep our distance." He began to advance on her again, and she was all too aware of a certain part of his anatomy. Evidently it hadn't gotten the news that there wouldn't be any under-the-sheets celebrations tonight.

Although...

"We can still fool around," she heard herself say as he pulled her back into his arms. He bent down and scraped a kiss across her jaw. "I think that's only natural." Her voice faltered as he nipped her earlobe.

"Oh, yeah?" Rob straightened. So did that certain piece of his anatomy she was trying so hard to ignore. "How much fooling around do you think is okay to do?" He pulled her in tighter.

Morgan laughed breathlessly. "As much as it takes."

He brushed another kiss over her forehead. "I'm up for fooling around."

Boy, was he. She scooted away, putting a few inches

between them. "I'm serious, though, Rob. If you so much as try to go farther than the limits I've set, I'll tell you to leave and I'll mean it. It's hard enough sticking to my guns without you pressuring me."

"Do you find it hard to stick to your guns?" He edged closer again.

"Only around you," she said.

A smile curved his mouth. "That's what I like to hear."

"So you think you can *get this done* without going all the way?" she pushed.

He grinned and her heart gave a funny flip-flop. Damn, he was handsome. Damn, she wanted him.

"Probably can think of something. But about that wedding..."

"Yes?" Now that they'd settled matters she couldn't wait to feel his touch again.

"Let's get hitched tomorrow." He cupped her ass and pulled her in tight.

"You got it, cowboy," she said with a happy sigh.

Chapter Four

HAD HE EVER WANTED A WOMAN as much as he wanted Morgan? Rob didn't think so. As he laid her back on the bed and fumbled with her nightie, he found that his fingers were trembling. He felt like he'd slipped downstairs early on Christmas morning and found all the presents he'd asked for under the tree. He couldn't wait to see her—all of her—as soon as he got rid of this stupid piece of satin.

Morgan seemed as eager to unwrap him. She reached for his buttons, but he was ahead of her. He shucked off his shirt and groaned with pleasure as she trailed kisses down his neck and chest.

"How the hell do you get this thing off," he growled in frustration, turning back to the nightie, ready to tear it off of her.

Morgan laughed, pushed his fingers away and made short work of stripping it up over her head.

The sound that came from his throat was half animal and all desire. He swept down to sweep his tongue around one full nipple and Morgan arched back with a little gasp. That was all the invitation he needed. Hunger growing inside him, he cupped her breasts and lavished them with attention.

He'd heard what she said, and he wouldn't push her boundaries, but otherwise all bets were off. He intended to show Morgan what he could do beneath the sheets, and meant to leave them both craving their wedding night. Nothing wrong with a little anticipation, and nothing wrong with a little fulfillment in the meantime. He was prepared to fulfill her every carnal wish.

Morgan slid her hands down his back as he took first one breast and then the other into his mouth. When Morgan cupped his ass and squeezed, he groaned aloud.

He wriggled lower, swooping kisses across her belly, running hands down her sides to curve over her hips. When he knew she was aching for a more intimate touch, he reached down and traced a finger over her folds. Morgan stiffened again.

"Shhh," he whispered into her belly. "I know the rules." With a hand on either side of her waist, he pushed himself up and kneed her legs apart, but instead of bending down then to minister to her, he sat back and gazed at her instead. He'd longed for weeks to see her like this, naked and disheveled, waiting for him, and he wanted to drink in the view.

After a moment she wriggled. "What are you doing?"

He knew what it cost her to bare herself to him this way, but that was what they'd promised each other out in the living room; that they would choose to love each other. Choose to make a life together.

Choose to give themselves to the other heart and soul.

"Looking at you." Morgan stared back at him, tense but aroused, too, judging by her flushed face and parted lips. "You're beautiful," he assured her. "I could look at you all night."

A smile curved her lips that was nearly irresistible. Every fiber in his body tugged at him to lean forward— to cross the divide between them and touch her.

Make love to her.

Still, he held back, and not out of a fear that he wouldn't be able to restrain himself once he did touch her. Rob wanted to see this woman he was pairing his life with. He wanted to know all of her. He'd never done this before; just sat and...looked.

"You're scaring me," Morgan whispered finally.

He shook his head. "You have no idea what you do to me."

"Show me."

It was almost a whimper, and the thought of his fiancée waiting for his touch—longing for it—finally propelled him to action.

As he bent to touch his mouth to her core, Rob had the feeling that marrying Morgan would be the easiest thing he ever did.

WHEN ROB'S MOUTH TOUCHED HER, Morgan very nearly came undone right then and there. She'd had no idea how much she ached for him, until he began his sensual attack. His tongue was sweet agony, and she gripped the bedspread to keep from thrashing under his attention. She wanted him inside her more than she'd ever wanted anything in her life. Only the promise she'd kept for so long held her back.

What would their wedding night be like? Would they try to conceive right away? She knew one thing; she'd gladly make love to him then. She could barely restrain herself now. As Rob moved his tongue farther into her folds, she moaned aloud. He paused, and she let go of the coverlet and wrapped her hands in his hair. "Don't stop," she cried, and he chuckled but resumed. Licking, touching, he slipped his hands beneath her ass and squeezed, crushing her against his mouth.

With a cry, Morgan went over the edge, bucking against him, shuddering with pleasure again and again until finally she was spent.

He kissed her thighs, brushed his mouth over her sensitive mound and propped himself on his elbows, the better to see her face. Morgan covered her eyes with her hands. "Sorry," she said. "I meant to wait for you."

He slid up beside her and nudged her hands away. "I liked watching you come."

Heat surged into her cheeks. No man had ever done what he'd done before—simply sat back and looked at her—all of her—for so long. At first she hadn't liked it; she felt stripped of every defense she had along with her clothes, but as the moments ticked by, she'd understood what Rob was feeling. His desire for her and his wonder at her body bathed her in warmth until she hummed with anticipation of the acts to come. She hoped he loved to watch her as much in ten years as he did now. She hoped their marriage stayed passionate.

But right now, she wanted to get a better look at him. "Your turn now," she said, pushing him down on the bed.

"If you insist."

Chapter Five

THE NEXT MORNING, Rob called his father's cell phone as he watched Morgan grab a box of fiber cereal from her barren cupboards and a small carton of one percent milk from the fridge. Yuck. That was her idea of breakfast?

"Rob? Where the hell are you?" Holt said. "It's past time for chores." Behind him, cattle lowed and bawled. He must be right among the herd.

"I know. I'm...out of town. Actually I'm out of the country."

"Out of the country? What the hell does that mean?"

"I'm in Canada—with Morgan. I've got some news." Rob grinned when Morgan lifted her head and smiled tentatively at him. "Dad, just listen, will you? I'm getting married."

He held his breath. From the look of things, Morgan was holding hers, too.

"Married."

"That's right, married," he said. "To Morgan Tate, Ethan and Claire's half-sister. I'm in Victoria right now.

Last night she agreed to be my wife." He flashed her a thumb's up.

"You're marrying that whore's daughter?"

Rob jerked and spun on his heel, striding to the far side of the living room, afraid Morgan might be able to hear his father's words. "Dad. That's no way to talk…"

"I'm calling it like I see it. If my wife ran around like Aria Cruz did, she'd see the backside of my hand. I certainly wouldn't hitch my wagon to a filly whose mare was that kind of wild." Holt was breathing hard, probably walking back to the barn or the house, to get away from the noise of the cattle.

"For God's sake." After a furtive look in Morgan's direction, Rob paced to the bedroom and shut the door behind him. "First of all, I never want to hear you speak about my wife or my wife's family like that again. Second of all, it's no fault of Morgan's if her parents' marriage was less than perfect. My parents' marriage ain't all sunshine and roses, either."

"You done?" Holt growled.

"For now," Rob growled right back. "If I think of anything else, I'll let you know."

"When's this so-called wedding?"

"Tonight if I can swing it. Tomorrow or the next day if I can't. We haven't figured out what it takes to get a civil marriage yet."

"Civil marriage? A civil marriage ain't going to do you any good. You want the land I told you about, you'll get married right here on our lawn."

"But…"

"But what? You afraid if she has to wait a month or two, she'll lose interest? Or are you paying her to marry you? You get a divorce, I'll expect that land back, you hear me? Should have known the first thing you'd do is pull off some joke."

Rob's anger surged. "I'm not joking, and we planned a civil wedding because we were in a hurry. And yeah, part of that hurry is I'm afraid Jake or Ned will beat me to it and grab that land. I don't trust you to keep your word."

He wondered if he'd gone too far. Holt had many faults, but he considered himself to be an honorable man.

"I won't go back on my word as long as the marriage is real. You bring back that girl of yours and you stand up before our family and friends and pledge your vows, and I'll give you the land then and there. But if I think you're playing a trick, the whole thing's off."

"Fine." Rob opened the bedroom door and walked out into the living room again in order to consult with Morgan. She was still eating her cereal, and raised her eyebrows at him. "We have to get married on the ranch," he told her. "How about two weeks from Saturday?"

"A week after Claire and Jamie get married?" Morgan asked. "Will they even be back from their honeymoon?"

"Shit."

"Those Cruzes are having a wedding in a week or so," Holt was saying in his ear, echoing Morgan's words. "Can't have two weddings in a row. You'd better wait a month." He heard paper shuffling on the other end of the phone. Holt must be consulting one of his many calendars. He got them free from local banks and feed companies each year, and posted one in every barn and outbuilding on the spread. "October eleventh. Might be chilly. We'll have to prepare for bad weather. I'll leave that up to your mother to sort out."

"October eleventh? That's…" He turned a pleading expression on Morgan.

"That's perfect," she said, and to his surprise she actually seemed happy. Maybe she hadn't been as thrilled at the prospect of a quick, civil wedding as he was. Women never were. She probably wanted all that dress and flower stuff.

"What if Jake or Ned or Luke decides to get married before I even get home?" he asked his father.

"Nah—you've staked your claim," Holt said. "I'll put you on the phone with your mother next. If you tell her she can start planning that wedding, then I won't let no one else jump the line ahead of you until after October eleventh. If you call the wedding off, though, the field's wide open again."

"Okay, well…all right. As long as they can't pull a fast one on me. I'll have Morgan home tomorrow night. Wait…she's trying to tell me something."

"I can't leave tomorrow—I have to give some notice at work and pack. I've already got tickets for September second, the night before Claire and Jamie's wedding. That's when we'll go."

Rob thought about arguing with her, then decided against it. He spoke into the phone again. "Morgan needs time to tie up some loose ends here, so we'll be home next Friday. Put Mom on. I'll let Morgan talk to her."

"All right. But don't expect your mother to waste her time planning a wedding until you and your bride actually roll into town. We know your track record. You don't have a chance in hell at pulling this off."

"Thanks a lot for that vote of confidence, Dad," he said, his anger finally getting the best of him. "Don't worry about tracking down Mom. I'll call her cell directly." He hung up with an oath.

"What did he say?" Morgan, finished with her breakfast, approached him, concern in her gaze.

"He can never let me do things my way," he finally said. "Not even my own damned wedding. He says it doesn't count unless we get married at the ranch. The whole town has to be present, too, and since Claire and Jamie are getting married on Labor Day we have to wait at least a month afterwards. That means October 11th. That's six weeks away!"

"That's not too long." Morgan looked pleased at the chance for a ranch wedding.

"Six weeks for my father to think of other ways to screw with me," Rob said. "Mark my words, he'll figure out some way to back out of giving me that land."

"Giving us that land, you mean," Morgan said, glancing at her watch and heading toward the bedroom. "You're not giving up, are you? Do you want to call it off?" She hesitated by the door.

"No." Rob's quick and vehement answer surprised

himself as much as her. "My brothers and mother all heard him say he'd give the land to the first son to get married. There'll be five of us against one if he pulls something. Almost a fair fight. I'm supposed to call my Mom and let her know what's going on. She'll want to start to plan the wedding."

"I have to get going or I'll be late for work. How about we call her tonight?"

MORGAN SAT IN HER TINY OFFICE at Cassidy Wineries, wondering if she could stay in it throughout the next week. She had handed in her resignation and Elliot was simply furious. So far she'd avoided Duncan, but she knew that couldn't last. He often didn't get to work until late in the morning, so any minute now he'd knock on her door and launch into his latest idiocy. She should have quit point blank and left for Montana a week and a half early, but her prudent side—the side that had seen her through a lifetime of needing to watch her own back, since no one else would watch it for her—dictated that she give her employer some notice to find her replacement. Best not to burn every bridge she currently had in the wine industry, in case things went sour with Rob and she found herself back here looking for a job. Besides, in four nights the winery was celebrating the launch of *her* vintage.

She should march back into Elliot's office and tell him exactly what had transpired last night, but what did she expect Elliot to do? He'd make another excuse, pat her arm like a compassionate uncle and sweep the whole affair under the rug. Duncan was his son, after all.

Unable to hide any longer, she slid her door open a crack and stepped into the distillery room, hoping against hope Duncan would stay away.

Nope. He must have been waiting for her.

"Morgan!" he called from behind one of the massive vats. "Vineyard. Now."

She sighed, slowing her pace to a crawl as she followed him outside.

"I spoke to your father this morning," she told his back.

"I hope for your sake you didn't tell any tales out of school, Tate."

"I handed in my resignation."

He stopped short and turned around. "Resignation? Where do you think you're going? No one's going to hire someone as insubordinate as you."

Just as she thought; he would do whatever it took to undermine any job search she made locally. Thank God she didn't have to—yet. "I'm not looking for another job."

"Oh yeah? What are you doing?"

Caution warred with the desire to see him squirm. "Getting married."

She stalked past him toward the vineyards, unprepared for how freeing that revelation felt. For once she didn't care what Duncan was doing behind her back. She didn't care if she was headed in the right direction or what he would tell her to do next. In a sudden surge of excitement, she realized she didn't have to do a damn thing he said for the rest of her time at Cassidy Wineries. What was he going to do—fire her?

She walked down the first long row of grapevines she reached, knowing that she would miss them, even if she didn't give Duncan another thought once she left Victoria. She knew these fields well, even if the bulk of her time was spent indoors. She didn't dislike overseeing the growth of the grapes; you couldn't be a vintner without a love of the fruit itself. But she far preferred the precision and science of the distillery. Duncan knew that, and he always tried to tear her away from the things she loved.

She figured he planned to get his revenge for last night's escape by marching her up and down the rows of perfectly developing grapes instead of letting her monitor the giant machinery that turned the humble fruit into the nectar of the gods.

He probably also wanted her out here to get time alone with her. Normally when they worked the fields, he took every opportunity to accidently brush by her, or take her hand to lead her, or wrap an arm about her as they surveyed the magnificence of the vines heavy with their fruit. Today he'd better not try any of those tricks.

Morgan pushed her heavy, dark hair away from her face. It was hot and dusty in the fields. She already felt sweat trickling down her back under the crisp material of her blouse.

"This could have been ours someday, you know," Duncan said, leaning in close. He touched her arm. "The old geezer won't last forever. I'll inherit everything.

Whoever you're marrying doesn't have anything to compare to this."

"He's got plenty," Morgan said, moving away. "And it's morbid to wait around for your father to die."

He pursued her. "It's practical. You love this vineyard and you've been working here forever. Marry me and you'll own half of it."

"I'm engaged." She waggled her ring in his face. "So drop it already."

"Come off it, Morgan—you know you're trying to make me jealous...who the hell is that?"

She turned to look in the direction he was facing and saw a tall man making his way along the row of grapevines towards them. A tall man in a cowboy hat.

Her heart thrilled, then sank. She didn't want Rob *here*.

Rob stopped to play with the winery's two dogs that raced out to see who this stranger was. In an instant he had them frolicking and bounding like puppies and she felt the corner of her mouth turning up. Animals loved Rob and he loved them back—she'd seen that on the Cruz ranch. She envied his easy comfort with them.

"Do you know him?" Duncan demanded, already moving forward. Morgan hustled after him. Visitors weren't allowed to walk in the fields. No one was allowed in the fields without the express permission of one of the Cassidys.

"Yes—that's my fiancé. He's visiting from Montana. He must have gotten bored back at my apartment."

Duncan stopped in his tracks and she nearly walked

into him. "You're serious, aren't you? You've got a fiancé? And you went out with me last night? How come you never mentioned him?"

"I didn't want to go out with you last night. You told me your father had called a meeting, remember?" She wasn't going to explain to him just how short a time she'd actually known Rob.

He got moving again, lengthening his strides until she practically had to run to keep up with him. They met Rob halfway down the row of grapes. Duncan stuck out his hand. "Hi—I'm Duncan Cassidy. My family owns this vineyard. Morgan says you're her fiancé."

Rob looked from one to the other of them, and met Duncan's handshake. "That's right. I'm Rob Matheson."

Morgan wanted to hide her head in her hands. Dammit, why hadn't she told Rob he absolutely couldn't come here? If he got any whiff of the fact that Duncan had tried to kidnap her last night, she didn't know what he'd do. She'd seen him beat the crap out of one man— the guy who'd attacked her when she and Claire went after her stolen possessions. The result hadn't been pretty. If he did the same thing to Duncan, her reputation in the industry would be toast.

But Duncan's fake smile of greeting broadened. "Rob—so good to finally meet you. Morgan's talked about you non-stop since she got back from her vacation."

Rob's eyebrows shot up. "Really? What's she been saying?"

"Something about you Montana boys putting us Canadians to shame." Duncan laughed heartily and clapped Rob on the shoulder. Morgan truly wanted to sink into the ground. She'd never said any such thing. Rob would think she was bragging about him. "What do you think of our operation?"

Rob surveyed the field of grapes. "Haven't seen much of it. How old are these vines? Four or five years?"

Duncan seemed surprised by his interest. "Six years, actually. Do you grow your own?"

"Grapes in Montana? Now that you mention it, I'm not sure if they grow there." He glanced at Morgan, as if wondering if that might throw a kink in the works.

"Actually, they do. There are a couple of wineries in the state," Morgan put in, happy to reassure Rob about that fact, and even happier to keep the conversation on a safe track. If she could get Rob away from Duncan before he did any more damage…

"How about I give you a tour?" Duncan asked Rob.

Rob settled his hat in a more comfortable position on his head. "Well, I was hoping Morgan might be up to that task."

"Of course," she began, pushing past Duncan to stand in between them.

"Unfortunately, Morgan needs to return to the distillery," Duncan said, easily elbowing her away. "She's working, you know, and we're only getting the benefit of her know-how for a few more days. I suppose you're the reason she's leaving, eh? As the owner, I love showing guests around our operation. We'll start outside and work our way in."

"That's mighty friendly of you." Rob looked at Morgan and gave a little shrug, as if to say, "It's better than nothing."

"I really don't have any pressing tasks in the distillery," Morgan tried again.

"It's unusual to have guests drop by during work hours, Morgan," Duncan said in a steely voice that brooked no opposition. "It's lucky I'm here to take over as tour guide so you don't have to send him straight home again."

"It is lucky," Rob said, seeming to grasp the situation fully now. "The last thing I want is to get Morgan here in trouble. You can't blame a man for wanting to be close to his girl, though, can you?" Rob persisted, nudging Duncan. Morgan thought she might keel over and die right then and there.

"No. You definitely can't blame a man for that," Duncan said, shooting her a significant look. "Run along now, Morgan. Back to work. I'll take care of your friend, here."

She was sure he would.

Chapter Six

As Rob watched Morgan walk away, he had the feeling he'd made a big mistake coming to the vineyard. He should have gone sight-seeing like she told him to, but alone in her apartment he'd felt like the walls were closing in.

Was he really ready for marriage and fatherhood? For starting a business and settling down? What if he failed? What if he screwed up with his kids?

He couldn't remember the last time he'd spent an entire day indoors, and within an hour he was pacing in circles around the living room. Morgan's bookcases caught his attention for a short time. Her interests ranged from horticulture to anthropology, art history to beekeeping, and everything in between. But when he tried to sit down and read, he soon found himself on his feet again. He supposed he could have gone for a walk, but the concrete sidewalks and crowded buildings didn't call him at all.

He wanted to be near Morgan. To touch her again. Needing to distract himself from that train of thought, he gestured to the grapes and asked Duncan, "How long has your family been in the business?"

"Three generations," Duncan said proudly. "My granddad bought this land. It's part of my blood."

"Like my ranch back home. The Mathesons have lived there since 1848," Rob said. "Feels strange to be away from it."

"So you and Morgan are getting hitched."

"Yep."

"Should have known there was someone in her life. Come on, let me show you around."

Rob thought he'd find the tour annoying, since he'd really come to see Morgan, but to his surprise he found it fascinating. At first Duncan seemed to want to talk more about Morgan than about the grapes, and Rob had the sneaking suspicion the man had the hots for her, but after he'd asked a few pointed questions about the rootstock, irrigation and the kinds of pests they had to deal with, Duncan launched into explanations and couldn't seem to stop talking. Rob imagined he rarely had an audience that was actually interested in the minutiae of growing such a finicky crop, but he'd spent enough time around his mother to know what questions to ask, and to process the information he received in return.

Most of the farmers he knew in Montana grew wheat. He'd never thought about the possibility of cultivating grapes. He itched to be back at Morgan's apartment, where he could look up the wineries she'd mentioned on the Internet and see if any were near to

Chance Creek. Most likely not. He'd have heard of them, wouldn't he?

Of course, he and his friends drank beer and whiskey, not wine.

His parents had quite a cellar-full laid in, though. Maybe they knew more about it.

"You must need a lot of workers to tend these fields," he said. Duncan raised a hand to shade his eyes and scanned the rows of grapes.

"There." He pointed and Rob squinted against the glare. He saw a number of men bent over the plants some rows away. "Most of them come up from Mexico for the harvest."

"Migrant workers?"

Duncan shrugged. "A few of them have done such a good job we've hired them permanently. We were able to help them immigrate to Canada and become citizens. The rest come and go. Let's see how they're doing."

Rob hung back when they approached the men hard at work. They all wore baseball caps to protect their faces from the sun. A few had tucked towels under their hats to hang down over their necks for further protection. They needed cowboy hats, he decided. Maybe seeing his would give them the right idea.

"Raoul, Thomas, Eduardo, meet Rob Matheson. He's visiting Victoria and I'm giving him a tour of the winery. Raoul and Thomas work for us permanently. Eduardo here is new this year."

The men all murmured greetings. Thomas took Duncan aside and launched into a discussion about the grapes and the exact day he thought they would be ready to harvest. Raoul and Eduardo gazed at Rob expectantly. He searched for a way to carry on the conversation.

"Do you like it here?" he asked.

Both men shook their heads yes emphatically. "Living here is like living in paradise," Raoul said. "I can feed my family, house them, they have medical care."

"Only thing is," Eduardo said, his accent more pronounced than Raoul's, "the food." He shook his head. "Very bad."

Raoul laughed. "Not enough Mexican food in Victoria," he agreed. "We need more immigrants. Maybe your wife someday, eh?" he nudged Eduardo. "Eduardo hopes Mr. Cassidy will take him on permanently, too. Help him immigrate, like he did me." He turned to his friend. "You have to work, work, work! First here in the morning, last gone at night, like I did all those years." To Rob he said. "I proved I was the best vineyard worker. Mr. Cassidy couldn't bear to see me go."

"You have to take time off, though," Rob said. "Live a little. Have some fun, right?" That had always been his mantra, anyhow.

Raoul became stern. "Fun is for people like you, Mr. Matheson. People who have all they need already. Me and Eduardo, we work, work, work to survive. Fun is being alive another day."

"Fun is food to eat at night," Eduardo put in wryly.

Rob scratched the back of his neck. He always seemed to be saying or doing the wrong thing these days. "Do you like the work, at least?"

"Work is work," Raoul said. "But yes, I like the growing things. I like to see the grapes reach the harvest. My muscle," he patted his arms, "my sweat—it is turned into food right before my eyes!"

Rob smiled at that. He'd never thought of work that way—that sometimes the result of the labor could be so tangible. He supposed it was like that on the ranch, but since he only did a task here, a job there, he didn't take in the whole process.

And whose fault is that?

He shifted uncomfortably. It was his own damn fault, he knew that. He barely showed up for the small tasks his father and brothers set him. He sure as hell didn't work, work, work like Raoul was advising Eduardo to do. He'd never proved himself the best man for the job in any tangible way.

Was that because he was too busy bucking his family's hierarchy, and getting back at his brothers for their earlier misdeeds, or was it because ranching didn't interest him all that much?

And if he wasn't interested in ranching, what did he want to do?

He surveyed the fields around him again.

No, he wasn't a farmer, or vintner, or whatever you called it. His love was horses and the rodeo. No way you'd find him mucking about in fields.

Even if it did look interesting.

"Mind if I try?" he asked Raoul, not sure why he wanted to prune grapevines. Something about watching the other men thin the foliage made his fingers itch to grab a pair of shears and get to work, though. Maybe it was the way the vines looked refreshed afterward—like they could breathe better.

Raoul had explained that the grapes were ripening and becoming sweet. Cutting back the leaves to the perfect balance of fruit to foliage pushed this process forward. According to Raoul, that was highly desired.

Duncan, coming back to his side after finishing his conversation, raised his eyebrows when he saw what Rob was doing. "You want to work?"

"Sure. I've got nothing better to do. Still an hour until lunchtime, right?"

Duncan looked at his watch. "Try two. You get bored, you come and find me; we'll finish that tour." But the man had a smirk on his face, probably thrilled to leave his rival toiling in the fields like one of the hired help. Rob didn't give that a second thought, though.

"Show me again which leaves to take off," he said to Raoul.

By the end of the afternoon, Rob's back ached in ways he hadn't thought possible. He had always considered himself a strong man, and for all his tendencies to put pleasure before responsibility, he knew how to do a full day's work, but the repetitive process of removing foliage from the bottom of the plants—leaving just enough leaves to shade the ripening grapes from the full-on sun—turned out to be harder than he would have expected.

Raoul and the other men shared their lunches with him during their short break, and only afterwards did

Rob realize he probably should have sought out Morgan and eaten with her.

Still, when he went to meet her in the parking lot at five o'clock, he felt the satisfaction of having worked with his hands and done a good job. Why didn't ranching ever feel like that?

Maybe it was time for a career change.

Chapter Seven

"I CAN'T BELIEVE YOU WORKED in the vineyards," Morgan said again as they entered her apartment.

"Yeah, well get used to it," Rob drawled. He'd been evasive about his intentions in helping out the Mexican field workers. She had no idea if he was trying to impress her, or get even with her for leaving him stranded in her apartment the day after they'd gotten engaged. He'd certainly confused Duncan, who'd loitered outside for a half-hour waiting for him to get bored and come back for the rest of that tour before coming inside to complain to her about her bizarre boyfriend.

"What do you mean, get used to it?"

"I'm going back tomorrow. Raoul said they could use another pair of hands, and Duncan said he'd pay me the going rate."

"You realize the going rate is minimum wage." She dropped her keys on the counter and flipped through her mail.

"It's more than I'll get if I sit here on my ass. Hold on, phone's ringing." He pulled out his cell phone and checked the screen. "It's my mom—probably for you." He shoved it into her hands and disappeared into the bedroom before she could protest. Morgan clicked it on and held it to her ear.

"Hello?"

"Morgan, is that you? I'm so glad you answered, honey. I wanted to talk to you about colors."

"Colors?"

"We've got to start somewhere, don't you think? October eleventh isn't that far off. What's your favorite color, honey?"

"Um…I don't know."

"You don't know your own favorite color?" Lisa laughed. "Sounds like that son of mine has got you all turned around up there."

She was partially right. Between Rob's sudden appearance and their whirlwind decision to spend their lives together, and his bizarre behavior at the winery today, she was a bit addled. But what truly left her speechless was Lisa's attitude. They hadn't even met yet and she was acting like they were old friends. Almost like a…mother.

"I really like mint green. I don't know if that helps."

"That helps a whole lot," Lisa said. "Now, I've started a guest list. I'm at 212 at the present. Both Holt's family and mine have lived in this area over 100 years, so we know almost everyone in the county. I'm trying not to let it get out of control. You'll need to send me your list. Do you have an estimate?"

Morgan steadied her breath, but the question pierced

her to the core. "Maybe…maybe you can give me some advice," she said finally. "I have a number of female friends in the area, but I don't expect them to spend the money to travel to Montana. Do I still invite them?"

"Of course—let them decide whether to make the trip or not. We've got extra rooms on the ranch, and I daresay your family does, too. We can put some of them up for the wedding. What about family?" Lisa's voice was kind and that made it all the worse.

"I hope my father will come. He's really the only family I have left."

"Of course he'll come. He'll have to walk you up the aisle, won't he?"

Morgan couldn't bear to say aloud that she wasn't at all sure he'd make the time. His wife wouldn't like him flying to Montana for such a task.

"Of course," she said, as firmly as she could.

"Now, Morgan, I want you to be straight with me," Lisa said. Morgan stiffened. Here it came—the accusation she'd been bracing herself against ever since Rob disappeared into his bedroom the previous evening when he was on the phone with his father. His parents had to be wondering if this was all a joke, or if they were being lied to. She was sure Lisa would press her for an answer. "I've waited so long for this," Lisa said. "I had a plain wedding—we had no money at all in those days. Just my parents and siblings and my best friend for my brides-maid. I vowed right then that if any of my children got married we'd throw them a fairy-tale wedding. Of course, I figured I'd have at least one girl," She trailed off wistfully for a moment, "but the good Lord saw fit to give me four ornery sons. Now that I'm finally getting to throw a wedding I want to do it right. But it's not my wedding. It's yours. You speak up now and tell me to butt right out of it if that's what you want."

Morgan laughed in relief. "Of course not. It's going to be at your house, for one thing."

"That doesn't mean I get to boss you around. The bride calls the shots; that's the way I see it."

"Are you sure this isn't too much trouble for you?" Morgan said. The truth was Lisa's exuberance was overwhelming her. She'd expected anger and suspicion. Instead she was getting enthusiasm.

"Trouble? Are you kidding? I'm over the moon! Of all my sons, Rob's the one I've wanted to see settle down. You have a good man there, Morgan. I hope you know that."

"You don't think it's too soon?" She glanced up to make sure Rob wasn't listening, but he'd disappeared into the bathroom and she could hear the shower running.

"The heart knows what the heart knows. There are some tricks to making a marriage work and I'd be happy to pass on what little wisdom I have, but at the heart of it are a few simple questions. Do your eyes light up when Rob walks into the room? Does your heart skip a beat? Do you feel drawn to him?"

"Yes," Morgan said, smiling a little.

"And when you're angry, are you really angry? Like, ready to blow your top angry?"

"That would be a good thing?" Morgan asked. She hadn't had time to be that angry with Rob yet.

"Yes. Passion. It's all about passion," Lisa said. "When you couldn't care less if he comes or goes, and you can't muster up the energy to get truly angry at him; that's when you've got a problem."

"Hmmm." She'd have to remember that.

"I'm going to let you go have your supper now. I'm going to email you some menu ideas. Are you on Pinterest? I have a whole board of bouquets! You have to *friend* me."

Morgan held the phone away from her ear. Friend her mother-in-law?

"As soon as you get here we'll go to Ellie's Bridals. If she doesn't have exactly what you want, we'll get it custom made. Rob sent me a photo of you; you'll make a lovely bride."

"Okay," Morgan said, trying to keep up. "But…we haven't talked about the cost. I have some money…"

"Honey, you stop worrying right now. Any woman who's head over heels in love with my baby is going to get pampered from here to next week by me! You won't be footing the bill for a single thing. That's my job. Aria and I were never exactly what you'd call close, but we were friendly and I know she'd want me to do this for you. If she were here, she'd throw you the wedding of the century. Since she can't, I will. Talk to you tomorrow."

And with that, she hung up.

"You okay?" Rob said, entering the room with a

towel wrapped around his waist. "What did she say to you?" He frowned with concern when she didn't answer right away.

Morgan shook herself out of her thoughts. She was floored by Lisa's friendliness and generosity. "I'm fine. She said all the right things." She smiled. This was going to work; finally, she was going to get the family and community she always wanted.

"OF COURSE I'M HAPPY FOR YOU," Ethan said when Rob called him. "But I'm stunned. You and Morgan only met last month. You sure you're not rushing into things?"

"You got married to Autumn after only knowing her a month."

"Well, sure—but I lived with her for that month, day and night."

"Emphasis on the nights, huh?"

"Stow it."

Rob chuckled, but Ethan's reaction made him uneasy. Everyone was going to question their sincerity when they heard about their engagement, and he didn't want Morgan to lose her nerve.

"So, one thing," Rob said carefully. "My Dad's going to give us some land as a wedding gift, and I promised Morgan we'd use half of it to start a vineyard."

"You're going to grow grapes in Montana?"

"Yeah—I looked into it. It's possible."

"Seems like a silly thing to do. Cattle's way more profitable."

Rob tamped down on the irritation that surged within him. He'd expected Ethan, at least, to be supportive. "She's my bride. I want to make her happy."

That shut Ethan up. "Okay. I guess I see your point."

"Anyway, for my gift to Morgan I'm giving her a down payment for her business. I want her to have everything she'll need to get prepared for next spring. Between tilling, rootstock, stakes and wires and the rest of it, she estimates it'll take twenty grand above and beyond what she's got to get things started."

"You got that kind of cash kicking around?"

Rob sighed. "You know I don't. Dad gives us room and board, but not much extra. I got a truck payment and a running tab down at the Boot. I figure I've got about eight thousand in the bank."

"In other words you're looking for either a handout or for work," Ethan said. "I've got work, but I don't pay twelve grand a month."

"I know, buddy. I'm hoping you have some ideas about who might."

Ethan was silent for a while. "You know, with all this settling down and wanting a job, I'm not sure I know who you are anymore."

"Ethan," Rob growled.

"All right, all right—I'll think it over and let you know what I come up with. Meanwhile, I've got one thing to say to you." Suddenly, Ethan sounded dead serious.

"What's that?"

"If you hurt my sister, you're going to be in a world of pain."

Chapter Eight

THREE DAYS LATER it was Saturday, the day of the party at Cassidy's to honor Morgan's first vintage. In some ways it had been the best week of her life. Even though the hours in the distillery were long, she knew that Rob was working in the fields with Raoul and the other men close at hand. At night, they went home to pack her things and then fall in to bed to explore each other's bodies and find every which way to wring pleasure out of them. On the other hand, the strain was telling on her. Elliot was angry with her for wanting to leave, and Duncan seemed to be going out of his way to make her life miserable. If it hadn't been for the celebration of her new vintage tonight, she would have walked out days ago.

Only a week to go, she told herself as she finished getting dressed. When she came out of the bedroom a moment later, Rob whistled.

"You look stunning."

Dressed in a scarlet sheath dress with a sweetheart neckline and a knee-length, pencil-thin fitted skirt, she felt sexy and curvy and knew he'd have a hard time keeping his hands off of her. Her matching stiletto heels and scarlet lipstick made a bold statement, and she'd done her dark hair up into a crisp chignon. Since this was her vintage being celebrated tonight, she had dressed for the limelight.

"You look very handsome," she said. Rob did look handsome. Unfortunately, he looked supremely uncomfortable, too, in the tailored suit they'd picked out for him when she realized he'd be here for the celebration.

"I still think my jeans and blazer would have done fine," he said.

"Pretend they are your jeans and blazer. Don't worry so much."

"I keep thinking I'm going to tear something. These pants don't fit right."

Morgan bit her lip to keep from laughing at the cowboy. Poor man. He was wrong, though; his pants fit fine.

She wrapped a silky shawl around her shoulders. "Come on, time to go."

ROB GUESSED THE MONKEY SUIT had been a good call, after all, as he mingled among the throngs of society folks who'd come out to try Cassidy Wineries' newest vintage. He had a glass of the stuff in his hand and he had to admit it tasted mighty good. Especially paired with the appetizers uniformed waitstaff were passing around to the guests. He snagged another one off a passing tray—some kind of cracker topped with ingredients he could barely begin to guess at. A cheesy paste of some sort. He popped it whole into his mouth.

Now that was tasty.

The company left something to be desired, though. Everyone seemed to know everyone else, while he knew nobody. He'd exchanged a few stilted sentences with a man near the entrance, and a woman in the middle of the room, but after they found out he was a cowboy from Montana, the conversations stopped cold.

He ran a hand through his hair. Morgan had nixed his cowboy hat. Said it wasn't done to wear one inside at an event like this. He felt half-bald without it, and of course no one knew what he was since it wasn't sitting on his head. If he'd been able to wear it, people interested in cattle and ranching could spot it from anywhere in the room and make a bee-line to him. Everything would be easy, then. As it was, how was he supposed to figure out who liked to talk ranching, and who didn't?

What did all these city people do, anyway? He decided to find out.

A quick scan of the room showed him a young lady reaching for an appetizer. She didn't seem to belong to any of the knots of conversations around her. A few steps brought him to her side and he selected another tidbit from the same tray.

"Good, aren't they?" he said, remembering just in time not to speak with his mouth full. Dinners at the Matheson ranch could become something of a free for all. Best to mind his manners here.

"Yes, they are," the woman said.

"I'm Rob Matheson." He stuck out his hand.

She switched her wine glass to her left hand and shook with him. "Eva Lorimer."

"What do you do, Eva?" All around them, gowned women and suited men drank and talked and laughed. The noise level was definitely rising the more wine was consumed.

"I'm in data analysis."

Data analysis? "What does a data analyst do all day?"

She raised an eyebrow. With cheekbones like that she should have been a model. "Analyze data."

Hell. "Want to explain what that means?"

"It means I sift through a lot of numbers and other information looking for trends that will help my clients improve their products and services."

Ah. "In other words, you sit at a desk all day and stare at a computer." He made a face. "Tough break."

Eva frowned. "I love my job."

"That's because you've never ridden a horse."

"Excuse me?"

"All you city people—you have no idea what real work is supposed to look like. I feel sorry for you."

"Yeah, well I feel sorry for you, asshole." She turned on her heel and disappeared into the crowd.

Hmmm, that didn't go too well.

He scanned the large, crowded room again until he spotted Morgan's red dress. She looked as unhappy as Eva had a second ago. Duncan was holding her arm and talking intently into her ear. He figured he'd better go find out what the bastard was saying to make Morgan so upset.

By the time he made it through the crowd, however, Morgan was heading toward one of the exits and Duncan was climbing onto the temporary stage that had been set up at one end of the hall. The musicians, who'd been providing some rather boring background music, became quiet and Duncan adjusted the microphone at the front of the stage and addressed the crowd.

"Welcome, one and all, to Cassidy Wineries' unveiling of its latest vintage…"

Rob reached the exit right as the door closed behind Morgan. He pushed through it, and called out to her retreating back, "Morgan. Wait!"

She slowed but didn't turn around.

"Hold up! What happened? What did he say to you?" When he finally caught up to her, his gut tightened in anger when he saw the tears sliding silently down her cheeks. "What the hell did he do?"

"He's taking credit for the vintage. My name won't be paired with it in any way. I mean, it's not like my name was going to be on the label or anything, but this was supposed to be my moment of glory—the night I got to stand up and be proud of what I did."

"Why isn't he giving you credit?"

"Because…I said no to him." She tried to turn away but he held her firmly.

"No to what?"

"No to…being with him. No to being his wife."

That son-of-a-bitch. Rage made it difficult to speak. If he said something now he'd sound like he was yelling at her. He paced away and fought to regain control of his temper. "Dry your eyes. I'm going to take care of this."

"No. Rob, don't…," she said, following him.

"Remember when I asked you to respect me? When we said our vows?" He knew it wasn't entirely fair to throw that in her face right now, but he'd be damned if he stood by and let Duncan Cassidy ride roughshod over her. He'd worked in the fields here for three days now and he knew how the hands felt about the Cassidys. Elliot was strict. Duncan was a jerk.

Morgan paused, opened her mouth and then closed it again. She searched his face with her gaze. "Okay," she said finally, although he could see that was an effort. "You said you'd think through your decisions. I'm trusting you to do that. What are you going to do?"

He nodded. "You'll see. Be back inside and ready in about thirty seconds, okay? Remember to smile. The bastards hate it when you smile." He strode back to the door and let himself in just in time to see Duncan grinning and preening in front of the crowd. Rob climbed the two steps to the stage, crossed it and stood side by side with the man, leaning in to the mic like he was part of the show and had something to add.

"Howdy folks, everyone having a good time tonight?" There was a ripple of amusement and surprise through the crowd at this unexpected interruption, but a smattering of applause and one good natured call back, as well. "I said, everyone having a good time tonight?" Rob repeated, more loudly. He'd emcee'd a concert or two at the Dancing Boot in his time. He knew how to rouse a crowd.

"Yes!" Cheers and clapping thundered through the

hall.

"What are you doing?" Duncan hissed, elbowing him away.

"What you should be doing," Rob said in a low voice, keeping a smile plastered on his face. He grabbed the mic with one hand and wrapped his other arm around Duncan, as if they were old buddies. He addressed the crowd. "As Duncan was saying, we're so glad you could join us and get a taste of Cassidy Wineries' latest vintage. But now it's time to meet the mastermind behind the wine. A beautiful young lady, and my fiancée…"

Duncan elbowed him again, and in one quick, practiced motion, Rob flipped up the tails of Duncan's coat, shoved his hand down the back of his pants and twisted his fist into the man's underwear. Yanking upwards as hard as he could, he gave Duncan the wedgie of the century. "Tell 'em, Mr. Cassidy. Who made this wonderful wine?"

Duncan let out a bray like a startled donkey, then managed to croak out, "Morgan Tate," in a voice several octaves higher than usual.

"You heard the man. Let's give a warm welcome to Morgan Tate!" He nodded toward the entrance, where Morgan stood uncertainly. "Come on, darling. Tell the crowd a little about your wine."

One hand still entwined in Duncan's underwear, an image sure to haunt him for days to come, Rob shoved Duncan away from the mic, towards the side of the stage. Morgan hesitantly took their place and began to speak.

"I came to Cassidy Wineries a decade ago, determined to learn everything there was to know about cultivating grapes and turning them into wine…" she began. As she went on, her voice became stronger and he saw the crowd becoming captivated by her story. Soon she had them on her side, as she detailed the journey she'd taken to rise through the ranks from a lowly position working in the tasting room to becoming manager of the distillery. "This summer I finally discovered the one place in the world where I belong," she said, with a glance and a smile toward Rob. "That's why this vintage is called Coming Home. I hope when you taste it, you'll be reminded of the complexity of the landscape and people that make up the one place in the world where you belong. Thank you." She dipped her head, and the crowd applauded her enthusiastically.

Rob released Duncan, but leaned in to say into his ear. "That's nothing compared to what I'll do if you ever turn her smile into a frown again. Got me?"

Duncan nodded and hurried from the stage. Rob hoped that was the last they'd see of him tonight.

"Ready to dance?" he asked Morgan when he slipped his arm through hers and led her to the parquet floor that was now filling with couples. The band struck up a waltz.

"Okay. But tell me—what did you say to Duncan? I can't believe he let me up on stage." She slid her arms around his neck and leaned comfortably against his chest.

Rob suppressed a chuckle. "I'll tell you all about it when we get home tonight."

Chapter Nine

"READY FOR THIS?" Rob asked as they prepared to deplane at Chance Creek Regional Airport six days later.

Morgan took a deep, steadying breath. The past week had been a whirlwind and she felt like she hadn't had a chance to get a hold of herself since the night of the winery party. Rob had never quite explained what he'd done to make Duncan keep quiet when he'd called her up to the stage. She hadn't seen the man for the rest of the evening, and on Monday morning she'd dreaded going to work. When she arrived at her office, however, she found a note from Elliot stating that Duncan was out of town for the week, and the distillery would be under her supervision. The days had flown by, her first peaceful experience in years at her job, and at lunchtimes she'd joined Rob and the field hands for an alfresco meal, getting to know the men in a way she never had before. It still left her speechless that Rob had taken to viticulture so smoothly and seemed to have so much fun working with the other men.

They spent their evenings packing up Morgan's apartment, getting their stories straight, and tumbling into bed and fooling around—without crossing the line into making love.

To Morgan's surprise, Rob didn't push her to go all the way, and she was grateful. It wouldn't take much persuasion now to get her on board with the notion. It was all she could do to hold back. Now she was more excited than she could say to reach Chance Creek and start a new life—and build her own winery—but she was nervous, too. What would everyone make of their whirlwind courtship?

As they gathered their belongings and took their turn inching down the aisle of the plane, Morgan's palms became wet. It was one thing to talk wedding plans with Lisa over the phone. It was another thing to meet Rob's family as his fiancée face-to-face. Would they like her? Would his brothers and father be as welcoming as his mother?

At least she wouldn't have to face them right away. Ethan and Autumn had volunteered to pick them up at the airport.

Once they made it past security they stopped and scanned the small crowd gathered to welcome the passengers.

"I don't see them," she said, looking from face to face again.

"Must be running late."

Before she could reply, a man she didn't recognize hurried up to them, waving a slip of paper. "Rob Matheson?"

"Yeah," Rob said, eyeing him curiously.

"Phone message from Ethan Cruz." He stuck the piece of paper into Rob's hand and hurried away, toward the ticket counters.

"What the hell?" Rob opened it up and showed her the writing.

Sorry, buddy—can't make it. You'll have to take a taxi.

Ethan

"He can't even pick me up from the damned airport?" Rob had his phone out in a second, and punched in a number furiously.

Morgan's stomach sank. Ethan must really not approve of their engagement if he'd leave them stranded this way. Maybe he and Claire didn't want her here, after all.

"Ethan? Get your ass out here…"

"SURPRISE!"

Morgan jumped as people leapt out from behind kiosks and baggage carousels. Autumn, Ethan, Claire, Jamie, Rob's brothers, Rose Bellingham and Tracey Richards, an older couple she had to assume were Mr. and Mrs. Matheson.

"Did you really think I'd make you take a taxi?" Ethan said, pulling Rob into a man-hug.

"You have before," Rob said, looking half-pissed, half-relieved.

"For a practical joker, you're pretty damn gullible."

"Rob! Morgan!" Mrs. Matheson—Lisa—approached

with open arms. Morgan found herself squished between her and Rob, being rocked back and forth in a stifling hug. "Let me look at you two. My bride and groom! Rob, you caught yourself a pretty one! Let me see the ring." She tugged Morgan's hand upward and exclaimed over the diamond and its beautiful setting. "We're going to have so much fun planning your wedding! We'll go to Ellie's Bridals tomorrow."

"Mom, give her a break; we just got here," Rob said.

"Son," Holt said. Morgan noticed he wasn't smiling. He shook Rob's hand as formally as if they'd never met before. "Congratulations. I look forward to your wedding day."

Was Morgan imagining things, or was there a veiled hint of a threat in that growled statement? Remembering the way Rob's conversation with him had gone when he had announced their engagement, she had a feeling Holt didn't expect them to last that long. Well, they'd last all right.

They would last a lifetime.

"Rob, put your luggage in your father's truck," Autumn said. "Then you'll ride with us to our ranch for the wedding rehearsal. Dinner's at DelMonaco's tonight, then I'm stealing Morgan for a pre-wedding sleepover to keep Claire company before the big day!"

Rob acquiesced, although he didn't like the idea of sleeping apart from Morgan. Still, this was Jamie and Claire's wedding weekend and they got to call the shots. He'd spend tonight with his buddies, and give Jamie a proper send-off. After his father's greeting, he didn't feel like spending much time with family right now.

Still, it was good to be home, among the people he knew best. The wedding rehearsal and dinner afterwards was full of good-natured teasing and banter. After dinner, the men and women split up. Claire, Autumn, Morgan, Tracey and Rose all returned to the Cruz ranch. The men retired to the Dancing Boot for a final night of drunken carousing.

Or so Rob expected, before Jamie announced he had no intention of spending his wedding day with a violent hangover.

"Plenty of time to toss my cookies in front of my bride later," was how he put it. Instead, they decided to create the ultimate pool tournament, and Luthor Redgrave, the owner of the Boot, even chipped in an old bowling trophy to use as a prize.

They hogged the sole table for the entire evening, and while they didn't drink overly much alcohol, they still made the most noise of anyone in the bar. Rob rode home with Cab later in a satisfied frame of mind.

"You really going to marry Morgan?" Cab asked as they drove out of town toward the Matheson place.

"Yep."

"That's too bad." Cab peered through the darkness of the country road.

"Too bad? What do you mean?" Rob was taken aback by his friend's quiet pronouncement.

Cab tapped his thick fingers on the steering wheel, then seemed to come to a conclusion. He slowed down and pulled off of the road onto the dirt shoulder. This far out of town there were no streetlights, and the quiet of a Montana night settled over them as the engine died. Cab hesitated again. He always was deliberate about his actions. Rob grew impatient, but before he could open his mouth to hurry Cab along, the man began to speak.

"I did a little checking into Morgan. It seemed strange when she appeared out of the blue last month, and then when I heard you two were getting married…something didn't add up." His shrug was barely visible in the darkness. "Sometimes I get a hunch, you know?"

Rob did know. "What'd you find out?" he asked reluctantly, his good mood evaporating. Once again he realized how much he was counting on this marriage—both for the prize of the land, and to be with Morgan.

"I don't know exactly how to say this, so I'm going to just say it, okay?"

Rob steeled himself. That didn't sound good. Although what Cab could possibly have found out about Morgan he couldn't guess. From everything he'd seen she was hardworking, quiet and kept to herself. What kind of trouble could she possibly have gotten into?

"She's implicated in an international diamond smuggling operation. I figure she's using this marriage to make it even easier for her to travel between the United States and Canada. A married woman can pretty much fly under any radar, know what I mean? She'll have a husband in the US, and family back in Victoria. Who would think to question her movements?"

His statement blindsided Rob. Diamond smuggling? That was so far from anything he'd guessed, he couldn't even form words into a sentence. "I...how...she what?" he finally managed to choke out.

Cab's laughter roared through the small interior of the truck. "Got you!" he gasped, wiping tears from his eyes. "I had you going good. You should have seen your face! Diamond smuggling? Morgan? Come on, man—how could you believe that for a minute?"

"She did appear from nowhere last month," Rob sputtered, trying to defend himself. "You have to admit it was pretty weird to find out Ethan and Claire had a sister we'd never heard about." Shit, he'd been had, twice in one day. His reputation was going to take a beating over this.

Relief flooded him, however, and he had to laugh at his own stupidity. *Diamond smuggling.*

"Yeah, I guess so," Cab said, his laughter subsiding into silent chuckles. "I did check her out, by the way. Clean as a whistle, as far as I can tell."

"Great." Rob tried to breathe normally again. He hoped no one else felt the need to get revenge for his past practical jokes any time soon, or he was going to have a heart attack.

Chapter Ten

I 'M SHAKING," Claire said as she checked her image in the full-length mirror again.

Morgan patted her arm. The beautiful bride was indeed shaking like a leaf. "You'll be fine."

"What if I'm not? What if I trip, or laugh when the minister's talking?"

"I was like this before my wedding," Autumn said, fluffing out Claire's veil. "The minute you walk down those stairs and out the door, you'll settle down."

"I think I'm going to be sick."

Claire did look pale, Morgan thought. Pale, but stunning. She'd surprised everyone when she showed them the dress she'd bought from Ellie's Bridals. Morgan had guessed Claire would choose a severe, unornamented sheath dress, to suit her sleek, black bob and no-nonsense fashion style. Instead, she bought a gown out of a fairy tale. Cream colored satin, a corset-boned bodice, long underskirt and an overlay of fabric pulled back into a generous bustle and train. With her imperial features and her dark hair swept back into a sophisticated updo, she could have stepped off the pages of a magazine.

"You won't be sick," Autumn said with authority. "What's nine times nine?"

"Eighty-one. Why are you asking…?"

"Six times eight."

"Forty-eight."

"Three times ten."

Claire started to laugh. "Multiplication tables? That's how you want me to conquer my nerves?"

"It works, doesn't it? It's how my Mom got me through getting shots when I was little."

Claire looked surprised. Morgan knew she was thinking of Teresa Leeds' cold personality.

"I know," Autumn sighed. "These days Mom would tell me to suck it up."

"She's pretty serious," Claire agreed.

"She didn't used to be. Anyway, you look beautiful, and the ceremony should start any minute. Let's get to the top of the stairs." She took one look at Claire's face and began to quiz her again. "Five times eleven."

"Fifty-five," Claire said as they left the room.

Morgan checked her own reflection one last time. As maid of honor, she'd need to get out there in a second. She and Autumn both wore light coral strapless bridesmaid dresses with flowing, floor length skirts and crisscrossed bodices. Plain, yet elegant enough to stand beside Claire.

"Morgan," Autumn called.

She hurried from the room and took her place at the

beginning of the procession. They met Ethan at the bottom of the stairs, and he took Claire's arm. Since Claire's parents were both dead, Ethan would give her away. Rob was to be Jamie's best man, with Cab his second groomsman.

"Ready?" Ethan asked Claire. Morgan smiled to see the look that passed between her half-brother and sister.

"I think so."

"I'm really happy for you," Ethan said, and dropped a kiss on the top of her head. Claire blinked back tears, and Morgan's eyes were damp, too. How wonderful for Ethan and Claire that their marriages kept them close to home and among friends. And now she and Rob were trying to make a go of it, too.

As the processional music swelled, she stepped to the doorway and out onto the front lawn of the Big House. Their path was strewn with rose petals and as she made her way between the rows of chairs set up on the lawn for the guests, Morgan heard the gasp from the assembled friends and relatives that signified they'd caught sight of Claire for the first time.

"Oh, isn't she beautiful," she heard a woman say.

She wanted to be that beautiful at her wedding. If all went well she would be making her way down the aisle in about a month. Soon she would belong here as much as Autumn, Claire, Ethan and Rob did.

She hoped.

As she took her place near the altar, she met Rob's gaze and smiled. His answering look promised another night of passion ahead of them when they were finally alone again. She knew he had to be frustrated they still hadn't consummated their relationship, but they were intimate often, and they'd both expressed how much fun they would have on their wedding night.

Rob cocked an eyebrow and her face warmed. She hoped he hadn't somehow read her mind.

She had a feeling he had.

ROB KNEW HE SHOULD BE ADMIRING the bride, but he couldn't keep his eyes off of Morgan. In her coral dress, she looked like a Grecian goddess, so feminine, so lovely. It was all he could do not to cross the aisle and take her into his arms.

He hoped he looked half as good in this damned suit. Twice in seven days he'd had to dress up. He hoped this wasn't a harbinger of things to come. A glance at Jamie told him his friend was dumbstruck by the vision his bride presented walking toward him. Good. That's what a wedding should be. That's what his would be like with Morgan.

Minus the suit.

He spotted his father in the crowd and looked away fast. He'd woken this morning to find Holt waiting for him in a chair on the front porch.

"You ready to get back to work?" were the first words out of his mouth.

Work? "Uh…not until after the wedding," Rob said.

"There're chores to do."

"I'm supposed to head right over to the Cruz ranch, help get everything set up. I need to square things away with Jamie, too. I'm his best man."

His father stood up. "Fine. Take another day off. But I expect your help with evening chores tonight, and first thing tomorrow you get right back to work like usual. You've already made your brothers shoulder your burden for far too long. I expect you to do your share. I'll post a list of chores in the barn."

A list?

Realization dawned over Rob and he'd rubbed a hand over his face, the bristles of his unshaven face scraping his skin. "Dad, I promised Morgan I'd help her start a business. I planned to spend the time between now and the wedding working a job to save up for that. I wasn't expecting to do chores here, as well."

"Ah, I see." Holt put his hands on his hips. "But you did expect room and board and laundry service, didn't you?"

"I expected my family would welcome me home," Rob said carefully.

"You expected a free ride, as usual. Well, you're not getting one. You want to live here, you'll work, too. Any extra jobs you want to take on can be in your own time."

"You all are going to have to get used to running the spread soon without me, anyhow," Rob said, annoyed.

"How do you figure that?" Holt loomed large, his ire up.

"Once I'm married and working my own land, I won't be working here anymore." Rob forced himself not to back down. They stood like two peacocks almost chest to chest. He was glad Morgan wasn't here to see this.

"I never said nothing about you shirking your obligations once I hand over that land. You'll still be a part of this family and this ranch. You'll help your brothers and that's final."

"Dad…"

Holt waved him away, and Rob expected he meant to storm off, but the steps of his porch seemed to give his father a little trouble. Holt leaned on the railing heavily as he made his way down, and while he stalked off, his pace was slower than usual. Rob bit back the angry words he'd meant to say.

When had his father gotten old?

It didn't matter; he knew what Holt was up to. He meant to keep Rob so busy he couldn't possibly earn enough money to give to Morgan before the wedding, let alone start his own business after they were married. He'd get his 200 acres, but they'd be worthless to him—he'd be right back in the same position he always was, working for his father, never his own man.

Normally he'd give his father hell for playing a trick like that. First he needed to figure out what was wrong with him.

Turning his attention back to the wedding unfolding in front of him, he watched Jamie and Claire exchange vows. He supposed he should have known his childhood friends would end up together, but the days when Claire used to try to boss them all around remained too clear in his head. Time was passing swiftly, and suddenly he understood why his father was in a hurry to see his sons married.

He wasn't going to live forever.

"I CAN'T BELIEVE you're moving here permanently," Autumn said as she and Morgan sat at the bridal table watching Jamie and Claire dance their first dance together.

"I know. I'm so happy."

"I'm happy, too." Autumn smiled at her.

Morgan wanted to hug her for that. Ethan seemed genuinely thrilled that she was going to be their neighbor, but Claire had been a little quiet last night when they'd talked about it. Perhaps it was only wedding nerves, but Morgan had a feeling something was going on. She hoped Claire wouldn't see her as intruding into her family.

"Be careful around Claire," Autumn said, echoing her thoughts.

"What do you mean?"

"It's just…" Autumn twirled her fork as she searched for words. "She's been going on about your mother—about how things don't add up."

"The money," Morgan said glumly.

"And the time. Claire thinks you're downplaying how much time Aria spent with you."

"And how much money she spent *on* me," Morgan said.

"Well," Autumn looked thoughtful. "She does seem a little obsessed about money."

"I understand why. It must have been awful to find

out the ranch was in debt after Aria and Alex died. I'd suspect me, too, I guess. But it's still depressing."

"Well, she'll get over it," Autumn said, doubtfully.

"No, she won't. But if she digs hard enough, maybe she'll find out the real answers."

Autumn speared a piece of chicken. "Does that idea scare you as much as it scares me?"

Morgan laughed. She already was coming to love her sister-in-law, especially her sense of humor. "It scares the crap out of me."

"YOU LEFT US SHORT-HANDED, you know," Ned said, shouldering up next to him as Rob waited for the bartender to hand him a bottle of beer.

"Had to get out of town for a little bit. I had a woman to propose to," Rob said. He was determined not to get into a fight with either his brothers or his father today.

"Yeah, you're pretty set on getting that free land. You even love Morgan, or did the two of you work out some kind of a bargain?"

"Watch it," Rob said, keeping his voice quiet.

"No, I don't think I will." A few wedding guests turned their way as Ned's voice rose. Rob wondered how many drinks he'd already had. Couldn't be too many. It was early yet. More likely Ned relished the chance to have a good argument. He liked arguing, especially with Rob. They always seemed to be in each other's way.

"If you haven't noticed, you're at a wedding," Rob said. "Show some respect."

"What do you know about respect?" Ned said. "When's the last time you ever showed any of your family any respect?"

"Hey, what's going on here?" Jake appeared out of the crowd and stepped between them. "This ain't no time for a fight."

"That's what I said."

Ned cast Rob a disparaging look. "Just telling him we missed him last week. Could've used the help."

Jake opened his mouth to speak, but Rob beat him to the punch. He wanted to say something cutting and sarcastic, put Ned in his place, but Raoul and the other men in the fields of Cassidy Wineries popped into his mind. Their respect for their jobs. Their respect for how the work they did put food on the tables of their families, and added something good to the world. As much as he hated to admit it right now, his father and brothers did work like that, too, and he'd walked away from the job without a second thought. If Raoul or the other men pulled a trick like that, they wouldn't have a job to come back to. Far more than their pride was on the line every day. He'd been acting like a spoiled brat for years, and though it galled him to admit it, Ned was right.

He'd been thinking about his father all day, and when he'd gotten over his anger, he'd had to admit that Holt was right, too. He had expected his folks to put him up in his cabin while he worked for someone else to save up the money for Morgan, and why should they? He was a grown man, after all. The deal he had with them was that he worked in exchange for his room and board. He needed to figure out another way to go about all of this, starting with the way he answered Ned.

"I know you could have used help, and I'm sorry I left you in the lurch," he said.

Ned gaped at him. Jake's brow smoothed. "Well, I don't blame you for being in a rush to get hitched, under the circumstances."

"You don't mind I beat you to the punch?" Rob said. Hell, this was practically turning into a conversation. When was the last time he'd had one with his brothers? Usually it was all orders and snide remarks.

"I didn't say that," Jake tilted his hat back and scratched his forehead. "I thought about it, but I couldn't come up with anyone I wanted to get hitched to that bad."

Ned sneered. "Rob's not really getting hitched. He and Morgan have some kind of a deal."

"That right?" Jake straightened and looked Rob in the eye.

"No. That ain't right. We're getting married and staying married. There's just one thing."

"What's that?" Jake asked.

"I promised Morgan I'd help her start her business, so I need more cash. I gotta find a job, quick. Dad says I need to keep working the ranch, though—even after I'm married. How am I supposed to work full time for him and get another job, too? And what's the point of getting that land if I'm never there to work it?"

"See, he's slacking off again," Ned said to Jake, scowling. "He was going to go off and get some job and leave us in the lurch."

"Stow it," Jake told him. He turned back to Rob. "How much you need?"

"Twelve grand."

"In one month?" Jake's eyebrows rose.

Rob tried to shove his hands in his pockets and remembered he was wearing a suit. "Yeah. I know. It's hard enough without Dad acting like a slave driver."

"What kind of business does Morgan want to start?"

Looking from one brother to the other, Rob realized he was about to have a whole new problem on his hands. When his father had said he wouldn't meddle once he'd turned over the 200 acres, Rob had taken him at his word. Now he saw what a fool he'd been.

"A winery," he mumbled.

"A winery?" Ned repeated, loudly. "What the hell does that mean?"

Jake stared him, comprehension dawning. "You're going to turn that pasture-land into a vineyard? Are you crazy?"

"Not all of it. Just Morgan's half."

"You're going to grow grapes?" Ned said. More guests were turning their way.

"Shut up. We'll talk about it later. I'm going to open up a rodeo training school, too. Maybe I'll partner up with Jamie, raising horses. It's no big deal."

"That Matheson land has been used for raising cattle for over 100 years," Jake said, leaning forward to emphasize his point. "It's not meant for cultivation. You better change your mind about that winery right now."

THE COWBOY IMPORTS A BRIDE

"Dad's going to blow his stack," Ned said. He seemed pretty happy about the idea.

"You keep your mouths shut," Rob said. "This is Claire and Jamie's wedding. Don't you turn it into a family feud."

Jake pressed his lips together. "Fine. We'll keep it under wraps. For today. But tomorrow I'm letting Dad know your plans for that land. We'll see what he has to say about it."

"And he'll have plenty to say," Ned said.

"I HAVEN'T FORGOTTEN, you know," Claire said several hours later, when darkness had fallen and couples swayed to the music on the lawn lit by fairy lights and candles on the tables. The effect was beautiful, and Morgan was bursting with happiness that she wouldn't have to fly back to Canada when the weekend was over. This was her home now; right here in Chance Creek, the most beautiful place in the world.

"What do you mean?"

"About the dates my mother was with you in Canada. You promised you'd write them down."

Morgan had, reluctantly. She had a typed up list in her luggage at the Matheson ranch, the dates as close as she'd been able to reconstruct from memory.

"Do we really need to do this?" she asked, trying to keep the pain from her voice. Couldn't Claire accept her existence and work with her to build the friendship that was growing between them? Why did she have to pursue a line of questioning that may well bring them both more

117

heartache?

"Yes. I'm sorry," Claire looked frustrated, "I know you don't agree with me, but I have to know what Aria was doing. I can't…rest until I know all her secrets."

"Do you really think we'll ever know them all?" Morgan asked. They were sitting in two of the folding chairs dropped off by the rental company this morning. Jamie had excused himself for a moment. Apparently Claire had been waiting for the opportunity to confront her.

"Maybe not, but I have to try. There are dates she was missing and money that's still gone. I need to know where it went." She glanced sideways at Morgan. "And if you know anything you're not telling me—even if it's something you think I won't want to hear—please tell me now. I'm going to keep digging until I find out, anyway."

Morgan frowned. "You think I'm holding something back?" Well, she was, wasn't she? She could have written down those dates weeks ago and sent them to her sister.

Claire looked at the hands clasped in her lap. "I don't want to think that, but I've barely known you a month. You came out of nowhere and you're one of the secrets my mother kept." Her voice wobbled a little, but then she steadied it again. "My mother is on my mind all the time these days. She should be here, you know? But since she isn't, I want to know everything I can about her—about what she was up to before she died."

She lifted a pleading gaze to Morgan, and Morgan had to relent. "Okay, I'll do whatever I can to help. I'll drop the list by your house tomorrow, and when you come back from your honeymoon, we can work on the mystery together, okay?"

"Thanks." Claire reached out and hugged her. "I'm glad you're here."

Morgan hugged her back, but she couldn't help feeling a flicker of dread.

As THE NIGHT'S SHADOWS deepened and the stars winked overhead, Rob decided he'd had enough socializing. All around him, couples swayed together on the lawn, or stole kisses from each other, and the whole atmosphere seemed charged with lust and possibilities.

He found Morgan chatting with Autumn, and made an excuse to separate her from her friend. Then he took her hand and led her toward the lane where his truck was parked.

"What are we doing? I don't want to miss it when Claire and Jamie leave," Morgan said, but she clung to his hand, a little unsteady from all the champagne he'd plied her with over the course of the evening.

"I want to show you something," he said.

"Now? In your truck?"

"We could walk, but driving is faster. And you said you wanted to be back in time to see the happy couple off." He nuzzled her neck and slipped a kiss behind her ear, then helped her into the passenger seat. Her long dress made her clumsy, and Rob took every opportunity to slide his hands over her body as he settled her in his seat. By the time he fastened her seatbelt and closed the door on her, his own body was thrumming with desire.

The ride out past Jamie and Claire's house only took a few minutes. Where the dirt track petered out, he parked the truck and went to help Morgan out again. She slid off the seat into his arms, and it was all he could do not to lean her against the truck and take her right then and there, but first he wanted to show her their land.

"You do realize I'm wearing high heels," she said a few minutes later as she wobbled over the range grass. He kept an arm firmly around her waist and made sure she didn't fall. The land sloped down to Chance Creek, the boundary between the Cruz and Matheson ranches. On the other side of the water was the 200 acres his father would give them. "Come on."

"Where are we going?" Morgan said a few moments later when they'd negotiated their way down the slope. She giggled after nearly taking another spill. Bending down, she took off first one shoe, then the other and tossed them away.

"I want to show you our land."

Morgan held back, gazing at the creek. "We can't cross that; I'm wearing a bridesmaid's dress."

"It's shallow here," Rob said. "This is the shortcut Ethan and I used when we were kids to get to each other's houses. It took far too long to go around by the road. Trust me; you'll be fine." He took off his shoes and rolled up his pant legs.

"Oh, it's cold!" Morgan shrieked when she stepped in.

"Come on, city girl, you can handle it." He supported

her carefully as they picked their way across the water, and then swung her into his arms as he climbed up the opposite bank. He strode up the hill on the other side and deposited her at the top. "See?"

Morgan looked around. "No, actually I don't. It's pretty dark."

"It's beautiful, trust me. People will be in awe when they come to the tasting room."

"Do you think there ever will be a tasting room?" Morgan asked wistfully. "It's hard to believe everything could work out so well."

"I guarantee you there will be a tasting room," he said, pulling her into his arms. He kissed her, cradling her head with his hand and taking the opportunity to hold every inch of her pressed against every inch of him. When he couldn't wait any longer, he released her, shrugged off his coat, lay it carefully on the ground, and began to unbutton his dress shirt.

"What are you doing?"

"As much as you'll let me," he said with a grin.

"Here?" She looked around them. "We can't…"

"Sure we can. No one will see us—they're all at the wedding. Let's consecrate this ground right now." He stripped the shirt off and tossed it aside, then got to work on his pants. "You going to join me, or stand there staring?" He could just make out the contours of her face in the dim light of the stars. She was smiling, but still unsure.

"I think I'll watch for now."

"For now," he agreed. He took his time unzipping

his pants and stepping out of them. Then he stripped off his boxers and stood naked, except for his hat, to accept her inspection.

"I think I need to take a closer look," she said, and moved toward him.

Rob waited as patiently as he could, and was rewarded with a stroke of her hand over his shoulder, his chest and down to his waist. She followed this with a series of kisses, moving feather-light over his skin. Up to his chin, down his neck and chest, over to one nipple, then to the other. When she finally dipped lower, he stifled a groan and laced his fingers together behind his head to keep from taking her face in them and guiding her to where he wanted her to go.

She went there on her own, caressing him with her mouth, taking him deep inside and moving him in and out until he could barely breathe anymore. She knelt before him, her beautiful dress puddled around her like the petals of a flower. As she tended to him, love for her swelled until he thought his heart would burst.

As Morgan slid her hands around him, cupped his ass and drew him deeper, he had to steady himself by holding her shoulders. He allowed one hand to tangle in her thick, dark curls and she moaned as he gently guided her, taking more of him into her mouth.

When he was so close he could hardly stand it, he withdrew from her despite her protests. It was her turn now. He wanted her as ready as he was; he wanted them to go over the edge together.

He pulled her to her feet, turned her around and undid the fastenings of her dress. Sliding it off of her, he wrapped his arms around her waist and pulled her back against him, slipping his hands under her bra to squeeze her breasts. Morgan moaned again and he tilted her forward to undo the clasp. She flung the bra away and pulled his hands back to cup her again, pressing against him as he played with her nipples.

To his delight, he realized she had been hiding a garter, sheer stockings and a thong under that dress. The garter straps framed her ass nicely and he decided she could keep that particular item of clothing on. The thong had to go, and he took care of it with a single, strong tug, then he pulled her back close, slid his hands to her thighs and ground her against him.

This time he was the one who moaned, although Morgan's breath hitched and he knew she wanted him as badly as he wanted her. He wished he could make love to her the good old-fashioned way, but he was determined not to cross her boundaries. Sliding one hand down her body, he found her as lush and ready for him as he was for her. He half-led, half-nudged her over to an old fallen log, all that was left of an enormous pine that stood sentinel here when he was a child. Guiding her to bend forward, he placed her hands on the horizontal trunk, nudged her legs apart with his own, and crouched behind her, tipping back his head and tasting her delicious warmth.

Morgan expelled a rush of air that told him he'd done the right thing. He loved the look of her ass high above him, loved the taste of her on his tongue. His hands on her spread thighs, he felt her begin to quiver as he continued his ministrations.

When she was wet and gasping, he reached under her to take one breast in his hand, kneading it and pinching her nipple until she was whimpering above him. Still he kept up his sensual attack, so turned on by the taste of her he ached with wanting a more intimate touch.

"Rob," Morgan said, her voice ragged.

With one last caress, he stood up behind her, positioned himself between her legs and began to slide back and forth, letting his hardness caress her slick folds. She let out another breath as she realized he wasn't going to try to cross the boundary she'd set. He placed his hands on her hips and she moaned aloud as he slid between her thighs.

A moment later, she lifted one of her own hands between her legs and cradled the length of him against her, adding another layer of friction to what was already becoming unbearably sensual. He sped up, sliding against her core and her hand, becoming so hard he thought he couldn't hang on.

Reaching around again to cup her breast, he rolled her nipple between his fingertips. Morgan cried aloud and shuddered into her release, calling out again and again as he bucked against her, going over the edge with her.

When they were done, they collapsed in a tangle of arms and legs against the side of the fallen log. Rob pulled Morgan onto his lap and wrapped his arms around her, kissing her softly.

After a moment, she laughed breathlessly.

"I keep thinking that when we finally make love we're going explode. I can't believe how good you feel."

"I'll gladly explode if it means I can make love to you." He kissed her again. "I'm bringing you back here on our wedding night, and I'm going to make love to you under the stars on this very ground."

"I can't wait," she said.

"Neither can I."

As THEY GATHERED their things and made their way back to the river, Morgan's legs were shaking and she had a feeling her biceps would be sore tomorrow from bracing herself against that log.

It was worth it, though. She'd never experienced anything like that before. Her desire for Rob seemed to be unquenchable. Only the feeling that she should be there when Claire and Jamie left for their honeymoon compelled her to hurry back to the wedding rather than stay here in the starlight with Rob.

Well, she'd have a lifetime of nights like this, wouldn't she? The thought made her smile. Rob wrapped an arm around her waist and hoisted her into his arms as they crossed back over the creek.

On the other side, they had quite a hunt to find the high-heeled slippers she'd tossed to the wind, but when they found them they made their way back up the hill to Rob's truck and climbed inside.

Morgan felt like a lifetime had passed since they'd pulled up on this hillside, instead of an hour. Something important had changed, and she struggled to define it, until in a flash it became clear:

She trusted Rob.

Not blindly, and not out of some foolish hope—but from her intimate experiences with him. Rob brought her to the highest heights, but he did so every time with the utmost respect for her, for her feelings and for her boundaries, as well. Many people who'd known her for years didn't respect her half so much, or spend nearly as much energy trying to bring her joy, for that matter.

As he climbed in the driver's seat and took her hand, she gripped it tightly. Eyes suddenly damp, she turned to him and hoped he could see the love shining there.

"I know," he said. "I feel it, too. We're supposed to be together, aren't we?" He leaned over and kissed her cheek softly.

Yes, she agreed with him silently. She thought they were.

"OVER MY DEAD BODY."

Rob tightened his hold on Morgan's waist and stared up at his father, a dark shape in the dim porch light. It was past two in the morning, and he and Morgan had said their good-byes to Ethan and Autumn after helping to do some preliminary cleanup as the wedding wound down. Claire and Jamie had left hours ago for a night at a hotel in town before they flew to Hawaii in the morning for their honeymoon. Holt must have been snoozing on one of the porch chairs, waiting for them. Damn Jake—couldn't he keep his mouth shut for one night?

No, damn Ned, Rob thought. Jake would have kept his mouth shut, but Ned wouldn't. He loved to make trouble; always had.

"Over your dead body, what, Dad?" He knew exactly what his father meant, but he wasn't going to make it easy on the old man.

"Over my dead body you're going to rip up this good rangeland and plant...grapes." Holt spit out the word.

Morgan stood stiffly beside Rob, and he could only imagine how she was feeling. "Dad, it's late, and my fiancée is tired..."

"Your fiancée has some nerve coming here thinking she can ruin this family's legacy," Holt boomed. Morgan jerked as if she'd been slapped and anger filled Rob until he could barely hold it in.

"You'll shut your trap and we'll work this out later, between the two of us," he said, tugging Morgan toward the stairs. "I'm putting Morgan to bed and then I'm coming back out to make sure you're gone. Don't even think about sticking around."

"You think you can talk to me that way?" Holt roared, taking a position at the top of the steps that would force them to push past him if they wanted to reach the front door.

"Rob?" Morgan's voice was thin with strain and he knew she'd be devastated by the way this was playing out.

"Damn it. Come on, Morgan," He grabbed her hand and pulled her back the way they'd come.

"Where are you going?" Holt hollered after them.

"Get back here. I haven't had my say!"

Rob helped Morgan back into the passenger seat of his Chevy, and rounded the cab to climb in the other side.

"Where *are* we going?" Morgan asked him, her face white.

"Back to Ethan's. He'll put us up for the night, and tomorrow I'll talk some sense into my old man. Don't mind him; he's more bluster than bite." But he knew she was too smart to believe the lie. Hell, he was deep in it now. He had no idea how he was going to turn this around.

But he was going to turn it around. He was going to get Morgan that vineyard.

No matter what his father said.

Chapter Eleven

"I WISH YOU TWO COULD STAY," Autumn said the following morning after breakfast. It was a rare morning off for her, since they hadn't booked guests for the weekend because of the wedding. As Jamie was gone for the remainder of the week, Rob was helping Ethan, and Morgan was in the kitchen unloading the dishwasher while Autumn put her feet up. "Jamie's old cabin is empty. You could take it. It's traditionally been for the ranch's horse trainer, but now that Jamie and Claire have built their house, no one's living there."

"Thanks, but we have to patch things up with Rob's family."

"Well, if that doesn't work out, you can hold your wedding here. We've done two so far this summer, I'm sure we can handle another one. I'm beginning to feel like a pro." She began to get up, but Morgan waved her down again.

"Rest. How are you feeling?"

Autumn dropped a hand to her still-flat belly. "Pretty good, actually. My morning sickness finally stopped, so I feel almost human. I'm really hungry these days and I've got this urge to clean everything. If you weren't here, I'd probably be sorting out the attic. I peeked up there last week and it looks like no one's touched a thing in ages."

"No shifting boxes around for you. You take it easy while you still can. You'll have enough to do when the baby gets here. I can't believe you're starting this business while you're pregnant."

"What about you? You'll be starting a winery. Are you and Rob going to put off having kids?"

The question brought a surge of heat through her body at the thought of making love to Rob, then a cold wash of anxiety as she remembered what had happened last night. "We'd planned to get right to it, actually, since a certain someone scared me to death with her stories about women waiting too long. All I can think about since you told me about your Mom's patients is having my kids as soon as humanly possible."

Autumn laughed. "Sorry. Mom talks about it so much I guess I blurt it out these days. I'm glad to hear you're not waiting, though. I want our kids to be able to play together."

"I hope it works out that way," Morgan said.

Autumn grew serious. "Tell me what you and Rob are going to do about Holt. What if he doesn't give you the land, after all?"

"We'll still get married," Morgan said. Rob had covered her with kisses last night when they'd finally settled in the spare room at Ethan's bunkhouse, and promised her he'd get her a vineyard no matter what it took. She'd tried to tell him it didn't matter, but secretly she was relieved he was so adamant about it. It did matter to her, and without Holt's gift of the land it was going to be nearly impossible to get one started. "Rob said he'll talk to his mother and get her to make Holt hold up his end of the bargain, but then what?" She appealed to Autumn. "It'll be awful living there if Holt and Rob's brothers hate us. I wanted to come here to be with family, not to be fighting with them."

"I'm sure things will settle down," Autumn said.

"But it's my fault," Morgan said. "I'm the one who wants to grow grapes. Apparently that's not done around here."

"You said there were other wineries in Montana, so it must be done somewhere around here. It's just a new idea, and ranchers don't like new ideas. Give Holt some time to get used to it. I bet Lisa can sweet talk him around, and as for those brothers of his—they're just mad they didn't marry fast enough to get the land for themselves."

"You actually think there's a chance it will be okay?"

"I'm sure there is. Meanwhile, I've got a proposition for you."

"I DON'T KNOW what I'm going to do," Rob said to Ethan as they rode out in Ethan's truck to check on the cattle. "The only reason Morgan and I jumped into everything so fast was to get that land. Don't get me wrong, I'm marrying her no matter what happens," he said when Ethan darted a look at him, "but she's got her heart set on that vineyard. She left her job for me. Hell, she left her country for me. I can't let her down. Besides," he kept his eyes on the road, unwilling to meet Ethan's gaze while making this confession, "I did a little work at the vineyard back in Victoria—the one where Morgan worked? And I liked it."

This time Ethan's eyebrows shot up. "Really? What kind of work?"

"Pruning the vines. You've got to get the balance right of foliage to grapes to get them to ripen efficiently. There's kind of an art to it."

"Huh." Ethan seemed nonplussed. "Never figured you for a farmer."

"Neither did I. But I wasn't making much of a rancher, either."

"You haven't seemed happy in a long time. Apart from the Morgan thing, I mean. I used to think you'd go on the rodeo circuit in a big way. Never seemed to happen, though."

Rob was relieved that Ethan understood. "I haven't been happy. Low man on the totem pole for too many years at my family's place, and never much cared for the work anyway. I just didn't know why. As for the rodeo, you're right—I probably should have made a real go at that. Maybe I'll try again before everything's said and done."

"Seems to me you and Morgan could be a great team building a winery together. You could tend the grapes and she could brew the wine. Have you talked to her about it?"

"Not yet. And now what's the point? We won't have any land, anyway. Hey—where are we going? You've got cattle over here?" He glanced out the window and realized Ethan had turned onto the same track he and Morgan had taken the previous night. Ethan drove past the acreage that now belonged to Claire and Jamie. Their brand new log cabin drew the eye, but Ethan kept on going.

"Nope. I want to show you something." He pulled to a halt at the end of the track just as Rob had the night before. When Ethan got out, Rob followed him, wondering what this was all about.

"Jamie's hundred acres end over there," Ethan pointed. "This area between here and the road, and down to the creek isn't being used. It's about 150 acres. You interested?"

"Interested?" Rob started forward. "What do you mean? What's the price?"

"What can you afford?"

"Aw, hell, Ethan, I'm not going to lean on you. I told you, I've only got eight grand in the bank."

"That'll do for a down payment. This land isn't making me any money, anyhow. You can work off the rest over time—I need some help. Claire was supposed to partner with Jamie to run the trail rides and activities for our guests, but she still wants to spend most of her time doing interior design projects. Carl's house alone is keeping her busy, and she told me yesterday a bunch of her old clients from when she worked at Ledstrom Designs have been calling her. I can only count on her part time, at best. Jamie can't do it all himself, and you were a whiz at entertaining the guests last month. What do you say? We'll draw up a contract and part of your *payment*," Ethan finger-quoted the air, "will go to your mortgage, and the rest you can keep."

"Shit, you'd do that for me?"

"I can't think of anyone I'd rather do business with. Come on—you, me and Jamie, all working together? Can't beat that! On the side, you and Jamie can build up that horse-breeding business if you like, and you can even teach rodeo skills to guests who are interested. Maybe run some classes for local kids, as well. It all fits together. Heck, even the winery fits in. We'll serve Morgan's wines at all our dinners, and our guests can tour the winery and go to her tasting room, too. Some of our more refined guests might prefer that to mucking out stalls."

Ethan looked pleased as punch, and Rob nodded his head. They could have a lot of good times if they all worked together. Then his stomach dipped. "Speaking of the vineyard, I still need that cash for Morgan. I wanted to have it by the wedding. I'll use my eight grand for a down payment on your land, and I'll do everything you need me to do here and more, but I've got to find something else, too—some other job that will pay me a lot of cash, fast. Twenty thousand dollars in the next month."

"Morgan will understand if it takes you a little longer to scrape up the money. She's going to be happy you found another way to get the land, right? I'll get Matt

Underwood to draw up a contract tomorrow. As soon as Jamie's back, we'll get the papers signed."

"Yeah, you're right," Rob said, but as happy as he was about this turn of events, he'd made a promise to his fiancée, and he was determined to see it through.

"HELLO! HELLO? YOO-HOO!"

Morgan rushed to the top of the Big House stairs to see who was barging through the front door. When Autumn had offered her a temporary job helping her cook and clean for the guests, she'd jumped at it.

"I know it's not as glamorous as running a winery," Autumn had said, "but I could really use the help. Tracey and Rose have been filling in for weeks, but they both have real jobs and they can't keep doing this. Eventually I'll hire someone permanently, but I can't really afford it yet. You won't get started with the winery for a while, right?"

"If ever," Morgan said gloomily.

"Think of this as something to fill the time, then," Autumn said. "Thankless hard work for slave wages. What could be better?"

"Well, when you put it that way, how can I resist?" Morgan said, laughing. "Sure, sign me up."

They worked it out that she would help Autumn daily from five in the morning to early afternoon. First they'd prep breakfast, serve it and clean up afterward. Then she and Autumn would do the rooms. They'd end the morning with lunch prep and cleanup.

It was late morning and she'd persuaded Autumn to

go back to the bunk house and relax while she finished readying the bedrooms for guests. Several families were descending on the ranch this afternoon. She figured after all the excitement of the wedding, Autumn could use a break before the next round of chaos hit. Autumn and Ethan seemed to work almost every hour of the day and she had resolved to help as much as she could. Autumn wasn't paying her much, but since sleeping in the bunkhouse wouldn't cost her anything, at least she wouldn't be dipping into her savings to pay her daily expenses.

When she peered down the large staircase, she saw Lisa poking her head through the door. *Uh oh, this could get ugly*, she thought, but descended the stairs anyway. No matter what happened, she and Rob were getting married, and Lisa would be her mother-in-law.

"Oh, honey," Lisa said when she spotted her. "I'm so sorry my husband's being a royal pain in the ass."

Morgan blinked. That wasn't what she'd been expecting at all.

"These men," Lisa went on. "It's all pissing and marking their territory, I swear. With five of them around the place it sure gets ugly sometimes. Don't you fret about it. I'm working on Holt and we'll simmer all of this down and get your wedding off the ground. You hear? But if you don't mind, could we put off our trip to Ellie's Bridals until Wednesday? Turns out I need to go help out an old friend this morning."

"Um…okay," Morgan said. "I'm free after two. I'll be helping Autumn in the morning."

"That's sweet of you. Poor girl is working her fingers to the bone. In the meantime, I'll keep looking into flowers and catering and everything else. You leave it all up to me! I'll see you on Wednesday at the shop."

Morgan waved good-bye, wondering if there was any hope that Lisa could actually patch things up between Rob and his father. From what she'd seen, she doubted it, but Lisa had been married to Holt for over thirty years. She must know a thing or two about how to handle the man.

When Rob arrived back at the bunkhouse later that afternoon, she was eager to tell him about his mother's visit, but before she could, he swept her off her feet and into an embrace.

"It's settled. Ethan's selling us 150 acres of land and I'll work off the cost over time. I'll help out with the guest ranch business and teach rodeo riding to local kids and visitors. I'll also team up with Jamie on his horse-breeding business, and I'll get your vineyard up and running for you."

Morgan tried to keep up. "What land?"

"The parcel next to Jamie's! We'll live right here with the rest of our friends."

"Really?" Morgan lit up. "You think we can afford it? Where will we get the money to start the winery?"

"I'll earn it, I swear I will. I already told Ethan I need to take on extra work." He hugged her again, then slid his hands lower and gave her ass a squeeze. "It'll all work out, so don't worry about a thing."

"I got a job, too—helping Autumn—so we'll both

be earning money."

Rob kissed her until she got weak in the knees. "The wedding is on," he said firmly when they split apart. "I asked Ethan and he said we'll hold it here if my Dad doesn't back down."

"Autumn said the same thing." She grinned. "But your mom stopped by and said she's working on Holt. She thinks he'll change his mind."

Rob shrugged. "Doesn't matter if he does, really. Our future is secure either way." He stopped and took her hands in his. "You know that, right, Morgan? I'm going to keep my promises to you, and make you my wife, whatever anyone throws at us. I'll make damn sure you have a winery to run, too."

Looking into his eyes, she could see he meant it. All the doubts she'd harbored slipped away and she stepped into his embrace again.

Chapter Twelve

WHEN MORGAN MADE HER WAY back to the bunkhouse the following afternoon, after spending most of the day helping Autumn with her guests, she was surprised to find Rob waiting for her.

"Come on—you and I have an errand to run."

"Now?"

"You have something better to do?"

"Let me grab my purse."

Twenty minutes later they arrived at the Chance Creek Pet Clinic, a small, neat building near the center of town. Morgan turned to Rob in surprise. "What are we doing here?"

"Visiting a friend of mine." He got out and came to open the door for her. She smiled at the gentlemanly gesture, and followed him to the entrance.

"It's closed," she said, pointing to the sign in the door.

"It's never closed," he said. "You'll see." He knocked and called out, "Bella? You in there?"

The door opened a moment later and a young woman appeared, her blonde hair piled atop her head in a mass of wild curls.

"Rob! I haven't seen you in ages," she said. "Come on in."

Morgan fought down a surge of jealousy at the pleased tone in her voice. She was pretty, curvy, and obviously happy to see Rob.

Rob gave Bella a quick hug and the ugly feeling grew. Had he brought her here to show her how attractive he was to other women? To give her a quick reminder that he had other options? The certainty she'd felt since his declarations last night began to slip away.

"How's your family?" Bella asked him.

Rob grimaced. "As ornery and controlling as ever. How's the business?"

Bella mirrored his expression. "Same as usual."

"In other words, you're still housing every stray animal for miles around?"

"Yeah." Her face fell, but then she brightened again. "You know, I think the number of strays is dropping. I haven't had as many brought in these past few weeks."

As she turned to adjust something on her counter, Rob rubbed a hand across his face. Morgan suspected he was trying to rub off the disbelieving smile that was lingering there. What was that all about?

"We've actually come to take one off your hands," was all he said.

Bella spun around. "Really?" Now her face was as bright as the sun with happiness. This woman really wore her feelings on her sleeve, Morgan thought. It made it hard to dislike her.

It got harder as Bella led them into the back of the clinic to an adjoining building that housed the animal shelter she also ran. It was the biggest facility Morgan had ever seen, with cages and cages of dogs and cats and a large exercise yard for them behind it all. Bella explained how local students volunteered and helped her exercise the animals and keep them acclimated to humans.

"How on earth do you feed them all?" Morgan asked.

Bella's face fell again. "It's hard," she admitted. "Somehow we manage."

"Well, you'll have to manage with one less animal," Rob said. "We're looking for a kitten."

"I've got kittens," Bella said. She led the way to one corner where indeed she had several mother cats with litters of kittens. "If you want to take one home today, these guys are your best bet." She took them past several cages in which the kittens were little more than piles of fluff huddled next to their mothers to one in which the kittens were noticeably older. They were alert, pouncing and playing. The mother cat was nowhere to be seen.

"These little guys are ten weeks. Ready for their own homes and families." Bella leaned over and opened the door. "What do you think?"

Five little gray faces turned toward them. Morgan melted at the sight of their big eyes and still-fluffy bodies. She'd never had a pet. Her grandparents wouldn't think of it, and her apartment building didn't allow them. "Can I hold one?"

"Of course." Bella beamed. "Put your hand in the door and see who comes looking. The best pets are the ones who pick you."

"Oh, it's not for me," Morgan said, but she did what she was told. A kitten with a white front paw scampered right over and nosed her fingers. She felt the rasp of its tiny tongue on her palm and shivered with delight. "It's so cute." When it climbed right into her hand, she pulled it out and cradled it to her chest, rubbing her chin over its soft fur. It licked her on the nose.

"That's it—she's chosen you," Bella said. "Now you have to take her."

"Who are you getting her for?" Morgan asked Rob.

"You, dummy. Who'd you think I was getting it for?"

Morgan lowered her hands. "But…"

"You're getting a pet," he insisted. "The minute I saw how you were living in Victoria, I promised myself I would get you one when I convinced you to move back here. People have to have pets. Anyway, we need a cat for the ranch. In fact, Ethan and Autumn don't have a cat yet, so we need two," he told Bella, then scanned the large room with all its cages. "Actually, make that five."

Bella beamed as she went off to find a cardboard box to carry them in.

"Five?" Morgan asked when she was gone.

"There's plenty of room for them," he said. "They'll keep the rat population down. I'll let Ethan and Autumn have a couple, keep one for Claire and Jamie, and we'll take the rest."

"There are so many animals here," Morgan said, daunted by the noise of them in their pens.

"She doesn't put them down—the strays, I mean. Most shelters have a time limit before they get rid of unwanted animals. Bella doesn't. She's going to bankrupt herself if she keeps on like this."

"She said the population of strays has gone down, though."

Rob laughed. "Seriously? You believed that? Most likely people are taking pity on her and bringing the strays to her brother, instead. He's a livestock vet—he doesn't do pets, but he's a realist. He takes care of the problem."

"That's awful!"

His faced softened. "It is awful, honey, but it's life. Unneutered cats breed like bunnies. There's no way to keep up with them all. Bella would have to be a million-aire to take in every last one."

"I guess." Morgan hugged the kitten in her hands tighter. This one was safe, at least.

"What're you going to name her?"

"Button." She nuzzled the kitten again. "My little Button."

Rob rolled his eyes. "Gunsmoke would be better."

"Button's a darling name," Bella said, returning with the box. "Let's load them up and get you guys out of here. It's past dinner time, and I'm starving, and I've still got a lot to do."

"Are you looking for any more volunteers?" Morgan

asked her.

"Are you kidding? How often can you come?"

"I'm not sure, but I'll try for once a week to start. I've never had pets," she confided to Bella.

"Then you need to make up for lost time, and this is certainly the place to do it," Bella said.

"Come on," Rob nudged her toward the door.

"I'm hungry, too," Morgan said as they returned to the car with their box of squirming, fluffy kittens. She looked back at the clinic, though, as Rob backed out of the parking lot and swung the truck toward home. It would be fun to go back and spend time with all of those animals.

"Let's pick up some cat food, grab some takeout, and get these critters home."

An hour later, Rob joined Ethan on the back porch of the bunkhouse to plan the following day's work, dropping one of the kittens into Ethan's lap.

"Here, I got you a present."

"Huh." Ethan lifted the kitten and rubbed its fur against his face. "Nice. I didn't even know I needed one of these."

"But you kinda do now, don't you?" Rob said.

"Matter of fact, I think I do." He nuzzled it again. "Gunsmoke. That's your name," he told the kitten.

Rob turned to him. "That's exactly what I said to Morgan. She didn't like it."

"Yeah? What did she name yours?"

"Button," Rob mumbled.

"Man, that's rough." Ethan chuckled and settled the kitten in his lap, petting it while they talked over their plans.

Rob found it hard to concentrate, though. The question of how to earn the money he'd promised Morgan was preying on his mind.

"Rob?" Ethan asked him. Rob realized he'd missed something.

"Huh?"

"You're a million miles away. Something wrong?"

"I've really got to find some extra work. Not that I don't appreciate what you've done," he hastened to say when he caught Ethan's eye. "It's a far sight better to buy the land from you than to have my father looking over my shoulder and bossing me around the rest of my days. It's just, I don't want to start my life together with Morgan by breaking a promise."

"Yeah, I get it." Ethan stared out over the landscape. "You know where most business deals get done, don't you?"

Rob raised an eyebrow at him.

"The feed store, horse auctions, and the bar. Try Rafters. Someone might know something."

"You think?"

Ethan shrugged. "Worth a shot. Twenty thousand dollars is a hell of a lot of money, though. Might need to go to North Dakota and work on one of those oil wells."

Rob looked thoughtful. "I could look into that."

"Start closer to home," Ethan advised him, standing up, still cradling the kitten. "You'll want to get going now—before all the old geezers with money get too drunk to spend it."

"WHAT ARE YOU DOING?"

Morgan glanced up as Ethan entered the living room. She was sitting on the couch, notepad in hand, writing down every expense she could think of for starting the vineyard and winery. They were adding up fast. Four kittens were exploring the room, climbing the furniture and playing with the curtains.

She put the notepad down. "Talking myself out of starting a winery."

"Why? I think it's a fantastic idea. A few years from now it will be a great partner to the guest ranch business. You can take our guests on tours—get them out of our hair for a few hours—and we can serve your wines at dinner."

"That's more than a few years away. We have to purchase rootstock, grow the grapes, erect a distillery and tasting room, buy the machinery…and even once we bottle some wine, it still needs to age."

Ethan sat down next to her. "So, every step you take is one step closer to your goal."

"I barely know Rob." She hadn't meant to say that out loud, but now that she had, she pushed forward, voicing the doubts that had crept back into her mind. She pushed a lock of hair out of her eyes and sighed. "What if he turns out to be a lousy business partner?" *What if he's a lousy husband?*

Ethan leaned back and stretched his arms out along

the top of the couch. "I think Rob's underrated. His family's never given him any real responsibility and everyone else thinks he's a playboy."

Her stomach contracted with unease at this reminder of the number of women Rob had dated over the years. Back before she'd gotten interested in him, Autumn had told her all about his checkered past. "You don't?"

"No. He's just been bored. Rob's smart, and no one gives him credit for that, either. Back in school he got all B's and a few A's."

"So?" That wasn't too impressive. She'd gotten good grades, herself.

"So, Rob never studied. Never did the homework, even though he loved school. His brothers would pick on him if he did. You have to understand Holt Matheson's all about work. He always said school was for sissies. He worked those boys to the bone and praised them to the hills when they carried their own weight, but if they brought home a report card they'd be lucky if he looked at it, let alone complimented them on their grades."

"That's too bad."

"Yeah. Rob could've been an engineer, or something like that. He should have gone to college."

This was a side of Rob she'd never thought about. "He seems like every other cowboy."

Ethan laughed. "Ignorant and oafish?"

She elbowed him. "More interested in horses than books."

He shrugged. "Leave some books around. See what

he does." He got up. "The way I see it, you promised to marry him and he promised you a winery. Everyone has second thoughts when they make big decisions. Don't let your cold feet stop you from getting what you want."

He retreated to the kitchen, leaving her to think over his words. Before she could think over it too much, the front door banged open, making her jump.

"Sorry, it's just me," Rob said, coming into the room.

Morgan's heart gave the little hitch it always did when she saw him. "Hey, come sit with me."

"Can't. I'm getting changed and heading out again."

"Where?" Morgan asked, glancing at her watch. It was past eight. Wasn't he ready to pack it in for the evening?

"I'm going to head downtown, check out the Dancing Boot and Rafters—see if anyone knows of a job that needs doing."

"I'll come, too," Morgan said, delighted at the prospect of putting aside her calculations for now.

"Sorry, honey. I'll take you out for a night on the town real soon," Rob promised her and gave her a peck on the cheek. "Tonight's going to be all business." He continued into the bedroom without waiting for her answer.

Morgan slumped down on the couch again. "All business at a bar?"

"A lot of business gets done at the bars around here," Ethan said, coming back into the living room. Rob reappeared, too, in a clean shirt.

"Don't wait up."

"Good luck," Morgan said as he headed for the door. A kitten struggled onto her lap and she petted it distractedly as Ethan sat on the other end of the couch and clicked on the television.

"Thanks. I'll need it."

THE DANCING BOOT was nearly dead on this weekday night, so Rob made his way over to Rafters, where the older cowboys and ranchers tended to congregate—men who wanted to sit and ruminate over past days or the price of cattle feed, rather than listen to music, or chase pretty girls. A quick scan of the bar from the doorway told him his father wasn't here. He didn't expect he would be—Holt saved his tame version of carousing for Friday and Saturday nights—but if he was, he'd turn around and go home.

Instead there were a handful of familiar faces, a couple he didn't know, and Carl Whitfield alone at a table in the corner.

Rob frowned. At least the man wasn't trying to buddy up with anyone, regaling them with how much money he made, like he had when he first arrived in town. Carl seemed different these days. A little more subdued. Rob stifled a chuckle. He guessed Lacey Taylor could do that to a man.

Lacey had dated Ethan for years, all through high school and beyond, and everyone assumed they were as good as married. When Lacey found out Ethan was having money problems after his parents died, however, she took off like a shot and left Ethan eating dirt. Pretty soon she hooked her carriage to Carl—self-made millionaire and wanna-be cowboy. People around here didn't like him much, since he bought his ranch for a song from a couple whose dreams had disappeared with their savings during the last recession. He hadn't thought the fellow would last long.

But here he was.

And of all the folks in the room, Carl was the one with money to spend. Rob tipped his hat to the men he knew as he walked by and made his way over to him.

"Can I join you?"

The man brightened. "Sure thing. What're you drinking?" He lifted a hand and signaled the waitress.

"Hi Rob," Trisha Bentley said, making her way over from the bar. "What'll you have?"

"Budweiser is fine," Rob said.

"Join me in a whiskey?" Carl offered.

"Not tonight—another time."

"Suit yourself. I'll have another one, honey."

"Coming right up," Trisha said and walked away.

"I haven't seen you here before," Carl said after a moment of awkward silence.

"Nah, I'm usually over at the Boot."

"I've decided to keep my distance from that establishment," Carl said. "I don't want Lacey to think I was out looking for women while she was away."

"Sounds wise," Rob said and draped an arm over the back of his chair. "I'm looking for work," he said, coming straight to the point. "Need some cash, so I'm trying to scare up some extra jobs I can do around my work for Ethan."

"You're working for Ethan? Figured you'd be helping your Dad on the Double-Bar-K," Carl said, playing with his glass.

"Not anymore. We've had a parting of ways. You know of anyone looking for extra helping hands?"

"Well, now that you mention it, I've got a job I could use a hand with myself. I figure Lacey's going to need something to do when she gets back. Something to keep her busy. I don't imagine she'll want to get a job…"

Not likely, Rob agreed.

"So I figure I'll set up a garden for her. A nice big one. Flowers. Vegetables. You know what I mean."

Rob couldn't help but raise his eyebrows. A garden? Carl thought Lacey was going to garden?

"Where you plan to put it?"

"Close to the house is best, I think. I figure an acre ought to do it."

Rob nearly spit out the mouthful of beer he'd just sipped. "An acre?" Did Carl have any idea how much work an acre garden would be to maintain? He'd be lucky if Lacey even deigned to walk in it. He opened his mouth to tell this to Carl, then shut it again. The man probably wanted the land cleared and tilled, flower and vegetable garden beds built, and then seeing how it was already fall, he'd probably want bulbs planted for next year and some annuals to pretty it up for now.

That was a lot of work.

"I'll do it," Rob said.

"Well, now, let's negotiate a price first," Carl said.

"There's a deadline, too. October first."

Rob calculated fast. Carl was a wealthy man, but he probably didn't get that way by being a fool. How much could he get away with charging? Hell, only one way to find out.

"That's a rush job. I'll need twenty thousand dollars—that's only the labor, not the cost of supplies," he said and held his breath. Any other rancher would laugh his ass right out of the bar. Then probably hunt him down later and use him for target practice, for good measure.

"Well, that seems fair," Carl said.

Chapter Thirteen

IT WAS DARK OUT when Morgan gave up on waiting for Rob to return and went to the kitchen to pour herself a glass of water before heading to bed. The kittens were curled up in a furry lump in one corner of the couch. Autumn and Ethan had turned in for the night long ago. The back door was open, letting a breeze waft into the kitchen. As she went to close it for the night, she heard footsteps crunch on the gravel outside, and a man-sized shadow appeared on the other side of the screen door. Morgan stifled a scream.

"Didn't mean to startle you," the man said. He looked familiar, but she couldn't place him at first. "You're Morgan, right?" The porch light behind him shadowed his face, and she fought the urge to turn and run.

"Yes, and you're…"

"Ned. Rob's brother."

She relaxed a little. "Is he okay?"

"Far as I know. I haven't seen him today."

She wondered what Ned could want at this time of

night. "He's out right now."

"That's okay. I didn't come to see him. I came to see you. Why don't you come on out and have a seat." He indicated the swing.

She had a bad feeling about this, although she couldn't say why, exactly. Ned hadn't been along for the ride when Rob, Jake, Jamie and Ethan came to her rescue the night she and Claire went after Claire's stolen things, but she had no reason to think he wasn't as nice as the other Matheson boys. This situation, though, didn't feel nice and she'd learned to trust her instincts.

"I don't think I want to," she said, not moving.

"Fine. Have it your way—we'll do this standing up," Ned said, folding his arms across his chest. Claire glanced at the old-fashioned metal hook and eyelet that were the only way to lock the screen door, and wished they weren't hanging uselessly undone, but she had a feeling such a flimsy mechanism wouldn't stop this man if he was really determined to get inside, anyway. Ned leaned forward. "You're destroying my family, you know that?"

"In what way?"

"Rob's supposed to work our ranch with the rest of us. When Dad passes on, the four of us are supposed to work together to keep it all going. It's been the plan all along, until you came around and ruined it."

"You'll need to talk to Rob about that," she said, stepping back.

"You've got him too wrapped up around your little finger to listen. This whole plan of yours? Making him build a winery for your spoiled little ass? It's crazy—don't you realize that? Any money and time Rob invests in it will be pissing in the wind. Meanwhile, we've got work that isn't done. Not to mention that there's no way in hell we're letting you tear up good rangeland for a bunch of stupid grapes."

"Okay, for one thing—I'm not spoiled," Morgan said, anger overcoming her fear. "Not by a long shot. For another, we're not going to tear up any of your rangeland, so you can butt out of it. We don't need your stupid 200 acres. We've got our own."

That shut him up. He looked at her through the screen door for a long moment. "You'd better explain that."

"Rob's buying 150 acres from Ethan, so don't worry; you're precious ranch will stay in one piece and you don't have to worry about my spoiled little ass anymore, because I'm never setting foot on the Double-Bar-K again."

Ned didn't look pleased. "If you keep my brother away from his family, you'll be sorry. My father's been beside himself since Rob left last night. He's not young anymore. Rob knows that."

"Rob knows that your father is hell-bent on controlling every last thing he does. Your father's a bully."

Ned scowled. "At least my mother's not a whore. Dad told Rob to stay away from the likes of you—now he's probably getting the idea why. You'll drain all his money and energy, and then move on to the next man, right? Just like your mother." He spit on the porch.

Morgan lost her cool. She barged through the screen door, which slammed into Ned, knocking him off balance.

"Hell!"

Whipping the door closed behind her, she lowered her shoulder and charged him before he could recover. Catching him in the sternum, she rammed him over the edge of the porch. He grabbed for the post as he went down, caught it for an instant, lost his grip, and crashed in a heap in the garden bed below. It wasn't much of a fall and she knew he'd be on his feet in an instant; she needed to make the most of this momentary advantage.

She grabbed a nearby watering can and chucked it at him.

He batted it out of the air. "Dammit. What're you doing?"

"Giving you the beating your Momma should have a long time ago. You arrogant son-of-a-bitch, get out of here!" She picked up the next thing to hand—a garden clog—and threw it with all her might.

"Stop that!" Ned tried to jerk out of its path, but failed and it clipped him on the arm. "God dammit!" This time he made it to his feet. For an instant, he hesitated and she knew he was weighing his options—come after her again, or beat a retreat.

"What the hell is going on out here?" Ethan appeared in the kitchen door in a pair of pajama pants and nothing else. Morgan froze, a flower pot in hand. She'd forgotten about him.

"She's crazy! That's what's going on here," Ned said.

"Morgan?"

She tightened her grip on the pot. "I took exception to something he said. I thought he needed to learn some manners."

"You're the one who needs to learn some manners," Ned began but Ethan strode down the steps, collared him and marched him around the side of the house. In the sudden quiet, Morgan realized she was shaking, and she sat down on the steps before her legs gave way. A few moments later, Ethan returned.

"You okay?" he said, sitting down beside her.

"Not really. Rob's family hates me."

"Nah."

"Yeah." She turned to him. "They're furious Rob's not going to ranch with them. Ned called Mom a whore. He said I was breaking up their family."

"Huh." She watched him process this bit of information. "I'll sort him out about Mom later."

"I told him Rob's buying the land from you and we'll be living here. I thought it would settle him down since he didn't want us to till up his ranchland for the vineyard. But he went berserk. What's with him?"

"The Mathesons are a pretty tight-knit clan. Family is everything to them. Holt probably sent him over to try to persuade Rob to change his mind, but he's wasting his time. You can't keep someone on a ranch who doesn't want to be there."

"But if it weren't for me, Rob wouldn't have left in the first place."

"Maybe, but if he'd stayed, he'd be miserable. Sooner

or later something would happen to make him leave. I'm glad he found a good reason to do so."

"Everyone thinks the winery is crazy," she said, remembering Ned's words.

"I don't," Ethan said. He put an arm around her shoulders and she leaned against him. "I know you two will make it a success. I think no one knows what Rob's capable of yet. Not even him."

She hoped he was right. But even after Rob got home and shared his good news about building a garden for Carl, it was a long time before she fell asleep.

Chapter Fourteen

THE FOLLOWING EVENING, after a day spent helping Ethan escort his guests on a long trail ride around the ranch, complete with picnic lunch, Rob prepared to head over to Carl's spread to get started on Lacey's garden.

"So let me get this straight," Ethan said when they met by Rob's truck. "You're going to build a massive garden for my ex-fiancée? Whose side are you on?"

"Don't pretend you give a crap about Lacey anymore, now that you're married to Autumn. That's like worrying about losing track of a skunk when you've been given a thoroughbred race horse."

"I think I understand what you mean," Ethan said wryly, "though I've never exactly heard it put that way before."

"Anyway, I need the cash and Carl's being real generous on this deal."

"Oh, yeah?"

"Yeah."

"All right, then. Have at it," Ethan said.

When Rob arrived at Carl's, he found the man had staked out the plot he had in mind in back of the enormous log house he was building. Unfortunately, he could barely see the tops of the stakes over the shoulder-high brush that grew all over this part of the property.

"You got some tools with you?" Carl said, when he came to meet him.

"Yep," Rob said. He figured he'd hack down the big stuff and then subcontract out to one of the locals who owned an industrial-strength tiller to come plow the whole acre. "You got any plans for the layout of the garden?"

"Not really." Carl scratched his head.

"How about a photo from a magazine or something—to give me a basic idea."

"Okay. Lacey's always looking through things like that. I've probably got something in the house," Carl said. "I'll go on inside and look around. You get busy."

Forty-five minutes later, Rob was ready to give up. The brush was so thick and high it was about impossible to cut through by hand. He was wasting precious time and energy doing it like this. He needed to hire someone with a tractor and rotary mower to power through all of it. Then a tiller could come through.

It was too late to call around, so he headed back for his truck. Carl met him in the driveway.

"I got it," he said. He waved a piece of paper at him. When he got closer, Rob saw that it was a page torn from a magazine. In the failing light he couldn't make out much of it, so he turned on the cab light in his

Chevy and examined it there.

"This is what you're after?" he asked after a moment.

"Yep—that's it exactly."

"You do realize it's September." The page showed an old-fashioned English garden with formal raised beds bursting with perennials in full bloom. There were perfectly clipped hedges, flagstone walkways, a fountain, statuary and a fence around the entire perimeter.

"I don't care what month it is. I'm paying you plenty—make it happen," Carl said.

"That fence alone will cost twenty thousand dollars."

"Fine. Make a list of the materials and costs, add on twenty thousand for your labor and show it to me tomorrow," Carl said. "We'll go from there."

What the hell had he gotten himself into? He'd never get this done in a single month. Should he confess that to Carl and negotiate a new time-table?

No, he needed that money before the wedding. Somehow, he'd have to perform a miracle.

"Will do."

MORGAN COULDN'T BELIEVE she was actually driving voluntarily onto enemy territory. She inched along the long lane that led to the main buildings on the Double-Bar-K, following the directions Autumn had given her. She drove Ethan's Ford F-150, and desperately missed the Honda Civic she'd placed in storage with her furniture back in Victoria before she'd left for Montana. Lisa Matheson had called her mid-morning to remind her about their date to go dress shopping, and asked if she could swing by and get her since her own vehicle was acting up.

The last place on earth she wanted to be after her fight with Ned was pulling up in front of the Matheson house. An impressive two-story home with a wrap-around porch, it had a slightly more old-money feel to it than the Cruz ranch did. She didn't need to be told this ranch had been in Matheson hands for a long, long time.

The front door opened and Lisa peered out. "I'll be ready in a minute—come on in!"

Sighing, Morgan gathered her purse. She'd hoped she could pull up, load Lisa into the truck, and leave before anyone else saw them. She guessed that would be expecting a miracle. She exited the Ford, climbed the steps to the porch and hesitated in the doorway.

"Come on in," Lisa sang out again from somewhere farther into the house. "I need to find my purse."

Morgan walked into a wide entryway. A formal living room lay through a door to her left. The dining room was to her right. A staircase in front of her swept up to a second floor balcony with halls extending from either end of it that must lead to a number of bedrooms. Somewhere farther back on the first floor must lie a kitchen and perhaps a family room. It was an elegant home and Lisa had every right to be proud of it.

"Found it!" Lisa called, and came bustling back up the central hall, as the door opened behind Morgan and a masculine voice said, "What are you doing here?"

Morgan spun around. It was Rob's oldest brother, Jake, and behind him, Rob's father was entering the house.

"Jake, behave yourself," Lisa said. "Morgan and I are going dress shopping. Lunch is all set in the kitchen. I'll be back in time for dinner."

"Dress shopping? With her?" Holt said. He glared at Morgan and she wished she could sink into the floorboards. Why, oh why hadn't she put Lisa off on this fool's errand?

"You behave yourself, too, Holt Matheson," Lisa said. "You go ahead and grumble all you like when it's family, but when there's a guest in our house, you mind your manners."

Morgan looked at Lisa in surprise. Holt frowned. "This woman is stealing our son. I guess I'll growl at her if I want to."

"She's marrying our son, not stealing him," Lisa said.

"What's the difference? She's taking him away, ain't she? Buying Cruz land, for God's sake. What's wrong with our spread, I'd like to know that."

"He's buying Cruz land because you didn't want him to build a vineyard for me here," Morgan said. "He loves me and wants me to be happy. Did it ever occur to any of you that he could use your support?"

"Did it ever occur to you we need his help here with this ranch?" Holt snapped back.

"No," she stated firmly. "That hasn't occurred to me, because according to Rob, none of you have ever needed him to do anything except your own dirty work. You miss having your slave to order around, because that's all he's ever been to you."

"I've never treated him like a slave," Holt said.

She simply stared him down. Eventually, he glanced away.

"Rob knows what I want," he said gruffly. "My four boys working this ranch together. That's always been my dream."

"Have you ever asked Rob what his dreams are? Or have you been too busy telling him what to do to ever ask?"

"Who the hell do you think you are coming to my house and speaking to me that way?" Holt drew himself up to his full height and Morgan could see where his sons got their stature and self-confidence.

"I'm the woman who loves your son. And pretty soon I'll be his wife and the mother of your grandkids, so you better get used to me. I'm not going anywhere." She turned to Lisa. "I'm sorry, but I think we'd better shop another day." She'd already said too much, and she knew if she stood for a minute longer in the entryway of the Matheson house, she'd say something they'd all regret. She pushed past Holt and opened the door, hurrying down the steps back to Ethan's truck.

She managed to hold back her tears until she'd reached the end of the long dirt lane, but then they began to fall. As she moved to turn back toward the Cruz ranch, she hesitated. If she drove back there, someone would ask questions and she knew she couldn't talk about what had happened without losing her composure all together. Making up her mind, she turned left instead of right, and drove into town.

Ten minutes later she entered the Chance Creek Pet Clinic, her eyes dry but rimmed with red. She hoped Bella would be there, but instead a young blond woman whose nametag read Hannah sat at the front desk.

"Can I help you?" she asked cheerfully. Several people sat in the waiting room, dogs on leashes and cats in carriers.

"I...don't have an appointment," Morgan said. "I was wondering...if I could hang out with the shelter animals?" She trailed off, feeling foolish. Bella probably wouldn't want people to drop in unannounced. This was a veterinary office, not just a pound.

"Sure thing!" Hannah smiled broadly. "We love it when people come and give the pets some attention. The animals love it, too. Are you a dog person or a cat person?"

"I guess I could be either."

Hannah considered her, and Morgan had a feeling she could see the traces of tears on her face. "Let's start with cats today," she said kindly. She led the way through to the shelter and once again Morgan found herself in the feline area of the big building. "Our animals have the best chance for adoption if they're good with being handled and unafraid of humans. If you take the cats out of their cages, one at a time, and just pet and hold them for a little while, that's really great."

"What if they don't want to be held?"

"Don't push things if they put up a fuss," Hannah said. "Some of the cats are feral. We give them shots, spay or neuter them, then try to find farms where they can be barn cats. Take your lead from the animals." She turned to leave.

"What if one gets away from me?" Morgan said, beginning to panic a little at the thought of being alone among all these cages.

"As long as you keep the main doors shut, you'll be fine." Hannah assured her. "Just come back up front when you're done."

Left among the animals, Morgan didn't know where to start, but she approached the cage of an orange tabby and cautiously opened it. The cat, interested, came over to inspect her, sniffed her outstretched hand and consented to be picked up. Morgan sat down on the floor and held the purring cat in her lap, stroking her fur and allowing her to sniff her, in return. The cat seemed in no hurry to run away from her so after a moment she relaxed and was rewarded when it curled up in her lap.

After a few minutes, she reluctantly put the animal back in its cage and took another one out, repeating the process. This one was more wiggly and she wasn't able to pet it as long before it made an effort to get away. Once she safely had it back in its cage, she moved on to the next one.

Soon she realized she was moving methodically through the cages because she wanted time with each animal before she had to leave. She began to understand how Bella could become obsessed with saving them all. How could you choose which one to keep or let go? They were all so beautiful.

A few crouched in the back of their cages, hissing

and spitting when she reached out to let them sniff her hand. Those she let be, but when she cuddled her tenth cat, a lovely black and white one who liked to nuzzle her under her chin, she had to laugh when she thought back to her confrontation with the Mathesons.

Who cared about Holt or Jake or Ned? These kitties didn't judge her because she was a Tate instead of a Matheson, or because she wanted a vineyard instead of cattle. They accepted her presence—reveled in it—without question.

Some humans could learn a thing or two from these fluffy balls of fur.

When she finally did leave, after cuddling every cat in the building that would let her near, she felt much better. Hannah smiled at her. "Are you hooked yet?"

"You bet. I still don't see how Bella can afford to feed all those animals, though."

"The bills are crazy," Hannah confided. "I've been working on some plans, though."

"Really? Anything I can do to help?"

Hannah brightened. "Do you mean that?"

"Sure." It was better than stewing about Holt.

"If you want to join me for lunch soon I could show you what I've got so far. I could use someone to bounce ideas off of."

"Sure. I'll call you later in the week." Morgan left the office much happier than she'd been when she arrived. Between the furry therapy she'd received from the cats, and the promise of a lunch date with Hannah, she thought she could take on Holt and all his sons.

Besides, she had made her first friend in Chance Creek unconnected to Rob or the Cruz ranch. In some small way, she'd sent down a thread of a root into the community she wanted so badly to join.

Chapter Fifteen

RIGHT BEFORE DINNER ON SUNDAY, Rob parked in the lot at the Chance Creek Regional Airport and climbed out of his Chevy. He couldn't believe only a little over a week had passed since he and Morgan landed here. So much had happened in the intervening days.

He was dog tired and he still had hours of work ahead of him at Carl's place tonight. He'd managed to get some equipment in and the acre plot was mowed and tilled within an inch of its life, but it had been much harder to find a mason. He had two kinds of rocks on order; rounded river rock for the perimeter fence, and flat shale for the raised beds. While the mason worked on the fence, he'd tackle those beds himself.

He'd done his best to lay out the garden's primary features in a pattern as similar as possible to the magazine photo Carl had given him. Carl himself had ordered the fountain, so tomorrow a contractor was to come in and lay the pipe. He'd also put in a sprinkler system throughout the garden. Rob would have to take an hour or two off of his day with Ethan to make sure the man understood the plans he'd dropped by his office.

Entering the airport, he waited for Jamie and Claire's flight to come in. He was excited to tell Jamie about moving onto the Cruz ranch, and looked forward to hashing out ways their business interests could line up. Morgan had lectured him about waiting at least until tomorrow to discuss that, however. She said Jamie and Claire would be too exhausted from their travels to talk business tonight.

He understood that. He was almost too tired, himself.

When the happy couple finally deplaned, they did look a little done in. Both were tanned, and they were holding hands, but Claire was quieter than usual.

"You two okay?" Rob asked, when they met up.

"Better now that we're off that plane," Jamie said.

"Three flights and I sat in front of a screaming baby twice," Claire said. "My head is pounding."

"Let's get you home," Rob said. He kept his mouth shut about all of his news, grateful for Morgan's advice now. This was definitely not the time to spring his plans on either of them. When they reached their new log home, he helped unload their luggage and prepared to take off.

"Any chance you could fill in for me again tomorrow morning?" Jamie said, leaning against his truck. "I want to make sure Claire's better before I get back to work."

"Sure thing."

"Great. I'll call Ethan and let him know."

"I can tell him myself," Rob said. "I'm heading back

that way now."

"Really? Helping him with evening chores?"

"Nah—just popping home for dinner." When Jamie looked confused, he elaborated. "Morgan and I are staying in the spare room at the bunkhouse; until we buy some furniture and get moved in over at your old cabin."

"My cabin? Why aren't you on your own ranch?"

Rob realized he'd put his foot in it. "I was going to tell you tomorrow; you two looked too bushed to talk it over tonight. I'm buying 150 acres from you and Ethan. That's where Morgan and I are going to settle down. We'll put in her vineyard and eventually build a winery there. Meanwhile I'll help you and Ethan and maybe the two of us can team up on that horse-breeding business. In time, I want to offer rodeo riding lessons. It'll all play into the guest ranch business." He grinned, happy now that he'd had a chance to lay it out for Jamie, after all.

"Ethan agreed to all that without even asking me?" Jamie said slowly.

Rob stilled. "You got a problem with it?"

"I don't know. I…thought he and I were partners. That's a pretty big change of plans."

"Heck, I thought I'd get a better reception than this." Disappointment made his tone sharp.

"It's nothing personal. Shit, I just went on my honeymoon." Jamie ran a hand through hair that was already standing on end. "I go away for a week and Ethan decides all of this? I…I better talk to him tomorrow."

"You do that." Rob started the truck. "See you around."

Jamie stepped back from the vehicle and watched him drive away.

Morgan was beginning to doubt she really had a fiancé. If she woke up in the middle of the night, Rob was by her side, fast asleep, but she hardly saw him during the day. He was gone by the time she got up in the morning and didn't come home until after she'd gone to bed. She knew he'd taken on this garden project for Carl in order to raise the money he'd promised her to start her winery. She'd begun to regret ever asking for it, but without his contribution, she'd have to put that dream on hold for another year. Given the amount of time it took to get a vineyard up and running, she didn't feel like she had another year. They needed to get the land prepped this fall so they could plant the rootstock first thing next spring.

Rob had been distant last night when he popped in for a quick dinner before heading out to Carl's. He'd driven Jamie and Claire to their house and said they looked tired but good. She was looking forward to hearing all about their trip to Hawaii. She'd never been there, herself.

When she let herself into the Big House, she found Claire sipping a mug of tea in the kitchen, keeping Autumn company while she prepped breakfast. There was an uncomfortable silence when Morgan entered, as if the two of them had been discussing something they didn't want her to hear.

Morgan handed Claire a kitten. "Rob and I got this

for you if you want it."

"Thanks," Claire said, but didn't meet Morgan's gaze. She took the kitten and held it carefully on her lap.

"I was telling Claire about how Ethan had to save Ned from you the other day," Autumn said.

Morgan looked from one to the other. Maybe they'd discussed that earlier, but judging by the tension in the room, something else had been the topic of conversation before she walked in.

"He was angry that Rob wouldn't go back to working on the Double-Bar-K. When he called Mom a whore, I decided to teach him a lesson."

"He called Mom a whore?" Claire set down her teacup, but Morgan didn't get the feeling she was mad at Ned. Instead, she had the distinct impression Claire was somehow blaming her.

"Like I said, he was angry."

"Well, I can understand that. People like to be consulted when plans change." She bent down and put the kitten on the floor where it began a tentative exploration of the large room.

Morgan narrowed her eyes. There it was again—that trace of hostility in Claire's voice. "Holt told Rob he couldn't use the land he was giving us for the vineyard. What did he expect Rob to do?"

"He probably didn't expect Rob to go run off and purchase 150 acres of our land behind our backs," Claire said.

Ah, there it was.

"That's what you think? That Rob was trying to do

something sneaky?" She moved all the way into the kitchen and put her purse on the counter. "The way I heard it, Ethan offered the land to Rob. It doubt it even occurred to Rob to ask if Ethan had checked with Jamie first. After all, this is Ethan's ranch."

"Like Ethan had any choice but to offer it to him once Rob started bitching and moaning about how his father had done him wrong," Claire said. "Anyway, Jamie's supposed to be Ethan's partner. Ethan can't go around selling bits of the ranch to people on a whim."

"I don't think it was on a whim," Autumn put in, crossing her arms on the other side of the counter. "Ethan loves the idea of the three of them working together on this ranch, and he thought the three of us could have a good time supporting each other, too. I agreed with him."

From her tone, it was clear she didn't anymore.

Claire frowned. "Did Ethan consult you before offering the land to Rob?"

"No. He didn't have to; he knew I'd be all for Rob and Morgan sharing the ranch with us. And for the record, Jamie didn't run it by Ethan or me before he decided to marry you and make you part owner again."

"That's different." Claire's voice was rising. "Marrying into ownership and buying into it are two totally separate things."

Morgan struggled not to turn on her heel and walk right back out the door. This was too important to walk out on, though. Why was Claire so dead set on not sharing the ranch when six months ago all she wanted to do was leave it behind, herself?

"Ethan still has the majority share in the ranch," Autumn began cautiously.

"And he thinks he can use that to lord it over everyone and call all the shots?"

"Who am I lording what over?" Ethan walked into the kitchen. Claire snapped her mouth shut, color flooding her face.

"Claire feels you should have discussed things with Jamie before offering to sell Rob part of the ranch," Morgan said quietly.

"I'm not the only one who feels that way. So does Jamie—he's pissed, and I am, too," Claire said. "You need to consult us before you do things like that!"

"Whoa, hold on, Claire. A month or two ago, Jamie and I paid you $600,000 for your share of the ranch. Seems to me if you're going to start bossing me around, you can pay me back," Ethan said. He bent down and scooped up the kitten, who was now sniffing around one of the easy chairs.

Claire's face flushed even more. "That's not how it works," she said. "If you're so tight for money, ask her where all the cash Mom stole went!" She pointed at Morgan.

"Mom didn't steal..." Ethan said.

"Bullshit! We all keep pussy-footing around it, but she did, and that's why the ranch is in debt, which is why you have to keep selling pieces of it!"

"Morgan's already said she doesn't know where the money is!" He sat down heavily on the easy chair and put the kitten in his lap where it crouched, quivering.

"Then who does? Where the hell did it go?"

Morgan couldn't stand it anymore. "Stop it! Stop yelling! If Rob buying the acreage is going to cause this much trouble, then forget it—we'll go somewhere else! But since I work for Autumn, right now I'm going to stay here and help her with breakfast. Aren't you supposed to be fixing up Carl's mansion, Claire? Seems to me it's time for you to get to work, too. We certainly shouldn't be fighting while there are guests upstairs trying to sleep."

Claire opened her mouth, glanced at Ethan and seemed to change her mind about what she was going to say. "Fine, I'm out of here. But I notice you still haven't dropped off the list of dates Mom spent with you, like you said you would. I'd like that by the end of today, and I'm going to keep searching for that missing money."

"Whatever," Morgan said and joined Autumn behind the counter. Ethan stood up and handed Claire her kitten.

"Don't forget this."

Claire frowned at the animal, then snuggled it close to her chin as she walked out.

"Sorry about that," Ethan said to Morgan. "I don't know what's gotten into her. You think something happened between her and Jamie?"

Autumn shrugged and Morgan shook her head. "Whatever it is, I hope they work it out quick."

WHEN ROB GOT in at two in the morning again, Morgan

was waiting for him in the living room of the bunkhouse.

"What's wrong?" he asked.

"Everything." She got up and crossed the room to hug him, leaning against him when he wrapped his arms around her and kissed the top of her head. "We can't plant our vineyard here."

He pulled back. "Why the hell not?"

"Shhh—Ethan and Autumn are asleep. Because Claire's pissed that Ethan offered the land to you without asking her or Jamie. And she thinks I know what happened to all the money my mom blew and that I'm lying to cover it up. Which doesn't even make sense. If I had all that cash squirreled away somewhere I'd buy my own vineyard."

"Huh." Rob moved to sit on the couch. He looked much too tired, his jeans and shirt covered with dust, stubble darkening his face, and hollow circles under his eyes. "Jamie wasn't too happy when I mentioned it yesterday, either. I assumed if Ethan said it was all right that it would be. I didn't think about needing to give Jamie a say first." He ran a hand through his blond hair, mussing it up. "Well, I'm sure it'll all sort out. Claire's mad they weren't asked, that's all. That doesn't mean she'll refuse to sell to me if we ask nicely." He grinned a lopsided grin, and it was all Morgan could do not to join him on the couch and snuggle up on his lap for a kiss.

"Maybe, but what if she doesn't?"

"I'm pretty sure Ethan ultimately gets to call the shots."

"Yeah, but if Claire and Jamie don't want us here, we

can't stay," Morgan said. "I couldn't stand that."

"I'm not letting Claire keep me from building a life with you," Rob said, leaning his elbows on his knees. "She better not try to stop us."

"It's not just Claire," Morgan said, sitting down next to him. "It's your father and brothers, too. Ned said that I was breaking up your family by forcing you to build me a winery."

"To hell with Ned," Rob said. "He likes to hear the sound of his own voice."

"Your father hates my guts. And they're right—you aren't speaking with any of them," she protested. "And it's all because of me."

"It's because they're pig-headed and they can't admit they're wrong. Now come to bed. Everything will look better in the morning." He stood up and tugged her across the room. "What did you say last night about missing me?"

She allowed Rob to lead her to the bedroom, and for a little while forgot their cares in his touch, but when they'd fooled around and he'd fallen asleep, she faced the fact that her presence in Chance Creek was tearing apart two families.

Maybe she'd been wrong to agree to marry Rob. Maybe this was what happened when you put the cart before the horse and agreed to marriage before you had a relationship. Had they been too thoughtless about the consequences of their actions when they'd pledged to spend their lives together? She had hoped that marrying Rob would bring her all the community she'd always craved. Instead, it was ripping both their families apart.

And what about what Rob had wanted? He was looking for a chance to be independent. She knew he'd thought their marriage would allow him to make something of his life—to become a success. Now he was slaving away for Ethan and Carl, little better than a hired hand. Maybe it was a step up from being his father's lackey, but he was working so hard to give her what she wanted that he wasn't making any progress toward his own goals.

Should she break off the engagement, return to Victoria and resume her old life, leaving Rob to patch things up with family and friends and weave his own way back into his community?

The thought made her throat ache with unshed tears.

She couldn't believe that Claire and Jamie had a problem with them moving onto the ranch. After all, Jamie and Rob were as much friends as Rob and Ethan were. From what she knew of Jamie, he was always one to offer help. And Claire's obsession was with Aria, not her. They'd had their differences in the beginning, but they'd also had some good times together. Did Claire really resent her coming to live here, or was it unfinished business with their mother she still needed to work out?

Morgan lay in bed, listening to Rob's quiet breathing beside her. One thing she was sure of; she didn't want to break off her engagement to this man. She had come to depend on his presence in her life and she loved their time together; especially when they were alone. She'd never met a man so interested in what interested her, and the way he was working to make her dreams come true left her speechless with gratitude.

No, she wouldn't let the Mathesons or the Cruzes break her and Rob apart.

Just when she'd decided to give up on sleep all together that night, an idea occurred to her. She wasn't prepared to let her marriage to Rob or the development of her winery destroy families and friendships that had held together over years. And she wasn't making any headway by trying to reason with everyone. She couldn't force them to like her, or want her vineyard on their properties.

But maybe she could show them exactly what they would be missing if she were gone.

Chapter Sixteen

ROB DIDN'T THINK he'd ever had such a long day in his life. He hadn't had more than four hours of sleep for the past few nights, and Jamie blindsided him in the barn first thing this morning to tell him again how little he appreciated him going behind his back to make deals with Ethan. When he tried to explain the circumstances, Jamie accused Morgan of being hateful to Claire. He hadn't taken kindly to Rob's suggestion that his bride was to blame for all the drama around the Cruz spread these days.

Ethan had intervened then, ordering Rob to spend the morning mending tack and straightening the barn while he had a head-to-head with Jamie. As the hours crept by, the strongest feeling of deja-vu swept over him: wasn't this exactly the type of work he'd been trying to escape when he left home?

At lunch time, he didn't feel like joining the rest of the crowd up at the Big House, so he only ducked into the kitchen, gave Morgan a peck on the cheek, and grabbed a ham sandwich off the pile she and Autumn had made.

"I'm going to eat on the run today," he said. Morgan only nodded. He left the house feeling even worse, but when he came back to the stable, Claire and Jamie were already there, talking in the shade of north wall.

"This isn't about Morgan and you know it," Jamie was saying. He leaned against the side of the stable. Claire paced in front of him.

"Yes it is."

"Baloney. It's about me wanting to start a family and you saying no."

Claire turned away from him and spotted Rob. "Damn it! Now you're eavesdropping?"

"Just trying to find a quiet place to eat," Rob said, holding up his sandwich. He backed up quickly, spun on his heel and hiked over to the bunkhouse before Claire could start another fight.

Why didn't Claire want to start a family? And what did it have to do with Morgan?

He couldn't fathom it, but he resolved to talk to Morgan about it the first chance he got. Meanwhile, he relaxed some about the tension on the ranch. If Claire was angry at Jamie, rather than at him, things would eventually work out.

He hoped.

Still, when dinner time rolled around and his work-day for Ethan was over, he looked forward to heading over to Carl's where things weren't so off-kilter. So when he arrived at the bunkhouse to gather his things and found Jake waiting for him on the front steps, his stomach sank.

"Whatever you've got to say, I don't want to hear it," he stated and tried to push past him. Jake stood up and blocked his way.

"You seriously going to let that girl break our family apart?"

"Morgan's not breaking anything apart. Dad's the one doing the destruction. And what do you care, anyway—I'd think the lot of you would be happy to see the last of me."

"How do you figure that?"

"Oh, come on," Rob said. "You've spent your whole lives trying to run me off the place. Picking at me, criticizing me, making sure I don't do anything meaningful over there."

Jake had the grace to look a little shamefaced. "That's Ned, mostly."

"Mostly," Rob echoed. "And Dad, and the rest of you."

"Dad set this whole thing up for you, you know that, don't you? That's how badly he wants you to stay on the ranch." Jake still wouldn't let him past.

"Set what whole thing up?"

"This…contest. The 200 acres. He told us point blank out in the barn after he announced it that it was meant for you—none of us were even supposed to try for it."

Rob blinked. "Why would he do that?"

Jake held his hands out wide. "Because he wants you to stay on the ranch. I just said that. He knew you were going to make a break for it."

Shaking his head, Rob turned around and stared out at the mountains in the distance. "Well, doesn't that beat all. I don't understand him. I don't understand any of you." He turned back. "If you want me to stay, why the hell do you try so hard to make me want to leave?"

"I'm not trying," Jake said. "I thought we got along all right."

"Until I try to do anything that's not your idea," Rob pointed out.

"Well, yeah. I guess so," Jake said. "Maybe I could work on that."

"Might as well not bother," Rob said gruffly. "Ned and Dad aren't going to change."

A funny look came over Jake's face. "I'm not so sure about Dad. He ain't been feeling so great lately. He's feeling his age. I think he wishes he'd done a few things differently."

"Dad's hated me my whole life," Rob said. "I doubt that's going to stop now. And I'm done trying to change his mind. I've got other people to worry about—like Morgan."

When he glanced Jake's way, however, his brother was staring at him open-mouthed. "Dad...hates you? You've got to be kidding me."

"What the hell are you on about now?" Rob said, bracing himself for a new round of cruelty. Jake was right—usually it was Ned sticking the blade in and twisting it in his guts, but Jake was no slouch when he was in the mind to get a dig in.

"You never heard him spouting off about his rodeo star son down at the bar?"

"When has he ever done that?" Rob stared at his brother in open derision. Heck, he hadn't even ridden much these past couple of years. Jake must be talking about ancient history.

"When doesn't he do that?" Jake scratched the back of his neck. "You're not at the right bar—you're always at the Dancing Boot."

He sure as heck wasn't going to hang around with a bunch of old fogies at Rafters, but he wasn't going to say that to Jake. "He's never even seen me ride. He always finds somewhere else to be when it's my turn."

"You don't get it, do you?" Jake said, leaning against the stair railing. "It's like you're totally blind. You're the damn baby of this family, Rob. You're the apple of Dad's eye. He didn't have time for the rest of us when we were young, but he was always hauling you around on top of his shoulders when he did his chores. I can remember when he taught you to ride. How damn proud he was of you. I wanted to knock you into next week. I'd been working on a trick to show him and he couldn't take his eyes off you long enough to see it."

"You're putting me on," Rob said, but his mind was busy dredging up old memories—a view of the stable-yard from way up high. Sitting on a horse that seemed as big as a Mack truck, his Daddy standing beside him, holding him steady. He hadn't thought about any of that in years.

"When you started riding in the rodeo, he had this

little book he kept in his pocket. He wrote down the dates and your scores. Shit, Rob."

"How the hell could he do that if he wasn't even watching?" Rob said.

"He was watching, you just couldn't see him. He couldn't sit in the stands. He couldn't sit still. He was so scared you'd…I don't know. Fall, or get hurt, or lose, or be sad. He can't stand it when you're unhappy, don't you know that?"

"So he yells at me all damn day long? Tells me how stupid I am for caring about anything other than ranching?" He couldn't believe what he was hearing—it made no sense. Jake was making all this up, he knew it. He just didn't know why his brother would take the time to spin such stories.

"He's never called you stupid."

"He tried to make me stupid," Rob countered. "He ripped up my report card the first time I brought home A's. He wants me stupid, ignorant, and stuck in his shadow for the rest of my life."

Jake sighed. "Shit. I remember that. You know why he did that, don't you? Nah, you probably don't." He wiped a hand over his face. "Aw, heck, I never realized until you disappeared to Canada how much we've screwed things up—me and Ned and Luke."

"What do you mean?" Rob turned away again. This whole conversation was making him mighty uncomfortable. The past was the past, and the only reason it kept dragging into the present was because his father was trying so hard to keep him under his thumb.

"What a mess," Jake said. "Okay, you're going to hate me, but try to understand—you're the youngest. We didn't mean to keep secrets from you."

"Secrets?" Rob didn't like the sound of that at all.

"Yeah, secrets. Although I have to admit I'm surprised you never guessed."

"Guessed what?" Shit, was Jake going to tell him he was adopted? He tensed, not sure he could handle that.

"Dad can't read. Not much, anyway. You really never figured that out?"

"Wait, hold on a minute." That was the last thing he expected Jake to say. "What do you mean he can't read?"

"Why do you think he dropped out of school at fourteen? Why'd you think he hates books so much?"

"But…"

"Think about it," Jake said, and Rob did. To his surprise, a number of things fell swiftly into place.

"Mom does all the paperwork," he said.

"Bingo. Now you're catching on. That day he tore up your report card?" Jake laughed, but it wasn't a happy sound. "You kept shoving it in his face. Wanting him to read all the things your teachers wrote about you."

"Hell." That day had been the end of his career as a straight-A student. Once Holt was through bellowing about sissies and wastes of time, he'd sent Rob out to the stables to muck out every single stall himself.

Rob had learned that lesson well.

"Why the heck didn't anybody tell me?" he asked now.

Jake studied his feet. "Didn't think you could keep

the secret, probably. No one but our family knows." He glanced up and caught Rob's eye. "No one can know."

Rob heard his unspoken message: this was a secret the Mathesons would take to their graves. If the rest of the town knew, they wouldn't be able to hold up their heads anymore.

"Why doesn't he learn how? Then there wouldn't have to be a secret." So many years of his life he'd blamed himself for his father's coldness. All because Holt couldn't read? No, there had to be more to it than that.

"From what I can figure out, he fooled his teachers for years this way and that, and no one figured it out until about the eighth grade. Then they sent him to some kind of specialist. The other kids gave him heck about it, though, until he quit school outright. So when Ned started having trouble, he refused to have anything to do with any doctors or interventions. He decided no kid of his was going to get teased."

I got teased, Rob wanted to say, but held his tongue. "Ned can't read, either?" Well, that made sense. Ned never was any good at school.

"Yep. Same problem as Dad. Gets his letters all turned around."

"They're dyslexic?" How the hell had he never known? "There's all kinds of things they do for that nowadays."

"Only if you admit you have it," Jake said. "And they won't admit it."

"So Dad protected Ned and left me hanging high

and dry," Rob said. "Helluva thing to do."

"Dad knew you'd do fine," Jake countered. "And you have, haven't you? You've always been able to protect yourself one way or the other. Everybody's been scared to death of you since you reached junior high. Remember what you did to the guy who attacked Morgan? You're a fighter, Rob—with your fists and your jokes. Now you're engaged to Morgan, you've got two jobs, a parcel of land…hell, I'm envious."

"Envious?" But as Jake's words sunk in, he realized his brother was right. He'd nursed his childhood grudges for way too many years, but no one had actually hurt him since…since…well, grade school, now that he thought of it. Even Ned hadn't touched him since they were kids. He still nagged him all the time, needled him and generally behaved like an ass, but he couldn't remember the last time they actually fought.

No. That wasn't true. He did remember. It had been the usual scrap, out by the barn, over chores or something along those lines. They'd tussled and rolled in the dirt and he'd finally landed a punch on Ned's chin that snapped his brother's head back. Ned had scrambled to his feet, kicked him clumsily, and run away.

He'd run away.

And instead of acting like the victor, Rob had kept telling himself the same old story—that he could never beat his older brothers, that he'd always be picked on, that there wasn't anything he could ever do to win.

Glancing around him, he wanted to laugh at his own stupidity. Or bang his head against a wall, maybe. Why was he still acting like his father could force him to do things he didn't want to do? At any time in the last decade or more he could have left home, gotten a job and run his own life exactly the way he wanted to. Instead, he'd blamed everyone else for his dissatisfaction and didn't lift a finger to change.

"You're in a hell of a lot better situation than I am," he told Jake honestly. "You've always known you wanted to be a rancher and you work like a son-of-a-gun. I'm still figuring out what I want to do."

"Maybe so," Jake said, "but my life ain't perfect, either. There are things I'd like to try with the ranch that I can't because Dad vetoes them. Still, even if our family's not perfect, it's something. I hope you won't turn your back on us, and for what it's worth," he took a deep breath, "if you really think planting grapes would make you happier than running cattle, then I'm on your side. It's your 200 acres. You do what you want with them." He stuck out his hand.

Rob slowly reached out and took it. "You mean that? What about Ned and Luke?"

"I don't think Luke cares one way or the other. You're on your own when it comes to Ned. Maybe it's time the two of you sorted a few things out."

"There's no way Dad will agree to the vineyard, though, and I won't come back on any other terms," Rob said.

"I heard a rumor Claire might not let you have the vineyard over here, either."

"You let me worry about that."

"I will. I hope you work something out. You've always been better at gardening than ranching."

As Jake walked off, Rob lingered where he was. Hell, he thought he'd been hiding his true nature all this time. Turns out he wasn't fooling anyone.

But everyone else had been fooling him.

"THANKS FOR ALL YOUR HELP," Autumn said. "I feel awful; you're supposed to be done after lunch time."

It was nearly nine in the evening, but Morgan didn't mind. She enjoyed working with Autumn and she wanted to pitch in as much as she could while she was still here. Autumn really shouldn't be working so hard while she was pregnant. Besides, Rob was so busy nowadays, she hardly saw him. If she wasn't working, she'd be bored.

"Don't worry about it," Morgan said.

"I wish Claire wasn't being such a…"

"Bitch?"

"Something like that." Autumn sighed. "I don't think her problem is with you, though."

"Sure seems that way."

"Something's on her mind. I wish I knew what it was," Autumn said.

"Go get some rest and stop worrying about everyone." Morgan patted her arm. Autumn's frown seemed perpetually in place these days.

"I was thinking about taking a look up in that attic."

"Now?"

"It's a mess and I want everything perfect before the

baby comes." Autumn flashed her a smile. "And yes, I know how insane I sound."

"You sound like a perfectly normal mom-to-be. But I'll point out that you have six more months to get the attic clean. Please rest tonight."

"I will. You, too. I'll see you first thing in the morning."

Morgan headed out the door with a smile on her face, but by the time she reached the bunkhouse she was frowning again. Autumn was right. It didn't make sense that Claire was so upset with her.

What was really bothering her?

MASONRY BY MOONLIGHT wasn't going to be the next big thing, Rob thought as he troweled on a layer of cement and fitted another stone in place. With Carl's help, he'd set up an array of lights run off an exterior extension cord. Still, his pace was hampered by the heavy shadows. At this rate he'd never get the garden done. Evenings were beginning to get cooler, too. It was late September. If he wanted a shot at beating Carl's deadline, he had to get these raised beds built in the next day or two.

It was close to three in the morning by the time he staggered home, so once he'd rinsed himself off under a hot shower and fumbled his way to the bedroom dressed in nothing but the towel around his waist, he was surprised to find Morgan still awake, reading by the light of a bedside lamp, several kittens tucked around her among the covers.

"Hey, you're finally home," she said, putting her book away and reaching for him.

He returned her hug and kiss. "Couldn't you sleep?"

"I wanted to talk to you. I've missed you."

"I've missed you, too." They hadn't fooled around in days and now his body reminded him of that fact. She looked good—warm, lush and inviting. He tore off the towel and pitched it into the corner of the room.

She watched him, eyes sparkling, but when he climbed onto the bed, she sat up straight and held him off. "We need to talk for a minute." She brushed her lips over his cheek, as if promising they'd do more than talk afterward. "We've got to do something about Claire and Jamie, and about your family, too."

"You think we should try to reason with them again?" He didn't see what else they could do.

"I was thinking more along the lines of a practical joke."

Rob's eyebrows shot up. "You serious?"

"I am." A wicked smile curved her lips. "I think it's time to get them all, good."

"Tell me about it." He couldn't wait any longer. He eased her down onto the mattress and covered her body with his own. Kissing her neck and then her jaw, then finally her mouth, he said. "Actually, hold that thought for a minute, would you?"

She let out a sigh as he traced his lips over her chin and down her neck, as he cupped one breast with his hand. "Okay," she said, and before he could even ask, she'd skimmed the shortie nightgown she wore up over her head and hurled it across the room to join his towel.

"That's more like it," Rob said. He took a moment to lift all the kittens off of the bed and deposit them on the floor. He would never grow tired of Morgan's body. Curvy in all the right places, he loved to touch her, taste her and tease her until she moaned beneath him in delight. He intended to do all three of those things right now, but he wished he could do more. He couldn't wait to make love to Morgan.

She seemed to be as much on fire for him as he was for her. She stroked his back, curving her palms over his ass, then traced her fingernails back up his skin.

Rob shivered and pulled her closer, lavishing his attentions of first one breast, then the other. He could spend all night right here…if he didn't have to get up in a couple of hours and start all over again.

With that thought in mind, he cut to the chase, wriggling lower and beginning to explore her center with his tongue.

Morgan arched and moaned, a sound that set him on fire. He wished…

"Rob," she breathed and tried to pull him back up closer to her.

"Honey, let me make you feel good," he said, and bent back to his delicious task.

"Rob." This time she tugged harder, her hands on his biceps. He sighed and inched back up to face her.

"What is it?" he said.

Her cheeks stained with color, a sight so beautiful it made his heart ache.

"I don't want to wait anymore to be with you. I want to make love to you tonight. Right now." She bit her lip, waiting for his answer.

His eyes narrowed. "You sure?" he said.

She nodded. "Definitely."

"What about waiting for our wedding?" he asked. Hell, he'd been ready to make love to her the day they'd met, but so much was screwed up right now, he didn't want to tip the balance against them. Women were funny sometimes. They got notions in their heads that were best to go along with. He didn't want Morgan to wake up disappointed tomorrow.

"I'm no virgin," she said. "And I know I'm going to be with you forever. I made up my mind the night you came to Victoria. You're the only man for me, Rob Matheson, and nothing's going to change that—not your family or mine. I've watched you these past few weeks doing everything you can to set up a life for us. No one's making it easy, but whatever they throw our way, you handle it and keep going. I respect you for that, so much. I know we can build something that will last." She searched his face and he figured she was wondering if he felt the same way.

He sure as hell did. "I don't care what any of them says. I'm marrying you and I'm staying married to you."

She took in a deep breath. "I think I love you."

Warmth surged into Rob's heart. He lowered his head to kiss her. "I know I love you."

"Show me," she whispered, and Rob nearly lost his grip right then. Slipping an arm behind her, he cupped her head and lifted it to meet her mouth with his. He kissed her long and hard, a possessive kiss, wanting her to feel the depth of his love for her right down to her toes. He didn't know when friendship, respect and desire for her had transformed into something deeper, but he did know he never wanted to let her go again. He would never accept circumstances that led to anything but their being together.

He ravished her again with his mouth, this time knowing that before they were done, he would possess all of her, body and soul. He took his time, exploring every inch of her, until Morgan twisted her hands in her hair and dragged him up to face her once more.

"I...can't...wait," she gasped out. "Now, Rob."

Gathering her close, he moved into position, wanting to stay here always, just on the verge of taking her, with the whole experience right in front of him. Morgan cried out in frustration and gripped him hard. Slipping her hands down to cup his ass once again, she tried to pull him inside her.

He held back only an instant, then slid into her, inch by agonizing inch.

Morgan moaned and he checked to make sure it was in pleasure. Yep, sure looked like it. She opened her eyes and glared at him. "What are you waiting for?"

He bent down and kissed her, then began to move. Slowly at first, he stroked in and out until Morgan clutched the bedclothes tightly in her fists. As he sped up, she opened her eyes again and met his gaze. The rise and fall of her breasts against him as moved within her set his skin on fire, but it was Morgan herself—seeing her watch him watch her—that nearly sent him over the edge.

She was getting close, judging by her ragged breathing. Wrapping her arms around his neck, she moved under him, matching him stroke for stroke. "Rob," she breathed, "Oh, God…"

When she cried out, he came with her, letting go all the passion he'd held in for so long. He barely stifled his own cries, only too conscious they weren't alone in the house. Someday soon they'd have their own place and he'd make love to Morgan for hours every night.

When they collapsed together, he found it hard not to start all over again. They had to get some sleep, though. Morgan had as early a morning ahead of her as he did.

"You are amazing," he whispered into her hair.

"You are amazing," she said. "I've never felt like that before."

"You ain't seen nothing yet." He moved to slide out of her, but she stopped him.

"Hold on, let me tell you my idea. I think you're going to like it," she said.

And as they lay together, entwined in the most intimate of ways, Rob listened to her plan and began to smile.

Chapter Seventeen

AT PRECISELY TWELVE-THIRTY SUNDAY AFTER-
NOON, two trucks pulled into the driveway of the
Cruz ranch, and the Matheson family climbed out.
Morgan, watching them from the front door of the Big
House, wondered how often the two families had gotten
together in the past. While the younger generation of
Mathesons and Cruzes had grown up as friends, the
parents seemed to have been something of rivals. Surely
from time to time, however, they'd gotten together and
shared a meal.

At any rate, they would do so today. Ethan had returned an hour ago from shuttling the latest group of
guests to the airport and they had several hours before a
new crop arrived. Morgan had timed her request for a
family get-together to take advantage of this break in the
action. She helped Autumn prepare a light lunch of
sandwiches and salads, and hoped that everyone would
stick around long enough to eat it.

"Mom, Dad, good to see you," Rob said, moving
past her and stepping out onto the porch.

Holt grunted and Lisa hugged him. Jake, Luke and Ned filed up the front steps after them, and Rob ushered them all inside.

Jamie, Claire, Ethan and Autumn were already in the great room. The table was set and the food ready to serve. Morgan had long debated whether to speak before or after the meal. In the end, she and Rob had agreed to speak first. They both knew they couldn't sit through an entire lunch knowing what was to come.

"Have a seat," Rob said to his family, gesturing to the comfortable couches that ringed the living room area. When they did, he held out his hand to Morgan and pulled her to stand next to him in front of the enormous stone fireplace. "Morgan and I have some news for you."

"You're having a baby?" Lisa popped up again and the others in the room exchanged glances, but Rob quickly regained control of the situation.

"No, we're not having a baby. Not yet, anyhow." Lisa sat down, looking disappointed. "You all know we plan to get married in October, and we're grateful for the support we've received."

Morgan bit back a snort. Some support. Although, to be fair, Ethan and Autumn had stood by them the whole time, and Lisa was their number one fan.

"Our presence in Chance Creek, however, hasn't made things easy on the rest of you."

Autumn opened her mouth as if to contradict this, but Morgan caught her eye and gave her head a little shake. She relaxed when her sister-in-law sat back against the couch cushions, but Autumn didn't look happy about it.

"We've been doing a lot of thinking," Rob went on. "At first we hoped to start a winery and riding school on the Matheson acreage," he nodded at his father, who crossed his arms over his chest, "and when that didn't work out, we hoped we could do the same on the Cruz ranch." He caught the eye of Jamie and Claire. "We've learned our lesson. Our plans don't quite fit in the scheme of things at either place." He waited a beat. "That's why we're moving to California."

The room erupted into instant chaos. Lisa surged to her feet again, her eyes flashing with anger. Jake shouted at Rob, something about, "I told you why!" Jamie and Claire stared at each other in horror. Ethan's mouth hung open, and tears ran openly down Autumn's face. Morgan wanted to run to her, but she couldn't. Not if they were to play this thing out to its conclusion.

"Hold on, everyone. Let me finish what I was saying," Rob said. His face was strained, but his voice remained strong. "Morgan's received a job offer in Napa. She's leaving this afternoon to check it out. They've offered her a week-long trial run to see if it's a good fit. I've been in touch with a riding school in the same area that's looking for someone to teach rodeo skills. Morgan's job comes with onsite housing, which makes things easy. We'll make up our minds at the end of the week based on her experience whether or not it's a good fit. If it is, we'll pack up our stuff and make the move at the beginning of October. Now I hope you all will enjoy your lunch. I've got to get Morgan to the airport, then

I'm heading over to Carl's." He squeezed Morgan's shoulders. "Once we move permanently to California, we plan to start our family, so we'll need all the cash we can get. As for the wedding," he turned his attention to his father. Holt, still as stone, stared back at him. "We don't want to put everyone out, so we've decided to make a layover in Vegas on our way out to our new digs. I've always wanted to get married in one of those Elvis chapels." He kissed her on the forehead.

When Rob released her, Morgan made a beeline for Autumn. Taking her sister-in-law into a warm hug, she said, "Don't be sad, I'll be back in a week. I've called Rose and Tracey—they've agreed to fill in for me." She squeezed her, hoping Autumn would somehow know their separation wouldn't be for good. This was why she didn't like practical jokes. Someone always got hurt.

But she hoped the end result would be worth it.

"I'm ready," she told Rob. "Let's go."

ROB WAS GLAD to see Morgan relax as they drove to the airport. When Autumn had started to cry, he thought she'd confess their deception right then and there. He knew her sister-in-law's reaction still upset her, but she was able to see the funny side of it all, too.

"Did you see the look on your mother's face when you said we'd get married in Vegas?" Morgan said.

"I thought my dad was going to keel over when I said we planned to have kids the minute we hit California. He's been angling for grandkids for years. Wants to bring them up on the ranch, like he did us."

"Autumn was pretty upset, though," Morgan said, sobering up again.

"I know. I wish she hadn't taken it so hard," Rob said. "I swore I'd never play another practical joke, and here we are pulling off the whopper of our lives."

"They deserve it," Morgan said. "Well, Ethan and Autumn don't. Neither does your Mom, but the rest of them do."

"Got that right."

"You going to be okay back there all by yourself? Think you can keep up appearances?"

"I'll be working like a dog. I won't have time to talk to anyone. How about you? You going to be okay out in California all by yourself?"

"Yep. I've never had this kind of vacation," Morgan said. "Thank God Tara Kramer still lives in the Bay Area, or this trip would cost a fortune. She said she's got her guest room ready for me, and she's dying to spend a day driving around Napa and tasting all the different wines. I only wish you could be there, too."

He felt a pang of loneliness even though they hadn't reached the airport yet. "Someone's got to build Carl's garden." He touched her thigh. "But I'll miss you, too."

Saying good-bye at the airport was one of the hardest things he'd ever done. Only two months ago, they'd played out this same scenario, her catching a flight to Victoria, leaving him behind. This time, though, they were engaged and he knew she'd be coming right back in seven days. It should have made it easier.

It didn't.

"You have to stay in character," she reminded him for the hundredth time. "Even when you think you're alone. If they know we're joking, none of this will work."

"I won't screw this up. I promise." He kissed her again. "Be good."

"Don't forget to feed the kittens."

"I won't."

"Love you."

"Love you, too." He could swear her eyes were shining with tears as she handed her tickets to the stewardess.

He couldn't wait for this week to be over.

As Morgan hauled her suitcases to Tara's spare room, she wondered again if she was doing the right thing. She looked forward to reconnecting with her old university friend, but she also longed for some time alone to think about her future. Tara planned to take the next few days off, but she would have to go in to work Wednesday through Friday. Rather than fill every minute with sightseeing, Morgan decided she would use that time to take a long hard look at her life.

She hoped her flight would bring Claire and Jamie to their senses and bring about a reconciliation between everyone she'd left behind at the Cruz ranch. She also hoped it would force the Mathesons to realize how much they'd miss Rob if he really left. She understood Holt's desire to keep his family together, but he had to give his son leeway to pursue his dreams, and he had to see that Rob was his own man now. She hoped he could.

Meanwhile, it was time for her to do some soul-searching of her own. If it didn't work out for them to build a winery on either the Matheson or Cruz ranches, then perhaps it was time to let that particular dream go.

She knew all the costs of starting such a business. She had taken into consideration the number of years it would take for the vines to grow to maturity, and the additional time it would take to create a vintage worth selling. She wasn't sure anymore if it was a dream that made sense.

What did she truly want in life?

A family. A community. A good job. Something extra to give back.

It was the day-to-day things in life—a hand held, a tear wiped away, a hug, a smile—that would fill her heart. Success at work was an additional bonus.

Wasn't it?

For one minute she thought she could make do without a winery of her own.

For one minute.

Then her ambition surged up again and showed her the truth; she'd be miserable if she couldn't pursue her dream. *Please*, she prayed to her family and her friends. *Please find a way to come together again.*

Chapter Eighteen

"YOU CAN'T LEAVE," Claire said, pacing the living room at the bunkhouse. In her elegant work clothes, she looked out of place in the homely room. Probably on her way to or from decorating Carl's new mansion, Rob thought. Jamie, in jeans, t-shirt and cowboy boots looked more at home as he sat on the couch.

"Why not? Isn't that exactly what you wanted? The minute you found out we'd be living here, you lit into Morgan like a pit bull."

Claire reared back, her black bob swinging. "I was pissed, but I didn't mean for this to happen."

"What the hell did you want?" Rob was exhausted, as usual, and Claire made a mighty fine target at the moment. He couldn't believe how much he missed Morgan, and she'd only been gone one day. Claire and Jamie had cornered him when he ducked in for some lunch, and now he couldn't shake them.

"I wanted...answers," she cried. "Dammit, how am I supposed to know how to be a good mother until I figure out what made Mom so bad?"

"Claire," Jamie reached for her. "You'll be a terrific mom."

"How do you know? Maybe poor parenting skills are inherited."

"What the hell does your mom have to do with anything?" Rob said.

Claire turned on her heel and strode out of the room, obviously on the verge of tears. Jamie watched her go, then dropped his head into his hands. "This is my fault," he said. "I want to start a family. I kept pushing on our honeymoon. I kept saying we should..." he waved a hand, "you know."

"Throw away Willy's hat?" Rob finished for him. He and Morgan had done that, and he couldn't wait to try it again.

"Yeah, something like that. Before we got married she was all for having kids, but once we went on the honeymoon, she kept saying she wanted to wait. I couldn't figure out why." He straightened up. "Autumn's already three months pregnant. If we went for it now, our kids would be in the same grade, you know? They'd grow up together. If we wait, they...won't."

Rob stared at him. Did Jamie think he'd be sympathetic about his marital problems when Claire had tried to run them off the ranch? Jamie must have seen his expression because he stood up. "I'm saying it so you'll understand why Claire's upset. She thinks that she'll be as bad a mother as Aria was. She's freaking out."

"So she takes it out on us?" Rob stood also. "I'm

sick of playing the scapegoat."

"She's sorry she's been so awful," Jamie said. "I'm sorry, too. I got mad because Claire was mad, and because I want to belong to this ranch all the way. I want to be Ethan's partner, not his hired hand. Can't you understand that?"

Rob let out a long sigh. Sure, he could understand that. Both wanting to call the shots and feeling protective of the woman he loved. He shoved his hands into his pockets and headed for the door.

"You'll change your minds, won't you?" Jamie called after him.

They certainly wanted to, but Jamie was the one apologizing, not Claire, and it was Claire's apology that really mattered. "Look, between Claire and my father, it's too tense for us to settle down here. Morgan and I want a place to belong, too. We'll keep looking until we find it."

"TRY THIS ONE," Tara said, holding out a glass filled with dark red liquid. Regardless of the sip and spit tradition in the tasting rooms they'd visited so far, Morgan was beginning to feel a comfortable buzz. Swirling the wine in her glass, she breathed in its bouquet of black currant and oak. Another wonderful California Cabernet Sauvignon.

"I'm glad you two came in. Mondays are slow," the man behind the counter said. He was in his late forties, with brown hair shot with grey, and a thickset frame.

"There's always work to do at a winery," Morgan

said with a smile.

"Sounds like you know what you're talking about," the man said, cocking his head. "You in the business?"

"Yes. Well, I was. I mean…I'm going to be." She shook her head and tried again. "I just resigned as distillery manager at a Victoria winery. I'm trying to set up my own shop in Montana."

"Montana. Wow, you like a challenge, don't you?" He leaned an elbow on the counter and waved her and Tara onto the stools on the other side.

"I do," Morgan said, nodding and taking a seat. "But I'm running into some problems."

"Can I ask why Montana? There are plenty of wineries looking for help around here. I should know," he added wryly.

"That's where my family is," she said. "Of course, right now they don't seem to be too interested in my plans. That's why I'm here."

"You said you were a distillery manager? Because I happen to be in the market for one of those. I'm Ted Hennessey. I'm the owner here."

"Oh, my goodness. I thought you were a server," Morgan said, taken aback. "You probably thought I was angling for a job."

"I was hoping you were. I mean, if you turn out to be qualified," Ted said. "Want a tour? A real tour—not the watered down one we give to customers. I'll tell you more about the position."

Morgan turned to Tara. "Want to?"

"Sure."

Ted turned out to be the perfect host, answering all of Morgan's most detailed questions about the winery's operations. He plied them with more wines to taste; everything from his oldest vintages to his newest experiments. Morgan loved the way he listened to her opinions and seemed to give weight to the few suggestions she had to make. By the end of the tour she knew that working at Hennessey's would be nothing like her time with Elliot and Duncan.

Ted wrote down the salary he was offering on a slip of paper, folded it and handed it to her. "Take this home and think about it. If you're interested, give me a call. We'll work out all the details."

Morgan and Tara were giggling like a pair of schoolgirls by the time they reached Tara's car.

"Oh, my gosh, if you take the job I'll be able to see you all the time," Tara squealed. "You've got to take it."

Reality hit Morgan squarely in the gut as she climbed into Tara's Subaru. Sure, it was fun to entertain the idea of moving to California to work for a major winery whose owner thought you had something important to contribute, but she already missed Chance Creek and her family.

She missed Rob.

"How much did he offer you?"

Morgan opened the slip of paper and whistled. "A lot," she admitted. Much more than Elliot paid her.

"Won't you even consider it?" Tara asked.

"Of course I will," she said. "And it's nice to have an ace in my pocket if everyone back home doesn't come to their senses."

"Hmmph," Tara said. "In other words, don't hold my breath."

Chapter Nineteen

"**W**HERE ARE YOU GOING?" Ethan asked Rob that evening, when they ran into each other outside the Big House.

"Carl's." The last thing Rob wanted was a conversation. He was struggling to keep up his end of the charade. He'd played many a practical joke in his lifetime, but never one that ran for so long. He was so terrified of being caught out he could barely speak these days.

"You're still finishing that job? I thought…" Ethan trailed off.

"You thought I'd quit because we're leaving town?"

"Well, you were doing it to raise money for Morgan's winery, right?"

"I said I'd do the job, so I'm doing it. Doesn't matter why I took it on." Rob climbed into the truck, knowing it wasn't fair to judge Ethan for thinking he might quit in this circumstance. He had a long row to hoe before people took for granted that he was a hard worker, rather than a layabout. He'd made his bed and he was sleeping in it now.

"I'm really sorry about the way things turned out," Ethan said. "I believed in you. I still do."

Rob swallowed. Ethan had been the only one who'd stuck by him through this whole mess. He should say something in return, but somehow he couldn't force out the words. He didn't want to lie to his friend more than he already had. Ethan turned toward the house.

"I hope you two will change your minds. No matter what Claire and Jamie say, there's always room for you and Morgan on this ranch."

"Thanks, man," Rob said, and started the truck before he spilled the beans.

MORGAN CLICKED THROUGH the texts on her cell phone after dinner, dread building with each message. She'd refused to answer any of them since she'd left Montana. Let everyone stew in their own juices for a while.

Then she got to the latest one that Lisa had left, and against her better judgment, opened it to see the whole message.

> *I know you can't be as heartless as you're acting. You can't take my baby away to California, raise my grandkids so far away, and deprive me of the one chance I have to throw a wedding. Please change your mind!*

She opened one of Claire's next.

> *I swear I'll never ask you about money again. I get it— you don't know where it went, and I should never have blamed you. When Jamie and I went on our honeymoon*

and talked about having kids right away, it all became too real and I got scared. I don't want to turn out like Mom did. Plz call!

There were several voice messages, too. When she brought up the first one, someone cleared his throat on the other end of the line. Then a gruff, masculine voice she didn't recognize at first said, "A winery's still the stupidest idea I ever heard, but I'll agree to it if that's what it takes to ransom my grandkids from that knee-jerk liberal excuse for a state. I don't want them to join the leftist commie legions trying to destroy this nation..." There was a scuffle and Lisa's voice in the background. "Don't you talk to my daughter-in-law that way, Holt!" A dial-tone rang in her ear. Morgan didn't know whether to laugh or cry.

The next message was from Rob. "I miss you," he said, and her entire body cried out with the desire to be in his embrace. "I think our plan might be working. Hang in there, okay? You wouldn't believe how much progress I'm making on Carl's garden since I can't stand being at home without you there. I'll talk to you soon."

She couldn't stand being without him, either. Couldn't wait to talk to him, and even more so, couldn't wait to share his bed. As much fun as she was having visiting Tara and exploring California, the week was crawling by. At the end of it, would the people she'd left behind be able to forge a better understanding?

Or was Napa Valley going to be her new home in truth? She dialed Rob's number.

"YOU WHAT?" Rob leaned against a metal rake in Carl's garden, and held his phone up to his ear. He'd been smoothing down the pathways between his newly finished raised beds to prepare them for the paving stones. He'd figured it was safe to talk to Claire out here in the middle of the night. No one else was around, that was for sure.

"I got a job offer," Morgan said.

"I thought you were sightseeing out there."

"Yeah, well, one of the wineries we visited wants to hire me."

"You said no, didn't you?"

"I told them I'd think about it, actually."

He gazed around the empty garden in disbelief. "Why the hell did you do that?"

"Because I can't live there if everyone's going to hate me for following my dreams. I actually thought about giving it all up, did you know that? I came out here determined to talk myself out of wanting a winery, but you know what? I do want one, and I'm not ashamed of that. The way I figure it, I get one shot at this life. If I give everything up now, I'm going to resent that later, and that doesn't help anyone."

"What about me?" Rob said.

"I want to be with you," she said, her voice softening. "I haven't changed my mind about that. All I'm saying is that you and I have to come first in all of this. We can't put your father or my sister ahead of us. I will give everything I have to help you reach your dreams, too. Don't you know that?"

"Yeah, I know it," he said after a pause. "So, we're really going to do this? Head out to California and start all over if that's what it takes?"

"I don't want that any more than you do," Morgan said softly. "But now we know we can if we have to."

Headlights scraped Carl's driveway and Rob straightened up. "Someone's coming. I've got to go."

"Talk to you tomorrow," Morgan said and clicked off the line.

Rob shoved the phone in his pocket as a familiar truck pulled to a stop and his father climbed out. Reluctantly, he met Holt halfway.

"Dad."

"You ready to come to your senses yet?" Holt rasped.

Anger swept through him, and Rob fought to keep control. This was the man who was screwing everything up between him and the woman he loved. What right did Holt have to keep throwing a monkey wrench in their plans? He'd thought when he agreed to buy the land from Ethan instead of getting it from his father, he'd finally know peace and security. It fried him that his position was as precarious as it had ever been and his father kept trying to make it even worse. "No. I'm not. In fact, I'm ready to go stark, raving mad."

"What the hell does that mean?" Holt puffed up his chest in anger, but Rob suddenly realized they weren't seeing eye to eye. He was looking down at his father. What the heck was wrong with the man? Why was he all hunched up like that?

Probably a bid for sympathy, Rob decided. Well, forget it. He was done with sympathy or any other weak emotion that kept him from getting what he wanted.

"It means that I don't like your definition of sanity. You think you should get to keep calling the shots for the rest of my life. I think you've proved you're not capable of running the show."

"You think you are?" Holt said. "When have you ever run anything? Except your mouth."

For crying out loud. Rob waved to the garden they were standing next to. Sure, it wasn't anywhere near finished, but the walls were up and so were the permanent raised beds. The plumbing for the fountain was in and the pathways all laid out. Another week like this one and it would be beautiful. How could his father look at this and still belittle him? "When have I ever run anything? Take a look around you, Dad."

Holt did and sneered. "You're building a garden. Very nice. When you're done playing in the dirt like a little child, how about you join the men in your family at the ranch you stand to inherit? Or is that too hard for a sissy like you?"

"You really take the cake, old man," Rob said. "You're blind to everything except your precious ranch. You can't stand it that I'm making my own way, can you? You can't stand losing control of anything, because you're afraid if you do someone will figure out you're not half the man you pretend to be."

"I have no idea what you're talking about," Holt said.

"I'm talking about the fact that you can't read, which

means the truth is, Mom's the one running the Double-Bar-K. She does the paperwork, she orders the feed and pays the taxes. She types the bills of sale, and keeps track of breeding stock. She handles just about everything that makes money on this ranch. And you're not even man enough to fess up about it, let alone to admit that maybe one of your sons wants to do something different. Or is your real fear that if I follow my dreams I might prove myself to be smarter than you? Oh wait—I am smarter than you; I know how to read…"

Holt quivered with rage and his face in the moonlight was a mottled purple. "Don't you dare talk to me like that. I'll…"

"What, Dad? Whip me within an inch of my life? Or will you turn me over to Ned, so he can do it?"

"He never beat…"

"For God's sake," Rob snarled. "Sure he did. Or can you not read faces, either? How many black eyes did I have as a kid before I learned to beat him back?"

"So you learned to fight," Holt said. "What man doesn't? If you can't make your point with words, sometimes you have to do it with your fists. I didn't raise any pansies."

Rob stared at him in disbelief. "No, you didn't raise any pansies, Pop. But you know what? I've just realized I don't want you anywhere near my kids. Morgan was right. We'll be better off in California."

"Ah, go on with you," Holt rasped. "That's a lie and you know it. Don't you think I can spot one of your jokes a mile away? I've seen enough of them."

"Well, you've seen the last of them, Dad. It's no joke. Morgan's got a job, and I'm joining her in California the minute I finish working for Carl." He'd said these exact same words before as a joke, but this time he meant them. He was done with his father, done with Chance Creek, done with everyone who'd ever worked to hold him back.

Holt fixed him with an angry stare, but Rob met his gaze and let the truth of his words speak through his eyes. His father must have realized all the jokes were truly over, because a change came over him. He stiffened, opened his mouth to speak, then closed it again.

Then he fell to his knees.

"Dad?" Rob bent forward as his father clapped a hand to his arm. His face contorted and he struggled to breathe. Rob dove to catch him before he went limp. "Dad!" All Holt's weight resting against him, he yanked the phone from his pocket and dialed 911. "Hello? Send an ambulance. My father's had a heart attack."

WHEN MORGAN COULDN'T ignore the vibration of her cell phone anymore, she asked Tara to pause the chick flick they were watching and picked it up.

"Oh, my God," she said as she read the frantic texts from Rob, Ethan, Autumn and Claire. "Rob's father is in the hospital. It looks like he had a heart attack."

The concern on Tara's face echoed her own. Morgan thought fast. "I'm going to call the airline and see if I can get a flight first thing tomorrow. I'm sorry, but I've got to go home."

LATE THE FOLLOWING DAY she found Rob in the waiting room of the Chance Creek hospital. He looked haggard, his clothes so rumpled, she wondered if he'd spent the night here.

"How's Holt doing?" she asked as she sat beside him and wrapped an arm around his back. She drank in his familiar scent and closed her eyes. They'd been apart much too long.

"He's in stable condition. It wasn't his heart after all; the doctors think he had some kind of panic attack. But it turns out my Dad found out about a month ago he needs open heart surgery. It's already scheduled for next week. He's got three blocked arteries and he never even told me."

She could see how much that hurt Rob. "I'm so sorry," she said. "Wait a minute," she thought fast. "He knew he needed open heart surgery before he offered 200 acres to the first one of you guys to get married? Do you think that's why he did it?"

"Yeah, I do. He's scared." She felt his muscles tighten under her hands. "He's trying to act like he's not, but I know him. I've never seen him like this before. A panic attack, for heaven's sake."

Morgan stroked his back. "He's going to be okay, Rob. You have to believe that."

Rob nodded, tension tightening his jaw. "Morgan, I'm sorry. I can't go to California. Not when my dad…"

"I don't want to go to California," Morgan said. "I want to live here, you know that. I just don't want everyone to be mad at me."

"Jamie's not mad at us anymore; he's been practically begging me to stay. Claire still wants to know what your mother did with all that money, but she knows you did nothing wrong." He sat back. "I learned something about my dad and Ned, too."

"Really? What?" She snuggled in by his side, her heart melting when he wrapped an arm around her shoulders. She touched his thigh. She liked the feel of his muscles; the strength of him.

"Neither of them can read. Can you credit that?"

She stilled. "That's why your Dad was so down on school and report cards?"

"A combination of fear I'd figure out what he was hiding, and that I'd show up Ned, who was hiding something, too."

"And that's why Ned picked on you so much."

Rob sighed. "I guess I'm supposed to forgive him for all that now, but I don't feel like it much."

"I don't blame you." She thought for a moment. "Maybe you don't have to forgive him so much as understand him a little better."

"Yeah." Rob grunted. "Guess I could do that."

Lisa appeared in the waiting room and her whole face brightened when she saw Morgan. "I'm so glad you came back, honey. You aren't taking that awful job in California, are you?" She crossed the room and hugged her tight.

"We were just talking about that," Morgan said.

"Well, why don't you both come in to see Holt and we'll talk about it together." Lisa tugged them both to a stand and led the way back down a maze of halls to a small, private room.

Morgan lagged behind Lisa and Rob when they entered the room, afraid to see the man who seemed to hate her so much. When they moved aside, and she got a glimpse of him, however, she was saddened to see him looking so frail beneath the bedclothes.

"You're back," he said, his gaze fixing on her.

Morgan stiffened, ready for another fight.

"Good," he said after a long pause. "California's no place to raise kids. Come here."

She advanced slowly until she was near enough to his bed for him to reach out and take her hand.

"I'm a stubborn old man who likes to get his way, but I know when I'm beat. My son wants to make a life with you, and in the end all I want is to see him happy. You think you can make him happy?"

"Dad," Rob said, moving closer. Holt waved him away.

"I'm sure going to try," Morgan said, taking Rob's hand with her free one.

"And you think you can grow grapes in Montana? Start this…winery business?"

"I think so. Others have done it."

"You'll put the Matheson name on it? None of this women's lib crap, keeping your own?"

"Holt!" Lisa warned. "She'll call it whatever she pleases."

"The Matheson name will go on the winery," Morgan promised with a smile. "It's a good name. Practically sells itself."

"You can have 300 acres near the river," Holt said, giving her hand a squeeze and letting it go. "In the northwest corner."

"You mean 200 acres, right, Dad?" Rob said, slipping an arm around Morgan's waist.

"I mean 300. I may be stuck in this hospital bed, but I haven't gone senile," Holt said. "Now get on with you. My program's on." He reached for the television remote as they turned to leave the room. "By the way," he added. He raised his voice and spoke distinctly. "Got you!"

Morgan stopped in her tracks. Rob spun around. "What do you mean?" he demanded.

"That wasn't no panic attack," Holt said. "That's what's known in the business as damn good acting."

"Dad," Rob said. "Come on, we both know that was real."

"What, you're the only one who can play a joke in this family?"

Morgan put her hand on his arm before Rob argued any further. Holt was trying to save face, anyone could see that. She gave his sleeve a little tug. "You got us good, Dad," she said.

Holt stiffened, then turned toward her. "What'd you call me?"

Morgan couldn't find her voice. Had she put her foot it in it again? "Dad," she said again, unsteadily.

Holt stared at the wall behind her head, his jaw working. "I like that," he said, and nodded once.

She figured they'd better leave while they were ahead. "Rest up," she said.

"See you later, Dad," Rob said.

Out in the corridor, he pulled her into a tight hug. "You're a genius."

"Thanks."

"But that panic attack wasn't no practical joke."

Chapter Twenty

W HEN THEY RETURNED TO THE BUNKHOUSE, she let Rob take her suitcase and followed him up the steps. Being back on the Cruz ranch felt like coming home and she hesitated on the porch, taking in the view. When she finally entered the living room, she came face to face with Autumn.

"You can't move to California. I cried my eyes out when you left," Autumn said, throwing her arms around Morgan's neck and refusing to let her go.

"We're not moving. We talked to Holt and he's giving us 300 acres and we can do whatever we want with it," Morgan rushed to say before Autumn strangled her. She felt awful about fooling her. Should she tell her it had all been a joke? Would Autumn hate her for it? "I'm so glad he gave in. I couldn't have left you guys and moved to California."

Autumn held her at arm's length. "I know that, dummy. You think you took me in with all that moving to Napa stuff? No way!"

Morgan stared at her. "You knew? You just said..."

"Hello! You're marrying the king of practical jokes! You fooled me for a few minutes," she conceded, "and I was really upset at first. Then I figured it out. Pretty smart, though; you had the rest of them fooled all the way."

"Does Ethan know?" Rob asked.

"I think he suspects, but he doesn't blame you. Your Dad was being pretty unreasonable. So was Claire. But speaking of Claire, I'm glad you're back because I finally got around to cleaning that attic, and I found something I think you'll both want to see."

"What is it?" Morgan asked when Autumn handed her a thick manila envelope.

"Take a look through it. I'm going to rustle you two up some dinner. I doubt either one of you has eaten yet."

She disappeared into the kitchen, and Rob and Morgan sat down on the sofa to examine the contents of the envelope. A kitten appeared and Morgan did a double-take. It was Button, and she'd grown like crazy in the few days she'd been gone. She snuggled the cat in close and turned back to the documents inside the envelope. The first page seemed to be an itemized list of expenses. Not making heads or tails of it, Morgan handed it to Rob. Underneath she found a pile of receipts and old plane, bus and train tickets, many of them in an exotic script. She leafed through them with growing confusion.

The tickets were all issued to a woman named Anne Smith. By the looks of it, she was a world traveler, flying from Chance Creek to New York City, to England, France, and then—Morgan's eyebrows shot up—in every case to Dubai, followed by a connecting flight to Afghanistan.

How had these ticket stubs made their way into the Cruz's attic? She passed them to Rob, and looked further. The next set of pages contained a list of names, dates and locations. *Badria Khan, b. June 8, 1986, Sangin to Kabul, May 15, 1997. Afshan Wazir, b. January 3, 1985, Khewa to Kabul, September 22, 1998.* The list went on and on, sometimes with several listings per year, other times only one or two. Kabul always figured in the entries. Morgan knew it was one of the largest cities in Afghanistan. She assumed the first words were names of people, and the second, towns. People moving from villages to Kabul? What on earth did it have to do with her family?

The answer came at the bottom of a pile, where she found a smaller, worn envelope, that when opened disclosed a Canadian passport, birth certificate, driver's license and social insurance number card. Her mother's face stared out from the passport and driver's license, but in each case the name on the document was Anne Smith.

Morgan let out a breath she hadn't known she was holding.

What had her mother done? Wordlessly, she showed the passport to Rob.

"Well, hell," he said.

Morgan took back all the documents again, sorting through the tickets and receipts for trains and buses.

Her mother had been moving people from villages to Kabul. Accompanying them in their travels.

Why?

Autumn popped back into the room. "What do you think?"

"She was helping people move. In Afghanistan. I don't understand why, though."

"I checked—all the names on that list are female," Autumn said. "She was helping women move—girls, actually. Look at the two sets of dates on each line. I think the first is a birthdate. The second is the day she delivered them to Kabul."

Morgan began to do the math as Autumn brought in plates laden with warmed-up pizza and set them on the coffee table before them. "They're teenagers," she exclaimed.

"Child brides, I bet. It's the only thing that makes sense to me," Autumn said.

"You think my mom was rescuing…" Morgan trailed off. This was too bizarre.

"She was saving young women who were probably married off against their will. I imagine she brought them to a safe house in Kabul."

"That…makes no sense at all," Morgan said helplessly. She glanced at Rob, who was puzzling over the list of names again.

"I'm beginning to really wish I knew your mother," Autumn said, heading back toward the kitchen. "She must have been a hell of a woman. She raised two amazing daughters, too."

"I wish I knew my mother," Morgan said softly to Rob. "The more I learn about her, the more I realize I hardly knew her at all." She wondered what she'd find when she compared the dates of her mother's visits to her with the dates of her trips to Afghanistan. Was she just the first stop on her mother's annual trips from Montana to Kabul? How had she gotten fake papers, and how on earth did she maneuver in such a dangerous country? And to think a simple car accident in Montana ended her life.

Rob put the papers down and wrapped an arm around her, pulling her tight against his side. "I think in your heart you know her pretty well," he said. "And I think your mom would be proud of you right now."

She smiled lopsidedly. "For playing an elaborate practical joke on my entire extended family?"

Rob pulled Aria's fake passport out of the pile and waved it at her. "Especially for that."

ROB WATCHED CLAIRE rein in and drop back along the line of riders until she was next to him. He'd wondered if she'd finally deign to speak to him on this three hour ride. Jamie led the way far in front of them, and a string of guests followed him with varying degrees of proficiency on their mounts. It was the first time he'd worked with both of them since Morgan had come back from her trip.

"I'm sorry," Claire said gruffly, and he had to hide a smile. Apologies came as rough to Claire as they did to his father. He was sure this one was costing her.

"That's all right."

"No, it isn't," she said. "I took my own problems out

on you and Morgan and that wasn't fair. Are you really going to take that land of your father's? You two belong here with us. You, Ethan and Jamie have been friends forever, you know?"

He realized that was probably all the apology he was going to get, but he was okay with that. He knew how your history could drive you a little crazy. Claire had spent a lifetime trying to figure her mother out. Now that Autumn and Morgan had shown her the paperwork and passports, she had her answer to where the missing money went. Aria must have funded those trips to Afghanistan herself, and paid who knew how much cash as bribes and expenses to move those women. Claire had told Morgan she planned to do some research and try to discover if her mother was working on her own or with an organization. If there was a group in Kabul dedicated to helping young women caught in arranged marriages, she wanted to send a donation in her mother's honor.

"Ethan still has my down payment for those 150 acres."

"Don't you want that back? I thought you and Morgan were short on cash."

"So you don't want us around that badly, huh?" Rob laughed at her expression. "I haven't had a chance to talk to Ethan about it."

Claire reached out like she would touch his arm, but her horse sidestepped and she had to bring it back under control. "I do want you around that badly. Morgan's my sister. I meant what I said—you belong on the Cruz ranch with us."

"I need that money, though," Rob said. "With the time I lost over my Dad's panic attack, and his preparation for his surgery, I'm way behind on Carl's garden. I won't finish it by his deadline, and I'll have to offer him some kind of discount for blowing it."

"She doesn't care about the money; she loves you," Claire said.

"I made her a promise," Rob repeated. "I know all of you expect me to break my promises, but she doesn't. That's important to me." An edge had crept into his voice. The only way he would have nearly enough money was if he got his deposit back from Ethan and borrowed the rest. The very idea of that made him want to spur his horse and ride away.

Claire nodded. "If you put your mind to it, you'll figure it out."

He looked at her askance. "You just saying that?"

"No." She met his gaze. "I believe it. You've got a good head on your shoulders, Rob. I'm impressed with what you've been doing here and at Carl's. Yesterday I was working on his place and I checked out the garden. It's beautiful. Totally wasted on Lacey, but spectacular just the same. You know," she looked thoughtful for a moment. "Maybe you and I should think about teaming up. At the very least I could pass your card around to some of my clients who might want your services."

"What services?" he asked, confused.

"Landscaping, silly."

LATER THAT EVENING it was Claire who called a meeting

in the Big House great room. She'd summoned Ethan, Autumn, Jamie, Morgan, Rob—even Cab Johnson. Tracey Richards and Rose Bellingham were escorting their guests to a street fair in town featuring local artists and musicians, so for an hour or two they were free to talk.

"I've been thinking over what you said the other day, Ethan," she began when they had all found seats on the easy chairs and couches. Morgan sat next to Rob, enjoying this moment of closeness with him. Between working for Ethan and his nights at Carl's, she still barely saw him. "And you're right; you and Jamie bought out my share of the ranch, but now I'm married to Jamie, which means I can claim part of it again. That's not really fair. I've decided I want to be a real partner in the ranch again. I'm making plenty of money with my interior design work, and I'm drawing a partial salary for helping with guests, as pitiful as that is," everyone chuckled, "so I'd like to buy back into the ranch, if you guys will let me."

Morgan noticed that Ethan was surveying his sister thoughtfully. "You've talked this over with Jamie, I assume?"

"Of course," Claire said, "and he's fine with it." Jamie nodded. "I thought that some of the money I invest could be used to pay down the mortgage to make everyone's life a little easier, and the rest could be put toward buying breeding stock." She waved a hand at Morgan and Rob. "I also want to say that I hope you two will become part of this ranch, as well. Rob already put a down payment on some of the land, and while I know Holt has given you 300 acres outright, I'd like you to consider moving forward with the purchase. Maybe the Tate Matheson Winery can be the first joint effort between the Matheson and Cruz ranches. I have a feeling it will benefit us all, and...well, I want us all to be a part of something together."

"Here, here," Jamie said.

"I feel the same way," Ethan said quietly. "I'm willing to structure that loan however you two need it to be to make this work."

Rob looked uncomfortable and he shifted in his seat beside her. "The only thing is...I'm not on track to finish Carl's garden by October first, which means I'm not on track to give Morgan the money I promised her for her wedding gift. Now hold on," he raised a hand to stop Morgan when she began to speak. "I don't want anyone here to misinterpret that. Morgan isn't marrying me just for my deep pockets," he paused to let everyone chuckle, "but we made promises to each other when we got engaged that were important to both of us. She's kept her promises and I mean to keep mine."

"You have kept yours," Morgan said in a low voice. It was hard to speak of things so intimate in front of a crowd, but the people gathered here in this room were the most important people in her life. "I told you I wanted to feel cherished, and I've never felt so cherished in my life. You've been working day and night to help me reach my dream, no matter what the cost to you in terms of your health, your sanity, or even your family.

You don't need to prove anything else to me. I love you. If it takes a few more months—or even a year—to save up for the rootstock, so what? It will happen someday."

"There've been too many times in my life when I haven't kept my word, though," Rob said. "I'm sorry, I need that deposit back, Ethan. It's the only way I have a hope in hell of keeping my word to my bride."

"It's not the only way," Claire said. "I've cleared my schedule. I'm available to help you out on Carl's garden for the next week."

"I'll help every evening after chores are done," Jamie said.

"Me, too," Ethan chimed in.

"Rose told me she's available Thursday and Saturday," Autumn said. "And Tracey can help out on Friday and Sunday."

"Count me in for the weekend," Cab said, "Tuesday and Thursday nights, too."

Rob sat back, looking stunned. "You all would do that for me?"

"You bet," Claire said, "And I've made some calls. I've got all kinds of people lined up to help next week. You better get used to managing a crew, because you'll have eight to ten people working with you every day. Don't worry about the ranch chores; we'll pick up the slack on those. You get that garden done."

Rob turned to Morgan and grinned. "What do you think? Want to own part of both ranches?"

"Yes. Absolutely," she said and kissed him. "I wouldn't miss this for the world." She kissed him again, savoring the feel of him.

"Get a room," Cab drawled and everyone laughed. Morgan turned to him, her cheeks pink.

"You're next, you know." She said, pointing from Ethan to Jamie to Rob. "All the rest of your friends are getting hitched. Now it's your turn to find the woman of your dreams."

The big man blanched in the sudden attention of everyone in the room.

"Aw, heck."

"WHERE ARE YOU GOING?" Rob asked the next day when Jamie turned left instead of right. They were supposed to be driving to Carl's ranch to get to work on the garden, but Jamie had just gone in the wrong direction.

"We have a stop to make," Jamie said. A few minutes later, he turned onto the lane that led to Rob's family's ranch.

"Here?"

"Yep. Let's find your brothers." Jamie pulled up in front of the house, parked the truck and hopped out before Rob could ask any more questions, and by the time he maneuvered his way out the door his friend had taken off in long strides toward the nearest barn.

When Rob caught up with him, Jamie had already corralled Jake and Luke. "Where's Ned?" he was asking.

"I'll get him," Luke said. As he disappeared into another outbuilding, Jake asked, "What's all this about?"

"Once Rob's married, he'll divide his time between

the ranches. He's got to help Morgan start her vineyard, Ethan with his trail rides, and me with my horse-breeding and riding school," Jamie said, "so he needs to nail down what part of this operation he'll be running, so he can schedule his time."

Rob nearly choked and Jake looked like he was having trouble swallowing this piece of news, as well. "The part he'll be running?"

"With your dad laid up and all, don't you think it's time he did his share?"

"Well, sure...but..." Jake seemed relieved when Luke returned with Ned. When Jamie repeated his piece, all three of them exchanged uncomfortable looks.

"It's not that we don't want you," Ned began, finally. "I've been trying to get you over here for weeks. It's just..."

"There are no other parts to take on," Luke finished for him.

"What are you talking about?" Rob said. "Ned's been on my back all this time about how much work is going undone. With Dad getting an operation there must be lots to do."

"After Dad went to the hospital, we decided we'd better get together and sort out the rest of the ranch," Jake agreed. "It was the darndest thing—when we sat down to do it, we figured out there was no extra work. We were already doing all of it."

"We realized Dad had been preparing us for years to take over the spread. He'd already handed out his responsibilities," Luke chimed in.

"But…" Rob sputtered. "What's he been doing all this time? And what about all the work you said there was for me to do?"

"Let's just say Dad was supervising a lot more than he was working," Ned said. "As for the rest of it, there's always work to be done, you know that. But there aren't any real jobs to take on—not supervisory ones—and we figured you wouldn't want us to boss you around for the rest of your life. We can hire another hand or two."

Rob shoved his hands into his pockets. Hell, now that they didn't want him, he felt a little offended.

"You'll always be part of the ranch," Jake said.

"Don't see how," Rob said.

His brothers exchanged another glance.

"Look," Jake said. "You're starting something of your own, and we've agreed we're all behind you 100 percent. It doesn't matter what you do, you'll always be a Matheson."

"I like the sound of that winery," Luke said. "It'll bring a little class to the place."

"Plus a lot of wine," Ned said, grinning.

The lead weight of worry and familial duty fell away, and for the first time Rob felt like he could pursue his dream without losing his family. He stood straighter as the truth hit him; he'd done everything he set out to do—everything but marry Morgan.

Chapter Twenty-One

"HOW ABOUT THIS ONE?" Lisa pulled a creamy satin gown from the rack where Ellie Donaldson was hanging the dresses she picked from all over her store for Morgan to try on. The minute she'd walked into Ellie's Bridals, the white-haired woman had looked her over and bustled off to find *just the thing*. She'd laden the rack outside her dressing room with gowns and Morgan was having the time of her life climbing into each one, then coming out to stand on the pedestal in the center of the store and model for Lisa, Autumn and Claire.

"Don't you think that's too fancy for the wedding I'm having?"

Lisa frowned, and Morgan wanted to kick herself for the way she'd phrased that. Holt hadn't been discharged from the hospital yet after his operation. Lisa had explained that normally he would have already been sent home, but he had other health complications, and he would need to remain in the hospital for several more weeks.

Accordingly, they'd decided to forego the fancy

wedding Lisa had wanted to put on at the Matheson ranch. Instead, the ceremony and reception would be held in one of the meeting rooms at the hospital, so Holt could take part. The Cruzes and Mathesons would all be there, plus as many friends and relatives as they could fit in the medium-sized room. Morgan squelched another pang of disappointment. After all, she was hardly contributing to the guest list. Even her father had been non-committal so far about whether or not he could make the wedding.

She lifted her chin. None of that mattered. What did matter was she was marrying the man she loved and creating the life she wanted with him right here in Chance Creek. There would be other occasions to celebrate at the ranch.

"I like this one." Autumn pulled out an elegant, slim gown. Morgan reached for it and went into the changing room. As soon as she stepped into the dress, she knew it was the one. The fitted bodice plumped her breasts up high, and the skirt draped and clung to her legs. It was the most sensual piece of clothing she'd ever worn, without being immodest in any way. Almost devoid of decoration, the dress was a masterpiece, and she felt as lush and radiant wearing it as she did when she made love to Rob.

A smile curved her lips at the thought. Soon she'd have the right to make love to him for the rest of their lives. What a gift that was. The thought of all those nights ahead of her made her tingle all over.

"Come on out and show us," Claire called, breaking

into her reverie. She turned and exited the small room, her smile widening when the others' gasps told her all she needed to know.

"That's definitely the one," Autumn said.

"No doubt about it," Lisa agreed.

Ellie nodded as if she'd known it all along.

THURSDAY EVENING, Rob was at Carl's to put the final touches on Lacey's garden. The walls were up, the pathways paved with stones, the beds built and planted and the fountain and statuary installed. Claire and Autumn had searched every garden store for miles finding shrubs, perennials and annuals, and they'd filled the boxes and borders as best they could given the time of year. Cab had promised to give everything a good dousing with water and make sure the pathways were swept before Carl's final inspection.

Once Carl gave him his check, he'd head straight to the bank the minute it opened in the morning to deposit it so he could give Morgan her wedding gift. He was overwhelmed by everyone's generosity. The garden had come together beautifully with so many hands ready to help. He couldn't believe how many friends and neighbors—even acquaintances—had pulled together to get the job done when Claire put out the call.

He smiled over at Morgan who was picking fallen leaves out of a flower bed. The whole gang had decided to meet at Carl's garden for the grand unveiling, as Autumn had started to call it. He hoped Carl didn't mind. Since everyone had pitched in to work on it, they all felt invested in the outcome. Already people were spilling into the garden, and Carl's driveway was full of cars.

Autumn and Ethan, Jamie and Claire, Cab, Jake, Ned and Luke. Even Rose and Tracey, and Bella and Hannah from the pet clinic had shown up. He went to greet them happily, until he caught sight of Claire's face.

Uh-oh. Something was wrong.

"You won't believe it," she said, hurrying up to him. "Lacey's home early. Carl texted me to say he's picking her up from the airport and they'll be here in fifteen minutes."

"Thank goodness we got the garden done," Morgan said, coming up beside Rob and taking his hand.

"But the house isn't done," Claire said. "Most of it is, but half of the furniture isn't here and all the extra little touches. It'll be like walking through an empty show-house. Damn it, I worked so hard on that!"

"I'm sure she won't mind," Morgan said.

"You don't know Lacey," Claire and Rob said at the same time.

"I'm going to make sure everything's as good as it can possibly be," Claire said, hurrying off.

"What do we do?" Morgan asked him.

"Wait, I guess."

SO THAT WAS the infamous Lacey Taylor, Morgan thought as she watched Carl open the door to his luxury truck and offer his hand to a tall, thin, fashionable woman. She seemed dazed to find a whole group of people in her driveway—including her ex-fiancé—but Carl took things into hand.

"Folks, I appreciate you coming out, but I'd like to show Lacey around the house first before we head out to the garden. If you all will give us a few minutes, we'll join you there shortly."

Claire hovered at the periphery of the crowd. Morgan thought she wasn't sure whether to join Carl and Lacey or leave them alone. Carl spotted her, though, and seemed to realize her predicament.

"Lacey," he said, "I used Claire's services for the interior design of our new home. Nothing but the best for my girl, eh?" He gave her a squeeze. "Would you like Claire to tour the house with us?"

"It's not complete," Claire rushed to say, her normal confident tones weak with nerves. Morgan's heart squeezed for her sister. She knew this particular contract meant a lot to her. "We thought we had a few more days—most of the furniture hasn't been delivered."

"I'm sure it's lovely," Lacey said. "If you don't mind, I'd like to see it first alone with Carl. I didn't expect company."

"Oh…that's fine. I understand," Claire said. "I'll wait in the garden."

"Thank you," Lacey said, took Carl's outstretched hand and followed him into the house.

"Well, she's changed," Rose said. There were murmured assents all around.

"Really?" Morgan said to Claire. "How?"

"Let me count the ways," Tracey said, cutting in.

"One, she's not dressed in some tacky miniskirt; two, she was actually polite and three; she was actually polite. Oh, and did I mention that she was actually polite?"

Everyone chuckled.

"We'd better head to the garden," Autumn said and led the way.

Ten minutes later the back door opened and Lacey stepped out onto the deck that overlooked the wide backyard and the whole garden behind it. With the fingers of pine forest running in from the hills forming a frame for the manicured space, Morgan was sure Lacey's view was spectacular. She held her breath, hoping against hope this difficult young woman would approve of it so Rob could get paid. She didn't know what Rob would do if after all his work, Carl was to renege.

"What do you think, sweetheart?" Carl asked her, escorting Lacey down the stairs into the garden. "I've taken care of everything, haven't I? And now that you're better there's nothing standing in the way of the two of us getting married. What do you say? Should we set the date?"

Morgan's breath caught when she saw Lacey's face. Why couldn't Carl see that Lacey was already overwhelmed by her homecoming, the enormous log home he'd built for her, and this outsized garden? Why did he have to push her for a date in so public a fashion?

In a horrible flash, she knew Lacey wasn't going to say yes.

"I'm so sorry, Carl," Lacey said, her voice wobbling.

"I thought we'd have time alone to discuss it. You see…"

"Honey, I'm the one who's sorry," Carl broke in. "You've had a long day and you're tired. We'll discuss this another time."

"No, I think we need to talk about it now," Lacey said. "I can't marry you, Carl. I'm sorry. When we started dating all I wanted was to be with a rich man, but now things are different. I'm different. I came home early to tell you I'm going to college in Billings. I'm going to get a degree in counseling and I'm going to help other women who've been through what I've been through. I can't be a trophy wife, and as beautiful as it is, I can't just take care of a garden. I want to take care of people." She smiled tremulously. "I've finally found my calling."

Carl sat down heavily on a marble bench. "You're not going to stay? Lacey—I don't mind if you go to school…I'll pay for it…"

"No." Lacey touched his arm. "I appreciate that but I need to do this for myself. You need to find someone whole, Carl. Someone who loves you for you. I wish it was me, but it's not. I'm sorry. Everyone—the garden you made for me is beautiful. I'm sorry your work was for nothing." With a sob, she ran for the house. A moment later, Carl went after her.

"Well," Rob said heavily. "Back to the drawing board."

"Carl will see you paid," Ethan assured him as everyone returned to their vehicles in silence. Morgan wasn't worried about the money anymore. She knew they'd figure things out even if Carl didn't come through.

She felt bad for the man, though. Even millionaires could have their hearts broken.

Chapter Twenty-Two

"WELL, HE PAID ME," Rob said to Ethan, Jamie, and Cab the next day as Carl's fancy truck drove away down the lane. "I hated to take it from him, but I did do the work even if Lacey didn't want a garden."

"I almost feel sorry for him," Ethan said. "Almost."

"I'm still finding it hard to picture Lacey as a counselor," Jamie said. "But I suppose stranger things have happened."

"Stranger things happen every day," Cab said. "For example, a certain friend of mine who swore he'd never get married is tying the knot."

Rob laughed as loudly as the others. "Yeah, that is kind of strange. Want to hear something stranger?"

"You're scaring me," Ethan said. "What could be stranger than that?"

"Out of all the things I've ever done for money, I liked making that garden for Carl the best." When the silence stretched out, Rob stuffed his hands into his pockets. "I still plan on helping with trail rides and horse-breeding and all the rest of it," he assured his friends, "but I think I'll be spending some time in that vineyard of Morgan's. And seeing as I have all those acres," he added, "probably can find somewhere to squeeze in a vegetable plant or two."

He turned back toward the Big House, knowing the others would need a little time to process that information.

"Is he joking or what?" he heard Ethan ask.

"I can't even tell anymore," Cab said.

"ARE YOU READY?" Autumn asked Morgan, as she and Claire flanked her in her bedroom at the bunkhouse, smoothing her veil and fluffing the skirts of her wedding dress. Something tugged at her hem, and she glanced down in time to see a gray ball of fur disappear under her floor-length skirt.

"I think so," Morgan said, "but we better get the cats out of the room before they tear my dress." In fact, she felt a kind of serenity she'd never expected to feel minutes before she walked down the aisle. So much had happened in the previous month, this small journey felt like a piece of cake in comparison.

"I can't believe you're getting married in the hospital," Claire said, scooping up the kittens and putting them into the living room. "You could have waited a few more weeks and still had it at the Matheson ranch."

"In a couple of weeks snow might be falling," Morgan said, but she glanced outside at the broad sunshiny day and felt a pang of regret.

"Come on," Autumn said and led the way downstairs to where a limousine waited. Lisa, bereft of her plans for a huge ranch wedding, had insisted on this piece of ceremony at the very least. As Morgan climbed into the back seat with her two bridesmaids, her stomach began to flutter with excitement. This was really happening; she was actually marrying the man she loved.

And she was getting her vineyard and winery. They now had 450 acres to do with what they wished. Ethan had refused to return the money Rob put down on his land. Instead, they'd worked out a contract with generous terms and a 30 year mortgage they could pay as they went. Rob and Jamie were full of plans for breeding horses and holding riding classes of all kinds. Both of them would work with Ethan and Autumn on their guest ranch business. She had no doubt the three men would make the ranch prosper beyond all bounds.

Meanwhile, she'd get down to business raising grapes and preparing to build the winery, with Rob's help of course. In fact, he talked a lot about the vineyard, and about gardening in general, these days. While her vines were growing, she'd help Autumn with her side of the guest ranch business. Claire still planned to divide her time between interior design and trail rides.

It was all coming together, she thought happily as the limo turned into the lane toward the Matheson ranch.

Morgan sat up. *The Matheson ranch?* "What are we doing? Did Lisa forget something? What do we need to pick up?"

Autumn and Claire exchanged a smile. "You'll see,"

Claire said.

They pulled up to the main house, where she'd fought with Holt and Ned a few weeks back. The driver parked the limousine and came to open their door. Autumn climbed out and held a hand to her. "Come on."

Confused, Morgan followed her out of the car, then gasped aloud when she saw the lawn ahead of her, filled with guests seated in white folding chairs. At the end of the lawn stood a white arbor decked with flowers. Beneath it stood Joe Halpern, Rob, Ethan, Jamie and Cab.

"Oh, my God," Morgan breathed, raising a hand to her mouth. Tears pricked her eyes as she realized what was going on. The ranch wedding she'd longed for—it was actually happening.

Lisa bustled up to her side as Autumn and Claire surrounded her. "Got you!" she cried, beaming with happiness. "You didn't suspect a thing, did you? I can't believe you thought I'd let my baby boy and his wonderful bride get married in a hospital!"

Morgan laughed along with her. She couldn't resist Lisa's obvious joy. "How did you do all this without me even knowing?"

"Who do you think Rob got all his trickiness from? It certainly wasn't from Holt!" Lisa crushed her in a hug, then gestured to the others. "Everybody's waiting. Let's get in line, girls. As soon as you're ready I'll take my place up front. Wait for the music and then walk down the aisle. Morgan, here's your bouquet." She handed her a lovely cluster of old-fashioned blooms.

Morgan searched for Rob again and met his gaze across the seated guests. He shrugged and held his hands out to his sides to say he had no idea, either, then smiled broadly. Lisa urged her to the rear of the rows of seats, where the guests were craning their necks to see her reaction to the surprise.

"Thank you," she managed to say before Lisa hurried off. Autumn stood first in line. Claire came second. Standing behind them, Morgan looked around her, helplessly. She couldn't believe what she was seeing. The care and thoughtfulness of Lisa's arrangements over-whelmed her.

The music swelled, and Morgan's breath caught. Wait a minute, wasn't someone supposed to walk her down the aisle? Cab had stood in for Autumn's father, and Ethan for Claire's in their weddings…

"Morgan," a deep voice said, as an arm linked with hers. She looked up to see Holt, frail but steady. "Your father should be here, and if I was feeling stronger I'd fly to Canada and give him the thrashing he deserves. Lisa tried to track him down, but his wife said he was out of the country."

Morgan bit her lip. She refused to let her father ruin this special day, but his absence hurt.

A lot.

"Would you allow me to escort you down the aisle?" Holt asked, and it was the first time she'd ever seen him look uncertain. "I have no daughters of my own," he said. "I'd be honored to fill in."

Tears threatened to spill over her lids, but she held them back somehow. "I'd like that, very much," she managed to say.

First Autumn, and then Claire began to move down the aisle. Holt patted her arm, and when they processed side by side she found comfort in his presence.

The seats around her were filled with guests. Some she knew, others she had yet to meet, but she was sure in the years ahead, as she lived, worked, and raised her family in Chance Creek, they'd become the community she'd always craved.

At the altar, Rob waited for her, his gaze never leaving hers. So much love shone there, and such promise of the good times ahead. Morgan's heart began to race as she joined him in front of the minister, and Holt took his seat.

Joe Halpern raised his bible and began the ceremony. Looking into the eyes of the man she loved, Morgan knew she was finally home.

ROB THOUGHT he'd never get to speak his vows and take his wife into his arms to kiss her before God and man. Finally, however, the ceremony started, Joe said his lines, and he and Morgan exchanged rings. He gave her a brand new wedding band to match the engagement ring already on her finger. She slid the exotic silver band she'd given him a month ago back on his finger. He'd grown so attached to it he refused to pick out something new.

When he bent to kiss her, he searched her face to see

if she truly meant her vows.

"I love you," she whispered.

He grinned and swooped in for that kiss. As their guests cheered, he cupped her face and kissed her on and on, finally breaking away to whisper back, "I love you, too."

Later, when they'd walked back up the aisle, and ducked into the main house for a moment alone, Morgan excused herself to freshen up and Rob waited for her by the front door.

Ned found him there and approached him before Rob could figure out an escape route.

"Glad everything worked out for you," Ned said, jamming his hands into his pockets.

"Yeah?" Rob still didn't feel like giving him an inch.

"Yeah. What I said a few weeks back…it wasn't right."

That was almost an apology, Rob thought in surprise. He surveyed his brother, who wouldn't meet his eye. "Maybe it's about time we figured out a way to get along."

Ned looked up, seeming relieved. "I don't mean to fight with you. It's just…we're different."

"What's wrong with that?" Rob wished Morgan was here. Or Autumn, or someone of the female persuasion. He had a feeling he and Ned weren't getting this quite right.

"Nothing, I guess." Ned shrugged. "That's what I wanted to tell you. You do your thing. I got your back."

Rob grinned in spite of himself. "Don't you mean

you'll pound my back?"

"Oh, I'll do that, too, if it needs doing," Ned said, grinning back at him. "But as long as you keep in line, I mean to be your brother, not your enemy."

Rob figured they'd better quit while they were ahead. Luckily Morgan descended the stairs looking as radiant as a goddess. Ned backed away. "Congratulations," he said to Morgan as she passed by and then disappeared down the hall to the back of the house.

"Wow, he actually spoke to me," she said, linking her arm through his.

"I think we've managed to set things right," Rob said.

"I'm glad. I want all of us to be one big, happy family," she said. "Speaking of which," she squeezed his arm. "With all the excitement, I haven't been paying much attention. I just realized I'm a week late. I think I might be pregnant."

Rob rounded on her. "For real? Or is this another practical joke?"

She stood on her tiptoes and gave him a kiss. "You'll have to wait nine months to see."

MORGAN KNEW THEIR FRIENDS expected them to head straight to Chance Creek airport and on to Aruba, where they'd decided to spend their honeymoon. Their flight didn't leave until early the next morning, however. First they planned a night out under the stars.

They snuck down the lane to the Double-Bar-K in Rob's truck until he swerved off on a dirt track that led out to their land. The thought of what they'd gotten up to last time they'd been out this way—a month ago at Claire and Jamie's wedding—had her pulse racing.

This time there were no boundaries they couldn't cross. This time they could do anything they chose. Although they'd been together before, she knew that this was the true start of their life together and the full expression of their love.

She couldn't wait.

When he cut the engine, Rob reached behind them and pulled out a canvas duffel bag and a picnic basket. Morgan joined him outside, shivering a little in the cool air.

"I won't build a fire—we don't want unwelcome guests," Rob said, "but I brought these." He pulled out a thick blanket and spread it out on the ground, then handed another one to her. She shook it out and draped it around her shoulders like a cloak, watching the man she loved pull out other provisions from the bag and basket. A bottle of champagne and two glasses, a loaf of bread and hunk of cheese, even a pillow. "I want you to be comfortable," he said with a grin.

"What would you have done if it rained?"

"I've got a tent in the truck. I can go get it if you want."

She shook her head. She wanted nothing between her and those stars. Nothing except Rob.

She appreciated the thought he'd put into this night, but right now she didn't want champagne or snacks; she wanted him. He must have guessed what she was thinking, for he pushed the food away and reached out for her.

Morgan joined him gladly on the blanket and sighed when he bent to kiss her.

"How are you doing, wife of mine?" he asked, tracing the contour of her jaw with a finger.

"I'm doing fine. How about you, husband?"

He swept her into his arms with a groan, and it was all too evident exactly how he was doing. Morgan came up from his embrace laughing with joy.

"Are you going to get me naked or not?"

"With pleasure." He turned her around and fumbled with the long row of tiny buttons that held her dress together. "What kind of torture is this?" he asked after a long moment.

"It's a test of your dexterity," she said, as eager as he was to get them undone.

"I'll prove my dexterity to you in a minute, as soon as I get this thing off of you," he growled, kissing the back of her neck and tickling her ear with his breath. "There. I think I've got it."

She turned around, slid the gown off and stood before him in a white lace bra and garter set. She remembered how much he'd liked this kind of get up the last time they were here and she hoped the sight of it would propel him to similar feats of passion.

"Don't you look a sight," he said, leaning back to take in the view.

"Your turn," she said, and stood watching, hands on hips, as he obediently stripped down.

"I'd ask you which way you want to do this," he said as he approached, took her hands in his own, and pulled her in tight, "except it doesn't matter because we're going to try them all before the night's through."

"Oh, yeah?" she said as he tugged her down to the blanket. He leaned her back, supporting her as she lay down, then covered her with his own body. He tugged the second blanket over the top of them since the night had grown cool.

"Yeah," he said, and kissed her again. Lifting her arms above her head, he captured them in one hand, then used the other one to stroke and knead and squeeze her until she hummed with desire. He kissed her everywhere, from her forehead to her nose, to first one breast, then the other, weaving back and forth until she felt that her skin would soon catch fire. When he slid lower, she kept her arms above her head, clutching at the tough grass and weeds that grew all over this rangeland. When Rob tossed the blanket away, she welcomed the cool touch of the night air on her skin. She wanted to be naked, wanted the sky and stars and all creation to witness this love of theirs.

Rob slid his hands under her ass and lifted her, dipping his head to taste her and drink in every inch of her beauty. She moved beneath him, slowly and sensually, joining him in this intimate dance.

When he moved back up to join her, pressing the length of him to her aching core, Morgan could barely contain herself. She wanted him inside her, wanted him to make love to her.

"Is this okay?" he asked, pushing forward an inch, nudging open her folds, giving her the tiniest taste of the sensations to come.

"Yes," she said, "but no fooling around this time. I want it hard and fast and powerful. I want it all."

"Yes, ma'am," Rob said, and plunged into her with a swift, hard stroke.

Morgan cried out as he pulled out and thrust in again, and then they were off and running, Rob's strong, fast strokes lifting her swiftly to a peak of desire. He wrapped his arms around her, crushing her against him, plunging in and out until Morgan could hardly breathe. She held on for dear life, trusting him utterly to bring both of them to the brink, and when they fell over the cliff together, they called out as one, their cries echoing in the night air.

Rob cradled her then, stroking her hair, her face, her body, until her breathing evened out again. He kissed her forehead and down her nose to her lips, lingered there for long minutes.

"Are you okay?" he asked finally. "I wasn't too rough?"

"No," she said, a smile curving the corners of her mouth. "Just rough enough."

"You want to sleep a little? Or eat something?"

She could tell from his tenderness Rob didn't quite believe her—that he was feeling tentative, maybe even ashamed of the physicality of the way he'd made love to her. She had to nip that right in the bud. She wriggled until he relaxed his hold on her, then got to her feet and reached out for his hand.

"Where are we going? Is something wrong?"

Morgan didn't bother to speak. Instead she led the way to the same fallen log she'd braced herself against a month ago, leaned forward to place her hands on it, and spread her legs. She heard his breath hitch and a moment later felt him take his place behind her.

"Are you sure you're up for this?" he asked.

"Are you?" she teased him. He chuckled in response and in a moment she felt that yes, indeed, he was up for it. As he stroked her body from behind, taking her heavy breasts into the palms of his hands, he slid easily into her again and she sighed.

"I love you, Mrs. Matheson," he said.

"I love you, Mr. Matheson. More than anything else in the world."

The **Cowboys of Chance Creek** series continues with
The Cowgirl Ropes a Billionaire.

Be the first to know about Cora Seton's new releases!
Sign up for her newsletter here!

Other books in the Cowboys of Chance Creek Series:

The Cowboy Inherits a Bride (Volume 0)
The Cowboy's E-Mail Order Bride (Volume 1)
The Cowboy Wins a Bride (Volume 2)
The Cowgirl Ropes a Billionaire (Volume 4)
The Sheriff Catches a Bride (Volume 5)
The Cowboy Lassos a Bride (Volume 6)
The Cowboy Rescues a Bride (Volume 7)
The Cowboy Earns a Bride (Volume 8)
The Cowboy's Christmas Bride (Volume 9)

Sign up for my newsletter HERE.

www.coraseton.com/sign-up-for-my-newsletter

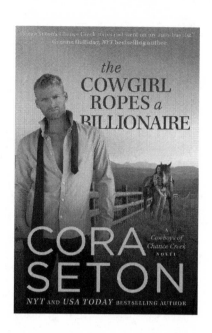

Read on for an excerpt of
The Cowgirl Ropes a Billionaire.

"NO—I CAN'T TAKE any more kittens!" Bella Chatham pointed to the closed sign posted prominently in the door of the Chance Creek Pet Clinic and Shelter. It was past seven o'clock in the evening and she'd already done a full day of appointments and surgeries. Now that she'd finished her errands, she looked forward to polishing off the fast food she'd picked up before she switched her attention to the animals waiting for their fair share of love and attention in the shelter out back. After a few hours of caring for her *long-term* guests, she'd make her way to the small airstream trailer she lived in at the far back of the property, take a shower and collapse into bed.

Dick Schneider stood on the other side of the door, however, holding a box emitting the all-too-familiar sound of kittens meowing. Their plaintive cries barely carried through the glass separating her from the cool October evening air. Dick owned a large spread about ten miles outside of town, and when the feral cat population became out of control out there, he caught all the kittens he could and delivered them to her.

"You'll have to come back tomorrow," she tried again.

She couldn't take in any more kittens. Her shelter cages were filled with kittens. Despite her best efforts at promoting a spay and release program for feral cats, Chance Creek, Montana was still full of them. And their offspring all ended up here at her combination clinic and pound. Feeding them ate all her income and more. Last month she'd had to pay part of her receptionist's earnings with the change from the big jug of coins she'd been adding to since she was a teenager.

She wasn't sure how she'd pay Hannah this month.

Dick shrugged. "I'll just take care of them myself," he called through the door and turned around.

For one brief second, Bella thought he meant he'd keep the kittens after all, but she quickly realized his true intentions. She yanked the door open. "Don't you dare kill those cats!"

Dick spun around on his heel and she caught his smile before he suppressed it. Darn it—this was her problem in a nutshell; everyone in Chance Creek knew she wouldn't turn away strays. She might deal with disease and death on a daily basis in her clinic, and she administered lethal doses to animals who needed their way smoothed as they died, but she could not bear to euthanize animals just because they'd had the misfortune to be born.

So she didn't.

And since most people hated the idea just as much as she did, they brought their unwanted kittens and puppies to Bella, knowing that even though they'd turned an animal in to the pound it would survive and their consciences could remain clean.

Bella propped the door open with her hip and accepted the box. "I don't suppose you'd consider a contribution to the clinic to help offset their care?"

Dick sighed heavily and pulled out his wallet. He carefully selected a ten dollar bill and handed it over.

"Ten dollars?" Bella bit back a curse at the piddly amount; she couldn't afford to alienate Dick, even if she knew darn well he could afford ten times what he'd given her. "Thank you!"

"You're welcome." He climbed back in his truck and pulled away.

Bella retreated into the clinic, placed the box on the floor, and sat down beside it. Now that she was stuck with them, she might as well see what she had. Pushing the cares of the day out of her head for just a moment, she opened the lid with the same sense of anticipation she'd opened her gifts on Christmas morning as a child.

She loved all animals. *Well, all except horses,* she thought, with the habitual frown she reserved for the four-legged monsters that were all too common in ranch country. Horses were dangerous, careless, overwrought beasts that had no business living among humans. She might sport cowboy boots and a hat just like all her neighbors, but she was terrified of them.

Five calico kittens stared back up at her. At least they were old enough to be weaned and she wouldn't be up all night with an eyedropper like she sometimes was. They mewed piteously and she picked them up one by one, rubbing their tiny faces with her cheek. Kitten cuddles were one of the best perks of this ridiculous job.

A ridiculous job she wouldn't hold onto much longer, at this rate.

"Another month and this will all be mine," Nate said as he barged into Evan Mortimer's ultramodern office and plunked a framed five-by-seven photograph of himself, his wife, Brenda, and his four-year-old daughter, Katy, on the gunmetal-gray desk.

Evan eyed the photograph with narrowed lids. "A month is plenty of time for me to get married, so don't start moving in your things just yet."

"Come on, if you were going to marry you'd have done it by now. You're incapable of dating a woman for longer than twenty-four hours, let alone getting engaged. Time to admit defeat and hand Mortimer Innovations over to me."

Evan would rot in hell before he did that, or he'd

marry the 72-year-old cleaning lady, for that matter. "What's got you so excited? You found some more farmland you want to destroy?"

"It's called fracking, and it's the next big thing," Nate said. "We're already late to the party. We should have invested years ago. Why aren't we in North Dakota right now, buying up those farms, blasting that bedrock and getting rich on oil?"

"Because we're already rich, and we're in San Jose, trying to promote technologies that will free us from our oil habit once and for all," Evan said. They'd been over this a million times.

"Hand your shares over, buddy, and let me get this company into the twenty-first century," Nate said.

Evan stood up, and was frustrated to find himself eye-to-eye with his younger brother. It had been so much easier when he stood a foot above Nate. "Sorry, man, but I'm not going anywhere. If I don't find a fiancée the old-fashioned way soon, I've got a backup plan."

Nate snorted. "What kind of backup plan? Are you going to marry a mannequin? I don't think that counts, buddy." Giving his family photograph a final pat, he left the office as abruptly as he came.

Evan couldn't believe he needed to marry at all. But the strictures around who got to run Mortimer Innovations were ironclad. He needed a wife.

Nate was right; time for plan B.

He reached for his phone and tapped the link for his secretary. "Amanda, get me on that show."

WHEN BELLA CHARGED through the door the following morning, late and disheveled, still twisting her unruly blonde hair into a ponytail, her cowboy hat—a tan affair she'd had since she was twelve—tucked under her arm instead of on her head, she noticed Morgan Matheson stood behind the reception counter with her sole employee, Hannah Ashton. Morgan's husband, Rob, sat on one of the waiting room chairs, his hands laced behind his head.

The two women looked guilty, like Bella had caught them dipping into the petty cash, and she felt the usual pang she did when she saw them together. Hannah was twenty-five and she had worked for Bella for four years. Bella counted her as her closest friend.

However, when Rob Matheson brought his fiancée in to pick out some kittens last month, Hannah and Morgan instantly took to each other. As soon as Morgan returned from her honeymoon, she began to stop by the shelter several times a week. She spent a lot of time with the animals, and even more time with Hannah—often inviting her out to lunch when she came by. It wasn't that the other two women excluded her exactly—Bella always worked through lunch, as Hannah knew all too well—but she still felt left out. Bella knew she'd neglected her friendship with Hannah; while they saw each other at work every day, they didn't hang out after hours, or go out to eat, or shop, or anything else women did together for fun. She simply didn't have time. She worked all day at the clinic, all night at the shelter, fell into bed as soon as she got home, and woke up and did it all over again.

Not to mention it was getting harder and harder to look Hannah in the eye when they both knew Bella would have to let her go soon. The one time she brought it up Hannah told her not to talk crazy, but the woman needed the money as badly as she did. She couldn't work for free.

She had to fix things, but she didn't know how. Her only option was to institute the same euthanization program all the other shelters had for their unwanted pets. She wasn't ready to do that.

"Bella! Great, you're here. I've figured it out!" Hannah said, breaking into her thoughts.

"Hi, Morgan, Rob." She nodded to the Mathesons and turned to Hannah. "What did you figure out?" She gratefully accepted the cup of coffee her receptionist offered her. Hannah lived a few miles out of town and passed the Bagel Bookshop—Chance Creek's best source of java—on her way in to the clinic. As much as it shamed her that her receptionist was buying her coffee these days, she hadn't been able to make Hannah stop, and she did love her coffee.

"How to get all the money we need!" Beside her Morgan nodded like she knew all about it, her thick, dark hair swinging. Bella suppressed another pang at the thought the two had discussed her situation behind her back. Judging by the grin on Rob's face, he was in on it, too. A tall, blond cowboy with wide shoulders, and an easy-going personality that had gotten more serious in the time he knew Morgan, he was one of four brothers who'd grown up on a ranch not far from town. Now Morgan and Rob were busy starting a winery and lived with two other couples on the Cruz ranch, next door to the spread where Rob lived as a child.

Bella grew up on a ranch, too. Her parents still lived there, although they'd had to sell about half of the land, but she hardly ever went home to visit, even if it was only ten minutes away. Her family wasn't close anymore; they hadn't been in a long time. She envied Morgan and Rob's tight-knit group of friends who all worked together to support each other. In these difficult times, a person needed friends like that. She knew the Cruzes, the Mathesons, and the Lassiters, but she wasn't among their inner circle.

Looked like Hannah was getting there, though.

Suppressing that catty thought, she grabbed the daily patient list off of the high counter that separated Hannah's reception station from the clinic waiting room. She was pretty sure she had some paying customers coming in today. That would offset the ongoing cost of spaying and neutering all the abandoned and feral animals she had in the kennels out back. Bella bit back a sigh. Maybe if she didn't spend all her time taking care of animals, she wouldn't have declined so many invitations and she'd be part of that inner circle, too.

"Bella?" Hannah said, breaking into her thoughts.

"What?"

"Don't you want to know how?"

"How?" she said as she scanned the front end of the clinic to make sure all was ready for the day. Shelves of pet food, common medicines and accessories stocked? Check. Floor swept and front windows clean of streaks? Check. "Oh, you mean how I'll get all that money? Sure—how can I strike it rich overnight?" She tried not to sound as impatient as she suddenly felt. She was going to lose everything she loved—her clinic, the shelter, the animals who depended on her…

"You'll be the winning contestant on *Can You Beat a Billionaire?*"

Bella had reached to tug the venetian blinds on the front window a little higher, but stopped mid-pull. "I'll be what?"

"You know that show—the one where they pit a poor person against a billionaire? If the poor person wins they get five million dollars. If the billionaire wins, he or she gets to pick some humiliating punishment for the loser. Last time the billionaire made the poor guy clean his house for three months. And it was a mansion! As in—huge!"

"You're kidding, right? You know those shows are all fake. I bet no one actually wins anything." She shook her head. Hannah was so gullible. Why didn't Morgan say anything? Morgan was in her thirties; old enough to know better.

She glanced at Rob, whose smile grew even wider. "Some of them win," he said.

"Actually, they do," Morgan said. "I'm sure some scripting goes on and the producers stick people in situations guaranteed to show their rough spots, but the contests are real and several people have walked away with the five million dollars."

"Remember that guy last year who used the money to refurbish a whole block in his inner city neighborhood?" Hannah chimed in. "I read a follow-up article about him. He turned around the lives of a bunch of people. They have testimonials from the families on the website."

Bella did vaguely remember that. She never watched the show—she didn't have time—but Hannah watched it religiously and filled her in on the latest gossip every week. Her receptionist cried with relief each time the poor contestant won and got the money, as had happened once already this season, if memory served her. And if the rich contestant won, she'd stomp around angry for a week.

"Okay, so maybe it's not all fake. So what? I'm just a country vet who's going broke. I bet they get thousands of interesting applicants—what makes you think they'd pick me?" Satisfied with the height of the blinds she turned around in time to catch the look Hannah and Morgan exchanged. Hannah began to blush, and since she was blonder than Bella—her hair a corn-silk tassel compared to Bella's honey locks—the red stain was all too obvious on her pale cheeks. Rob leaned forward, as if eager to see how this next bit played out.

Uh oh. Warning bells went off in Bella's head. "What did you do?" she demanded.

"Submitted your application," Hannah said in a small voice. "Three months ago."

Bella's mouth dropped open. "Take it back! Make

them delete it—I don't want to be on some stupid reality TV show!"

"It's too late." Hannah cringed as if she thought Bella would jump the divider and tackle her. "They already picked you."

Morgan hurried to add her two cents. "When Hannah first told me what she'd done I reacted like you did, but after I thought about it, I decided it's a great idea!"

"Yeah, ought to be fun," Rob said.

"No way." Bella shook her head, instinctively taking a step back. "You started this and you can put an end to it. Call them up and tell them I'm not interested. I'm sure they'll understand."

"I can't." If Hannah slumped any further in her chair she'd be under her desk, Bella thought. "They're on their way over right now for your first interview. Besides, you need the money. You know you do!"

Bella's cheeks heated at the words Hannah didn't say—they both needed the money. Otherwise, they'd both be out of a job, something Hannah couldn't afford, even if Bella was determined to go down with her sinking ship.

"I've got appointments all day," she said, grasping at straws. "I can't do interviews. I don't want to do interviews!"

"Actually I rescheduled all of today's appointments," Hannah said. She stood up and came around the partition to take the clipboard out of Bella's hand. "Come on, I knew you'd be upset so I left a little time for us to talk. Let's go out back—I want to show you something."

"I don't want to talk!" But Hannah took one arm and Morgan the other, and with Rob taking up the rear, Bella had no other choice but to allow them to lead her through the clinic to the shelter in the back. The facility had both indoor and outdoor spaces for the pets awaiting placement in adoptive homes. Additionally, Bella had built ad hoc sheds around the wide yard to house the pets that probably wouldn't ever be adopted. A whole band of volunteer schoolchildren took turns coming in the afternoons to feed and play and walk and socialize with the animals, so Bella knew they received adequate love and attention. She also knew that every pet deserved a forever home with a loving person they could call their own, and her heart ached for the ones that didn't get one. "What am I looking at?" she said brusquely. She couldn't believe Hannah had added another responsibility to her already crushing schedule. That she thought such a hare-brained scheme could possibly work.

And that she'd told Morgan all about it and never mentioned it to her.

"All of these animals depend on you, and more come in every day. These beauties weren't here when I left yesterday." Hannah pointed to the calico kittens, safe now in their own small cage. "Think about what five million dollars could do for these animals. Think of the food it would buy. Think of how much you could expand the spay and neutering program. We could get a truck and do a mobile clinic so people wouldn't have to try to lug feral cats into town. Maybe we could actually solve the feral cat problem!"

Bella took a deep breath as she considered Hannah's words. Five million dollars would go a long, long way. If she didn't have to worry about money every minute of the day, she could do so much good for the animals of Chance Creek.

"Right? It's a good idea, isn't it?" Hannah prompted her.

"Maybe," Bella conceded. "But filming a whole television show? That must take weeks. I have to come to the clinic every day."

"It only takes one week," Hannah said and held up a hand to forestall her protests. "Yes, you can take a week off. When was the last time you took any vacation at all? If you keep working like this, you're going to have a heart attack, and then where will the animals be? Look, I've already moved all your appointments for the next two weeks back and I've put a notice in the paper that we'll be closed until you're done. The volunteers and I will take care of the rest of these beasts while you're gone, and your brother's agreed to take any emergency cases that come up."

Bella grimaced. She hadn't talked to Craig in months. He probably thought she should just close down her clinic for good. Her older brother was the *real* veterinarian in town—at least, that's what she'd heard more than one rancher say—the veterinarian who wasn't deathly afraid of horses. You called Craig when your cattle had hoof rot. You called Craig when your mare was foaling for the first time. You called Craig for any and all problems concerning livestock—the bread and butter of the ranches that ringed Chance Creek. She was just the *pet doctor*—the one who gave Spot and Mittens their shots, rid them of their fleas, and made their last days a little easier. She knew no one took what she did seriously, but she also knew someone had to care for Chance Creek's pets—they couldn't all be hotshot livestock vets like her brother.

"We'll all help out while you're gone," Morgan said.

Rob nodded and put an arm around his wife's waist. "Don't you worry about a thing. We've got your back, Bella."

"The show's coordinator is coming in twenty minutes," Hannah said. "She'll ask you a lot of questions, go over the paperwork and you'll have to sign a bunch of forms. Your flight to Canada leaves tonight at seven."

"Tonight?" Bella squeaked. This was all happening way too fast. "I haven't even agreed I'll do the show! And why Canada?"

Hannah bent forward and gripped her face in her hands. "Five million dollars, Bella. Focus on the five million dollars. All you have to do is win a couple of contests. It's in Canada because it's located in Jasper National Park—you know they use a new exotic location for each show. Just be grateful you don't have to fly to Australia."

"Although Australia would be pretty cool," Morgan put in. "But Jasper's great, too. I've been there a bunch of times."

Fine, she was grateful. *Not.* She couldn't believe Hannah and Morgan were ganging up on her, and just because Morgan—a Canadian by birth—vacationed in Jasper, didn't mean it would be any fun at all to film a reality television show there. In fact, it sounded downright cold. "What if I lose?"

"Uh… you'll have to…" Hannah held the clipboard in front of her face and mumbled something unintelligible.

"I'll have to what?" Bella demanded.

Hannah's face grew red again. "I already agreed to that part—there's no way to change it now," she said, lowering the clipboard slowly. "If you lose, you have to marry the billionaire for a year."

EVAN MORTIMER PICKED up his cell phone on the first ring. "Speak to me." He sat at an oversized mahogany desk in the plush headquarters of Mortimer Innovations and he'd been waiting for this call from his longtime personal assistant, Amanda Hollister. Amanda was the one person he could count on—he knew this because he paid her ten times her worth, footed the bill for all six of her grandchildren to attend private universities and matched her contributions every year to her rather hefty pension plan. Every expense was worth it. He had to have an ally he could trust implicitly in this cutthroat industry. He'd learned the hard way that people like Amanda were few and far between.

"I still can't believe you're doing this crazy show," she said.

"We've been over all of that. What's the dirt on this Bella woman?"

"She's a cowgirl," Amanda said flatly. "Wait until you see her photograph—hat and everything."

A cowgirl? Evan stifled a chuckle. "What else?"

"She's thirty-one, lives in Chance Creek, Montana, and seems like a nice girl," Amanda said, making the adjective sound like a dirty word. "Smart—graduated top of her class in Chance Creek Senior High. Did well in veterinary school, too. Attended Montana State University for undergrad, Colorado State University for the vet program. Came back home to Chance Creek to start her own clinic. Specializes in house pets."

"House pets? You said she lives in Montana—shouldn't she be handling livestock? I bet she'd make more money."

"You'd bet right," Amanda said. "Here's where it gets interesting. Bella has an older brother, Craig. Five years older. Looks like big brother sewed up the livestock veterinary business and left Bella to take care of the cats and dogs."

"You'd think Montana might require more than one livestock vet." Evan ran a hand through his thick, dark hair and gazed out the window at downtown San Jose. If he lived on the east coast, he'd be high over some city in a penthouse office, but no one built skyscrapers in earthquake country. Still, this was home—always had been. San Jose suited him. Some of the best minds in the world toiled away just minutes from his office, and he was positioned to capitalize off the fruit of their mental labor. Mortimer Innovations bought up patents from aspiring scientists and inventors and held on to them until the market suited his exact needs—only then did he resell the patents; right at the point he could make the most money off of the companies dying to get their hands on them. The millions he made each year went to funding his own innovative projects. Evan had a dream that one day instead of factories that ate up resources and produced waste and products that ended up in landfills, he would build closed systems that produced useful objects whose components could be reused again and again.

He remembered the day he'd stumbled on the concept of a factory cleaning the water it used; returning it to the surrounding watershed in better condition than when it entered the plant. He'd been in college, his growing awareness of the damage his family's holdings were doing to the environment piling up on him like so much trash in a dump, and the idea that it could be different—that industry could help the environment instead of hurt it—fueled him to study engineering and put his family's money to good use.

Nate thought he was crazy, but while there might be money in oil and natural gas, Evan was sure there was money in green technology, too, and it was the kind of innovation that could put Americans back to work. He saw himself as part of a new breed—both environmentalist and capitalist. He intended to make his money work—for himself, his family, his company, and the rest of the good ol' U.S. of A.

This Bella person was an idiot if she'd let her brother push her out of the most lucrative segment of her business. But most people were idiots when it came to money. He'd realized as a teenager that his grandfather and father didn't have any special characteristics that set them above the crowd; they were just willing to think about money morning, noon and night. "What you focus on is what you get," Grandpa always said. By the time he was fifteen he'd decided to focus on his dual loves of cash and nature. A shy child, and an awkward teenager, he was never happier than when he was either alone in the wilderness, or supervising experiments.

"I don't know about that. What I do know is Bella isn't a businesswoman. I managed to get a hold of her tax returns for the last five years—she's losing money fast."

"Losing money?" He wrinkled his nose. "A vet should turn a profit, even if her specialty is pets—what's the problem?"

"A tender heart," Amanda said sarcastically. "People bring her strays, but she won't euthanize them."

"Can you blame her? Putting down kittens doesn't sound like a fun time."

"Maybe not, but it's part of the job," Amanda countered.

Evan shrugged. She was right. "So she keeps every stray she sees, feeds them all, provides medical care…."

"And the money going out tops the money coming in. Her bank account's nearly empty. She's got a couple more months and it's good-bye clinic, good-bye trailer, see you later, cowgirl," Amanda finished for him.

"Trailer?" Evan rolled his eyes. He owned a five-bedroom, five bathroom luxury home in the San Jose hills, complete with a pool. Who the hell lived in a trailer?

"Trailer—at the back of the same lot her clinic is on. We're talking white trash here, Evan."

"Doesn't matter. In fact it's for the best."

"Seriously? You're going to marry this Betty Bumpkin?"

"I'll do what I've got to do to keep control of the company, you know that."

Evan's great-grandfather, Abe Mortimer, was a Bible-thumping, stiff-necked, pain in the ass by all accounts, but he started Mortimer Innovations and set up the corporation so that the family's shares could only be held by one family member at a time—the oldest male, who was required to be married or forfeit control to the next in line. If the oldest male family member was under twenty-five, the stock would be held in trust for him until he reached his twenty-fifth birthday, at which time he had a year to find a wife. If he was older than twenty-five, but unmarried, he had six months from the moment he inherited to get hitched. Evan's grandfather had already been married when he took the helm, as had his father. Now that his dad had passed away five months ago, Evan was running out of time to find a wife.

Trouble was, he didn't want one.

After a whole lot of looking, he'd found a loophole within all the legal gobbledygook that was going to save him from that fate—the marriage requirement only lasted a year. Evidently women in Abe's time often expired early due to complications of childbirth, and Abe had taken that into account. He wasn't required to stay married, therefore. No—all Evan had to do was find a woman whose time he could purchase for one year, or better yet, win for free. Betty Bumpkin might not know it at the moment, but she was doomed to be Mrs. Evan Mortimer for at least twelve months, right after he beat the pants off her on this stupid reality TV show.

"Yes, Amanda—I'm going to marry her."

"Thank God for prenups."

He'd made sure Hammer Communications, the parent company of the network that ran *Can You Beat a Billionaire*, knew there was no way he would expose half of Mortimer Innovations assets to some TV contestant. They'd fallen over themselves to agree—thrilled they'd managed to catch one of the West Coast's richest bachelors.

"Amen to that," Evan said, leaning back in his chair.

"Why don't you just buy some prostitute? They're a dime a dozen."

Evan rolled his eyes. They'd been over this before, too. "And let the newspapers have a field day when they figure it out? Nope—not into it."

The TV show gave him a bizarre, yet legitimate, excuse to get a wife no one had ever heard of before— someone his competition couldn't possibly have tainted beforehand—and dump her a year later. The network assured him no one would care what actually happened to the couple once the show was off the air.

"What if she refuses to divorce you?"

"First of all, no court will make a couple stay married these days if one person wants out. Second, look at her résumé—the one time she left Montana it was for school, after which she made a beeline back home. She'll hate it out here in California. The minute I let her go, she'll be gone!"

"If you say so—not many women will walk away from a lifestyle like yours."

"I'll give her a nice donation to start her clinic back up again. I'll give her some business tips, too."

"Like—you can't save all the kittens in the world?" Amanda said dryly.

"Something like that. What's she look like, anyway?"

"I told you about the hat, right?" Amanda laughed. "I'm sending over her photo right now." She hung up on him and he turned to his computer and clicked the refresh button on his email. He clicked again on the image Amanda attached to her message and stared at Bella Chatham.

Hello.

A golden-haired beauty stared back at him. Well, maybe beauty was too strong a word. She was fresh, wholesome, wore little makeup that he could see. She stood in a yard filled with large enclosures, surrounded by dogs, cats, rabbits and other animals. She held a puppy in her arms that was obviously squirming and she was laughing—all bright eyes, thick, wavy hair, legs that went on for a mile, and a cowboy hat perched atop her head. She could be the poster child for middle-

America—a healthy, happy, well-adjusted country girl.

His total opposite.

He'd never dated anyone like her, not that he'd dated much. When your family was worth billions a certain amount of suspicion crept into your personality. His mother, especially, thought they were surrounded by vultures ready to rip them apart at the slightest sign of weakness. She'd practically hand-picked Nate's wife from the children of her small circle of friends. While Nate and Brenda seemed happy enough, Evan had no interest in marriage to a woman like that.

His own attempts at dating had been disastrous. A few girls back in college who made it clear they expected a steady stream of expensive gifts, and called him cheap when they weren't forthcoming. Several more women in his twenties who didn't mention money at all, but talked frequently of their friends' impending weddings, all the while shooting him furtive looks from gleaming eyes that he swore held the reflection of dollar signs.

He never got past a few weeks of dinners, dancing and trips to museums or concerts before he broke it off. A constricting feeling would build in his chest until the idea of seeing them again made him physically ill. He was ashamed to admit he broke up with most of those women over the phone, several by texting, but that feeling of being caught—of being trussed up with no way to escape... He couldn't bear it, and couldn't take the risk that if he met with them in person, he'd end up running away.

That had happened once—only once—but he'd never forget it, and he'd never put himself in that position again.

He shook his head and dragged his thoughts back to the present. His money was a blessing. No way Evan would feel sorry for himself because it hampered normal relationships.

Bella was nothing like the sophisticated, calculating women who'd given him so much trouble in the past. He'd have no problem keeping her at arm's length and controlling the outcome of the show.

She'd do fine for his wife.

Just fine.

End of Excerpt

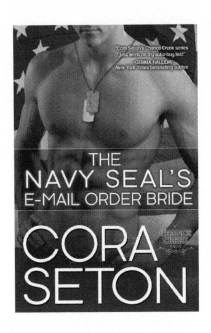

Read on for an excerpt of Volume 1 of
The Heroes of Chance Creek series –
The Navy SEAL's E-Mail Order Bride.

"BOYS," LIEUTENANT COMMANDER Mason Hall said, "we're going home."

He sat back in his folding chair and waited for a reaction from his brothers. The recreation hall at Bagram Airfield was as busy as always with men hunched over laptops, watching the widescreen television, or lounging in groups of three or four shooting the breeze. His brothers—three tall, broad shouldered men in uniform—stared back at him from his computer screen, the feeds from their four-way video conversation all relaying a similar reaction to his words.

Utter confusion.

"Home?" Austin was the first to speak. A Special Forces officer just a year younger than Mason, he was currently in Kabul.

"Home," Mason confirmed. "I got a letter from Great Aunt Heloise. Uncle Zeke passed away over the weekend without designating an heir. That means the ranch reverts back to her. She thinks we'll do a better job running it than Darren will." Darren, their first cousin, wasn't known for his responsible behavior and he hated ranching. Mason, on the other hand, loved it. He had missed the ranch, the cattle, the Montana sky and his family's home ever since they'd left it twelve years ago.

"She's giving Crescent Hall to us?" That was Zane, Austin's twin, a Marine currently in Kandahar. The excitement in his tone told Mason all he needed to know—Zane stilled loved the old place as much as he did. When Mason had gotten Heloise's letter, he'd had to read it more than once before he believed it. The Hall would belong to them once more—when he'd thought they'd lost it for good. Suddenly he'd felt like he could breathe fully again after so many years of holding in his anger and frustration over his uncle's behavior. The timing was perfect, too. He was due to ship stateside any day now. By April he'd be a civilian again.

Except it wasn't as easy as all that. Mason took a deep breath. "There are a few conditions."

Colt, his youngest brother, snorted. "Of course— we're talking about Heloise, aren't we? What's she up to this time?" He was an Air Force combat controller who had served both in Afghanistan and as part of the relief effort a few years back after the massive earthquake which devastated Haiti. He was currently back on United States soil in Florida, training with his unit.

Mason knew what he meant. Calling Heloise eccentric would be an understatement. In her eighties, she had definite opinions and brooked no opposition to her plans and schemes. She meant well, but as his father had always said, she was capable of leaving a swath of destruction in family affairs that rivaled Sherman's march to Atlanta.

"The first condition is that we have to stock the ranch with one hundred pair of cattle within twelve months of taking possession."

"We should be able to do that," Austin said.

"It's going to take some doing to get that ranch up and running again," Zane countered. "Zeke was already letting the place go years ago."

"You have something better to do than fix the place up when you get out?" Mason asked him. He hoped Zane understood the real question: was he in or out?

"I'm in; I'm just saying," Zane said.

Mason suppressed a smile. Zane always knew what he was thinking.

"Good luck with all that," Colt said.

"Thanks," Mason told him. He'd anticipated that inheriting the Hall wouldn't change Colt's mind about staying in the Air Force. He focused on the other two who were both already in the process of winding down their military careers. "If we're going to do this, it'll take a commitment. We're going to have to pool our funds and put our shoulders to the wheel for as long as it takes. Are you up for that?"

"I'll join you there as soon as I'm able to in June," Austin said. "It'll just be like another year in the service. I can handle that."

"I already said I'm in," Zane said. "I'll have boots on the ground in September."

Here's where it got tricky. "There's just one other thing," Mason said. "Aunt Heloise has one more requirement of each of us."

"What's that?" Austin asked when he didn't go on.

"She's worried about the lack of heirs on our side of the family. Darren has children. We don't."

"Plenty of time for that," Zane said. "We're still young, right?"

"Not according to Heloise." Mason decided to get it over and done with. "She's decided that in order for us to inherit the Hall free and clear, we each have to be married within the year. One of us has to have a child."

Stunned silence met this announcement until Colt started to laugh. "Staying in the Air Force doesn't look so bad now, does it?"

"That means you, too," Mason said.

"What? Hold up, now." Colt was startled into soberness. "I won't even live on the ranch. Why do I have to get hitched?"

"Because Heloise says it's time to stop screwing around. And she controls the land. And you know

Heloise."

"How are we going to get around that?" Austin asked.

"We're not." Mason got right to the point. "We're going to find ourselves some women and we're going to marry them."

"In Afghanistan?" Zane's tone made it clear what he thought about that idea.

Tension tightened Mason's jaw. He'd known this was going to be a messy conversation. "Online. I created an online personal ad for all of us. Each of us has a photo, a description and a reply address. A woman can get in touch with whichever of us she chooses and start a conversation. Just weed through your replies until you find the one you want."

"Are you out of your mind?" Zane peered at him through the video screen.

"I don't see what you're upset about. I'm the one who has to have a child. None of you will be out of the service in time."

"Wait a minute—I thought you just got the letter from Heloise." As usual, Austin zeroed in on the inconsistency.

"The letter came about a week ago. I didn't want to get anyone's hopes up until I checked a few things out." Mason shifted in his seat. "Heloise said the place is in rougher shape than we thought. Sounds like Zeke sold off the last of his cattle last year. We're going to have to start from scratch, and we're going to have to move fast to meet her deadline—on both counts. I did all the leg work on the online ad. All you need to do is read some e-mails, look at some photos and pick one. How hard can that be?"

"I'm beginning to think there's a reason you've been single all these years, Straightshot," Austin said. Mason winced at the use of his nickname. The men in his unit had christened him with it during his early days in the service, but as Colt said when his brothers had first heard about it, it made perfect sense. The name had little to do with his accuracy with a rifle, and everything to do with his tendency to find the shortest route from here to done on any mission he was tasked with. Regardless of what obstacles stood in his way.

Colt snickered. "Told you two it was safer to stay in the military. Mason's Matchmaking Service. It has a ring to it. I guess you've found yourself a new career, Mase."

"Stow it." Mason tapped a finger on the table. "Just because I've put the ad up doesn't mean that any of you have to make contact with the women who write you. If it doesn't work, it doesn't work. But you need to marry within the year. If you don't find a wife for yourself, I'll find one for you."

"He would, too," Austin said to the others. "You know he would."

"When does the ad go live?" Zane asked.

"It went live five days ago. You've each got several hundred responses so far. I'll forward them to you as soon as we break the call."

Austin must have leaned toward his webcam because suddenly he filled the screen. "Several hundred?"

"That's right."

Colt's laughter rang out over the line.

"Don't know what you're finding so funny, Colton," Mason said in his best imitation of their late father's voice. "You've got several hundred responses, too."

"What? I told you I was staying…"

"Read through them and answer all the likely ones. I'll be in touch in a few days to check your progress." Mason cut the call.

REGAN ANDERSON WANTED a baby. Right now. Not five years from now. Not even next year.

Right now.

And since she'd just quit her stuffy loan officer job, moved out of her overpriced one bedroom New York City apartment, and completed all her preliminary appointments, she was going to get one via the modern technology of artificial insemination.

As she raced up the three flights of steps to her tiny new studio, she took the pins out of her severe updo and let her thick, auburn hair swirl around her shoulders. By the time she reached the door, she was breathing hard. Inside, she shut and locked it behind her, tossed her briefcase and blazer on the bed which took up the lion's share of the living space, and kicked off her high heels. Her blouse and pencil skirt came next, and thirty seconds later she was down to her skivvies.

Thank God.

She was done with Town and Country Bank. Done

with originating loans for people who would scrape and slave away for the next thirty years just to cling to a lousy flat near a subway stop. She was done, done, done being a cog in the wheel of a financial system she couldn't stand to be a part of anymore.

She was starting a new business. Starting a new life.

And she was starting a family, too.

Alone.

After years of looking for Mr. Right, she'd decided he simply didn't exist in New York City. So after several medical exams and consultations, she had scheduled her first round of artificial insemination for the end of April. She couldn't wait.

Meanwhile, she'd throw herself into the task of building her consulting business. She would make it her job to help non-profits assist regular people start new stores and services, buy homes that made sense, and manage their money so that they could get ahead. It might not be as lucrative as being a loan officer, but at least she'd be able to sleep at night.

She wasn't going to think about any of that right now, though. She'd survived her last day at work, survived her exit interview, survived her boss, Jack Richey, pretending to care that she was leaving. Now she was giving herself the weekend off. No work, no nothing—just forty-eight hours of rest and relaxation.

Having grabbed takeout from her favorite Thai restaurant on the way home, Regan spooned it out onto a plate and carried it to her bed. Lined with pillows, it doubled as her couch during waking hours. She sat cross-legged on top of the duvet and savored her food and her freedom. She had bought herself a nice bottle of wine to drink this weekend, figuring it might be her last for an awfully long time. She was all too aware her Chardonnay-sipping days were coming to an end. As soon as her weekend break from reality was over, she planned to spend the next ten months starting her business, while scrimping and saving every penny she could. She would have to move to a bigger apartment right before the baby was born, but given the cost of renting in the city, the temporary downgrade was worth it. She pushed all thoughts of business and the future out of her mind. Rest and relax—that was her job for now.

Two hours and two glasses of wine later, however, rest and relaxation was beginning to feel a lot like loneliness and boredom. In truth, she'd been fighting loneliness for months. She'd broken up with her last boyfriend before Christmas. Here it was March and she was still single. Two of her closest friends had gotten married and moved away in the past twelve months, Laurel to New Hampshire and Rita to New Jersey. They rarely saw each other now and when she'd jokingly mentioned the idea of going ahead and having a child without a husband the last time they'd gotten together, both women had scoffed.

"No way could I have gotten through this pregnancy without Ryan." Laurel ran a hand over her large belly. "I've felt awful the whole time."

"No way I'm going back to work." Rita's baby was six weeks old. "Thank God Alan brings in enough cash to see us through."

Regan decided not to tell them about her plans until the pregnancy was a done deal. She knew what she was getting into—she didn't need them to tell her how hard it might be. If there'd been any way for her to have a baby normally—with a man she loved—she'd have chosen that path in a heartbeat. But there didn't seem to be a man for her to love in New York. Unfortunately, keeping her secret meant it was hard to call either Rita or Laurel just to chat, and she needed someone to chat with tonight. As dusk descended on the city, Regan felt fear for the first time since making her decision to go ahead with having a child.

What if she'd made a mistake? What if her consultancy business failed? What if she became a welfare mother? What if she had to move back home?

When the thoughts and worries circling her mind grew overwhelming, she topped up her wine, opened up her laptop and clicked on a YouTube video of a cat stuck headfirst in a cereal box. Thank goodness she'd hooked up wi-fi the minute she secured the studio. Simultaneously scanning her Facebook feed, she read an update from an acquaintance named Susan who was exhibiting her art in one of the local galleries. She'd have to stop by this weekend.

She watched a couple more videos—the latest installment in a travel series she loved, and one about over-the-top weddings that made her sad. Determined to cheer up, she hopped onto Pinterest and added more images to her nursery pinboard. Sipping her wine, she checked the news, posted a question on the single parents' forum she frequented, checked her e-mail again, and then tapped a finger on the keys, wondering what to do next. The evening stretched out before her, vacant even of the work she normally took home to do over the weekend. She hadn't felt at such loose ends in years.

Pacing her tiny apartment didn't help. Nor did an attempt at unpacking more of her things. She had finished moving in just last night and boxes still lined one wall. She opened one to reveal books, took a look at her limited shelf space and packed them up again. A second box revealed her collection of vintage fans. No room for them here, either.

She stuck her iTouch into a docking station and turned up some tunes, then drained her glass, poured herself another, and flopped onto her bed. The wine was beginning to take effect—giving her a nice, soft, fuzzy feeling. It hadn't done away with her loneliness, but when she turned back to Facebook on her laptop, the images and YouTube links seemed funnier this time.

Heartened, she scrolled further down her feed until she spotted another post one of her friends had shared. It was an image of a handsome man standing ramrod straight in combat fatigues. *Hello.* He was cute. In fact, he looked like exactly the kind of man she'd always hoped she'd meet. He wasn't thin and arrogant like the up-and-coming Wall Street crowd, or paunchy and cynical like the upper-management men who hung around the bars near work. Instead he looked healthy, muscle-bound, clear-sighted, and vital. What was the post about? She clicked the link underneath it. Maybe there'd be more fantasy-fodder like this man wherever it took her.

There *was* more fantasy fodder. Regan wriggled happily. She had landed on a page that showcased four men. Brothers, she saw, looking more closely—two of them identical twins. Each one seemed to represent a different branch of the United States military. Were they models? Was this some kind of recruitment ploy?

Practical Wives Wanted read the heading at the top. Regan nearly spit out a sip of her wine. Wives Wanted? Practical ones? She considered the men again, then read more.

Looking for a change? the text went on. *Ready for a real challenge? Join four hardworking, clean living men and help bring our family's ranch back to life.*

Skills required—any or all of the following: Riding, roping, construction, animal care, roofing, farming, market gardening, cooking, cleaning, metalworking, small motor repair…

The list went on and on. Regan bit back at a laugh which quickly dissolved into giggles. Small engine repair? How very romantic. Was this supposed to be satire or was it real? It was certainly one of the most intriguing things she'd seen online in a long, long time.

Must be willing to commit to a man and the project. No weekends/ no holidays/ no sick days. Weaklings need not apply.

Regan snorted. It was beginning to sound like an employment ad. Good luck finding a woman to fill those conditions. She'd tried to find a suitable man for years and came up with Erik—the perennial mooch who'd finally admitted just before Christmas that he liked her old Village apartment more than he liked her. That's why she planned to get pregnant all by herself. There wasn't anyone worth marrying in the whole city. Probably the whole state. And if the men were all worthless, the women probably were, too. She reached for her wine without turning from the screen, missed, and nearly knocked over her glass. She tried again, secured the wine, drained the glass a third time and set it down again.

What she would give to find a real partner. Someone strong, both physically and emotionally. An equal in intelligence and heart. A real man.

But those didn't exist.

If you're sick of wasting your time in a dead-end job, tired of tearing things down instead of building something up, or just ready to get your hands dirty with clean, honest work, write and tell us why you'd make a worthy wife for a man who has spent the last decade in uniform.

There wasn't much to laugh at in this paragraph. Regan read it again, then got up and wandered to the kitchen to top up her glass. She'd never seen a singles ad like this one. She could see why it was going viral. If it was real, these men were something special. Who wanted to do clean, honest work these days? What kind of man was selfless enough to serve in the military instead of sponging off their girlfriends? If she'd known there were guys like this in the world, she might not have been so quick to schedule the artificial insemination appointment.

She wouldn't cancel it, though, because these guys couldn't be for real, and she wasn't waiting another minute to start her family. She had dreamed of having children ever since she was a child herself and organized pretend schools in her backyard for the neighborhood little ones. Babies loved her. Toddlers thought she was the next best thing to teddy bears. Her co-workers at the bank had never appreciated her as much as the average five-year-old did.

Further down the page there were photographs of the ranch the brothers meant to bring back to life. The land was beautiful, if overgrown, but its toppled fences and sagging buildings were a testament to its neglect. The photograph of the main house caught her eye and kept her riveted, though. A large gothic structure, it could be beautiful with the proper care. She could see why these men would dedicate themselves to returning it to its former glory. She tried to imagine what it would be like to live on the ranch with one of them, and immediately her body craved an open sunny sky—the kind you were hard pressed to see in the city. She sunk into the daydream, picturing herself sitting on a back porch sipping lemonade while her cowboy worked and the baby napped. Her husband would have his shirt off while he chopped wood, or mended a fence or whatever it was ranchers did. At the end of the day they'd fall into bed and make love until morning.

Regan sighed. It was a wonderful daydream, but it had no bearing on her life. Disgruntled, she switched over to Netflix and set up a foreign film. She fetched the bottle of wine back to bed with her and leaned against her many pillows. She'd managed to hang her small flatscreen on the opposite wall. In an apartment this tiny, every piece of furniture needed to serve double-duty.

As the movie started, Regan found herself composing messages to the military men in the Wife Wanted ad, in which she described herself as trim and petite, or lithe and strong, or horny and good-enough-looking to do the trick.

An hour later, when the film failed to hold her attention, she grabbed her laptop again. She pulled up the Wife Wanted page and reread it, keeping an eye on the foreign couple on the television screen who alternately argued and kissed.

Crazy what some people did. What was wrong with these men that they needed to advertise for wives instead of going out and meeting them like normal people?

She thought of the online dating sites she'd tried in the past. She'd had some awkward experiences, some horrible first dates, and finally one relationship that lasted for a couple of months before the man was transferred to Tucson and it fizzled out. It hadn't worked for her, but she supposed lots of people found love online these days. They might not advertise directly for spouses, but that was their ultimate intention, right? So maybe this ad wasn't all that unusual.

Most men who posted singles ads weren't as hot as these men were, though. Definitely not the ones she'd met. She poured herself another glass. A small twinge of her conscience told her she'd already had far too much wine for a single night.

To hell with that, Regan thought. As soon as she got

pregnant she'd have to stay sober and sane for the next eighteen years. She wouldn't have a husband to trade off with—she'd always be the designated driver, the adult in charge, the sober, wise mother who made sure nothing bad ever happened to her child. Just this one last time she was allowed to blow off steam.

But even as she thought it, a twinge of fear wormed through her belly.

What if she wasn't good enough?

She stood up, strode the two steps to the kitchenette and made herself a bowl of popcorn. She drowned it in butter and salt, returned to the bed in time for the ending credits of the movie, and lined up *Pride and Prejudice* with Colin Firth. Time for comfort food and a comfort movie. *Pride and Prejudice* always did the trick when she felt blue. She checked the Wife Wanted page again on her laptop. If she was going to pick one of the men— which she wasn't—who would she choose?

Mason, the oldest, due to leave the Navy in a matter of weeks, drew her eye first. With his dark crew cut, hard jaw and uncompromising blue eyes he looked like the epitome of a military man. He stated his interests as ranching—of course—history, natural sciences and tactical operations, whatever the hell that was. That left her little more informed than before she'd read it, and she wondered what the man was really like. Did he read the newspaper in bed on Sunday mornings? Did he prefer lasagna or spaghetti? Would he listen to country music in his truck or talk radio? She stared at his photo, willing him to answer.

The next two brothers, Austin and Zane, were less fierce, but looked no less intelligent and determined. Still, they didn't draw her eye the way the way Mason did. Colt, the youngest, was blond with a grin she bet drew women like flies. That one was trouble, and she didn't need trouble.

She read Mason's description again and decided he was the leader of this endeavor. If she was going to pick one, it would be him.

But she wasn't going to pick one. She had given up all that. She'd made a promise to her imaginary child that she would not allow any chaos into its life. No dating until her baby wore a graduation gown, at the very least. She felt another twinge. Was she ready to give up men for nearly two decades? That was a long time.

It's worth it, she told herself. She had no doubt about her desire to be a mother. She had no doubt she'd be a great mom. She was smart, capable and had a good head on her shoulders. She was funny, silly and patient, too. She loved children.

She was just lousy with men.

But that didn't matter anymore. She pushed the laptop aside and returned her attention to *Pride and Prejudice*, quickly falling into an old drinking game she and Laurel had devised one night that required taking a swig of wine each time one of the actresses lifted her eyebrows in polite surprise. When she finished the bottle, she headed to the tiny kitchenette to track down another one, trilling, "Jane! Elizabeth!" at the top of her voice along with Mrs. Bennett in the film. There was no more wine, so she switched to tequila.

By the time Elizabeth Bennett discovered the miracle of Mr. Darcy's palace-sized mansion, and decided she'd been too hasty in turning down his offer of marriage, Regan had decided she too needed to cast off her prejudices and find herself a man. A hot hunk of a military man. She grabbed the laptop, fumbled with the link that would let her leave Mason Hall a message and drafted a brilliant missive worthy of Jane Austen herself.

Dear Lt. Cmdr. Hall,

In her mind she pronounced lieutenant with an "f" like the Brits in the movie onscreen.

It is a truth universally acknowledged, that a single man in possession of a good ranch, must be in want of a wife. Furthermore, it must be self-evident that the wife in question should possess certain qualities numbering amongst them riding, roping, construction, roofing, farming, market gardening, cooking, cleaning, metalworking, animal care, and—most importantly, by Heaven—small motor repair.

Seeing as I am in possession of all these qualities, not to mention many others you can only have left out through unavoidable oversight or sheer obtuseness—such as glassblowing, cheesemaking, towel origami, heraldry, hovercraft piloting, and an uncanny sense of what cats are thinking—I feel almost forced to catapult myself into your purview.

You will see from my photograph that I am most eminently and majestically suitable for your wife.

She inserted a digital photo of her foot.

In fact, one might wonder why such a paragon of virtue such as I should deign to answer such a peculiar advertisement. The truth is, sir, that I long for adventure. To get my hands dirty with clean, hard work. To build something up instead of tearing it down.

In short, you are really hot. I'd like to lick you.

Yours,
Regan Anderson

On screen, Elizabeth Bennett lifted an eyebrow. Regan knocked back another shot of Jose Cuervo and passed out.

End of Excerpt

The Cowboys of Chance Creek Series:

The Cowboy Inherits a Bride (Volume 0)
The Cowboy's E-Mail Order Bride (Volume 1)
The Cowboy Wins a Bride (Volume 2)
The Cowboy Imports a Bride (Volume 3)
The Cowgirl Ropes a Billionaire (Volume 4)
The Sheriff Catches a Bride (Volume 5)
The Cowboy Lassos a Bride (Volume 6)
The Cowboy Rescues a Bride (Volume 7)
The Cowboy Earns a Bride (Volume 8)
The Cowboy's Christmas Bride (Volume 9)

The Heroes of Chance Creek Series:

The Navy SEAL's E-Mail Order Bride (Volume 1)
The Soldier's E-Mail Order Bride (Volume 2)
The Marine's E-Mail Order Bride (Volume 3)
The Navy SEAL's Christmas Bride (Volume 4)
The Airman's E-Mail Order Bride (Volume 5)

The SEALs of Chance Creek Series:

A SEAL's Oath
A SEAL's Vow
A SEAL's Pledge
A SEAL's Consent

About the Author

Cora Seton loves cowboys, country life, gardening, bike-riding, and lazing around with a good book. Mother of four, wife to a computer programmer/ eco-farmer, she ditched her California lifestyle nine years ago and moved to a remote logging town in northwestern British Columbia. Like the characters in her novels, Cora enjoys old-fashioned pursuits and modern technology, spending mornings transforming an ordinary one-acre lot into a paradise of orchards, berry bushes and market gardens, and afternoons writing the latest Chance Creek romance novel on her iPad mini. Visit www.coraseton.com to read about new releases and learn about contests and other events!

Blog:

www.coraseton.com

Facebook:

www.facebook.com/coraseton

Twitter:

www.twitter.com/coraseton

Newsletter:

www.coraseton.com/sign-up-for-my-newsletter

Made in the USA
San Bernardino, CA
29 June 2017

© Dr. Abdallah H. Al-Kahtany 2009

King Fahd National Library Cataloging in-Publication Data

Al-Kahtany, Abdallah H

Women's Rights: A Historical Perspective

ISBN: 9960-9441-5-8

L.D. No. 1424/3712
ISBN: 9960-9441-5-8

First Edition 2003
Second Edition 2009
ISBN: 9960-9441-5-8

Cover Design & Layout by C.P. Muneer Ahmed, Kerala, India

CONTENTS

Address of the author:

Abdallah H. Al-Kahtany
P.O. Box: 9012
King Khalid University
Abha, Saudi Arabia
E-mail: aalkahtany@gmail.com

DEDICATION

I dedicate this second edition of my book, Women's Rights: A Historical Perspective, to the man who was behind the publication of the first edition of this book. He is living in our world no more but his efforts in informing people about Islam are still very salient. I ask Allah to reward him abundantly for his great efforts and gather us with our Prophet in Paradise.

ACKNOWLEDGEMENTS

I am very grateful to Allah the Almighty for His guidance and infinite bounties. Without His generosity, inspiration and infinite bounties, I would be helpless.

My sincere thanks are due to those many people who helped in turning the compilation of this book into existence among whom are the one's below:

■ My sincere brother Dr. Abdallah Abu-Ishi for his effort in reviewing the final draft. His moving words of encouragement and guidance were of great help.

■ Sister Om Muhammad for her very accurate effort in spotting the smallest of mistakes and patience in following the thread of arguments. May Allah reward her for the tiring and the time consuming task!

■ My loving thanks to the women who inspired the writing of this book and were always there to give all the needed support and dua': my late grandmother, my mother Fatimah, my wife Aysha, my sister Amra, my two daughters Areej and Fatimah , and Mona, my sister in Islam.

INTRODUCTION

Different societies have now been forced to take a position regarding the stakes of their women. It is hardly ever mentioned in the literature that Islam had addressed the subject of women's rights over 1400 years, long before it became a serious preoccupation in many other cultures, especially in the west recently.

The issue of women's rights received much attention in western and western-like societies for the past number of decades. Only prophet Muhammad (S.A.A.W.), through Divine revelation, was able to restore dignity and rights to women who were living in very degrading circumstances centuries before women in other nations were given parts of their rights.

Many feminist writers are enthusiastic in condemning the treatment of Muslim Women. Sometimes, they mix between the pure Islamic teachings and the irresponsible personal or cultural practices of some Muslims. However, some may have been intentionally prejudiced due to the publicity their works receive and probably the high income they receive as revenues for the sales of their books. This business is prospering nowadays while the Islamic fundamental teachings are being unfairly attacked. Such works have not paid attention to the teachings of Islam on the subject. As a result, they make no attempt to distinguish between the behavior of some Muslims and of the religion of which they may be very ignorant.

Feminist scholarship would have done better by focusing on the miserable situation that women, children and the family are going through all over the world, including western countries. Regardless of the very tiring efforts by western women to win and secure their rights, recent statistics and academic research only expose frustrating results of molestation and discrimination against women and children. The unjust competition between men and women in a male dominated work world has had a negative result in the most important institution, the family. In modern societies, a woman is entitled to honor and respect only to the extent to which she succeeds in performing the functions of a man while at the same time exhibiting her maximum beauty and charm to the public. The result is that the role of the two sexes in contemporary societies is thoroughly confused[1] .

One of the main rationales behind assuming this search was the unjust misrepresentation of Islamic teachings regarding women by a number of writers. They only focused on excerpts that were taken out of both text and context. Or, they blamed unacceptable practices by some ignorant Muslims on Islam. Most of those writers have not objectively conducted serious objective comparative study regarding

---

1 - Maryam Jameelah. Islam in Theory and Practice. H. Farooq Associates Ltd: Lahore, 1983, p.85.

the position of women in the teachings of Islam and in other religions and ideologies. Via the information present in this research, the readers will be able to deduce by themselves the strong correlation between the genuine teachings of these sacred books and doctrines and the mistreatment that women have been experiencing in these societies over the ages. Simply, because women have been manipulated by man while being blamed on God; and therefore called 'Divine'. When it comes to Islam, the equation is reversed. The Islamic teachings are not reflected on the wrong practices by some Muslims' treatment of women. Nevertheless, they were blamed on Islam. Edward Said alluded to this unfair allegation by saying in reference to V. S. Naipaul's biased writings about Islam: "For Naipaul and his readers, 'Islam' somehow is made to cover everything that one most disapproves of from the standpoint of civilized and Western rationality.[2] "Allah did not give man the full liberty to legislate. He instead, provided very well defined guidance to protect human beings from going astray and hence violating others' rights.

The purpose of this book is to provide a historical overview of the rights of women in the major religions of the world. More attention will be given to the status of women in contemporary western societies with comparison to the Islamic view regarding women. However, I do not intend to provide an extensive account of such a novel topic but rather present a general framework in which a complete picture regarding women in a historical perspective can be drawn. ●

---

2 - Edward Said, Covering Islam. Vintage, 1997, p.8. Said has also mentioned that ' Assiduous research has shown that there is hardly a prime-time television show without several episodes of plenty of racist and insulting caricatures of Muslims and Islam in general.

Women in the Teachings of Hinduism

A recent report disclosed by the UN mentioned that women in India are facing a number of problems including malnutrition, poor health care and lack of education. This is reflected on the ratio of the number of men to women, 960 women for 1000 men[3] . Another problem is that men are demanding high dowry from the bride's family, which has put a lot of economical pressure on the bride's family[4] . Such unfair practice was one of the factors behind the escalating rates of infanticide. Female children face a higher probability of abortion at late pregnancy due to the ability to diagnose the sex of the baby via ultrasound. Selective abortion is also done because of preference to male babies. Female infanticide has become a common practice. As a matter of fact, the burning of the widow Sati alive after the death of her

3 - BBC online, 2/7/2000
4 - Fred Plog and Daniel G. Bates. Cultural Anthropology. New York: Knopf, 1982, p. 209.

husband is part of the Hindu teachings that has been practiced against women through history. It was very prevalent
in India until the British government prohibited it in 1930.

In his book Modern Hinduism, Wilkins (1975) asserted
that Rashtra women in Hinduism would never acquire liberty whatsoever. Simply, because the highly respected teachings of the Hindu Avtar, Manu, that is called Dharma Shastra
ordains that:

> By a girl, or by a young woman, or
> by a woman advanced in years,
> nothing must be, even in the dwell-
> ing-place, according to her mere
> pleasure. In childhood, a female
> must be dependent on her mere fa-
> ther, in youth on her husband, her
> lord (husband) being dead, on her
> sons. A woman must not seek inde-
> pendence. (Dharma Shastra, Ch. V.
> pp. 162-3)[5]

According to Manu's teachings, there are certain types
of beings who do not deserve any rights

> Three persons, a wife, a son and a
> slave, are declared by law to have
> in general no wealth of their own. The
> wealth, which they may earn, is
> regularly acquired for the man to
> whom they belong.[6]

Women in Manu's teachings are even denied the right

---

5 - W. J. Wilkins, Modern Hinduism. London, 1975, p. 180.
6 - George Buhlerg, The Law of Manu. Motilal Banarsidass: Delhi, 1982,
p.326, Chapter VIII, verse 416.

to worship Hindu gods in their own name, they must pray in their husbands' names.

> The wife is forbidden the comfort of approaching the gods in her own name. No sacrifice is allowed to women apart from their husbands, no religious rite, no fasting.[7]

They do not seem to have a personality of their own. They are just attached to man. They are also not allowed to read religious books. According to the Dharma Shastra of Manu,

> For women no (sacramental) rite (is performed) with sacred texts, thus the law is settled; women who are destitute of strength and destitute of (the knowledge of) Vedic texts, (are as impure as) falsehood (itself), that is a fixed rule.[8]

In accordance with these teachings, The Dalit Voice, 1-15 of February, 1994 reported that Shankarachari of Puri Swami Nischalanda publicly stopped a woman from reciting verses of the Vedas at a gathering in Calcutta on January 16th, 1994.[9]

The strict caste system imposed by the Brahmins (the learned Hindu priests and upper caste) has resulted in the degradation of other castes. Women were affected the most, especially those of lower casts. Dr. Chatterjee (1993) re-

---

7 - Wilkins, p. 181.
8 - Buhlerg, p. 330, Chapter IX, verse 18.
9 - In M. J. Fazlie, Hindu Chauvinism and Muslims in India. Abul Qassim Publishing House: Jeddah, 1995, p. 51.

ferred to a report by the Times of India in which they referred to Devadasi system (religious prostitution) imposed by priests." Poor low-class girls, initially sold at private auctions, were later dedicated to the temples. They were then initiated into prostitution".[10] In another report The Times of India, in its issue of the 10th of November, 1987 has confirm the wide spread of Devadasi system. The system involves dedicating "young Harijian girls (Mahars, Mangs, Dowris and Chambhar) at childhood to a goddess, and their initiation into prostitution when they attain puberty continues to thrive in Karnataka, Andhra Pradesh and other parts of South India. This is due to social backwardness, poverty, and illiteracy".

The report mentioned that this system of prostitution flourishes as a result of conspiracy between the feudal class and the Brahmins. With their ideological and religious influence, they had control over the illiterate peasants and craftsmen, and prostitution was religiously sanctioned. The report referred to a study by two doctors from the Indian Health Organization that girls from poor families were sold after puberty at private auctions to a master who initially paid a sum of money to the families ranging from Rs. 500 to 5000.[11]

According to Vedic teachings, the women have no rights. They are just blessed to be subservient to their husbands.

> Whatever be the qualities of the man with whom a woman is united according to the law, such qualities even she assumes is like a river (united) with the ocean.[12]

---

10 - Dr. M. A. Chatterjee, Oh You Hindu Awake! Indian Patriots Council. 1993, p.28.

11 - Chatterjee, p.29

12 - Buhlerg, p. 331, Chapter IX, verse 22.

In another verse the Vedic teachings of Manu give no value, whatsoever, to women.

> Neither by sale nor by repudiation is a wife released from her husband; such we know the law to be, which the lord of creatures (Pragapati) made of old.[13]

Women according to authentic Hindu Vedic teachings are just like property that can be inherited and used by one's relative.

> The wife of an elder brother is for his younger (brother) the wife of a Guru... [14]

Manu implemented a similar law regarding the inheritance of the wife of the deceased husband by his

If the (future) husband of a maiden dies after troth verbally plighted, her brother-in-law shall wed her ... [15]

The rigid and unfair caste system has favored the Brahmins at the expense of other castes. Women of lower casts and their offspring have suffered in many ways. Receiving unfair share of inheritance was only one issue. According to Manu's law;

> The *Brahmana* (son) shall take four shares, the son of the *Kashatriya*

---

13 - Buhlerg, p. 335, Chapter IX, verse 46.
14 - Buhlerg, p. 337, Chapter IX, verse 57.
15 - Buhlerg, p. 339, Chapter IX, verse 69.

(wife) three, the son of the *Vaisya* shall have two parts, the son of the *Sudra* may take one share.[16]

Women according to Manu's Hindu teachings do not have the right to question their husbands or take legitimate measures to correct their husband's behavior.

She who shows disrespect to (a husband) who is addicted to (some evil) passion, is a drunkard, or diseased, shall be deserted for three months (and be) deprived of her ornaments and furniture.[17]

Unrestricted polygyny is legalized by Hindu teachings. Ram father has several wives in addition to many concubines.[18] Krishna, the hero of *Mahabharat* and an incarnation of *Vishnu* (Hindu god) had eight chief wives. He married another sixteen thousand and one hundred women on the same day.[19] Swami Vamdev of VHP, is in favor of issuing permission to Hindu males to have a maximum of 25 wives.[20]

> **Unrestricted polygyny is legalized by Hindu teachings. Ram father has several wives in addition to many concubines. Krishna, the hero of *Mahabharat* and an incarnation of *Vishnu* (Hindu god) had eight chief wives.**

---

16 - Buhlerg, p. 358, Chapter IX, verse 154. Deciding the unfair share for the offsprings of non-Baramana continues in verses 154- 161. If this the fate of the sons, we can imagine the fate of the daughters.

17 - Buhlerg, p. 341, Chapter IX, verse 78.

18 - Dr. Babasaheb R. Ambedkar, **Riddle of Rama & Krishna**, Bangalore, 1988, p.8, in Fazlie 1995, p.107.

19 - **Ambedka Statistical**, p.25.

20 - Fazile, p.107.

In Hindu society, on the other hand, the life of women whose husbands have perished becomes unbearable to the extent that they have to commit suttee, a form of suicide. Gustave le Bon wrote about this aspect of the Indian society by saying:[21]

> The immolation of widows on the funeral of their husbands is not mentioned in the Shastra, but it appears that the practice had become quite common in India, for we find references to it in the accounts of Greek Chroniclers.

This disdain for females is also seen in reports by the Indian media, which report that great numbers of young girls are buried alive because the females are viewed as an economic burden to their parents. **UNICEF** revealed that the phenomenon of infanticide is widespread in most of India's 60,000 villages where 70% of Indians live. 40% of girls at school age do not go to school. Thus, the vast majority of the 84% India's illiterate population is made of women.[22]

The Times reported the one-child-only policy applied in China nowadays has led many Chinese to desire a male child. Consequently, they abort female babies, kill their female toddlers or sell their older girls to mobile slave merchants. In this regard, the Chinese police have recently arrested 49 members of a gang whose job it was to buy, smuggle, and sell girls all over China. As a result of this savage treatment of female children in China, the Chinese Committee for State Planning reported that the number of males is 36 million more than the number of females.[23] O'Connell 1994 reported that

---

21 - Gustave le Bon. Les Civilization de Inde. P. 238.
22 - Al-Usrah, No. 51, Jumada II 1418.
23 - In The Family, 15, September. P. 7.

O'Connell 1994 reported that more than one million female babies were killed in China as a result of the one-child policy that was imposed by the state.

more than one million female babies were killed in China as a result of the one-child policy that was imposed by the state. [24]

In this section, a general view of some aspects of the status of women in Hindu teachings was briefly introduced. The complex caste system that divides people into certain socio-economic categories with unequal rights has very much affected the position of women in the Hindu teachings. I am turning my focus on the image and status of women in the Old Testament. The following section will bring into perspective the way women are presented in the Old Testament.

●

---

24 - In Zedrikly 1997, p20.

B Women in the Old Testament

The image of women in the Old Testament is not flattering. Many Old Testament verses represent women in the most evil image. In one place, they are shown as the source of deception, which led to the calamities of mankind. Eve was blamed as the one who persuaded Adam to eat from the forbidden tree with the result that Adam and his progeny were banished from paradise. This sin of disobeying the orders of God has resulted in what is known as the Original Sin and the Christian dogma of redemption through Christ, 'the savior'.

This perception of Eve as temptress in the Bible has resulted in an extremely negative impact on women throughout the Judo-Christian tradition. All women were believed to have inherited from their mother, the Biblical Eve, both her guilt and her guile. Consequently, they were all untrustworthy, morally inferior, and wicked. Menstruation, pregnancy, and childbearing were considered the just punishment for the eternal guilt of the cursed female sex. In order to appreciate how negative the impact of the Biblical Eve was on all her female descendants we have to look at the writings of some of the most important Jews and Christians of all time. Let us start with the Old Testament and look at excerpts from what is called the Wisdom Literature in which we find:

"I find bitterer than death the woman who is a snare, whose heart is a trap and whose hands are chains. The man who pleases God will escape her, but the sinner she will ensnare....while I was still searching but not finding, I found one upright man among a thousand but not one upright woman among them all" (Ecclesiastes 7:26-28).

In another part of the Hebrew literature which is found in the Catholic Bible we read:

"No wickedness comes anywhere near the wickedness of a woman.....Sin began with a woman and thanks to her we all must die" (Ecclesiasticus 25:19, 24).[25]

According to the OT, women have been punished for the sin of their mother, Eve, by carrying the burden of pregnancy and the pains of childbirth.

(Genesis3:16)

---

25 - Dr. Sherif Abdel Azeem, in http://www.twf.org/library/women ICJ.htm/

16 Unto the woman he said, I will
greatly multiply thy sorrow and thy
conception; in sorrow thou shalt
bring forth children; and thy desire
shall be to thy husband, and he shall
rule over thee. [26]

Such blame and sever punishment contradicts with
the Qur'anic reporting of responsibility for people's actions
regardless of their sex, male or female. As a matter of fact,
The Qur'an never blamed Eve alone for eating from the forbidden tree.

Al-A'raaf : 22-23

So, he (Satan) misled them (Adam and Eve) with deception . . . . And their Lord called out to them (saying): "Did
I not forbid you that tree and tell you: Verily, Satan is an open
enemy unto you?"

They said: "our Lord! We have
wronged ourselves. If you forgive us
not, and bestow not upon us Your
mercy, we shall certainly be of the
losers."

---

26 - What I found very consistent is that in many places in the Bible
offspring are taken for their ancestor's sin. I will only quote a few inci-
dents.
Exodus 20:5
> For I the Lord of thy God am a jealous God.
> Visiting the iniquity of the father upon the
> children unto the third and fourth genera-
> tion. (Reiterated in Exodus 34:7)
Deuteronomy 23:2
> A bastard shall not enter into the congre-
> gation of the Lord; even to his tenth gen-
> eration.

The Qur'an emphasizes that each Person is personally responsible for his/her deeds.

> No person earns any (sin) except against himself (only), and no bearer of burdens shall bear the burden of another. Then unto your lord is your return, so He will tell you that wherein you have been differing. (Al-An'aam: 164)

The concept of The Original Sin is totally foreign to Islamic and responsibility teachings because of three reasons. One, it contradicts the uniqueness of every human being. Two, it is unfair to blame and put wrath on the whole of humanity because of the wrong doing of a person. Three, the concept of the Original Sin was a pretext for finding another problematic teaching which links salvation to atonement through Christ. The Qur'an rejects the fatalist view of the destiny of human beings and urges people to assume responsibility for their conduct and choices.

The Qur'an rejects the fatalist view of the destiny of human beings and urges people to assume responsibility for their conduct and choices.

Al-Israa': 14

> Whoever goes right, then he goes right only for the benefit of his own self. And whoever goes astray, then

he goes astray to his own loss. No one laden with burdens can bear another's burden. And We never punish until We have sent a messenger (to give warning).

Al-Nahel: 97

Whoever works righteousness, whether male of female, while he (or she) is a true believer (of Islamic Monotheism) verily, to him We will give a good life, and We shall pay them certainly a reward in proportions to the best of what they used to do (i.e. Paradise in the Hereafter).

Kendath (1983) reported that Orthodox Jewish men in their daily prayer recite "Blessed be God King of the universe that Thou has not made me a women." On the other hand, women thank God every morning for "making me according to Thy will."[27] According to the Jewish Talmud, "Women are exempted from the study of the Torah." Swidler (1976) mentioned that Rabbi Eliezer said: "If a man teaches his daughter Torah it is as though he taught her lechery."[28] This prohibition is due to the unbelievable fabricated stories regarding daughters and wives of the prophets that they might find in the scriptures.

Jewish Rabbis listed nine curses inflicted on women

27 - Thena Kendath, *Memories of an Orthodox Youth*. In Susannah Heschel, ed. **On being a Jewish Feminist**. New York: Schocken Books, 1983, pp. 96-7.
28 - Leonard J. Swidler, **Women in Judaism: The Status of Women in Formative Judaism**. Metuchen, N.J. : Scarecrow Press, 1976, pp. 83-93.

as a result of the Fall:

> "To the woman He gave nine curses and death: the burden of the blood of menstruation and the blood of virginity; the burden of pregnancy; the burden of childbirth; the burden of bringing up the children; her head is covered as one in mourning; she pierces her ear like a permanent slave or slave girl who serves her master; she is not to be believed as a witness; and after everything--death." [29]

Contrary to the Biblical teachings, The Qur'an does not view childbirth and pregnancy as a punishment for women but rather as an honorable duty that the mothers should be appreciated for.

The Qur'an does not view childbirth and pregnancy as a punishment for women but rather as an honorable duty that the mothers should be appreciated for.

> And We have enjoined upon man (to be dutiful and good) to his parents. His mother bore him in weakness and hardship, and his weaning is in two years - give thanks to Me and to your parents,- unto Me is the final destination. (Luqmaan: 14)

---

29 - Leonard J. Swidler, Women in Judaism: the Status of Women in Formative Judaism (Metuchen, N.J: Scarecrow Press, 1976) p. 115. (in Abdel Azeem).

By studying the verses from the Old Testament, the book in which both Jews and Christian believe, regarding the punishment of a rapist, one wonders who is really punished? Is it the man who raped the innocent woman or the woman who has been raped and violated? If this is the way dignity and chastity of women are perceived, what would prevent someone from looking for the best looking women in town, rape her, tell everybody about it, and then have the court force her to be his wife for the rest of her life? This is a quote from Deuteronomy regarding such a case.

According to the Old Testament, daughters inherit their father only if they have no brothers. Widows, mothers, and sisters are deprived of inheritance.

KJV Deuteronomy 22:29-30

29. Then the man that lay with her shall give unto the damsel's father fifty shekels of silver, and she shall be his wife; because he hath humbled her, he may not put her away all his days.

According to the Old Testament, daughters inherit their father only if they have no brothers. Widows, mothers, and sisters are deprived of inheritance.

KJV Numbers 27:6-10

6. And the Lord spake unto Moses, saying, 7. The daughters of Zelophehad speak right: thou shalt

surely give them a possession of an inheritance among their father's brethren; and thou shalt cause the inheritance of their father to pass unto them. 8. And thou shalt speak unto the children of Israel, saying, If a man die, and have no son, then ye shall cause his inheritance to pass unto his daughter. 9. And if he have no daughter, then ye shall give his inheritance unto his brethren. 10. And if he have no brethren, then ye shall give his inheritance unto his father's brethren.

I have briefly reviewed some of the teachings of the Old Testament regarding women. In the course of my research, I kept wondering how it was possible for so many immoral stories to be attributed to God's noble envoys, the prophets (peace and blessing of Allah be upon them all).

●

C Women in the Teachings of Christianity

In her book Islam and Christianity, Ulfat Azizusamad attributed the introduction of monogyny into Christianity, and hence admiring celibacy, to the negative attitudes many Christian religious leaders held towards women and marriage in general. St. Paul, the real founder of the current form of Christianity, regarded women as temptresses. He laid the entire blame for the fall of man and the genesis of sin on women. We find in the New Testament statements that underscore such negative attitudes towards women; among which are the following:

KJV 1 Timothy 2:11-15

11 Let the woman learn in silence with all subjection. 12 But I suffer not a woman to teach, nor to usurp authority over the man, but to be in silence. 13 For Adam was first formed,

then Eve. 14 And Adam was not deceived, but the woman being deceived was in the transgression. 15 Not withstanding she shall be saved in childbearing, if they continue in faith, charity, and holiness with sobriety.

In order to understand the reason behind the contempt of women in the West for many centuries, we need to analyze the extreme position canonized saints of Christianity held against women. Some of these teachings are listed below:

"Woman is a daughter of falsehood, a sentinel of Hell, the enemy of peace; through her Adam lost Paradise." (St. John Damascene, P.79)

"Woman is the instrument which the Devil uses to gain possession of our souls." (St. Cyprian, P.79)

"Woman has the poison of an asp, the malice of a dragon." (St. Gregory the Great, P.79)[30]

The supreme engineer of the New Testament, St. Paul, addressed women with a much more severe language.

"A woman should learn in quietness and full submission. I don't permit a woman to teach or to have authority over a man; she must be silent. For

---

30 - Ulfat Aziz-us-sammad, Islam and Christianity, Presidency of Islamic Research: Riyadh, 1984, p. 79.

Adam was formed first, then Eve.
And Adam was not the one deceived;
it was the woman who was deceived
and became a sinner" (I Timothy
2:11-14).

St. Tertullian was even blunter and more candid than
St. Paul, while he was addressing his 'best beloved sisters'
in the faith, he said:

"Do you not know that you are each
an Eve? The sentence of God on
this sex of yours lives in this age:
the guilt must of necessity live too.
You are the Devil's gateway: You are
the unsealer of the forbidden tree:
You are the first deserter of the divine law: You are she who persuaded him whom the devil was not
valiant enough to attack. You destroyed so easily God's image, man.
On account of your desert even the
Son of God had to die."

St. Augustine was faithful to the legacy of his prede-
cessors, he wrote to a friend:

"What is the difference whether it is
in a wife or a mother, it is still Eve
the temptress that we must beware
of in any woman......I fail to see what
use woman can be to man, if one
excludes the function of bearing children."

Centuries later, St. Thomas Aquinas still considered

women as defective:

> "As regards the individual nature, woman is defective and misbegotten, for the active force in the male seed tends to the production of a perfect likeness in the masculine sex; while the production of woman comes from a defect in the active force or from some material indisposition, or even from some external influence."

Azeem, as an expert in women rights alludes to some of the most prominent Christian reforms by stating:" the renowned reformer Martin Luther could not see any benefit from a woman but bringing into the world as many children as possible regardless of any side effects:

> "If they become tired or even die, that does not matter. Let them die in childbirth, that's why they are there"[31]

Again and again all women are denigrated because of the image of Eve the temptress, thanks to the Genesis account. To sum up, the Judaeo-Christian conception of women has been poisoned by the belief in the sinful nature of Eve and her female offspring".

Understandably, many Christian monks preferred the life of celibacy to getting married to women. Marriage was

---

31 - For all the sayings of the prominent Saints, see Karen Armstrong (a former Catholic nun), The Gospel According to Woman (London: Elm Tree Books, 1986) pp. 52-62. See also Nancy van Vuuren, The Subversion of Women as Practiced by Churches, Witch-Hunters, and Other Sexists (Philadelphia: Westminster Press) pp. 28-30.

looked at as a practice, which is too worldly. It will divert the person from devoting his full time to God. In modern times, this system of worship has proved to be fraught with problems. Very few people today are willing to embrace celibacy and join the priesthood. The number of young people seen in nunneries and monasteries is dwindling.

Following the Jewish tradition as represented by the Old Testament and having in mind that Prophet Jesus (SAAW) never prohibited polygyny, early Jews and Christians were polygnous. It was given as an option for those who can carry the responsibility of marriage and family life not for those seeking the pleasures of sex. Some sects of Christianity still practice

Very few people today are willing to embrace celibacy and join the priesthood. The number of young people seen in nunneries and monasteries is dwindling.

this tradition (i.e. the Mormons of Utah in the US). It is reported in the Old Testament that King Solomon (SAAW) had many wives.

KJV 1 Kings 11:1-8

> 1.But king Solomon loved many strange women, together with the daughter of Pharaoh, women of the Moabites, Ammonites, Edomites, Zidonians, and Hittites. 2. Of the nations concerning which the Lord said unto the children of Israel, Ye shall not

go in to them, neither shall they come in unto you: for surely they will turn away your heart after their gods: Solomon clave unto these in love. [Is it possible for the great prophet of Allah, Solomon, to disobey God in such an irresponsible manner?)3. And he had seven hundred wives, princesses, and three hundred concubines: and his wives turned away his heart. 4. For it came to pass, when Solomon was old, that his wives turned away his heart after other gods: and his heart was not perfect with the Lord his God, as was the heart of David his father. 5. For Solomon went after Ashtoreth the goddess of the Zidonians, and after Milcom the abomination of the Ammonites. 6. And Solomon did evil in the sight of the Lord, and went not fully after the Lord, as did David his father. 7. Then did Solomon build an high place for Chemosh, the abomination of Moab, in the hill that is before Jerusalem, and for Molech, the abomination of the children of Ammon. 8. And likewise did he for all his strange wives, which burnt incense and sacrificed unto their gods.[32]

32 - Much of what is said about Prophet Solomon (SAAW) in this excerpt from the Old Testament is considered to be false by The Teachings of Islam. A prophet of Allah will never turn to idolatry. The Jews consider Solomon not as a great prophet of God but merely a king.

Prophet Abraham had two wives, Sarah and Hagar. Luther, on one occasion, spoke of polygyny with considerable toleration and was known to have approved the polygynous status of Philip of Hesse.[33] So, why does current Christianity reject polygyny in contradiction with its holy books? Christian religious leaders who claimed certain prophetic powers and characteristics including revelation (direct verbal contact with God) intervened to change the laws of family relations for the benefit of men who did not want to bear the responsibility of marriage.

why does current Christianity reject polygyny in contradiction with its holy books?

Another reason behind the negative attitudes of Christianity towards the practice of polygyny is related to the historical contact Christianity had with the more advanced philosophy of the Greek-Roman culture. Christianity was influenced by their concepts of bizarre kind of strange monogyny. The majority of the population was considered as slaves who could be used freely. So, there is no need for any form of polygyny that would restrict such liberty of men and impose certain rights for women in the society. Many Greek philosophers regarded utility and happiness as the sole criteria for morality. They waged a vicious war against ethics and values that stand in the way of full satisfaction and pleasure in life. Man to them should be left to seek as much pleasure as he wants. There-

33 - J. Jones and B. Philips 1985, p.3.

fore, they perceived no value in Christian traditional demands for chastity.

Bear in mind that the negative impact of different extreme approaches towards institutionalized polygyny in Roman-Christian society (free Roman bohemian sex and refrain from marriage and the negative attitude towards women by Christian clergy) resulted in today's social disasters. These social ills include: the alarming rates of single mothers, sexual harassment, teenage births, children born out of wedlock, etc. Islam is the only universal way of life that provides a pragmatic, universal, workable and natural system and solution to the world's current dilemmas.

Islam is the only universal way of life that provides a pragmatic, universal, workable and natural system and solution to the world's current dilemmas.

Though it was common that women, children and old people did not participate in war, according to the teachings of The Bible their right to live is not protected. The slaying of women and children of the Israelites' enemies was considered a normal practice. Many biblical verses described the practice:

KJV Numbers 31:15-24

> 17. Now therefore kill every male among the little ones, and kill every woman that hath known man by lying with him.

18. But all the women children, that have not known a man by lying with him, keep alive for yourselves.

KJV Luke 19:26-27

27. But those mine enemies, which would not that I should reign over them, bring hither, and slay them before me.

KJV Ezekiel 9:4-7

4. And the Lord said unto him, Go through the midst of the city, through the midst of Jerusalem, and set a mark upon the foreheads of the men that sigh and that cry for all the abominations that be done in the midst thereof. 5. And to the others he said in mine hearing, Go ye after him through the city, and smite: let not your eye spare, neither have ye pity: 6.Slay utterly old and young, both maids, and little children, and women: but come not near any man upon whom is the mark; and begin at my sanctuary. Then they began at the ancient men which were before the house.

KJV 1 Samuel 15:1-3

3.Now go and smite Amalek, and utterly destroy all that they have, and spare them not; but slay both man and woman, infant and suckling, ox and sheep, camel and ass.

KJV Isaiah 13:15-16

15. Every one that is found shall be thrust through; and every one that is joined unto them shall fall by the sword.16. Their children also shall be dashed to pieces before their eyes; their houses shall be spoiled, and their wives ravished.

KJV Hosea 13:16

16.Samaria shall become desolate; for she hath rebelled against her God: they shall fall by the sword: their infants shall be dashed in pieces, and their women with child shall be ripped up.

Such verses probably have given the Serbs and the Zionists the legitimacy to kill women and children indiscriminately. The existence of such verses regarding the command to massacre even infants is what has hindered The Pope from renouncing the atrocities committed against Muslims women and children in Bosnia and Kosova.

No doubt those original Judeo-Christian teachings preached by prophets Moses and Jesus (peace and blessing be upon them) abhor such kind of practices and consider them acts of immorality, but unfortunately these principles of morality and chastity are not even implemented by people who claim teaching the word of God. Many have warned against the soaring of immoral practices under the

guise of personal free-
dom. At the time when
we hear of homosexual
priests and open mar-
riages, anything can be
expected since virginity
and chastity are looked
at as out of fashion and
as characteristics of
backwardness. I re-
member Edwin Cook's
(a former American
Surgeon General) re-

Edwin Cook's (a former American Surgeon General) response to a question on radio about the best way to stop the spread of AIDS and other sexually transmitted diseases; "MORALITY!" was the answer.

sponse to a question on radio about the best way to stop the
spread of AIDS and other sexually transmitted diseases; "MO-
RALITY!" was the answer. At a time when the feminists are
proceeding to demand full equality between men and women,
they have met with considerable opposition form many
women who are not in favor of 'substantial changes in traditional sex role distinctions. Phyllis Schlafly, for example, is a
vocal opponent of the Equal Rights Amendment and believes
that women could actually lose certain important rights as a
consequence. She also feels that women find their greatest
fulfillment at home with family .'[34]

Needless to say, the churches and their religious hierarchy have become corrupt and concerned with wealth and
fame more than morality. They care more about quantitative
evangelization through investing on the misery of the poor
and the agony of the sick. Instead, they should focus their

---

34 - in T. Sullivan, K. Thomson, R. Wright, G. Gross and D. Spady, Social
Problems: Divergent Perspectives. John Wiley & Sons: New York, 1980,
pp.456-7.

Phyllis Schlafly is a vocal opponent of the Equal Rights Amendment and believes that women could actually lose certain important rights as a consequence. She also feels that women find their greatest fulfillment at home with family .

message on combating immorality and re-instituting chastity and ethics. President Clinton's appeal for forgiveness after his denial regarding relations with the White House employee, Monica Lewinsky, is very similar to Rev. Jimmy Swagart's crocodile's tears to deceive more people and get more of their money. Diane Sawyer had shown in a number of series in her Prime Time on ABC TV that many of these televangelists' aims were merely accumulating massive wealth at the expenses of the deceived faithful. These very dangerous systems are flooding larger parts of the world and being exported to other parts of the world under the guise of human rights and liberalism.

Can God, the Merciful, The Compassionate and the all Forgiving say such verses and give such vicious commands as referred to God and the Prophets of God in the existing Bible? Definitely NOT! Unless, His is not the same god that has directed Muhammad (SAAW) not kill a child, a women or an old man but only those who fight in the battle field and cause aggression. I would not be unfair to say that such unbelievable views against women in Hinduism, Judaism and Christianity were behind many of the miseries that women have been facing throughout history, which led to the extremes of today's immorality, liberalism, feminism and secularism. ●

D Women in Contemporary Times

Maryam Jameelah reported that the first champions of the movement for women's 'emancipation' were no other than the very well known western thinkers, Marx and Engel. They were undoubtedly the founders of Communism that proved to be a disastrous system of life. Their communist Manifesto (1948) preached that marriage, home and family were nothing more than a curse which has kept women in perpetual slavery. Thus, they insisted that the women must be liberated from domestic servitude and achieve full economic independence through whole-time employment in industry. The main aim of those women liberation champions and other adamant supporters of feminism was to grant women as much freedom to indulge in illicit sex as the men through mixed education, employment outside the home side by side with men, social functions and courtship before marriage in semi-nude fashion, mixed social functions which include drinking, drug-taking and dancing.[35] This included

35 - Maryam Jameelah. **Islam in Theory and Practice**. H. Farooq Associates Ltd: Lahore, 1983, pp. 94-5.

the widespread use of contraceptives, sterilizations, and abortion to prevent unwanted pregnancies, at the expense of the women who carry the burden of emancipation. Families are broken. Children are neglected and abused. Morality has become an old unwanted commodity.

Many concerned intellectuals have openly uttered their concern regarding the unlimited personal freedom that has resulted in great damage to the society as a whole, and probably to humanity at large. Among those intellectuals is Max Lerner, an acknowledged American historian and columnist. In an article in the *Readers' Digest* as early as April 1968, he uttered his deep concern regarding the dramatic negative changes that took place under the guise of personal freedom by writing:

The Communist Manifesto preached that marriage, home and family were nothing more than a curse which has kept women in perpetual slavery.

> We are living in a Babylonian society, ... the emphasis is on the senses and the release of sexuality. All the old codes have been broken down. Until recently, the church, the government, the family and the com-

munity have dictated what can and cannot be expressed in public. However, now these institutions have been overrun by the demands of a mass society that demands to see and hear everything. Across the United States of America, audiences pack art houses and neighborhood theaters to watch the multiple orgasms of a seldom-clothed young Swedish actress in I, a Woman. Italian director, Michelangelo Antonioni breaks the taboo against head-on, total nudity in Blow-up. In Barbarella, a film built around the endless seductions of a French comic-strip heroine, Jane Fonda hops from one nude scene to the next in celebration of the erotic life. Portrait of Jason, a remarkable voyage into the twisted soul of a black, male prostitute, compresses in less than two hours all the raw language and candid corners of life that today find free expression in almost every independent American film. The Jesuit theologian, Father Walter J. Ong, says: 'We are going to have to live with a degree of freedom much greater than anything we've known in the past... "[36]

36 - Max Lerner, *Our Anything Goes Society-Where is it Going.* **Readers' Digest**, April 1968.

In the following part of this book, I will be simply summarizing some of the consequences that today's unrestricted liberalism has caused to the family, the society and to the whole world.

1. Infidelity

Infidelity and extramarital sex are becoming part of individual personal freedoms in most western and westernized societies. Fidelity in today's marriages has become idealistic. Such extramarital sex practices have caused many problems in the society at large. Abortion rates are escalating; more children are born out of wedlock. Social and psychological traumas have severely affected the family as a heaven for its members. One factor behind such extramarital practices is related to the imbalance in the number of men and women in most western communities.

According to **The National Opinion Research Center** (1995), 25% of American married men had sex partner(s), (from one to six), beside their wives during the past twelve months. During the same period, about 15% of American married women had other sex partners beside their husbands (from one to six). During their lifetime, American men usually have an average of six sex partners.[37]

The Clinton-Lewinsky drama may take place with ordinary people but is not expected of the commander-in-Chief of the most powerful nation on earth. It involved very outrageous sexual acts and discussed in the most disgusting way that parents had to keep their children away from watching their TV sets or listening to the horrible details of such immoral relations. Why is this taking place in a society that is in great need of family ethics and morality and where fatal

---

37 - Reported in **The Macmillan Visual Almanac**, 1996, p.104

Women's Rights: A Historical Perspective

diseases like AIDS are serious threats?

The answer is very simple. These immoral practices are expected to happen in any society that has lost its divinely revealed values and morals, which control the fragile relationship between women and men. Infidelity and other unchaste practices are expected to become the norm in societies that perceive morality, virginity and chastity as radical, backward and abnormal. The National Center for Health Statistics conducted interviews with 60,201 women in response to National Survey of Family Growth between January and October 1995. Only 10.5% of women interviewed did not have partners beside their husbands. The remaining 89.5% of women reported having extramarital relations.[38]

2. Teenage Births

As long as programs like "Dr. Ruth Live" are unleashed to teach open sex on the air and other similar programs, only horrible statistics like the following are expected. In 1990 alone about, 67% of teenage births were to unmarried mothers; this is excluding abortions. What is more disastrous is

---

38 - Abstract of the United States 1998, 118th edition. Issue October 1998, p.86.

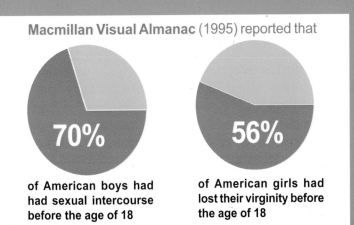

Macmillan Visual Almanac (1995) reported that

70% of American boys had had sexual intercourse before the age of 18

56% of American girls had lost their virginity before the age of 18

that in the majority of teenager births, the mothers are left alone to carry the financial and emotional responsibilities of raising the newly born babies. The males just abandon them both, and probably look for other easy preys. **Macmillan Visual Almanac** (1995) reported that 70% of American boys had had sexual intercourse before the age of 18, while 56% of the girls had lost their virginity by that age.

Men and women mix and mingle freely with one another with no reasonable restrictions in such a society where these kinds of relations between men and women are prevalent. Men and women could lock themselves alone in houses, offices or any other private locations; just as President Clinton did with Monica in the Oval office with the excuse that they were involved in serious work for the good of the nation. Western and western-like societies, have for long time, had blindly demolished moral principles to accommodate false values and principles deceived by the mirage of modernization and liberalism which pushed men and women into dark tunnels of adultery and hypocrisy.

3. Sexual Harassment

Equal Employment Opportunity Commission stated that reported sexual harassment complaints by female employees were 10,578 cases during the year 1992. In 1993, the number increased to be 12,537 cases.[39] The problem is not only restricted to the USA, but rather a global one, especially in societies that put no restrictions in men/women relations. According to a recent report by the **International Labor Organization** (ILO), entitled 'Combating Sexual Harassment at Work', November 1992, thousands of women are victims of sexual harassment at the workplace in the industrialized world every year. Between *15-30 percent of women questioned in surveys by ILO say they have been subject to frequent, gross sexual harassment. Of all women surveyed in* the United States, *42% of women reported some kind of sexual harassment.* The report included countries like Australia, Austria, Denmark, France, Germany, Japan and the United Kingdom. **The Labor Research Department** made a survey in 1987 in which 75% of women responding to the questionnaire reported that they had undergone some form of sexual harassment in their workplaces.[40] According to the Center of Health and Gender Equality (CHANGE) for Population Reports, 25% of women in Australia reported sexual abuse in the year 1997. The same percentage was reported in Switzerland during the year 1996. In Costa Rica, 32% of women surveyed reported some form of sexual harassment, while 8% of women studied in Malaysia reported that they had been sexually harassed.

---

39 - **The Macmillan Visual Almanac**, 1996 p.37
40 - The 1994 Information Please Almanac, InfoSoft Int'l, Inc.

Sexual abuse against women reported in various countries		
Country	Percentage (%)	Year
United States	42	1992
Australia	25	1997
Switzerland	25	1996
Costa Rica	32	1996
Malaysia	8	1996

4. Single Parent Family

Single parenting was not a common type of human social relations throughout history. It was only during the later part of the last century that this type of family relations has developed. Escalating rates of divorce and the birth of children to unmarried mothers have been the major factors behind the emergence of single parenting. The decay of morality in western and western-like societies because of very alarming rates of children born out of wedlock has reached about 50 % of all births in a country like Sweden. A more proper term for such a family type should have been mother headed family. Mothers head more that 90% of these single parent families.

> **Escalating rates of divorce and the birth of children to unmarried mothers have been the major factors behind the emergence of single parenting.**

The UK has occupied the highest rank in the number of single parent families in the whole of Europe. The Times issue of the 27th of September

1991, reported that the percentage of single parent families has doubled during the nineties; 16.7% in comparison to 8.3% during the early seventies. Women compose 90% of these families. Similar situations were also reported in Australia.[41] Jean Lewis (1992) has blamed the escalating number of single parent families on three emerging social changes: (1) fast increase in the number of working women outside the home, (2) escalating rates of divorce during the 70's & 80's and (3) the dramatic increase in the birth of illegitimate children.[42]

5. Violence against Women and Children

Violence in the family against women and children in particular has greatly increased. Though such a problem is not confined to Western societies, it has become the norm of life. In the US, for example, more than two million women have reported to the police violent aggression by a husband or a partner. Aburdene and Naisbitt (1993) have also stated that four women are beaten to death on a daily basis in the US.[43] One in five women victimized by their spouses or exspouses report they had been victimized over and over again by the same person.[44]

The following report by National Crime Victimization Survey Report summarizes the magnitude of violence against women in the US.

A study of violence against women shows that two-thirds of these at-

---

41 - Prof. Shatha S. Zedrikly, **Muslim Women and Contemporary Challenges**. Majdalawi Press: Amman, 1997, p. 95.
42 - Zedrikly, p. 95.
43 - In Zedrikly, p.97.
44 - The Basics of Batterer Treatment, Common Purpose, Inc., Jamaica Plain, MA

tacks were committed by someone the victim knew--such as a husband, boyfriend, other family member or acquaintance--a much higher figure than for men.

The survey, conducted by the Justice Department's Bureau of Justice Statistics, found approximately 2.5 million of the nation's 107 million females 12 years old and older were raped, robbed or assaulted in a typical year, or were the victim of a threat or an attempt to commit such a crime. Twenty-eight percent of the offenders were intimates, such as husbands or boyfriends, and another 39 percent were acquaintances or relatives . . .. The findings were drawn from more than 400,000 interviews conducted between 1987 and 1991.

The report pointed out that although violent crimes against males have decreased since the Bureau of Justice Statistics started its annual victimization surveys in 1973, the rate against females has remained relatively constant . .

Although black females were more than twice as likely as were white females to be robbery victims, there were no significant racial differences in per capita rates among female victims of rape or assault .[45]

Senator Joseph Biden reported that nationally, 50 percent of all homeless women and children are on the streets because of violence in the home.[46] Bennett and La Violette (1993) estimated around four million women report experiencing some kind of physical assault yearly. This takes place at a time where only half a million car accidents take place. Seventy five percent of violence takes place because the woman asks for divorce.[47]

According to United Nations' 1991 Report on Women in India, the social custom that the bride's family should pay dowry to the bridegroom has proven to

In India about 1786 women were killed because of falling short of meeting the dowry demands of their husbands, in the year 1987 alone.

work against promoting harmony in the marriage. Many men demand high dowry and valuable gifts even after marriage. When the families of poor women cannot meet the demand of the greedy husbands, they face brutal and sometimes deadly assaults. In the year 1987 alone, about 1786 women

---

45 - Single copies of the BJS National Crime Victimization Survey Report, "Violence Against Women" (NCJ-145325)

46 - Senator Joseph Biden, U.S. Senate Committee on the Judiciary, Violence Against Women: Victims of the System, 1991.

47 - In Zedrikly, p. 97.

were killed because of falling short of meeting the dowry demands of their husbands.[48]

The social problem of violence against women in such very large and increasing scales is not peculiar to the US but rather a common phenomenon in other western and western-like societies. In Austria, 59% of divorce cases were blamed on violence within the household during the year 1984.[49] During the year 1992, Aburdene and Nasibit (1993) mentioned that 50% of women were killed in England by their husbands or partners.[50] All these reported atrocities taking place made only 22% of the abused women in the same year. It is estimated that 88% of the cases of violence against women went unreported.[51]

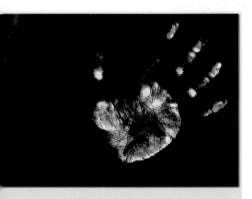

It is estimated that 88% of the cases of violence against women went unreported.

According to Russian government records, in the year 1993 alone, "14,500 Russian women were murdered by their husbands. Another 56.400 were disabled or seriously injured." Domestic violence statistics of crimes against women in England and the United States are alarming." According

---

48 - The United Nations Report on women in India, 1991.
49 - Zedrikly, p. 97.
50 - Zedrikly, p. 97.
51 - **Population Reports**, Vol. XXVII, No.4, Dec. 1999.

The treatment of women and children in present secularist societies - whether in America, Europe, India, Russia, China or even Muslim societies that does not apply Islam in their lives- is very similar to that of the pre-Islamic society (jahiliyah). Islam came to abolish the abuse of women and children and to restore dignity to women, young and old alike.

to Home Office Research, 18 percent of homicides in England and Wales are of wives killed by their husbands, with a quarter of all recorded violent crimes blamed on domestic violence."[52]

The treatment of women and children in present secularist societies - whether in America, Europe, India, Russia, China or even Muslim societies that does not apply Islam in their lives- is very similar to that of the pre-Islamic society

---

52 - James Meek. "Moscow wakes up to the toll of violence in the home" **The Guardian**, Thursday, June 22, 1995.

(jahiliyah). Islam came to abolish the abuse of women and children and to restore dignity to women, young and old alike.

Because of the social chaos that is taking place in many societies of the world, abuse is not only directed towards the weak members of the society as indicated above but rather towards those in charge of educating and disciplining. Based on a report by the Carnegie Foundation, the percentage of teachers in the U.S. who say that they have been verbally abused was 51%. As for those who have been threatened with injury, the proportion was 16% but those who have been physically attacked were 7%.[53]

---

53 - **The Macmilan Visual Almanac**. 1996 (PP. 367)

E Islamic View of Women

The Muslim view of women has been so misrepresented in the West that it is still a prevalent idea in Europe and America that Muslims think that women have no souls! In the Holy Qur'an no difference whatsoever is made between the sexes in relation to Allah; both are promised the same reward for good, the same punishment of evil conduct.[54]

> "Verily the men who surrender (to Allah) and women who surrender, and men who believe, and women who believe, and men who obey and women who obey, and men who are sincere and women who are sin-

---

54 - Marmaduke Pickthall. .The Relation of the Sexes 1925 lecture on the "pitiful condition of Muslim womanhood" in www.islam for today.com

cere, and men who endure and women who endure, and men who are humble and women who are humble, and men who give alms and women who give alms, and men who fast and women who fast, and men who are modest and women who are modest, and women who remember (Him), Allah hath prepared for them pardon and a great reward." [Qur'an 33:35]

It is only in relation to each other that a difference is made - the difference which actually exists - difference of function. In a verse which must have stupefied the pagan Arabs, who regarded women as devoid of human rights, it is stated:

"They (women) have right like those (of men) against them; though men are a degree above them. Allah is Almighty, All-Knowing." [Qur'an 2:228]

Aburdene and Naisbitt (1993), two prominent feminist researchers, were astonished to discover that the Qur'an does not consider women of a lower status than men; as is the case in all other religious writings. They have come to realize that male-practices against women in the Muslim World are basically based on non-Islamic social customs or misinterpretation of Islamic teachings.[55] Carroll (1983) admitted that she was surprised to find out that the Muslim woman is the first woman in the universe to be recognized for her economical and legal rights. She also added that the family system in Islam was legislated 1400 years ago in or-

---

55 - Zedrikly, p. 97. Zedrikly, p. 39.]

der to protect the corner stone of the society, the family.[56] Reference to the role of men and women along with their rights are detailed in The Qur'an and in the teachings of prophet Mohamed.

1. Women in the Qur'an

The Qur'an spoke of the different roles women play in life. It, for the first time in history, established women's rights to inheritance, respect, and dignity. The Qur'an spoke of women's role in supporting the truth, in giving birth to prophets and in suffering. The Qur'an has also spoken about the agony of

Carroll (1983) admitted that she was surprised to find out that the Muslim woman is the first woman in the universe to be recognized for her economical and legal rights. She also added that the family system in Islam was legislated 1400 years ago in order to protect the corner stone of the society, the family.

women at the different walks of life and through history. Below are only very few excerpts that show to what extent such rights have been recognized in Islam.

The Qur'an introduces the Pharaoh's wife as an example for the faithful person who accepted all types of suffering for the sake of Allah.

Al-Tahrim: 11

And Allah has set forth an example for those who believe: the wife of

---

56 - Zedrikly, p. 97.

Firaun(Pharaoh), when she said: "My Lord! Build for me a home with You in Paradise, and save me from Firaun(Pharaoh) and his work, and save me from the people who are oppressors.

The Qur'an narrated in detail the story of Mary and her miraculous birth of Jesus Christ and how she responded to her people's (the Jews) accusation of being unchaste. In deed, a whole chapter of the Qur'an is named after her. Another long chapter of the Qur'an is titled 'The Women', An-Nisaa. The Qur'an has talked about the role of women in repentance and accepting the truth. For example the repentance of al-Aziz's wife regarding her accusation of Prophet Joseph. (Yusuf: 51-53).The Queen of Sheba's acceptance of Prophet Solomon's (SAAW) invitation to Islam was also mentioned in details in the chapter of An-Naml: 44.

Mary was accorded great respect in the Qur'an. In fact, a whole chapter was devoted to her fascinating story in contrast to the blasphemous accusations   mentioned in the Talmud about her and her son,[57] Prophet Jesus peace and blessings of Allah be upon him.

---

57 - R. Papa observed: This is what men say (regarding Mary), she who descended of princes and governors played the harlot with a carpenter 5.... Did the children of Israel sly with the sword among them that [referring to Jesus] were slain by them? ... [The Babylonian Talmud, The Soncino Press, London, p. 725 (106a-106b)].

"It is the tendency of all these sources (The Talmud and other Jewish sources) to belittle the person of Jesus by ascribing to him illegitimate birth, magic, and shameful death ... All of the Toledo editions contain a story of dispute which Jesus carried on with the scribes, who on the ground of that dispute declared him to be a bastard." The Jewish Encyclopedia (p.170).

Al-Imraan: 35-37

> (Remember) when the wife of Imran said: "O my Lord! I have vowed to You what (the child that) is in my womb to be dedicated for Your service (free from all worldy work; to serve Your Place of worship), so accept this from me. Verily, You are the All-Hearer, the All-Knowing."

> Then when she gave birth to her [child Maryam(Mary)], she said: "O my Lord! I have given birth to a female child,"-- and Allah knew better what she brought forth,--"And the male is not like the female, and I have named her Maryam(Mary), and I seek refuge with You (Allah) for her and for her offspring from Shaitan(Satan), the outcast."

> So her Lord (Allah) accepted her with goodly acceptance. He made her grow in a good manner and put her under the care of Zakariya (Zachariya). Each time he entered Al-Mihrab to(visit) her, he found her supplied with sustenance. He said: "O Maryam (Mary)! From where have you got this?" She said, "This is from Allah." Verily, Allah provides sustenance to whom He wills, without limit.

The Qur'an recognizes both men and women as spiri-

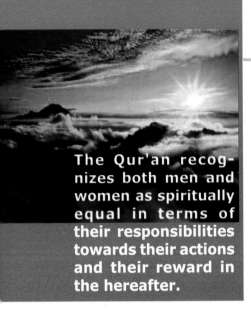

The Qur'an recognizes both men and women as spiritually equal in terms of their responsibilities towards their actions and their reward in the hereafter.

tually equal in terms of their responsibilities towards their actions and their reward in the hereafter.

Al-Nisaa: 124

And whoever does righteous good deeds male or female, and is a (true) believer {in the oneness of Allah (Muslim)}, such will enter Paradise and not the least injustice, even to the size of a speck on the back of a date-stone, will be done to them.

Al-Hadeed: 12

On the Day you shall see the believing men and the believing women: their light running forward before them and by their right hands. Glad tidings for you this Day! Gardens under which rivers flow (Paradise), to dwell therein forever! Truly, this is the great success!

Ar-Rum: 21

And among His signs is this that He created for you wives from among yourselves, that you may find repose in them, and He has put between you affection and mercy. Verily, in that are indeed signs for a people who re-flect.

2. Women in the Teachings of the Prophet

Prophet Muhammad confronted many unjust practices that were institutionalized by the pre-Islamic society against women. Men of that society were benefiting greatly from the roles they have prescribed for women. When the Prophet started preaching against the male treatment of women, the Quraishi's adamantly opposed him. Nevertheless, it was Divine Revelation that he had to pass onto people regard-less of their unjust interest.

Abu Hurairah reported that Prophet Muhammad said:

"Let him be a loser, let him be a loser, let him be a loser." Someone said, "Who is he, Oh Messenger of Allah? He said, "The one who has lived to see his parents or one of them and did not enter paradise."

Jabir said I heard the Messenger of Allah saying:

"The one who is deprived of kind-ness is deprived of goodness ."[58]

Anas Ibn Malik said that the Messenger of Allah had said:

"Whoever brings up two daughters, he and I will come side by side in the Day of Judgment… "[59]

---

58 - Narrated by Muslim, 1758, P. 469.
59 - Narrated by Muslim, 1761, P. 465.

3. Women and Education

Right to Education in Islam was granted hundreds of years ago while most prestigious schools of the world denied it.

Abu Saeed Al-Khudri reported that some women requested the Prophet to fix a day for them as the men were taking most of his time. On that he promised them to devote a day for teaching them... [60]

Seager and Olson 1986 reported that most universities in western countries waited very long before admitting female students. Madam Curie was refused membership in the French Academy of Science, though she was the first female professor in The Sorbonne in 1911.

In another hadeeth, it was reported that the Prophet had said: "Seeking knowledge is incumbent on every Muslim"

Seager and Olson 1986 reported that most universities in western countries waited very long before admitting female students. Madam Curie was refused membership in the French Academy of Science, though she was the first female professor in The Sorbonne in 1911. We have got to bear in mind that she was awarded the Noble Prize in 1903. [61]

---

60 - Narrated by Al-Bukhari, **The Book of Knowledge**, Hadeeth # 87, p. 97.
61 - McGrayne,1993 in Zerekly 60-61

4. Polygyny in Islam

People sometimes talk as if polygyny were an institution of Islam. It is no more an institution of Islam than it is of Christianity (it was the custom in Christendom for centuries after Christ) but it is still an existing human tendency to be reckoned with, and in the interests of men and women (women chiefly), to be regulated. Strict monogamy has never really been observed in Western lands, but for the sake of the fetish of monogamy, a countless multitude of women and their children have been sacrificed and made to suffer cruelty. Islam destroys all fetishes, which always tend to outcast numbers of God's creatures. In Europe, side by side with woman worship, we see the degradation and despair of women.

In Arabia, the lot of poor widows was particularly hopeless prior to the coming of Islam. The Holy Qur'an sanctions the remarriage of widows. It legalizes divorce and marriage from another husband, thus transforming marriage from a state of bondage for the women to a civil contract between equals, terminable by the will of either party (with certain restrictions, greater in women's case for natural reasons, intended to make people reflect seriously before deciding upon separation) and by death. The Prophet, when he was the sovereign of Arabia, married several windows, in order to destroy the old contempt for them and to provide for them as ruler of the State.[62]

Islam is the only religion limiting the number of permissible wives to four. To this fact John Esposito, a renowned professor of religion and international affairs and Islamic studies at Georgetown University, writes:

---

62 - Pickthall, www.Islam for today.com

Although it is found in many religious and cultural traditions, polygamy (or more precisely polygyny) is most often identified with Islam in the minds of Westerners. In fact, the Qur'an and Islamic law sought to control and regulate the number of spouses rather than give free license. In a society where there no limitations existed, Muslims were not told to marry four wives but instead to marry no more than four. The Qur'an permits a man to marry up to four wives, provided he can support and treat them equally. Muslims regard this Qura'nic command (4:3) as strengthening the status of women and the family, for it sought to ensure the welfare of single women and widows in a society whose male population was diminished by warfare, and to curb unrestricted polygamy.[63]

The idea of limited polygyny was introduced by the Qur'an as a solution to social dilemmas like the increased number of widows and fatherless orphans following wars. It also plays a great role satisfying the natural needs of a large sector of people, especially in societies where the number of women is exceeding that of men.

An-Nisa: 3

"And if you fear you will not be just to

---

63 - John L. Esposito. Islam: The Straight Path. Oxford: Oxford University Press, 1988, p.97.

the orphans, then marry what is good for you among the women- two, three, or four. But if you fear that you will not be just [to them], then only one, or whom your right hands possess. That is more likely that you will not do injustice."

The idea of limited polygyny was introduced by the Qur'an as a solution to social dilemmas like the increased number of widows and fatherless orphans following wars. It also plays a great role satisfying the natural needs of a large sector of people, especially in societies where the number of women is exceeding that of men.

When this regulation regarding polygyny was firstly introduced, it was in reality a restriction to the unlimited polygyny the pre-Islamic Arabs used to practice. Though, the regulation gives men the right, for good reasons, to practice polygyny but they should adhere to the strict conditions and responsibilities behind it. Polygyny was restricted by Islam and not fully banned to satisfy the polygynous nature of men while restricting and severely punishing men who seek extramarital relations. Islam, by restricting polygyny and decreeing strict conditions regarding its practice, took a moderate stance between the unrestricted polygyny of the Old Testament and the practice of Romans, Persians and pre-Islamic Arabs and the unobserved celibacy that some latter Christian saints preached.

Therefore, to solve the problem of fatherless households, the Qur'an is encouraging men who can bear the responsibility and be just to take into their care the destitute families by marrying the eligible widows and female orphans who are victims of tragedies. One rationale behind this measure is to save the society in general from indulging into immoral practices either because of poverty or the natural sexual desire on the part of the unmarried women.

Open-minded people can accept natural and reasonable solutions to their problems while recognizing full right and legitimacy to the women and their children. In his book **Struggling to Surrender**, Jeffrey Lang, (1995), reported on a program aired on Public Television at that time investigating whether or not men were innately polygamous and women innately monogamous. In 1987, the student newspaper at the University of California, Berkley, polled a number of students, asking whether they thought men should be legally permitted to have more than one wife in response to a perceived shortage of male marriage candidates in California. To the surprise of many feminists, almost all of those polled approved of the idea. One woman even stated that a polygamous marriage would meet her emotional and sexual needs.[64] A segment of the Church, the Mormons, which has become one of the established churches in the United States, propagates polygyny among its increasing members.[65]

Jane Goodwin (1994), an American sociologist, thinks that many American women would prefer the status of a second wife rather than living a lonely life in a gloomy apartment in New York or Chicago in the society of *freedom*.[66] As a matter of fact, males in general continue to be protected

64 - Jeffrey Lang. **Struggling to Surrender**. Beltsville, Maryland: Amana Publications, 1995,pp. 162-3.
65 - T. Sullivan, K. Thomson, R. Wright, G. Gross and D. Spady, p. 658.
66 - in Zerekly 1997,p.80

by monogamy, especially in a society that does not punish extramarital practices, while prostitutes, call girls, mistresses, secretaries, models, actresses, store clerks, waitresses and girl friends remain their playground. In reality, polygyny is vehemently opposed by the male-dominated western society because it would force men to adopt fidelity.

Regardless of my opinion towards the issue of polygamy, Dr. Le Bon advocates: "A return to polygamy, that natural relationship between sexes, would remedy many evils; prostitution, venereal diseases, Aids, abortions, the misery of the illegitimate children, the misfortune of the millions of unmarried women and widows, resulting from the disproportion between the sexes and wars, even adultery and jealousy. "[67]

The Islamic system, when completely practiced does away with the dangers of seduction, the horrors of prostitution and the hard fate which befalls countless number of women and children in the West, as the consequence of unavowed polygyny. "Islam's basic principle is that a man is held fully responsible for his behavior towards every woman, and for the consequences of his behavior. If it does away likewise with much of the romance which has been woven round the facts of sexual intercourse by Western writers, the romance is an illusion, and we need never mourn the loss of an illusion.

Take the most widely read modern European literature, and you will find the object of man's life on earth is depicted as the love of women (i.e., in the ideal form as the

---

67 - Suayman A. S. A-Shaqasy." How Islam Elevated the Status of Women - III" A paper presented at the Muslim Sisters' Convention, Mombasa, and December, 1990. Published in Al-Islam 1991, Vol. 15, No. 4, p. 38.

love of one woman, the elect, whom he discovers after trying more than one). When that one woman is discovered, the reader is led to suppose that a "union of souls" takes place between the two. And that is the goal of life. That is not common sense - it is rubbish. But it is traceably a product of the teaching of the Christian Church regarding marriage. Woman is an alluring but forbidden creature, by nature sinful, except when a mystical union, typifying that of Christ and his Church has happened, thanks to priestly benediction".[68]

5. Who is Benefiting from Monogamy?

In polygyny, as presented by the Islamic family system, it is the husband who bears the full financial and other social responsibilities towards his wife or wives. Therefore, strict monogamy as practiced in western societies is in the interest of men. Jones and Phillips (1985) indicated that "some males self-righteously assert that monogamy is maintained to protect the rights of women. But, since when has the western male been concerned about women's rights? Western society is riddled through and through with socio-economic practices, which oppressed women and led to the upsurge of women's liberation movements in recent years, from suffragettes of the early nineteen hundreds to the ERAs of today. The real-

> In polygyny, as presented by the Islamic family system, it is the husband who bears the full financial and other social responsibilities towards his wife or wives. Therefore, strict monogamy as practiced in western societies is in the interest of men.

---

68 - Pickthall, www.Islam for today.com

ity is that monogamy protects the males' right to play around without any responsibility, since the incidence of infidelity among them is usually much higher than among females."[69]

Although many western women were caught up in the so-called sexual revolution, they are the ones who suffer the most from the side effects of contraceptives, the trauma of abortion and the shame of childbirth out of wedlock. In The United States alone, in every one thousand births forty-five were born to unmarried women between the ages of 15-44, in 1991 alone. This costs taxpayers more than $ 25 billion dollars in welfare payments.[70]

Mrs. Jones and Mr. Phillips (1985) talked about other logical reasons for the need of an institutionalized Polygyny. They mentioned that the preponderance of females in the world is an established fact. Infant mortality rate is much higher among boys. Women on the whole tend to live longer than men; not to mention the large number of young men who die daily in the various wars around the world. "However, the ratio varies from one country to another, women still outnumber men. Hence, there are more females competing for a diminishing number of males. Consequently, there will always remain a large segment of women unable to fulfill their sexual and psychological needs through legitimate means in monogamous societies. Their presence in an increasingly permissive society also contributes to the break down of western family structure."[71] From the brief discussion we had about the issue of polygyny, women seem to have a vested interest in legally institutionalized and rec-

---

69 - J.Jones and B. Philips. Plural Marriage In Islam. 1985, p. 5
70 - National Center for Health Statistics, in **The Macmillan Visual Almanac**, 1996, pp. 320-322
71 - J. Jones and B. Philips 1985, pp. 6-7.

ognized polygyny as acknowledged by Islam because of the obvious socio-economic protection it provides, as well as, the real life problems it deals with to satisfy both sexes.

6. Separation is Better

If it is true, as life experience suggests (and the advocates of woman's rights in Europe and America are never tired of declaring that women's interests are separate from those of men) that women are really happier among themselves in daily life, and are capable of progress as a sex rather than in close subservience to men, then the Islamic rule which makes the woman the mistress in her sphere does not discord with human nature. While every provision is made for the continuation of the human race, and while the relation of a woman to her husband and near kinsfolk is just as tender and as intimate as in the West, the social life of women is among themselves. There is no 'mixed bathing,' no mixed dancing, no promiscuous flirtation, no publicity. But according to the proper teachings of Islam, there ought to be no bounds to woman's opportunities for self development and progress in her own sphere. Therefore, there is nothing to prevent women from becoming doctors, lawyers, professors, preachers, merchants, … etc, but they should graduate in women's colleges and practice on behalf of women.[72]

Separation between men and women has been recognized to be of great benefit for women. As a matter of fact, this principle was adapted by The Pentagon as a solution to many problems including sexual harassment, without giving credit to Islam as the system of life that is propagating this practice to maintain morality and social peace and security. Nevertheless, Prince Charles has emphasized the great contributions Islam can provide the non-Muslim societies to over-

---

72 - Pickthall, www.islamfortoday.com

come their most serious moral and social problems, during a number of his speeches on Islam and the West

William Cohen, American Secretary of Defense, announced the first phase of a comprehensive plan to maintain a reasonable level of morality among male and female soldiers. The plan stressed the importance of constructing permanent partitions to separate male and female soldiers in the current mixed buildings. This is only a temporary solution until newly separate buildings are constructed. The Navy also issued a number of strict instructions that prohibit the presence of female and male navy officers behind closed doors. These instructions were presented as rules that should be respected by all soldiers, especially on board Navy ships. The Defense Secretary emphasized that the rationale behind such measures was to provide a reasonable level of privacy and security for members of the different sectors of Defense. Among these new regulations, the restriction of sleeping while wearing underwear or naked and those doors should be tightly locked during sleeping hours. They also forbid watching pornographic films in the presence of female soldiers, and imposed clearly detailed regulations regarding the type of clothes to be worn when swimming or when sun bathing.[73]

The question that we raise here is this: why are such regulations (that many would look at as radical and anti-modernization) imposed by the most modern country in the world? The answer is very simple: sexual harassment has reached an unbelievably alarming level and has become a threat to national security and morality. Thousands of complaints of sexual harassment by female employees rang an alarming bell. The American and other lawmakers around

73 - The Family, June 1998, Issue No. 59,p.3

the world should think seriously about imposing similar regulations at all governmental offices, including the White House, especially in the aftermath of the Clinton-Monica affair.

McGrayre, 1993[74] addressed the fact that separation in education is for the benefit of female students who experience unbearable harassment and pain at the hands of boys. Eight out of the nine female scientists who were awarded Nobel Prize were graduates of female only high schools.

The New York Times published, in May 1993, a report which was entitled *Separation Is Better.*[75] The report was written by Susan Ostrich who herself was a graduate of one of the few women's colleges in the U.S. It was a shock to most Americans to find that girls in female colleges achieve better academically than their counterparts at mixed colleges. She supported her claim with the following statistics:

1. Eighty percent of girls at female only colleges study science and math for four years, in comparison to two years of study in the mixed colleges.

2. Female school students achieve higher GPA than the girls in mixed schools. This leads a higher number of female students to be admitted to universities. In fact, more Ph.Ds were acquired by such female students.

3. According to Fortune Magazine

74 - in Zedrekly, 1997,72
75 - **The Family**. August, 1994, 14, P. 7.

one third of the female members in the boards of trustees in the largest 1000 American companies are graduates of female only colleges. To realize the significance of this number, we need to know that graduates of female only colleges make only 4% of the number of female college students graduating every year.

4. 43% of female professors with Ph.Ds in math and 50% of female professors with Ph.Ds in engineering were graduates of female only colleges.

Only Islam has the workable solutions to these complicated problems of immorality and destroyed family values. It provides a complete system of life, which grants dignity and happiness to all members of society by taking human needs into consideration and satisfying them in the most honorable and respectable way.

This is another evidence from the Western world itself that lends support to the validity and applicability of Islamic principles as universal laws guiding or regulating human behavior. The Indian politician and reporter, Kofhi Laljapa, concluded:
No other religion but Islam has the ability to solve the

> problems of modern life. Islam is indeed unique for that ... [76]

Only Islam has the workable solutions to these complicated problems of immorality and destroyed family values. It provides a complete system of life, which grants dignity and happiness to all members of society by taking human needs into consideration and satisfying them in the most honorable and respectable way. This complete system is not subject to man's manipulation in order to satisfy his temporal interest, but rather Divinely proposed to take into account human nature. In so doing, Islam sets clearly and strictly defined rules and rights for all members of the society, regardless of their race, sex and religion, based on a just system of mutual responsibilities and authority. Nevertheless, Islam is avoided and even looked at with suspicion because of a number of reasons: (a) the Jewish controlled media has great interest in picturing Islam as a savage religion that was not even good for the middle ages. *Jihad in America* and *The Siege* are only specimens of what the movie industry does to distort the image of Islam in the minds of people who have no true knowledge about Islam. Experts in Middle Eastern studies like the orientalists Bernard Lewis, Daniel Pipes and Judith Miller played an irresponsible role in inducing wrong attitudes about the genuine message of Islam in the minds of people who are in great need of its way of life. Nevertheless, many intellectuals were not deceived by this propaganda and were able to find their way to the truth, after a long search and after overcoming many hurdles. Jeffrey Lang (Professor of Mathematics at Kansas University) and M. Hoffman (the German Ambassador to Morocco)

---

76 - Emad Khalil. **They Said About Islam**, 1994, in The Islamic Future, 27, May 1994. P. 12.

are good examples. (b) A minority of Muslims enhances the already distorted image of Islam by their un-Islamic malpractices, which is greatly exaggerated and generalized by the already biased media. (c) The inability of concerned Muslims to present Islam in an attractive manner to the world and to clarify misconceptions and misunderstandings about its universal teachings.

Women of the West have had to agitate for themselves in recent years for simple legal rights, such as that of married women to own property, which has always been secured for women in Islam. They have had to wage a bitter fight to bring to the intelligence of Western men the fact that women's interests are not identical with those of men (a fact for which the Sacred Law makes full allowance.) Women in the West have had to agitate in order to obtain recognition of their legal and civil existence, which was always recognized in Islam. Their men secured the rights of women in Islam, and men will champion and secure what further rights they may require today in order to fulfil the spirit of the Shari'ah. In this emancipation, there will be no strife between the sexes. Therefore there is really no analogy with the case of women in the West.

●

F Western Women Accepting Islam

Regardless of the vicious politically motivated attack by some subjective western media against Islam (especially in issues related to the treatment of women) *The Daily Mail*, Dec. 2, 1993, p. 39, reported that more than 20,000 Britons were estimated to have accepted Islam as their way of life by that time. Most of them were middle class educated women. Why would these women accept Islam if they believed what the media was propagating? One of them reported that:

"Becoming a Moslem has transformed my life and brought me a lot of peace and contentment ...I do not see what I'd done as going backwards, I see it as liberation."[77]

Another revert who is a writer and the daughter a nuclear plant supervisor said in relation to the role of separation between men and women and the wearing of hijab:

"Unlike the confused messages of Western culture - which encourages women to look sexy, yet condemns them for provoking men to rape-*hijab* gave out a clear signal that women are not put on this earth to flaunt themselves."[78]

When Mrs. Sisly Catholy an Australian lady who embraced Islam along with her daughter was asked: "Why did you embrace Islam?" She responded by saying:

"First, I would like to say that I embraced Islam because I was a Muslim inside myself without knowing it. Since I was a child, I had lost my faith in Christianity for reasons. The most important one was that whenever I asked a Christian whether he is one of those called the clergy or the public about anything of the church. "You have to believe in them." At the time of believing in Christianity, I was influenced by what has been said to us that Islam was

---

77 - The Daily Mail, the 2nd of December 1993, p. 39
78 - **The Daily Mail**, the 2nd of December 1993, p 42

a joke. But when I read about it, the wrong ideas went away. It was not long when I started to look for some Muslims to ask them about the issues which were not clear to me. Here, the barriers between Islam and me were torn away. Whatever question I had, I received a convincing answer, the very opposite of that ... which I used to hear when I asked about Christianity. After a long reading and study, I decided, along with my daughter, to embrace Islam, and we named ourselves Rashidah and Mahmoudah."[79]

Lady Avenin Zainb Cophand, an English woman, was also asked for the reason she accepted Islam. She reported:

"... as my study and readings about Islam increase, my certainty that it is very distinctive from other religions increases. It is the most suitable religion for practical life and it is the most able one to lead humanity to the path of happiness and peace. So, I did not hesitate to believe that Allah, the Almighty is one, and that Moses, Jesus, Muhammad (peace be upon them) and those before were prophets who received revela-

79 - Bawani, 1984, pp. 134-6, in Khalid Al-Qasim. **A letter to a Christian**. Dar Al-Watan: Riyadh, 1995, p. 76.

tions from their Lord. ..We are not born sinful; neither do we need someone to take away our sins or to mediate between us and Allah, the Almighty. ... It does not have any of the complex heavy theological doctrines.... "[80]

Margaret Marcus, a former Jewish American intellectual and writer, candidly explained the rationale behind her acceptance of Islam after discussing her Reform Jewish up bringing in a totally secular society by saying:

I did not embrace Islam out of any hatred for my ancestral heritage or my people. It was not a desire so much to reject as to fulfill. To me, it meant a transition from a moribund and parochial to a dynamic and revolutionary faith content with nothing less than universal primacy.

Each new Muslimah has gone through a trial and accepted many challenges to surrender to Allah. Amira, an American girl from Arkansas is just one of them.

I was born to American Christian parents in Arkansas in the United States and that is where I was raised also. I am known as white-American to my Arab friends but alhamdolilah that Islam knows no color, race, or nationality. The first time I ever saw

---

80 - Bawani, 1984, pp. 130-1, in Khalid Al-Qasim. **A Letter to a Christian**. Dar Al-Watan: Riyadh, 1995, p. 75.

a Muslim was while I was in college at the University of Arkansas. I will admit that at first I stared at the strange clothing the Muslim women wore.... and could not believe that they covered their hair. But I am a curious person so I introduced myself to a Muslim girl in one of my classes the first chance I had. It was a meeting that would change the course of my life. I will never forget her. Her name was Yasmine and she was from Palestine. I would sit for hours and listen to her tell me about her country, culture, family and friends that she loved so much, but even more so was the love that she had for her religion, Islam. Yasmine had an inner peace about her like no one I had ever met. She would tell me stories of the Prophets (pbut) and about the one-ness of Allah (swt). This was when I learned that they didn't worship some other God; it was just that in Arabic, Allah meant God. Everything she told me made so much sense to me and was so pure. ...

In a report by the staff writer for the Christian Science Monitor, Peter Ford, titled 'Why European women are turning to Islam?" a French woman explained her raison d'être for accepting Islam:

Islam demands closeness to God. Islam is simpler, more rigorous, and it's easier because it is explicit. I was looking for a framework; man needs rules and behavior to follow. Christianity did not give me the same reference points.[81]

Haifa Jawad, a teacher at Birmingham University, indicates that some of the reasons behind European women acceptance of Islam are:

a. A lot of women are reacting to the moral uncertainties of Western society.

b. They like the sense of belonging and caring and sharing that Islam offers.

Karin van Nieuwkerk, who has studied Dutch women converts to Islam, argues that "there is more space for family and motherhood in Islam and women are not sex objects."

Sarah Joseph, an English convert to Islam, argues that "the idea that all women converts are looking for a nice cocooned lifestyle away from the excesses of Western feminism is not exactly accurate."[82]

---

81 - Peter Ford. "Why European women are turning to Islam?" **Christian Science Monitor**, December 27, 2004 edition, p. 1.
82 - Ford., 2004, p.1

CONCLUSIONS

In the previous discussion, I tried to draw a general picture regarding the way women were viewed by major religions and ideologies that have been having a great influence in the life of humanity. By doing so, I thought, we can have a historical as well as analytical framework through which we can have a better understanding of women's rights. The research relied on original sources of Hinduism, Christianity and Islam in order to investigate their teachings regarding the roles women were assigned and the treatments they deserve. I also touched upon the dramatic consequences as a result of misunderstanding the very essential role women play in maintaining a balanced and a healthy family and society. The harmonious and integrative roles of men and women have resulted in a fierce competition and individualist aspiration in fulfilling egocentric desires, out of which women turned out to be the great losers.

Women's emancipation through extreme feminism

and liberalism has backfired, caused more calamities, and added suffering in a world that is controlled by men. Indeed, it was those men who deceived women by pulling them out of their homes and cutting their family ties to be mistreated in low paying and unwanted jobs. They were given added burdens to bearing and rearing children and taking care of the family to be forced into cheap labor and to be forced to support themselves and their families. Margaret Marcus (now Maryam Jameelah) has reiterated such consequences by stating that:

> ...Yet this same propaganda insists that the emancipated women's primary duty is still her home! In other words, this means that the modern woman must bear a double burden! In addition to earning her own living in fulltime employment outside the home, she must at the same time somehow perform the near-impossible task of fulfilling all her obligations to her husband and children and keep a spotless house single-handed! Is this justice?[83]

When alluding to the catastrophic status the family had reached in Western and Western-like societies, especially in relation to the family and the type of abuse against women and children, I do not mean that other societies who follow the same pattern of unleashed liberty, dissolution from morality and rejection of authentic teachings of the Creator are immune against such ills. The cheap slogans of women's rights, emancipation and progress only serve as a smokescreen to obscure its real intentions. The movement

---

83 - Maryam Jameelah, 1983, p. 97.

for female emancipation in the Muslim world cannot but lead to the same catastrophe that has already happened elsewhere. Universal indulgences in illicit sexual affairs shock the wild beasts of the jungle. The inevitable results have been the destruction of home and families and indeed, the whole social framework, an epidemic of juvenile delinquency, crime and an atmosphere saturated with violence, unrest and lawlessness. The history of civilizations of the past is sufficient proof that when vice and immorality run rampant, no society can longer happily survive.[84]

I invite the respected readers to investigate by themselves the teachings of Islam at their original sources; not regarding women only but in encompassing the human life in general. Islam is the system of life that was designed by the Creator to provide guidance for humanity and to attain happiness in this life and in the hereafter.

This book is concluded with an excerpt from Prince Charles' speech about 'Islam and the West' at the Oxford Center for Islamic Studies:

> Another obvious western prejudice is to judge the position of women in Islam by extreme cases. The rights of Muslim women to property and inheritance, to some protection if divorced, and to the conducting of business were rights prescribed by the Qur'an 1400 years ago. In Britain, at least some of these were novel to even my grandmother's generation.[85]   ●

---

84 - Maryam Jameelah, 1983, p. 99.
85 - Prince Charles, "Islam and the West." **Arab News**, October 27, 1993. In R. Hill Abdulsalam. **Women's Ideal Liberation**. Abul-Qasim Publishing House: Jeddah, pp. 41-3.

REFERENCES

The Glorious Qur'an

Abdulsalam, R. Hill. *Women's Ideal Liberation*. Abul-Qasim Publishing House: Jeddah, 1993.

Abstract of the United States 1998, 118th edition. Issue October 1998

Al-BuKhari, The Book of Knowledge.

Al-Qasim, Khalid. *A letter to a Christian*. Dar Al-Watan: Riyadh, 1995

Ambedkar, Dr. Babasaheb R. *Riddle of Rama & Krishna*, Bangalore, 1988

Aziz-us-sammad, Ulfat. Islam and Christianity, Presidency of Islamic Research: Riyadh, 1984

BBC online, 2/7/2000

Biden, Senator Joseph. The U.S. Senate Committee on the Judiciary, Violence Against Women: Victims of the System, 1991.

Buhlerg, George *The Law of Manu*. Motilal Banarsidass: Delhi, 1982

Chatterjee Dr. M. A, *Oh You Hindu Awake!* Indian Patriots Council. 1993

Daily Mail, the 2nd of December 1993.

Fazlie, M. J. *Hindu Chauvinism and Muslims in India*. Abul Qassim Publishing House: Jeddah, 1995

Ford, Peter. "Why European women are turning to Islam?" *Christian Science Monitor*, December 27, 2004 edition, p. 1.

Information Please Almanac, InfoSoft Int'l, Inc.

Jameelah, Maryam. *Islam in Theory and Practice*. H. Farooq Associates Ltd: Lahore, 1983

Kendath, Thena. *Memories of an Orthodox Youth*. In Susannah Heschel, ed. *On being a Jewish Feminist*. New York: Schocken Books, 1983

Khalil, Emad. *They Said About Islam*, 1994, in The Islamic Future, 27, May 1994. P. 12

Lang, Jeffrey. *Struggling to Surrender*. Beltsville, Maryland: Amana Publications, 1995

le Bon, Gustave. *Les Civilization de Inde*.

Lerner, Max. Our Anything Goes Society-Where is it Going. *Readers' Digest*, April 1968

Muslim, Summarized Sahih Muslim. By Al-Munthiri, tr. Dar-usSalam, Riyadh, 2000.

National Center for Health Statistics, in *The Macmillan Visual Almanac*, 1996
Pickthal, Mohammad Marmaduke. The Relation of the Sexes. A 1925 lecture on the "pitiful condition of Muslim womanhood"

Plog, Fred and Daniel G. Bates.*Cultural Anthropology.* New York: Knopf, 1982

Said, Edward *Covering Islam*. Vintage, 1997

Single copies of the BJS National Crime Victimization Survey Report, *"Violence Against Women"* (NCJ-145325)

Sullivan, T., K. Thomson, R. Wright, G. Gross and D. Spady, *Social Problems: Divergent Perspectives*. John Wiley & Sons: New York, 1980

Swidler, Leonard J. *Women in Judaism: The Status of Women in Formative Judaism*. Metuchen, N.J.: Scarecrow Press, 1976, pp. 83-93.

The Babylonian Talmud, The Soncino Press, London.

The Basics of Batterer Treatment, Common Purpose, Inc., Jamaica Plain, MA

The Family, June 1998, Issue No. 59

The Family. August, 1994,Issue No. 14

The Macmillan Visual Almanac, 1996, Abstract of the United States 1998, 118th edition.

http://www.twf.org/library/women ICJ.htm/

The United Nations Report on women in India, 1991.*Population Reports*, Vol. XXVII, No.4, Dec. 1999

W. J. Wilkins, *Modern Hinduism*. London, 1975

Zedrikly, Prof. Shatha S. *Muslim Women and Contemporary Challenges*. Majdalawi Press: Amman, 1997